FABRICK

FABRICK

ANDREW POST

MEDALLION
P R E S S
Medallion Press, Inc.
Printed in USA

For Traci

Published 2013 by Medallion Press, Inc.

The MEDALLION PRESS LOGO
is a registered trademark of Medallion Press, Inc.

Copyright © 2013 by Andrew Post
Cover illustration by Patrick Reilly
Edited by Emily Steele

Typeset in Hoefler Text
Printed in the United States of America

ISBN# 978-160542501-6

10 9 8 7 6 5 4 3 2 1
First Edition

CHAPTER 1

Tea, Disrupted

They were at the table set for two with scones and a pot of mint tea. Just the two men, one young and one old, out in the expansive and elegant gardens behind the senior man's chateau in the early afternoon; Clyde and his master, whom he'd known only as sir. It was a relaxing affair, the slow decline of the day into an evening calm, a time to unwind and reflect and laugh and converse—until they were struck by what Clyde took to be lightning. The violent concussion tossed them apart, sent the scones sailing, and detonated the antique teapot along with the table it had rested upon. The two men landed on their backs.

Clyde's ears rang. He managed to sit up.

His master tried to do the same, struggling like an overturned tortoise, moaning and bleeding freely from a gash across his forehead, his ever-present spectacles gone. The last thing his master said to him, looking into Clyde's bottomless black eyes that shined like polished briquettes of coal, was *"Run."*

Exactly sixteen and a half minutes before that, everything was serene. A regular weekday afternoon. Before the teapot was broken, the frosted scones still on their silver platter, all well, Clyde watched the old man spoon sugar into his teacup before pouring, as he always did. Clyde smiled, for he enjoyed noticing little things. He considered himself a highly observant fellow, and his master's many routines were easy to pick up on.

The two didn't talk, didn't need to. The birds were singing; the grass was greener than it had been all summer. Clyde admired the gardens, the vibrant pinks and violets, the lush blues. The house itself, he had learned from an architecture book in his chambers, was a chateau. Between the beautiful, warm golden stones, the mortar grayed with age. The garden around them was enclosed with high walls of immaculate shrubbery, well groomed and not at all like a wall—not really. More like a gentle border. He'd never been allowed beyond it and didn't mind, for he had never asked or desired to. It was home. Why leave if it was perfect?

Today, not unlike any other day, he wore his butler uniform, an elegant garment he had found neatly folded in the attic one day, a spare for one of the servicemen. He loved it immediately. A black tuxedo complete with bow tie and tails, the cuff links something his master had given him as a present upon the one-year anniversary of his arrival. The tuxedo was something of a splendor that could be worn. Before coming here he only donned stained tunics and ill-fitting trousers, which he had to cinch at the waist with a hank of cord to keep them from falling down. The cuff links were the crowning thing, though. Both bore a serif *P* for reasons Clyde didn't then understand. He figured it must've been the initial letter of his master's first or last name, neither of which he knew; he didn't feel it was his place to request that information. Clyde shined the cuff links against his pant legs now, one and then the other.

He angled his face, ashen as the rest of his flesh, to the suns in the easterly sky. He closed his eyes and felt the warmth on his eyelids and heavily pomaded raven hair, which was piled into a high, tidy pompadour.

"What a beautiful afternoon," he observed.

A trio of starships scudded overhead, heaving out of sight over the rooftop of the chateau. A moment later a series of pops and dull thuds shook the air. Several of the manor's glass panes rattled in their frames.

"Strange, don't you think, sir? A fireworks display during the daytime? And it's nowhere near Citizen's Day. They didn't wait for nightfall, when the fireworks could be seen. What do you suppose the occasion might be? Something marvelous, I'd bet."

In uncharacteristic reply, his master merely grunted. The older man ran a hand over his freckled bald pate and down a fringe of silver hair. He was typically a jolly, soft-spoken man, but today he was particularly quiet. With trembling hands, he set to refilling Clyde's cup, then poured tea atop the sugar in his own.

Clyde sat forward. Something was amiss here. "Where has Miss Selby gone, sir? Does she have the remainder of the day off?"

"Yes," his master answered flatly, "Miss Selby has gone."

Edging forward, Clyde became transfixed on his master's shaking hand as the old man freed a bent finger from the hoop of the ceramic teacup. It was as if he were a metal man in desperate need of a few pumps from the oilcan.

Clyde grimaced. "Is something wrong, sir?"

His master set the teapot aside and took a very deep

breath. "I'm afraid so, my boy." He folded his hands, clearly having something big to say.

"You know that I've enjoyed these years we've spent together and that I regret every *second* you were cooped up here like some caged bird, never even able to set those mysterious eyes of yours on anything past the road in front of this house. For that, I sincerely apologize. It has not been a very fulfilling life, I'm sure, having to live under lock and key with a dusty old duffer like me."

"No need to apologize, sir. I like my life here. But I'm afraid—and I apologize for any impatience—you did not answer my question."

The old man broke eye contact and gazed languidly into the plate of scones as if the answer lay deep within. "You're a very dear friend of mine, my boy. And I know, for whatever curses that've been laid upon you, you cannot tell me the same when I tell you that . . . that I love you very much." He cleared his throat. "I consider you not an employee but as dear to me as one of my own children. I do hope you know that."

A nod. "I thank you, sir. Those are very kind words."

"But I believe I have done something atrocious, something for which neither my children nor you would ever be capable of forgiving me, I fear."

Clyde forced brightness into his voice. "Nonsense, sir. It is what I do, remember? Tell me anything you wish, and I will swab your mind clean as easily as one removes bird business from a windowpane." He said this with gusto, for it was his gift—his duty—to be the conscience sponge to his master. Whenever the older man needed to clear his mind, Clyde was there to listen and sweep all nasty, nagging thoughts under the proverbial rug. Albeit with minor consequences, but his master never did anything so bad that a nasty jinxing would occur after he was sponged.

His master bit a knuckle and stared toward the hedges at the far end of the lawn. "This is something altogether different, I'm afraid to say. I have done something"—he winced—"unpardonable. And if I know you, although my mind will be clear once I say what I must, my life may be placed in the balance."

Clyde put a hand atop his master's. "I'm sure you couldn't do anything *that* bad, sir. If you wish me to sweep up, just say so." It was their code for conscience sponging. "If not, it can wait. I have nowhere to be."

His master's hand fell away. His eyes revealed his deep worry, a swallowing darkness Clyde had never seen. "I'm afraid our time together is at an end, Clyde."

"What do you—?"

Inside the house, a door opened and closed, but Clyde was too preoccupied with what his master was saying to pay it even a mote of attention. He caught the older man's hand, held it tight, and gave it a squeeze. "Sir?"

And with that final whisper came a whistling. An object fell from the sky, trailing over the top of the house. It landed at their feet in the grass with a soft thud and rolled: just a smooth metallic cylinder.

Feeling a sudden tension in the hand clutching his own, he looked up and saw his master's head bowed and his eyes tightly closed. He was about to ask what was wrong, what the object on the ground was. Was it a game? He nearly began his line of new questions when the table, the teapot, the plate of scones—all of it—shattered in a deafening thunderclap.

His master's hand let go again.

Above, the bright early-afternoon sky, blue and beautiful, spiraled up and past as Clyde was tossed through the air, his body feeling ripped asunder. He felt the impact of the lawn on his back but didn't hear it. His ears rang as if a dozen Klaxons had been installed directly inside his skull and simultaneously set off. The world beyond the wall of noise was garbled and far away.

When he sat up, he saw the table reduced to splinters, teapot shards scattered on the lawn. His master, cast clear across the yard from him, managed to sit up feebly before falling back to the ground. He could lift his head, barely. Terror simmered in his eyes as he stared at something distant. Clyde followed his master's gaze to the floating ball of greenish-gray light that hung in a perfect sphere of fog, like swamp gas trapped in a glass bubble, right where the table was a scant instant ago.

Staring into it, Clyde felt all the world condense around him. Looking away was impossible. The ethereal orb of swirling, diseased green and gray wanted, *commanded* him to look into it forever. With some difficulty, Clyde clamped a hand over his eyes. It was the only way to chisel his gaze from it. Even from behind his fingers, his onyx eyes remained directed toward the orb.

Clyde shouted for his friend, his voice sounding dampened to his own ears. There was no reply, so he repeated his bellowing call, "Sir? Are you all right? Master? Sir?" Clyde dared a peek, blocking the orb's light with the flat of one upheld hand.

His master was still there but transfixed, as Clyde had been.

"Sir!"

Finally, the old man also freed his gaze from the spooky ethereal sphere and looked at him. The corners of his mouth turned down, and there was an apology behind his kindly eyes. "To your chambers, my boy. Run. Stay hidden until it's all over."

"But for how long?" Clyde shouted. He liked specificity, but he dropped his request when he noticed movement through the back windows of the chateau. Man-shaped shadows moved about, distorted penumbras swathing the furniture, darting along walls. As a row of them passed the hall mirror, he caught glimpses. They were dressed darkly, their faces concealed by reflective black masks, their shoulders exaggerated by padded garb.

He turned to his master, whose attention had been sucked into the weird orb again. He was muttering, ostensibly unable to stop, "Three weeks, I suppose. Stay hidden for at least *three weeks*. Go now. Three weeks." Suddenly, he gasped, apparently able to pull himself from his torpor when the orb allowed. His scream was clear then. *"Run."*

Knowing he should never disregard his master's orders, Clyde scrambled to his feet, every inch of his body hurting, as if a single miscalculated step may shatter him like glass. He took the path of pavers along the back of the chateau, avoiding going inside, where the strangers were. He ducked below window level and rushed past. He got to the far corner, just about to go around to the exterior entrance of the cellar, but he stopped.

He couldn't just *leave* him.

Keeping hidden around the corner, Clyde dared a peek. The old man lay in the grass, the left side of his face painted bloodred from brow to ear. He freed himself from the orb enough to shield his eyes. He was turning his head away from it when four shadows fell over him, and the old man's expression changed from frustration to utter dismay.

The ball of light evaporated in a puff, and his master's face slackened.

In his blood-and-tea-spattered waistcoat, Clyde weakly slunk back.

Four black shadows loomed in the grass around his master—a devilish paw of outstretched fingers folding around him, lying square in the clutch of the dark talons as the men approached. Clyde's old friend tried to crawl away, pushing off on the burnt grass with the heels of his loafers, to little avail.

Unable to bear the sight a moment longer, Clyde followed his orders—even if it meant volunteering for what he felt was cowardice—and ran. He charged down the steps into the foundation of the chateau, nearly tumbling but keeping as quiet as he could. Inside, he barred the doors, moving piles of books in front of them one load at a time. There were plenty of books, the only objects in his cellar chamber besides the bed and nightstand. After five or six armloads, both the door to the garden and the door to the house were as secure as he could get them.

A dull bang sounded from somewhere aboveground. Clyde stopped to listen. Wherever the sound had been made, it was very loud if it could be heard down here.

He hoped it was all just a prank like Miss Selby liked to play sometimes. No, Miss Selby played a prank but once a year, on the sir's birthday, and that wasn't for another seventy-nine days.

He wanted to rush outside, but just as he was about to shove one of the towers of books aside, he stopped himself. He had to do as he was told: remain hidden for three complete weeks. But he wouldn't for a second longer. Certainly it would be torturous to stay down there all that time not knowing whether those men meant harm to his master, but he would do as he was commanded. The master's orders were, after all, the master's orders.

Trying to quell his heart, Clyde hugged himself until he believed everything would be okay.

CHAPTER 2

The Conscience Sponge

There was no way to be absolutely certain it had been three complete weeks. Clyde's room had not a single clock, window, or calendar. But he could perceive time's passage within the stones at his back as they were heated by the suns and cooled at night.

Pressing an ear against the masonry, he listened for hours for any movement. With a hand placed against the wall to feel for vibration, he waited for the smallest indication of any other occupants within the house.

Soon, he gave up. The house was sturdy, with incredibly thick walls and floors, and he had never heard anything from beyond this closed room before. He sighed. Resting his hands in his lap, he returned to counting minutes.

Very much unlike the house, which sounded still enough, Clyde's mind rattled ceaselessly with increasingly panicked thoughts. Was he okay? Were those men just playing a joke on his master? If so, it was a potentially dangerous one. Among all his questions, there was one he couldn't keep at bay. Who *were* they?

Clyde felt as if he were being impatient with his master's orders and gave up trying to hear anything. Perhaps it was all some strange custom or a form of celebration the master had set in order. Perhaps the table breaking apart like that and the loud bang were how old men *liked* to commence their birthday celebrations.

Another question. What was that light? Clyde could still see it in his mind's eye—gray and green and terrible. Looking into it was like watching the water spiral at the bottom of the tub, going around and around, as if it were trying to summon you to fall headlong down with it, but much worse. *It won't hurt,* even the mere memory of it seemed to whisper. Its voice, which he hoped was just his imagination, scared Clyde, and he decided then and there not to think about it anymore. He returned to counting the minutes, picking up roughly where he left off and adding a few extra seconds for those in which he'd been distracted.

Three weeks, he kept telling himself. *The master told me three weeks. I have to heed his demands. I must.*

"But how would I know for sure?" he found himself saying in his soft voice. "How could I know three weeks haven't already passed? And why three weeks? I've never been asked to stay in here *that* long." Again, he checked the walls for a clock he somehow may've never noticed. Just his room, stone walls, electric braziers, a small space heater, and the books. The piles and piles of books. He picked one up to distract himself, but the words went all wonky and wouldn't cooperate with him. Frustrated, he slammed it shut with a loud thwack.

He hissed, remembering he was supposed to be hidden, which meant he should probably be quiet. He opened the book again and reclosed it, this time silently.

A hundred and fifty-four minutes, he counted.

The lights flickered and went out. A minute later, they came back on. The grill of his space heater went dark, then glowed orange again. The bulbs behind the metal mesh of the braziers flickered, their coiled filaments barely darkening completely before they surged back to life.

This happened several times.

And he noticed every time, for he never slept. Not now, in this dire situation, and never anytime before. It went along with his curious personality, his master had told him. And because of that, Clyde felt every moment pass.

With nothing to do, he allowed his mind to travel backwards and play snippets from his life with the sir. By no means did he have a perfect memory or anything resembling one, but he hoped the happier times were as brilliant and wonderful as he remembered them.

Considering himself a person of manners, Clyde never asked why he was being kept there. Questions like *How much did you pay for me?* or *How long do you plan on keeping me?* were things a brute would ask. But he took it as an oddity that the master hadn't treated him like his other keepers had. He was nice, for one. He visited him for reasons other than the unique service Clyde could provide. Often they'd just chat, read stories or poetry, have tea in the garden. The stories, especially, were among Clyde's fondest memories. His master was the one who taught him how to read. He took to it about as well as a fish breathes cement, but his master was patient.

Yes, his current master—the only one befitting the title, in Clyde's honest opinion—was unlike his others. He was an earnest, good man. A good man who *never* deserved to be startled like that, have his best bistro set ruined, the beautiful antique teapot he asked to be used only for special occasions smashed. *There,* he thought with finality. The broken earthenware teapot that his master had inherited from his mother's mother's mother. *There* was the straw that broke the camel's back. The sight of it in bits and pieces was just too sad to bear. The men who did this didn't care if anyone got hurt, which meant they were bad people. Clyde's eyes snapped open.

"I can wait no longer," he told the stale air.

He sprang to his feet, sidestepped his columns of stacked books, and went to the door to the house.

Halting, he put his ear against the cold steel. Beyond, a faint buzzing of the fluorescent lights of the cellar corridor could be detected; the whoosh and thamp of the air circulation system activated sporadically. He listened steadfastly, calling out in the gaps of silence when the circulator shut itself off. Not a soul answered. No footfalls sounded from above. No one came to tell him it was all right to return upstairs. No tremble in the walls indicated an automobile was nearby. No ragged coughing announced the master was up and about in the early morning.

"No, not yet," Clyde said to himself. "What if I go up prematurely and spoil some surprise the master has for me? What if I'm sent away?" His master was a patient man, but one could never tell what would be the clincher, the thing to best a man's patience. He'd been sent away for less. Forcing himself to turn away from the unlocked chamber door was hard, especially when it would be so easy to turn the knob, step right out—

"I must do as he asked."

Making himself sit down, Clyde summoned all the courage he had sponged from the master over their time together, motes of personality he'd absorbed and made his own pinch by pinch. He needed it to force himself to think about all this and be honest with himself. He sighed, for he was fairly certain by this point the master had either abandoned him or, heaven forbid, passed on to the next world or, heaven forbid again, been *made* to pass into the next world by those men. He closed his eyes. *Please not that.*

But Clyde remembered some of the candlelit confessions, the master sitting across from him in his chamber, unraveling all the unethical tales of business he had done in the name of economic strategy. He never mentioned by name the men he had accidentally cheated but divulged guilt to Clyde in a slow way, tackling each painful memory meanderingly, until the choice parts that were troubling him were told, the story complete. He would look at Clyde, not seeking confirmation that he had heard him or anticipating a blessing or a stoic pass of the hand as a sign that all had been forgiven. He knew how it worked with Clyde, and to merely say his piece meant the transaction was complete. Slowly he'd stand. Sometimes Clyde would have to help the old man to his feet and see him out. And the master would pull the chamber door behind him as he left, never locking it, as his previous keepers had, only closing it so Clyde could have his privacy. He'd wish Clyde good night and return upstairs cleansed, perhaps even smiling.

As close as they were, Clyde never knew what his master really did with his time outside the manor. Perhaps he was a banker or some kind of broker or possibly an entrepreneur. The details of his occupation were always carefully omitted. All Clyde had were the subtle clues picked up between the lines, shining hints laid in the trail of each sentence, words that jumped out.

His old friend felt bad about the things he had done,

ruining other men's lives accidentally when a *prospect* didn't go right, whatever that was. Looking up the term in the dictionary didn't help any. Regardless, his master had made a bad call on some *prospects* and some *investors* squandered their fortunes, making his master feel like an inept cheat, an accidental *scoundrel*. But in the end, Clyde would be there to make it all better, and after a round or two with the thesaurus, Clyde would come away with a better vocabulary, his own sort of prize for helping his master.

But there was always the jinx that a confessor would endure in return for telling things to Clyde. Sometimes their gizmos like the toaster or television wouldn't work right or batteries would die despite being fresh out of the package. The jinx was never the same twice, always unpredictable. It could scarcely be blamed on Clyde because of the subtle way the jinxing would inject itself into one's day-to-day activities.

Clyde remembered once how his master got something off his chest; he had accidentally forgotten to pay for a haircut because he and the barber were old friends and they'd gotten to talking and the financial side of the visit was completely skipped. "I plumb forgot!" he said during his confession with a jolly chortle. He still felt bad about it, apparently, and Clyde was glad to listen. But without Clyde's consent, since his strange gift was beyond his control, his master would be jinxed in a small way for that absentminded—and somewhat laughable—crime, if one could even call it that. But apparently whatever strange spirit decided such things chose to have his master plagued with a sudden rash on the crown of his head that looked like a dozen little spider bites. His master didn't blame

Clyde but merely laughed it off, itchiness and all.

Clyde's reminiscing smile faded, and he shot to his feet.

Had it been . . . *his fault?*

Had the unpredictable arrangement of the jinxing summoned those intruders to the manor to harm a kindly old man? Was this *his* doing?

Clyde had to do something, three weeks or no, especially if he was partly to blame. His master would tell Clyde to calm himself each time he'd gotten a cold because of confessing too much, that it wasn't his fault . . . but this? *This* was different.

Clyde exited his chamber, took the cellar stairs two at a stride. He cursed his ignorance, or what Miss Selby frequently called his *lamblike innocence*. For the duration of the climb, Clyde hated himself.

CHAPTER 3

A Mouflon Guest

Every room was dark, even when he flipped up the light switches. In the dining room, broken glass crunched underfoot. Moonlight cut in through the windows in reaching slabs, splashing the interior of the house in dead white. Though the illumination was inconsistent and left shadows scattered about, Clyde glimpsed grimy trails crisscrossing all the rooms. Thick muddy shoe prints had turned themselves into dirt molds, and Clyde dashed them apart as he followed them. From the front doors that still hung open, he saw the driveway absent of vehicles.

He followed the prints to the second floor. He searched the library and the observatory and the den where they led him. He walked through the guest bedrooms, the five water closets, even Miss Selby's personal quarters. The tracks brought him to no one, just empty spaces that echoed each and every call of, "Sir?"

He didn't need to be following the footprints; he knew this place, his home. But this space felt alien now, he realized, returning downstairs. He knew every fiber of carpet, every knick in the banister, and every decorative drawer pull. It was always quiet, certainly, but it had life in it before. Now the manor was a soulless place.

He repeated, "Sir?" to the spaces the footprints hadn't traveled. The music room, the drawing room, and the library, his question beginning to sound defeated and hopeless, even to his own ears.

There was still one place he hadn't looked.

Clyde drew a deep breath, steeling himself. Just as he was about to pass through the kitchen for the back doors, the lights flickered once, and he was momentarily blinded and twitching at the alarming brilliance. Every lamp, every chandelier, every electric brazier exploded with light. Starbursts leaped at his eyes from every direction.

He saw his own hazy silhouette in the panes of the back doors leading to the gardens. For a second he thought it was his master, until he noticed the reflection was wearing a tuxedo.

The flash was gone as fast as it'd come, though, like lightning without the accompanying rumble. It felt like a sign. A gentle prodding.

"Fine, then." His voice bounced throughout the house and echoed back to him. Solemn, he marched to the back doors, admitting that it was just the inevitable he was delaying: checking the last place he'd seen his master.

Outside, the air was cold, the night impenetrable. After his eyes adjusted, Clyde saw exactly what he was hoping he wouldn't see.

There he was.

Right where he had last laid eyes on him.

Clyde realized that his fears had been woefully met. The tears came at once, his chest tightening like a wet towel being mercilessly wrung. He fell to his knees in the dew-soaked grass. Staring at the crumpled heap that had once been his beloved friend, Clyde let himself fall apart.

The only man who had treated him with dignity. His

one genuine friend. And now? Now he was gone.

After he had cried himself dry, Clyde realized his perception of time had been incorrect, his patience greater
than he had originally thought. He had been in the cellar
for quite beyond three weeks.

It was clear to him now, seeing what remained of his
friend in the ethereal light of the moon. He'd read in a
biology textbook about decomposition. If it had been
only three weeks, there would be more of his master left,
wouldn't there? What a horrid thing to think about, but he
decided it didn't matter. He sidled forward on his knees.

A shrunken gray husk, facedown among the tatty remnants of clothing, was all that remained. With a slender
white hand, Clyde touched the hoary bones. A few ribs
were shattered, the back of the skull had a jagged cra-
ter buried in it—*Could a gun have done this?*—but it was
obviously his master. Clyde recalled the loud bang, and
his heart sank. Desperate, he thought perhaps this wasn't
his friend, but then . . . No. No question about it: round
spectacles, broken, lay beside the body. If his master had
survived, he would've picked those up immediately. He
wouldn't have been able to go anywhere without them.

He thumbed the garment's lapel: tweed, soaked
through with rainwater and dried blood. Clyde pinched
a swatch of the man's jacket that hadn't been ruined. A
stamp-sized piece of fabric tore away. Mindlessly, he deposited it into his own pocket. It just felt like the appropriate
thing to do.

Nothing else to tend to, he stood and adjusted his bow
tie—a nervous habit—and said a few words of requiem.
His own weeping interrupted him, and he ushered out the

rest of the prayer falteringly. Succumbing to the sorrow, he collapsed yet again onto the lawn, palming his face tightly with both hands and weeping in hitching sobs. He was still in the thick of it when a metallic click sounded behind him.

Jumping to his feet, he faced the individual he was sure had been his master's murderer. Anger boiled his blood, but he didn't let it show as he studied the armed man. It was hard to keep his expression serene, though, when he saw that the killer before him . . . *wasn't a man at all*.

Standing there was a furry creature, easily seven feet tall and wearing blocky leather armor. Massive horns sprouted from its head and coiled on either side of its wide cranium like two glued-on nautilus shells. Its face was broad and pug-like, and the creature stared back at him with wide, horizontal pupils. In its rust-colored fur, tiny spikes lined the bridge of its nose, crossed its forehead, each quill topped with a black tip. It was stout, almost paunchy. Clyde's gaze ended at the creature's feet, seeing not ten toes but three, each ending in a thick claw. Clyde's anger was immediately quashed by an avalanche of bafflement.

Apparently realizing Clyde was no threat, the creature angled the flared barrel of the blunderbuss away.

"What are—?"

"Are you human?" it interrupted in a surprisingly even voice, neither gruff nor ineloquent. In fact, an occupation in radio might befit the furry, horned man if this whole gambit as a looter or murderer didn't pan out.

Terrified, Clyde stood frozen. He knew he had the attributes of a human: arms, legs, generally hairless body save for what grew atop his head and in a thick band over each eye. The minor, if obvious, differences unsettled all who looked upon him. His impossible paleness, his whiteless onyx eyes. He didn't know what else to consider himself if not human, so he nodded.

"Do you live here?" the creature asked, taking a cautious step to the left to see around Clyde. Its focus flicked from Clyde to the skeleton behind him, then back to Clyde.

"I do, yes."

"Who's that?"

"It is . . . *was* my master."

"Master? You a slave or something?" The creature zeroed in on Clyde's butler uniform. "Or were you paid to call him that?"

The bulky creature slowly took a step to the side. It kept the blunderbuss's butt pressed against a hip, gripping the weapon as nonchalantly as anyone from Clyde's comfortable little world would wield a throw pillow. But that world was gone now, and now this creature that smelled like burnt cinnamon and old sweat was in it, right here in the backyard—the place for tea, long talks, and shared laughs. Well, the place that *used* to be the place for those things.

Clyde remembered he'd been asked a question, then shrugged absently, for he had no answer and felt too drained to conjure up one. Instead, he posed a question of his own. "Did you do this?" He had no idea what he would do if the creature admitted his involvement, but it would start off with a thorough tongue-lashing—that much was for sure.

"Kill that poor soul behind you there? No. Just got to this ward about an hour ago," it replied casually, circling Clyde slowly.

Clyde turned to keep him in sight.

The creature's wide-set eyes narrowed, studying

Clyde's frame as if he were a tailor assessing measurements from a distance. "You're not armed, are you?"

"No." Clyde took this partly as an insult, for he had stumbled upon a theme in his books: only bad guys used guns.

At this, the thick thumb of the creature found the blunderbuss's hammer and lowered it with care. The weapon was on a strap, and when the towering creature let it go, it swung down to its fuzzy flank. With its freed hand, it withdrew a metallic rod from a narrow leather sleeve. It gave the rod one swing through the air, and it glowed a ghostly cobalt blue. "Seems about right. You don't look the type."

Because I'm not. Clyde huffed.

"I should be off. Sorry to have bothered you."

"What were you doing here anyway, in my master's chateau?" Clyde asked hurriedly, trying to be polite.

"Scavenging. But I see that you stayed, despite what happened, and I'll move right along. I promise you I didn't take anything. Do you happen to know if any of your neighbors here in this ward are home? I don't want to surprise anyone else . . . or get shot for intruding." He chuckled.

"I don't know." He had never seen any neighbors.

The creature sighed. "I guess that's the price one pays for the gentleman scavenger's life. Risk over reward and such, yeah? Well, take care. I'm sure the Patrol will be by eventually to bring you into their warm, warm bosom."

There was a strange tone in that. Sarcasm? Was that what it was called?

The creature turned again to leave.

"Wait," Clyde blurted. "The Patrol? What are you talking about?"

The creature stopped again and turned around all the

way. "The Royal Patrol. You know, the prime minister's guard?" Slowing it down, he said, "You *do* know about the king's *guard*, yeah? The armor, the guns, the autos with no windows, the metal barricades that have sprung up all over Geyser?"

Those were a lot of words and terms he didn't understand, *Geyser* being chief among them. The creature seemed to have used it as the name of a place. Clyde had read the dictionary a few times all the way through and really remembered only the ones he had difficulty picturing. A geyser, as he recalled, was an underground spring that shot up occasional spouts of hot water and steam. He didn't know about any of those other things. *King's guard, prime minister, Royal Patrol? What?*

"Good Meech on this cloud! You suffer a bonk on the head or something? Where've you been?"

"In the cellar."

"Since the day you were born, it'd seem."

"I thought it was only three weeks, but seeing how my master looks," he muttered, "I must've lost count of the hours at some point."

"Looks to me it's been a wee bit longer than that, yeah," the creature said with a humorless chuckle. After a nasty glare from Clyde, it stepped forward, ducked its head slightly, and said almost apologetically, "Do you even know where you *are*, Pasty?"

"My name is Clyde, and yes, I know exactly where I am. I am at the chateau. Plainly." He thrust his arms outward for emphasis, indicating the gardens, the fountains, and the sculpted shrubberies, which, he now noticed, looked quite overgrown.

"No, I can tell you know that much, but I mean *here*,

as in the big picture. What continent we're on, what place we're currently at. You seem a bit . . . confused."

"You're the confused one. This is clearly private property, and you're trespassing as if you own the place." He stopped and scoffed at himself. "Why would one trespass if they owned the place?" He worried a little about himself then. How long *had* he been down there? He seemed to have gone a little wonky. He returned to the point. "How do I know you didn't steal anything?"

"Calm down. I didn't take anything. I just got here, like I said. I like to go 'round the place first, make sure no one's home before I pick through what's inside. It'd be quite embarrassing to be stuffing my rucksack full of good-ies when a resident came out of the powder room, wouldn't it? Listen, I don't think you know the severity of what's going on here. Why didn't you leave with the others?"

"Why would I have left?"

The creature nodded toward Clyde's decomposed master. "Because a whole lot of that happened. Listen, fella . . ." The creature took a step forward.

Clyde promptly took a step back.

The creature rolled his eyes. "Come here. I'm not going to hurt you, Pasty."

Clyde was sure to stand between the intruder and his beloved master. It took a moment before he realized the defensive gesture was sadly pointless. What more could be done to his master now? He allowed the horned, furry creature to step closer.

"How long has it been?" Clyde said.

"Since I did a jig? You got to be more specific."

He gestured over his shoulder to the corpse of his friend.

The creature nodded. "I can't really give you an exact

time for him, but . . . a lot of the badness started just about six months ago."

Clyde gaped. "Six months . . ."

Setting a heavy hand on Clyde's shoulder, the creature continued, "I don't think you should stay here. The Patrol can do only so much, and to be honest with you, you don't exactly look like the type that'd fare well in their refugee program. But then again, I'd rather be relocated than be around when the Odium returns, as they surely will."

"The Odium?"

"Meech. You really are a clueless one, aren't you? It's a bloody surprise you've managed to eke out an existence *this* long. Speaking of which, what do you have to eat here? You may be thin, but you must've sustained yourself on *something,* yes?"

"There may be something in the kitchen. I don't know." Clyde waved a hand in the general direction of the kitchen. He was still fixated on how good his patience truly had been. Six. Entire. Months.

"You mean to tell me you don't know? You may be pale, but you are still a man, yes? Men eat. I know they do. Sure, they may decide to eat the strangest things—and in the smallest portions—but I've seen them do it. You eat, right?"

He snapped out of it. "I don't, actually."

The creature blinked. "Ever?"

"No."

It looked for a few moments at Clyde, biting its lip. It concluded, voice going dreamy, "Well, isn't that strange." Then it shrugged. "Ah, well, never mind that, then. Come along. You can tell me all about how you *don't* eat while I *do*."

CHAPTER 4

Flam and Cake

In the kitchen, lit by only the cerulean glow of his light stick, the brute went from cupboard to cupboard, taking items out that he found of interest and setting them on the tiled kitchen island before going to collect more. A loaf of bread half swallowed by powdery white mold, a couple of prepackaged brine bars leaking out of their plastic, an entire pint of briar flower juice that looked like it'd settled and soured, and a frozen mushroom the size of an automobile wheel that Miss Selby served like pie to Clyde's master topped with melted sweet cheese. Clyde wanted to protest that the creature was going to eat them out of house and home but said nothing, remembering for the umpteenth time that his master wouldn't require any more meals ever again.

Once the creature had assembled a considerable banquet for itself, it moved a stool out and sat carefully, testing to ensure it could support its weight. Once assured, it smiled and began to *eat*, for lack of a better term. More like *massacre,* Clyde thought, recalling one of his vocabulary words.

"Good briar flower juice. Can't get this for less than fifty spots in most places."

"Do you know who may be responsible?" Clyde asked, standing nearby.

"For what? Your master out there on the garden or . . .

all of it? Probably one and the same. That is, unless your master was killed during the city's razing by an old grudge holder or something, some sour bloke that just used the Odium invasion as a way to cover up his deed. A lot of that happened, apparently. A time for disgruntled folks to get things off their chests and let the Patrol believe it was *all* the Odium's doing." He bit the moldy bread loaf in two and continued with a full mouth, "Not speaking from experience or anything. I'm the peaceful sort."

"Odd, seeing as how you walk about armed to the teeth with that thing." Clyde eyed the blunderbuss, nearly as tall as he was, resting against the kitchen wall.

"My two cents: I wouldn't bet a single spot on the culprit being anyone but a member of the Odium. Wicked bunch, them."

"Do you have an affiliation with this . . . Odium?" He already didn't like saying the name aloud.

"Me?" The creature brayed, spraying crumbs. "Meech, no! I avoid the Odium to the best of my ability. They don't care for us Mouflons all that much. Consider us a crass, stubborn bunch—and they're probably partly right!" The creature ate a brine bar, wrapper and all, and chased it with a swallow of juice. It gave Clyde a measured look. "I think they'd care for you even less. Couldn't imagine you'd even be able to lift one of their breastplates above your head, let alone wear all that gear they tote about. Did you get a look at them, though? Do you even know who to look for?"

"I saw their shadows and that is all, I'm afraid."

"Don't think a sketch artist will be able to fetch you much of a picture based on shadows. Everyone looks the same, unless they got horns like mine." He swallowed, and his face went grave. "*Did* they have horns?"

"Not that I can recall. They looked like men, regular men."

"Well, that's unfortunate. Humans outnumber any other race on Gleese ten to one." It carefully pinched some crumbs off Clyde's lapel and vacuumed them from its fingertips in one quick slurp. "I very much doubt it was a Mouflon, because Mouflons know better than to kill a human. We can barely stay out of jail as it is, what with human laws favoring humans, naturally. But if it *was* a Mouflon, at least you would have *something* to go on. But since it was humans who killed that poor old sod out there, that lowers your odds a bit."

"Regardless, I want to find who did it."

"Good for you. Should probably know what city you're in first, go and speak to a frigate pilot, see if you can hire one crazy enough to chase after the Odium, which, to be perfectly honest with you, will probably be a bit of a challenge. That is, if it *was* them. Most frigate pilots would rather go the *other* way, like everyone else with any sense in their heads."

"What about you? Will you assist me?"

The creature's considerable jaw paused midgrind. It swallowed and set the loaf of bread aside. "You'd never catch me dead, alive, or anywhere in between looking for the Odium, Pasty. I'm merely a magpie that follows in their wake, picking up what they leave behind. Call it dishonorable, call it being a profiteer of tragedy, but there's a life in it if you're smart." It finished the bread off and chased the mouthful with the last slug of the juice.

"You're not going to help—?"

It stood, a crumb avalanche cascading off its lap. "Well, I wish you the best, young man. I do pray to Meech high above that you find what you're looking for. Thanks for the nibble. If I'm back in Geyser anytime in the near future, the next one's on me. Seems like a lot of this was, too." It brushed itself off.

"You're just going to *leave?*" Clyde moved in closer.

"Yep. Even though you got nothing I can fence, at least I got a meal out of it, some temporary company." It mussed Clyde's hair. "A sheltered bloke such as you should probably get yourself to the Patrol, just hand yourself over to them. Shantytown living may not have much pride in it, no, but at least you'll be safe."

Clyde had to think fast. He turned toward the cupboard in which Miss Selby often stored pastries. It was his only hope. He darted to the cupboard doors and, wrenching them open, found a lidded cake stand with a frosted double chocolate cake. It was frosted again with mold, but the creature hadn't been deterred before by such a thing. Clyde turned with it and presented it to the creature, held high like a prize. The lid chimed like a bell when Clyde removed it, giving the cold, dark house a millisecond of singsong levity.

And apparently it elicited something in the creature as well.

It stepped forward eagerly, wide eyes matching its hungry smile, but then stopped as if this were the hardest thing in the world to do. Its expression shifted wildly to downright fury as it said, "That look—I've seen it before. You *want* something, I can tell. Men are easy to read as a Meech-damned book, even when they have a face as weird as yours."

"I'll give you the cake, but you have to agree to help me."

The creature frowned. It kept looking at the cake, talking to it more than to Clyde. "Look, I'll brief you on Geyser, point you in the right direction, but going after the Odium—I apologize—is *not* going to happen. I'd sooner wrap myself in jerky and cast myself into the biter-infested waters of Lake Candlewood."

Clyde mulled this over for a moment. "Fine." Any knowledge was good, even if it was just pointers on what areas to avoid. He set the cake stand on the kitchen island in front of the creature.

It sat down—again, carefully—and tore off a wad of cake with its bare hand. "First off, I'll ask you a question," it said after one fistful had disappeared.

"All right."

"Okay, so I know you know that we're in your master's place—we established that—but do you know where you are in the world? Because that would be somewhat vital information to start off with."

"You mentioned we're in Geyser."

"Right. We're in Geyser. One of the last places that has seen fresh water in quite some time. Of course, those times have passed, and, well, water seekers have all gone north and south and they've pretty much figured out how to make water with machines, too. But . . . I'm getting ahead of myself. So you know this is a unique city, right? Unlike any other, on account of its foundation, right?"

Clyde shook his head. His frame of reference ended at the edge of the back garden. He'd seen the street out front of the house. He'd seen the autos puttering up and down it through the dense grove of trees crowding the front lawn, but only from the second-story window. Other masters' homes before this one had offered even less than that.

He watched the creature as it looked around the kitchen, searching for something. When it returned its focus to the cake, it brightened. "Here! Geyser is a lot like this."

"Chocolate cake?"

"No, the thing beneath it, twit. See, it's like this." He tore the remainder of the cake away until only a peak remained in the middle. "You see, that bit I left there is like the geyser itself. The platter is where the sediment has settled and has become hard enough to hold structures upon. Close to three million folks once lived here, mostly humans but occasionally some like myself and a few Cyno."

Clyde interrupted, "I'm sorry, but what's a . . . *Sy-noh?*"

"Cyno. Cynoscion. Water folk," it explained. "Like me and you, they walk on two legs, except they live underwater. Pincers and eye stalks and shells as hard as their personalities but good with an abacus. Generally jerks of the highest order, most of them, thinking themselves better—again, like humans—but they're good for Geyser. Well, they were good for Geyser. You see, while the water was still flowing, the platter would expand every few years because of the sediment—just a centimeter at most per moon cycle. And it was up to the Cynoscion to shape the sediment, using real precise arithmetic, which they are quite good at, unlike me, to make sure it was expanding evenly."

"Why would it need to expand evenly?"

"Because, again, much like this cake stand, Geyser is suspended in the air. The platter is only halfway down the geyser peak, and there's about a mile from the edge down to the floor of the island below." The creature trailed a crumb-clotted fingernail over the edge and tapped the countertop for emphasis. "Don't want something that high up, with a bunch of folks living on it, to lean. Get me?"

"And the city is perfectly circular like this?" Clyde gestured at the cake stand.

"Sure is. The mathematical wizardry of the Cynoscion—proof positive."

"But you said the water stopped flowing. Is that why everyone left?"

"Can't be a town without any water. Water tapered off, the flow slowed, and that's when the folks turned tail for more fertile places. Of course, a few decided to try and stick it out, but with less citizenry came less security, and with less security the Odium could get in easier—and that was *just* what they did. You could call Geyser sacked, if you want to put it bluntly. But I wouldn't go around saying it like that; people are sensitive. They refer to Geyser as a site of great loss, but a kingdom that got pummeled by a band of hooligans is good, old-fashioned *sacked* if you ask yours truly."

"And who is mine truly? Who *are* you?" Clyde saw a deep knowledge, if only of the street-smart caliber, within the creature sitting across from him. He looked the armored creature up and down, in the azure aurora of the light stick, focusing on the scarring across his snout—shiny flesh, betraying a history of scuffles. He had been places, clearly, and had been forcibly expelled from a few of them, too, by the look of it.

"Flam." The creature extended a cakey paw. "Didn't realize I didn't give it. Mother'd tan my hide—forgetting my manners like that."

Clyde surveyed Flam's palm. Flam looked at the mess as well, lowered it, and then offered his cleaner hand. They shook, Clyde's tiny white hand lost in the brute's.

"You mentioned a kingdom. Was there a king of Geyser? Is he still here?"

"Not a king. Not anymore. Got a prime minister, though." Flam looked down, shook his horned head. "Hasn't been a king in Geyser for quite some time. Kind of a scandal, to tell you the truth. Pitka Gorett—that's the prime minister—was quite the right-hand man to the king. Pyne—that'd be the king—got sick and, wouldn't you know it, none of the princes could be tracked down in time. The tradition goes that when the king passes away, whoever is there inherits his soul as well as his title. Naturally, Gorett was there. Some say he deliberately got the king's kids stuck en route to Geyser and was able to 'catch' the king's soul. Bunch of guano, if you ask me, the whole bit about souls and spirits and passing them on to the next in line for the throne. But there it is, the long and short of it. Gorett got it. Immediately began demanding everyone refer to him as sire and lord and King Gorett, but no one did, except those directly beneath him. Probably part of the reason the Odium came here, but that's just my thought on it all."

"Was the king the king of all the lands—or just Geyser?"

"Geyser is like the capital of this continent. It's based on an island, but it's the only thing of value save for the woods at the base of Geyser's stem. But on my way in, those woods didn't look nearly as good as they used to."

"So what's the rest of the island called?"

"Geyser."

"No, not the city. The island."

"Yeah. Geyser. It's all called Geyser. City as well as the island."

"That's confusing."

"I know, but really . . . Here, let me explain it this way: No one comes to the island to see just the island, since everything but the city is rock, a few mines and quarries, and the occasional mud-choked river. If you come to the island of Geyser, you're really coming to the city of Geyser, the geyser itself. So you say one thing, and everyone knows. Kind of a nuisance, I imagine, especially for someone new to all this, like yourself. Speaking of which, how is it that you don't know any of this? You've obviously been living here for a while; you knew right where the cake was hidden."

"I was brought here blindfolded, in chains."

Flam's spiky forehead crinkled. "Excuse me?"

"My previous masters were the distrustful sort. I guess they were afraid that if I saw too much or moved about freely, my gift would be spoiled."

"Whoa, wait a minute." Flam eased back on the stool slightly. "Gift. You a Fractioner? A Bulbist?"

Clyde stared. Those were terms he'd never heard or read in any book. He repeated them, trying them on for size. "Bulbist? Fractioner? What're those?"

"You know, a Bulbist. Makes the plants grow. They're weavers they put in gardens like gargoyles. Some kind of light fabrick. Fractioners take things apart, put them together again . . . You know something about that, I'm sure, if nothing else; I saw you got a TV in the other room."

"Wait. What's that?"

"TV? Television? Plastic box that talks and tells humans to buy things?"

"I'm well aware what TV is. I meant that other word you said. Fabrick." He had heard the word before, or a similar one, having run across it in one of Miss Selby's sewing books, but the way Flam said it now, it had a harder K sound at the end and an air of mystery slathered across it, whereas whenever the word *fabric* was used in *The Royal Stitcher's Guide to Patches and Other Small Garment Fixes,* it seemed rather dull. Cotton. Polyblend. Etcetera. Perplexed, Clyde asked, "What is *fabrick*?"

Flam relaxed a little and chuckled. "Forget I said anything."

"No, I mean, with me . . . I can put minds at ease." Clyde recited the bits and pieces he'd overheard throughout his life about himself. "Someone can tell me something and their conscience is cleared. Whatever they cannot forgive themselves of, they tell it to me and the baggage of whatever thing they did is erased from their minds. They can't ever completely forget they did the thing they did, no, but they feel better about it, at any rate."

"Meech. Sure sounds like fabrick to me."

"There's that word again."

"Before you even ask, don't. Because that, my friend, is an even harder nut to crack. Not even a cake stand will do for a visual aid on that one, I'm afraid." He reached into his belt, where a series of satchels and pouches hung. He withdrew a long metal tube along with a leather pinch pouch that reminded Clyde of Miss Selby's coin purse. Flam carefully picked out what appeared to be black knots of mold clusters. He pushed one into the end of the pipe and paused.

"Just having a smoke, Pasty. I'm not a fabrick weaver."
Flam apparently could feel Clyde's unflinching gaze. "I am
most definitely unwoven, as the saying goes. Happily, I
might add. You want to see that in action, you best ask an
individual who isn't a Mouflon. None of us do any of that
business. Wouldn't even if given a choice, speaking for the
whole of my people quite confidently."

Flam lit the pipe with a match and puffed a few times.
A malodorous smoke filled the kitchen almost instantly.
Clyde flashed back to the time he'd volunteered to make
breakfast, gotten distracted, and the omelet he'd been trying to perfect somehow transformed into a flaky black discus
and stunk the manor up for a month. His master ate it
anyway, without complaint.

"Well, I do believe that pretty much settles things,"
Flam said. "A woven pale-faced man and a Mouflon traveling in a pair would go over about as well as trying to give
yourself a haircut with a paring knife in a funhouse hall of
mirrors while drunk." He reached past Clyde, hoisted the
blunderbuss from the kitchen counter, and threw its strap
over his shoulder. He turned in the doorway, the pipe held
by his large square teeth. He slurred, "Happy trails. Hope
you find what you're after."

He started to leave, glowing light stick in hand. Darkness crept in from the corners of the room. The cake stand
was drowned in shadow, every angle of the cupboards
gloomy. The window displaying the side yard gardens
betrayed no light. Without the glow of Flam's light stick,
the kitchen would be in absolute darkness.

"T-take me with you."

Flam kept moving. "My auto seats only one, Pasty. My

suggestion: bite the bullet and go to the Patrol guard towers. They're six blocks to the north. From there, I don't know what to tell you. Perhaps when you get to the refugee center outside Adeshka, where they got everyone else stashed, you can speak to someone there about your friend's murder. I'd take you there myself, but I'm sure the Patrol wouldn't be one bit too pleased about a scavenger picking about in the rich folks' ward. And trust me: they *will* ask where I found you."

"You mentioned the frigates. What about them? Can you take me to them?" Clyde had chased Flam into the foyer and now stood next to him, his hands outstretched. He had never begged. Never had to, not while living with his most recent master. And doing so with the previous ones would have only yielded smacks. With his sir, the only one deserving of being called sir, Clyde didn't require much besides lots to read, a fire to get warm by, and a roof over his head, but he always languished when he went too long without being able to serve a purpose. After too long without sponging a confession from a master, he would begin to feel a certain languor inching inward on his spirit. Maybe there was some legitimate biological reason behind the catatonic way he could find himself—which, as it was now obvious to him—could last longer than even he was privy to. Even six months, evidently.

"The closest frigate station is eighty meters to the north, across Jagged Bay, and over the mountain ranges, and those passes—let me tell you—ain't full of bandits intent on tickling passersby. And again, my auto only seats one. I think you should take this opportunity and consider yourself freed. Isn't a soul who can call themselves your master now." He gestured to the world beyond the front door, adding, "Enjoy it. I mean, I'm not a great *visual* example of entrepreneurship, but I assure you there is no greater pleasure than being your own boss, living *your* way."

Clyde brushed that away, waving his snow-white hands to the side as if escorting Flam's words off. Freedom could come later, when his friend's killer was brought to justice. Changing his tack would be the only way to get Flam's help. He needed it.

"You've done very bad things."

Flam straightened. "Meech. That's a mean thing to say. Plus, I believe that's my business and none of yours—"

"It's okay. It's fine. We all do them. We make bad choices; we foul up. We want to do the right thing and end up doing the opposite. The right choice isn't always clear." He felt that he was quoting his master directly, but it was fine; Flam didn't know. "But you're an individual who's been out in the world. Your scars tell me you've gotten into a few fights. Even that. You tell me about those times you got into a scuffle . . . and I'll help you feel better."

"Oh, no. No, no, no, no. You're not going to pull any of that fabrick on *me*." Flam raised his stony hands and backpedaled out of the foyer and into the parlor, blackness rushing away and being replaced with blue from his light stick with each step. The harp in the corner, the toothless maw of the fireplace—all blue. "You keep away from me, whatever you are. You wanted a tutoring lesson about Geyser; I gave it to you. But by no means are you going to fabricate anything in my head—make me spend the rest of my days believing I'm a brine cluster or something!"

"Just tell me anything. Something you did wrong once.

Please. It doesn't even have to be anything terrible, just something you regret a little." He was edging closer to Flam, hands reaching.

Flam backed into the wall. A picture fell, smashed.

"Please just let me be of use. Let me help; let me do this."

It came on fast. Flam began muttering, but it quickly developed into words and the confession found its narrative. He stared at the broken glass on the floor. "I was just a pup. I went into the candy shop up the street one day on summer break. I didn't have any change because it was just me, my brothers, and my mum. And I stole a piece of chark, just one stupid little piece of chark. I took it, I did. And . . . I brought it home . . . and my brother saw it, and he asked where I got it . . . and I told him I got money from Mrs. Wright. I sometimes did chores for her, but not during Middlemonth, which it was, the day I took the chark . . . He called me a liar and went to tell Mum . . . She was so mad . . . She made me go back down to the store and . . . I said I was sorry and swept the floors like the fella who ran the place asked. It felt like days. And then and only then, when I got home . . . Mum gave me a hug and told me it was . . . going to be . . . *okay*."

Clyde knew how it was for those getting sponged. The words came out, like thin alpine air, easy. The woody vines that had wrapped themselves around that memory for them would miraculously detangle, embedded thorns retracting, popping free of raw divots that soon, now vacated, could finally heal. He saw when Flam opened his eyes that he experienced the same sensation. The story had spilled out as if on greased tracks, one word after another until a complete confession was out.

"How do you feel?" Clyde asked, feeling much better himself, as if he could now hear better, stand straighter. A nestled sensation occupied his heart, a cradling warmth he had missed these past six months. *Sustenance:* a word from the dictionary that applied now.

"What's going on? Why do I feel strange? Is this when a frog's gonna fall out of my bum?"

"No, nothing like that's going to happen. But how do you *feel?*" This could be the ticket, the thing that would convince Flam to take him along.

"I feel as if I just got something off my chest, for certain, but I've told that story dozens of times. I'll admit, I've never been able to say it so . . . easily."

"You won't feel bad about that ever again."

"I guess you weren't fibbing before." Flam eyed Clyde. "What do they call this form of fabrick? Because that's certainly what this is."

"Is it fabrick what I do?" Clyde asked, looking down at his hands. He felt as if they were required during the sponging of a person who didn't want to give up the memory easily. Sometimes, if he concentrated hard enough when one of his masters was unfurling a wicked personal tale, he could almost feel the sharp edges of their transgressions cutting into his palms.

"I reckon that's what they'd call it." Flam put the pad of a finger to his forehead, minding the barbs, to check his own temperature. He then pressed the finger to the space of neck under the outcropping of his broad jaw.

"I can be of use," Clyde suggested.

Chin still up, Flam peered at Clyde. He took his fingers away from his neck and developed a strange—if a little wicked—smile.

"Why are you looking at me like that?"

"I'm seeing a booth all of a sudden. In some market somewhere, charging twenty spots per visit with the pale Calmer of Consciences. Plenty of folk out on the road with skeletons in their closets that could use a good brooming, I can tell ya." He beamed down at Clyde.

As much as Clyde wanted to say he absolutely wouldn't be used in that way, Flam would only say what he'd done with his fabrick up till this point wasn't much different. Besides, when asking a favor of someone, it was probably best not to shoot down his ideas.

One eye going squinty, Flam seemed to be working out the details. "All right," he said at last. "Come on."

Clyde stepped forward with relief, glad to have gotten through to the Mouflon.

"I feel incredible. This is great. I could almost sing," the Mouflon was saying as he pushed open the front doors to the chateau—and promptly tumbled down the fifteen steps to the front drive. He seemed unable to stop himself or throw out a hand to slow his fumbling descent. All the way down, Flam grunted, oofed, and thudded. Once at the bottom, he jumped to his feet, brushed himself off, and glared up at the threshold of the chateau where Clyde still stood.

Clyde looked. There had been nothing to trip on. Nothing at all.

"Consider myself a bit more nimble than that," Flam mumbled. "Even given my size, I tend to be pretty light on my feet."

Clyde put his hands in his pockets. Trying to keep a grim look of apology from his face, he pretended to study the steps for masonry errors.

"What is it?" Flam's shoulders drooped. "Don't tell me. Oh, Meech, do *not* tell me . . ."

Clyde gave a solemn nod. "Yeah. That's part of it."

Flam patted himself, perhaps checking for a second tail or a colony of boils surfacing on his lower back. "Oh, you weren't honest with me, were you? Shoulda *known!* Never trust a fabrick weaver! Never ever!"

Into Flam's deluge of curses, Clyde interjected, "Minor misfortunes."

This halted the Mouflon. Flam came back up a few steps, hooves clicking. "And what do you mean by 'minor misfortunes'?" He picked up his pipe from one of the steps. "Well? Speak up."

"Bad luck." Clyde spread his hands. "Rest assured, it's only temporary. Probably that tumble did it. That's probably all you'll get, especially given how little the confession was. But, yeah, that's the downside. Bad luck comes when the slate's wiped clean, I'm sorry to say . . . Could I ask you to stop making that face at me?"

"And a little too late!" He pointed a thick fingernail at Clyde. "You see? Fabrick of the worst kind right there. You're made with it; it's entwined in you—I can see it now. I knew it was too good to be true. I knew there had to be the other side of the coin. Meech, save me."

Clyde realized his journey had begun and ended before he'd even crossed the property line. "I suppose that means you've reconsidered and won't be taking me with you now."

Back turned, hands on hips, head bowed, Flam said, "I have to."

"You have to?"

"Yes, I *have* to." He spun about. "It's a Meech-damned Mouflon custom. We give our word on something, we gotta do it. That's why I was so stubborn about not wanting to do it. But there it is, fabrick doing what it does best, cursing some innocent wanderer for his generosity. To quote my gran: 'Mouflon and magic mustn't mix.' But"—he sighed, eyeing Clyde as if he were a mountain to be dragged to the other side of the planet by a length of chain—"a promise is a promise."

"I'm sorry," Clyde tried, the apology sounding more like a question.

"Forget it." Flam turned and, head hanging, paced across the front cobblestone drive to the gate, swearing with words Clyde had never heard, ending with, "Meech, curse my avarice." He kicked the gate open, which clanged loudly. Without turning back, he said, "Come on, then, Pasty. Night's a-wasting."

Clyde's heart skipped a beat. He stepped onto the front steps, pulled the chateau door closed behind him, and hurried to catch up.

CHAPTER 5

The Name on the Blade

Clyde had never been outside the front of the house without the cowl and chains on. He had seen the back gardens, the sky that a craft might dart by on the odd day—but seeing the front gardens, the barren streets, and the flickering lamplight, he could now imagine the sounds he had heard from within the house matched that of the street at night back when it thrived. The honk of auto horns, the chatter of people, the screech and clank of robots marching up and down, doing their duty to keep the gutters tidy, bending to fill dustpans or obliterate a wad of chewing gum with a quick zot of a laser.

He walked behind Flam, staying close, taking in all the sights his beady black eyes could capture. Magnificent, massive homes with turreted studies just like his master's chateau. Gardens with dry fountains, manicured walkways, gazebos of stone and wood, not to mention the ones of sediment shaped into beautiful, intricate designs.

He pointed at them. "Cynoscions do that as well?"

Flam glanced. "Aye," he grunted and kept walking.

More than once Clyde had to peel his gaze off something to catch up to his escort, who grumbled and kicked at trash in the street. A tin can danced out ahead of them, colliding with a railing and then falling into the gutter. Flam redirected his stride and gave it another punishing kick with his hooves.

Having kicked it out of range, the Mouflon led the way in a straight line. Despite his size, Flam moved surprisingly quietly. There was only the soft rustle of his armor, the brushing sound as his hairy limbs swayed—left, right, left.

Clyde noticed that even the traffic lights flickered, just like the street lamps. Flam pointed to his auto, camouflaged among other abandoned vehicles. His didn't look all that different from those it was parked among: battered and weathered with its chipping paint and dented fenders and one headlight gouged out of its fishlike front end. It stood as tall as Clyde, had a dusty glass bubble enclosure for a cockpit, a set of narrow wheels up front, and a third wheel in the back that was as tall as Flam, nubby and clotted with dirt from many days of travel. It was sleek and blocky simultaneously and appeared to be a hodgepodge of several other vehicles.

Setting his satchel on the ground, Flam popped the hatch on the auto's hull. He unloaded several items, some of which were delicate and wrapped in rags. Clyde didn't know what a lot of the objects were but watched as they were each placed within the auto's holds for safekeeping. One item went by that he did recognize: a short instrument in its scabbard, its ornate handle crafted from green-hued metal.

It belonged to his master.

"That's not yours. You said you wouldn't steal from my master. I've seen him with that letter opener; I know it's his."

Flam turned the short knife in his hand to get a better look at it in the moonlight. The street lamp flickered once, throwing a harsh white glare off of it temporarily. "I didn't steal this from your master's place. It's merely something they gave each person who moved into one of these homes, a sort of human tradition. Geyser government's way of letting the well-to-do folks believe they're part of the royal guard. *Honored,* I suppose is the term. And it's a dagger, not a letter opener."

"So it's not my master's?"

"No, his is probably still back where I found you, unless it was thieved by someone else. This particular one came from a pulse-deprived fellow across the way. Here, I'll show you." He withdrew the dagger from its scabbard, metal scratching the silence in the barren street. He turned it in his palm. "Presented to cherished citizen Mr. Mercurio Bansphere in honor of his commitment to Geyser. See? Bansphere. He wasn't your master . . . What was his name?"

Clyde blinked. "I never learned it."

"You're kidding me. You served how long, mopping the conscience of a man whose name you never even knew?"

"It wasn't my place to know it. Not his or any of my masters' before him."

"But I thought you said he had one of these." He waggled the dagger. "Didn't you ever get curious and read it?"

"I wasn't permitted to touch his things unless he said so. I only ever saw the handle. He never took it from its sheath. Not anytime I ever saw anyway. I assumed it was a letter opener; he didn't seem like the type to keep weapons in his house."

"Well, how in the plummets do you plan to find the individual responsible for killing him if you don't even know his name? Go 'round and ask everyone if they knew who killed the bloke that resided at . . . 4970 Wilkshire Lane in Geyser?" Flam said, guesstimating the address with a glance at the nearest street sign.

"His dagger," Clyde said, brightening. "I will go back and find it, and if it's the same as that one with an inscription, then I'll know my master's name."

Flam studied the sky. "We really need to move on. The power seems to be the most cooperative during the morning hours, so we should find some place to bed down for the night and start the fight to get the elevator working in the morning."

"Elevator?"

"Yes, the elevator—down to sea level, to the forest below Geyser. You didn't think we'd just jump off the edge, did you? From there, we'll take the ferry to the mainland, go through a few of the ghost towns, and I'll drop you off within a few miles of Adeshka. I would join you there, but there's a warrant for my arrest in that particular metropolis. There you'll find the frigate pilot you can beg to chase after the Odium, if that's what you want to do—but before we can do any of that, we need to take the elevator. And before we do *that*, apparently, you need to learn the name of the man you're seeking to avenge, so go!"

Clyde didn't need another word. He turned and ran up Wilkshire Lane toward the gates of his master's chateau.

Flam remained behind, watching the strange young man bolt up the street, clearer in intervals when the streetlights flickered.

The Mouflon, still holding the citizen dagger, drew it from its scabbard again and eyed the inscription. It was built for man and too tiny for Flam's hands. It might as well have been a toothpick. He turned and dropped it into the cargo compartment of his auto. It'd fetch a few spots. Enough for a meal, maybe two. Such was the life of the scavenger.

He looked back up the street. When the street lamps pulsed, the strange little man was nowhere to be seen. Probably already back at the house. Tiny people could move so fast. Flam removed the auto key from his satchel and rested his hand on the latch of the glass bubble of the cockpit. He opened it, raised one foot to get in. He considered leaving, going against his Mouflon promise and ditching the poor fool. He set his foot back down, slammed the cockpit shut, and loaded the rest of the loot.

To busy his hands and keep himself from thinking about leaving Clyde with nothing to return to but a dust cloud in his auto's absence, Flam smoked a pipe's worth of mold and idled about until the man in the butler uniform charged back down the street with the citizen dagger in his grip. He ran with such abandon, like a little kid, arms and legs flapping about as if he had no bones at all. Like this was for fun. But his face . . . it showed resolve. His strange little hairdo, that floppy pompadour that bounced down in front of his face with each stride, those mousy eyes, all black. Where in the world had this goof come from?

This will be my end. This will be what taps out my last bit of luck: toting this pale little turd around. It's like kismet, fate, pre-ordination—whatever you'd want to call it. I made the promise, and then he reveals he's a jinxing fabrick weaver. Lovely. It's like Meech himself is on high, sending down the telegraph: "Flam, you are hereby and forever screwed."

Clyde slowed his pace with slapping footsteps, then

plodded back. He doubled over to catch his breath. With his face cast downward, his words punched from his mouth between ragged gasps: "His name was Albert Wilkshire."

"Wilkshire," Flam echoed, turning and checking the street sign of the lane they stood upon. The same. "You think he owned this whole area, where all these mansions are? What did your master do for a living?"

Clyde stood tall, hands on hips, still breathing hard. "He was a great man, wise and kind. He worked in money in some capacity. That's all I know."

"Must've been great sums of it, given that he either owned this street or had it named after him. Either way, you know who you're avenging now, and you have a weapon of your own." Flam pointed at the dagger. "Keep it close, but don't have it showing. Do like I do, yeah?" Flam demonstrated moving a panel of his leather armor over the blunderbuss hanging at his side. "The Patrol will often shoot first and ask questions afterward if they see you're carrying anything more than a spoon. I once saw a poor fool gunned down while he was just holding a banana like a pistol."

"Like this?" Clyde asked, clipping the dagger's scabbard to the belt loop of his trousers and then covering it with his baggy suit coat.

Flam nodded, hopped into the cockpit of his auto, but left the glass bubble up so they could talk as he drove down the street. Flam occasionally tapped the accelerator to get the big wheel at the auto's rear a boost of momentum. Sometimes his foot suggested he should just floor it—the little fella would never catch up—but he didn't.

When they reached the next intersection and started turning left to head north to the city proper, Clyde looked over his shoulder toward the chateau. He regretted not burying Mr. Wilkshire, not committing him to the ground so he could rest in peace, but if Flam was to be believed, there was no time. Clyde didn't know whether to wave to the house or salute it and decided to give it the same grateful gesture he would give Albert Wilkshire himself: a simple bow, eyes closed, chin to chest.

When they turned the next corner, the chateau dropped from sight, but Clyde would always be able to see it in one way or another.

"I'll find whoever did it, Mr. Wilkshire. I promise."

CHAPTER 6

The Opposite of Up

The geyser from which the city got its name was within easy sight of South Main Street. Clyde thought it looked like a giant finger pushing up out of the middle of the city. When the electricity flickered on, the glowing spheres upon its rocky shell illustrated its striking height and cautioned potential night flyers of its presence.

Flam said, "Yep, there it is. Quite the sight back when it was still pushing a flow out. The whole city used to be under a cover of never-ending mist from it. Now look at it, as dead and dry as bone."

They moved closer down South Main Street, approaching the geyser a few blocks off. They were still in the seemingly endless thick of a residential ward, but by this point the houses and yards were shrinking. The closer to the town square they came, the more everything seemed to condense, as if the houses themselves were crowding toward the geyser for warmth. But whatever warmth it had been throwing off was gone. Just like the darkened houses encircling it, the geyser looked arid and spiritless.

"What stopped it?"

Flam tapped his hoofed toe to the auto's accelerator. "No one knows for sure. Sediment may have blocked it up; perhaps the well it was based upon finally dried up. No one really cared, it seemed. Once it stopped flowing, people moved on regardless of whether it could be fixed. Or so I assume; I haven't been in these parts for a while. That's just the wine of the grapevine."

The lights studding the geyser flickered once, a temporary flash. The effect moved in a ringing wave. The geyser would light up and darken first, followed by all the streetlights around them. Light, then all was dark once more.

"That keeps happening," Clyde murmured.

"We shouldn't get any closer." Flam braked, then made a wide U-turn in the street, passing in front of Clyde, apparently in hopes of peeling his focus away from the geyser.

"Why not? I want to see it."

Flam came to a full stop directly in Clyde's path. "The Patrol. They keep to the town square looking for stragglers or anyone *thick* enough to come to Geyser for assistance. We get spotted, and that's it. Whether we like it or not, we'll be headed straight to the refugee camp. Me, it'll probably be a prison autobus with a one-way ticket to Adeshka."

"What did you do there, anyway?"

The auto gave a malfunctioning chortle. The dashboard within the cockpit went into a frenzy of flashing lights.

Flam gave it a thump with a balled fist, and the vehicle's instrument panel returned to normal. He chuckled. "I won't tell you nothing about that, Pasty. Unless you want my auto to die out completely."

"I didn't mean it like that. I was just curious."

"Do you have control over it?"

Clyde's brow furrowed.

"Like," Flam continued, "can someone tell you something bad they did and you just be a good listener and not jinx them, or is it just . . . automatic?"

"Once it's in my ears, it's out of control." He ran a hand through his raven hair. "I wish it weren't so. It'd make swapping stories a lot more fun."

"Well, in that case, the story about what I did in Adeshka will have to wait. Maybe when we have a few days off, after our business venture is up and running, when there are no stairs to trip down or we don't have to rely on an auto to get anywhere."

Clyde wasn't certain, but it seemed as if Flam was trying to be . . . reassuring?

"In any case, let's get going. I don't like the look of this street."

Clyde agreed.

They moved along, avoiding going north any farther, and turned left.

Clyde wanted to see the geyser up close, to stand at its base and look straight up, as one would watch starships. But, like Flam's story about Adeshka, it would have to wait.

An hour later, they arrived at the elevator station in the south ward of Geyser. All around were shops and buildings, darkness inside their windows. Several autos were parked along the paved drives, all in worse condition than Flam's. The street was strewn with trash, a couple of forsaken pieces of luggage. A crumpled newspaper danced down the street, propelled by a cold and salty wind. The street lamps gave a plaintive splash of light, then died again. Every single time, Clyde hoped they'd stay lit just this once, but they never did.

Flam parked his auto before the chain-link gate of the

elevator. It was a massive space within, big enough to house dozens of people. Flam stepped out of his auto. He grunted as he lifted the gate and, with surprising ease, pushed the auto into the elevator car. He went over to the elevator station's control booth. Just like the streetlights and the glass spheres dotting the town's geyser, the panel for the elevator flickered on and off. Flam kept his hand on the power button, ready to push it when the time was right.

"We're not going down with your auto?" Clyde inquired.

"No," Flam said, distracted, missing a chance to mash the button when a surge came and went. "We'll lower the car first, just in case there are any bandits waiting for us below. The auto has a security feature in it that will alert me if anyone tries to open its cockpit once it's down there," he said and referred to a small device clipped to the bandolier crossing his breastplate. "Okay, here we go. I can feel it. Got some juice coming our way . . . right . . . about . . . *now!*" He hit the button, timing it precisely, and the elevator car burst with fierce fluorescent light, throwing the haggard automobile into illumination. The elevator made a deep groan of metal on metal, and the car lowered at a glacial rate.

Flam came out from the control box and watched through the chain-link gate as his auto made its slow stop-and-go descent.

"Is it really a mile down?" Clyde asked, looping his fingers through the links of the gate.

The unraveling rusty cables groaned loudly.

Flam looked around the surrounding neighborhood. "Yes, indeed. Had a few close calls nearly falling off the side. And let me tell you, both required me to go trouser shopping afterward."

"What keeps the bandits from coming up?"

"Nothing, but they're not as stupid as I am." Flam smiled. "See, I had family here once, so I'm in the citizen registry, even if just by proxy. If I get caught, I'll be treated with reasonable respect until they look up my record. The bandits with no registered family wouldn't be so fortunate. One has to either have kin in Geyser or be an employee to be welcomed." He shrugged. "Well, that was the way it worked before, anyhow."

The elevator's inner workings made a terrible howl. The gears were turning in infrequent shudders, spinning along smoothly and then frantically. A smell of burning oil came from the machine, and a thin smoke rose from its vents.

"Meech damn!" Flam said, pushing his face into the grate to see his auto in the elevator car below. There was a snap as loud as a gunshot, and the elevator car dropped. From above, one of the massive metal spools on which the elevator cable was suspended whizzed by. Flam roared, beat the fencing, watching the elevator car, with his auto, drop down, down, down. After nearly a full minute, there was a smash below. Flam lowered his head.

Beneath Geyser, the world was too dark to see anything but a brown smoke with a bright spot smoldering in the middle, the funeral pyre of Flam's auto.

"How many pieces of chark did you say you stole?" Clyde said.

"Shut it." Flam sighed and pushed away from the elevator to walk to Clyde. "How long does it usually last, anyway? This jinxing you've laid on me."

Clyde shrugged.

The tiny sparkle of fire burning far down grew.

"The longer ago it was, the worse the bad luck. The worse you felt about it and the longer you carried it with you, even *worse* the jinxing still."

"I should hope that my auto being destroyed was the end of my tab. I don't think I can take much more of this." He ran a paw down his face. "You know how long I had that auto? I still owe Ricky ten spots for that thing, too." Flam leaned against the wall of the elevator control booth and slid down until he was sitting on the sidewalk. He took out his pipe and sighed.

"Is there another elevator we can take down?"

"Sure." Flam laughed morosely. "It's on the north end of town, smack-dab in the middle of the Patrol fortification. Go ahead and waltz down there, give their gate a knock, ask if you can take a quick trip down if they're not too busy with it."

"Is there another way down without using an elevator?"

"Got a parachute? Yeah, me neither."

"And there's only the two elevators?"

"Yep."

Looking toward the central part of Geyser, Clyde could see the rocky tower through the trees lining the street. The lights came on upon its surface, then dimmed. "What about the geyser itself? It's not flowing as much anymore. Perhaps we could climb to the top, shimmy down inside, and maybe find a way to—"

"Now you're just being thick." Flam puffed smoke. "You go inside that thing, it's a straight shot to the underground lake. Water so hot down there you'd be turned to powder before you even made a splash. Sediment and toxic gas, completely unbreathable. It's the doorway to the plummets if I ever saw it."

"You've been in there?"

Against the night sky, the geyser momentarily materialized out of the murk, as if happy it was being mentioned in conversation and wanted to say hello.

Flam made a smoke ring, his eyelids at half-mast. He stared across the street toward the darkened storefronts, the gray circles of smoke drifting from his mouth. "Like I said, I had relatives who lived here. My uncle was an engineer for the Geyser sub works. Sometimes when Mum got good and tired of my shenanigans, she'd send me out here to stay with him. I'd work with him sometimes, repair the turbines or go down the sewer lines to breach a clog. Trust me, it wasn't as much fun as it sounds."

"So you've been inside."

"That I have."

"There has to be a way down besides the elevators, then."

Flam tore his gaze from the abandoned storefronts, his furry mug dented with impatience. He plucked the pipe from his mouth, the metal tip clicking on his teeth. "Look, Pasty, I don't think you're listening. The platter, the *cake stand* this city is built upon, isn't connected to the geyser itself. It's built around it. Sure, some of the turbines reach inside the geyser's floodway, but no man, no Mouflon, not even a Meech-damned Cynoscion could survive that heat."

"But if we timed it, like we did with the electricity to the elevator—"

"Because that turned out so swimmingly."

"—then we could, possibly, dodge the water when the geyser activates."

"Did you *see* how hard it was to get the elevator to work? How I had to time it just right? The geyser isn't on a set schedule. It's not clockwork; it's not automated or set by any watch. It bursts when it wants to. Besides, getting to the top and going down inside—that's half a mile below just to where the platter is. And another half mile to the island, and then . . . This is daft. I don't even know why we're considering this. Scratch that; I don't even know why *you're* considering this. Once you get in there, it's a straight fall to the plummets."

"Perhaps in the plummets there's a way back to the surface," Clyde pondered aloud. "Go down and *then* up?"

Flam snorted. "The plummets is a figure of speech, Pasty. It's not a real place. Well, some believe it's a real place. It's myth. It's where Meech sends all the bad folk when they die. I'm sure you've heard of it: swimming in boiling tar and banging your head on razor rock every single time you dare surface, for all eternity?"

Clyde stared. How horrid.

"No big surprise there. Can't imagine your master was much of a religious sort. Money pads the mind, after all."

"And what's that supposed to mean?"

"Nothing. Forget I said anything." Flam stood up, grunting. "Come on. We'll figure all this bosh tomorrow morning." He began making his way across the street to a shuttered haberdashery.

"No, tell me what you meant by that," Clyde spat, matching Flam's stride. "My master was an honorable man. He said that every bad thing he did was a hard decision, that he was looking out for his company's best interest. That by hurting a few, he could save plenty more."

"Plenty more money, maybe. Everyone knows the rich folk don't do anything unless it increases the number of spots in their wallets. It's not your fault. You probably had no choice who you worked for."

"What are you implying? You believe that when my master died, he went to the plummets?"

"I don't imply anything. I know it. It's the best place for all the rich folk to go. Even if they didn't get a wake-up call in life, they sure as plummets got one when they died. Deservedly, too. Never saw a single pampered rich individual do anything he wouldn't benefit from. And don't tell me your master was different, that he gave to the poor and volunteered to ladle stew at the orphanages. He had *you* around to clear his conscience. From where I'm standing, that's evidence enough he wasn't a good bloke."

The speed of Clyde's stride died halfway across the boulevard from the haberdashery. He was stunned by the accusation. He could scarcely believe he was actually giving it thought now. Ahead, Flam stopped as well, about-faced, and caught the look of hate written in the pale man's onyx eyes.

"Listen, Pasty—"

"You take that back this instant." It was barely more than a whisper.

"Or what? You'll use your fabrick and make me say something else I did that was naughty in my time, so that when I go to use the pot, the thing will clog and overflow on me? Save your threats, Weaver. I didn't mean anything by it. You should know that all of us Mouflons are like this—blatantly honest—unlike humans, who spin secrets and gossip and stab one another in the back. Just look at this place, and you'll see what I mean. You don't suppose the Odium is made up of anything but humans, do you?"

"I'm not talking about the Odium. I'm talking about Mr. Wilkshire."

"Pasty. It's honorable. Really, it is—you regarding your former keeper as a great man. And I'm sure he was one spectacular bloke in life. Liked by all who knew him. But you should learn this now about the world while you're still new to it. *Rich* men and *good* men are, without question, mutually exclusive. All those rich bastards, when they die? Not a single one goes to Meech. Where they go is the *opposite* of up."

"I don't want you to say anything else about him. You promised to help me, and if you want to, that's part of it. Speaking ill of Mr. Wilkshire is as bad as not helping me, and you said it's a custom of your people to stick to what you promise."

"Fine. Whatever you say, Your Majesty. Forgive my trespasses upon Mr. Wilkshire, hallowed be his name." He bowed, lowering his head until his horns nearly touched his knees. Without ceremony, he stood upright and stepped onto the curb in front of the haberdashery's front doors. He shouldered them open with a thunderous crack of wood.

He glanced back at Clyde, still standing stock-still in the middle of the street. "Well, come on, Pasty. We should probably get some shut-eye if we're going to find a way down tomorrow so you can begin your journey to avenge the regal Mr. Wilkshire."

Despite really wanting to spit back that he never slept, Clyde refrained. He turned his back on Flam to take one last glance at the geyser towering over the city, an enduring sentinel that could do nothing but observe. The lights came on, went dead again, a glum wisp of steam popped up off its summit, immediately chased away in the wind.

A moment later, the lights around him, even within the haberdashery itself, came on and again went dead. Reluctantly, he followed his guide inside.

CHAPTER 7

The Bullet Eater

A wake.

Immediately the odors drifted in, replacing the pleasant ones of Aksel's flowery dreams. Gone was the new car smell, freshly oiled leather, musky colognes, the glorious aromas of crisp money, fresh-baked bread, good dark coffee, pepper-crusted cuttle steaks. Now it was just the encyclopedic tour of the stinks outside his shack. Stagnant ponds of human waste, spoiled meals, and food that had been cooked despite being rotten and smelling like, well, a ladleful of the first thing. He hated this place—the camp, the shantytown. He was an accidental refugee, and that, too, he hated.

Aksel sat up and took stock of his surroundings. The clapboard walls, the panel of rusty, corrugated steel that he'd lashed down with some twine for a makeshift roof. Nothing new, different, or missing. But mostly he looked over his personal belongings littering the earthen floor. There was no way to securely lock his shack, since doors were a commodity not afforded in any of the temporary shelters.

He sat up and, as on any other morning, grabbed his eye patch from where he had left it for the night, dangling from a nail driven into the wall, and pulled it on. Next, he put on his threadbare duster jacket, which had only one complete sleeve. He tugged on his trousers, which in a previous life may have been a sack for transporting pota-toes. His boots were good and were the thing that got him into the most fights, no matter how much he took a rock to them to make them look scuffed or how many mud puddles he went out of his way to step in to sully their appearance. Everyone had been here long enough—if the tick marks on his shack wall could be trusted, a little over half a year—and reliable footwear was a hard thing to hide.

Outside, the suns were high already. The heat was stifling. He wondered why it was that everyone from Geyser was taken here, to Adeshka, where it was always so damn warm. Of course, it wasn't as they said it would be. None of the refugees from Geyser were permitted inside Adeshka's walls. The camp was a good half mile up the road, cor-doned off by high fences, the gates always manned. He'd had a hard life, but this was downright dishonorable. He felt like a caged animal awaiting his turn to get the shove up the ramp of the abattoir. Hell, after this heat, the hatchet would almost be welcome. But they killed no one at the refugee camp. Well, the guards didn't kill anyone. Didn't mean the refugees themselves didn't.

He tried to ignore it—the heat, the smells, the babies crying and families arguing—forcing his imagination to paint him elsewhere. On holiday somewhere. Somewhere nice. Eye closed, ignoring everything around him to the best of his ability and just focusing on the suns' warmth bathing his face, he may've very well been on another planet entirely. A planet whose sole existence was to be a place for rich folk to vacation, weeks upon weeks spent sprawling on beaches, sipping generously spiked fruit drinks from a chark husk, listening to the tropical music, riffs and clangs of homemade instruments played with incandescent joy, joy, joy.

He opened his eye, and that vacay spot in his imagination vaporized, the music echoing for one blessed second longer, the last victim to reality crashing in.

No, the only music here were gunshots, the all-too-frequent spat over rations, supplies, a chance at the showers, or when they'd get to return home to the city—and beyond that, persistently, babies' cries. Although Aksel looked a brute, a dirty, haggard savage with no heart, he hated the sound of babies crying; it always made his remaining eye water up. Try as he might to hide it, there it'd come. Somewhere under his leathery exterior, well concealed, was a golden, pumping heart.

The sister city of Adeshka looked like a giant glass blister on the horizon. Weather didn't affect them, nor did the dust storms that struck the refugee camp weekly. Not with that nice atmo bubble over their heads.

Aksel stood on a pile of trash to get a better vantage over the fences. He surveyed the mighty city, biggest in all Gleese, with its faceless blocky-shaped buildings, its three layers of crisscrossed elevated roadways that from above looked like a bowl of spaghetti. There were aircrafts darting about as well, but from this distance, they appeared to be mere bugs with determined trajectories, looping in and out among the enormous buildings—buildings with fresh running water, soft beds, food that appeared with a click of a button and a swipe of a piece of plastic.

He had spots to him, hidden in a hollowed boot heel. Probably enough for a burger—maybe a burger and a small order of fries. It was strange. Things he never knew he'd miss he now stayed up nights torturing himself about. Grilled slab cut from a freshly butchered cuttle, a mix of white and dark meat picked clean of scales, slathered with mustard, honest-to-goodness real mayonnaise, a buttered bun toasted on the griddle . . .

"Enough," he told himself. There was no point in it—longing for good food—not while they were still all here for their indefinite and undeserved sentence. He hopped and slid on his heels down the mountain of trash. He bypassed the muddy river that some people voluntarily drank from knowing there was scarcely a better way to give themselves bone worms. There was clean water to be had—just had to know the right fellow to ask.

Ricard "Ricky" Pembrawn was just such a fellow. He was like Aksel in the way that he'd been brought to the camp by accident. Neither man had been an actual Geyser citizen but had acquired a trader's pass, came in with their assorted junk to sell and hawk in the town square, and when the announcement came over the city-wide loud-speaker that everyone had to get to the elevators, go down to sea level, and board a shuttle bound for Adeshka, well, there wasn't enough explaining under the suns that'd get them out of having to go along. They'd both tried to let the Patrol rounding them up know—"I don't actually live here, you see. I'm just a trader!"—but they got pushed right along with the rest, their goods slapped out of their hands as they were ushered into the cramped interior of the water-capable aircraft and whisked off to the mainland, jettisoned to the camp on autobuses, and then through the gates: slam, click, welcome home.

Ricky was where Aksel always found him, square in

the middle of the camp, where a sort of hub had naturally developed early on. It was like an agora of sorts, where people hung out and talked, some scheming, most complaining, some fighting over a sliver of shade where it could be found, wrestling along with it as it slowly shortened and disappeared. Even after it was dark and there was shade everywhere, the fight would continue, because what else was there to do?

But Ricky was a dyed-in-the-wool businessman and, even though his cart had been left behind, he mostly sold automobile parts (under the term *gently used*, though all his dedicated patrons knew that was just a different way of saying *stolen*), traveling most star systems in and around Gleese using Adeshka and Geyser as a center point of his travels. He never strayed much farther, having found a reliable income stream to dip his line in here. Good for him, sticking to it like that.

Aksel, on the other hand, set up no shop here. He decided to consider his time as a refugee as a sort of sabbatical from hustling junk to knaves. *I really am that desperate for a vacation, aren't I?* he mused.

Walking closer, Aksel noticed that Ricky's storefront in the camp wasn't as good as the others', despite Ricky's constant attempts at improving it. It still looked like a poor attempt at a lemonade stand, complete with crooked counter. Its leaning sign, painted with a grease pen, meant to announce Ricky's General Store, Seller of Fine Wares and Whatnots, but had every word misspelled save for the proprietor's name, bless his heart.

"Morning," Ricky said, tipping the visor he'd made from a scrap of a lamp shade and elastic he'd pinched from a woman's discarded brassiere. The greeting was dull, much like any other exchange you'd hear in the cheerless camp.

"Got something to drink?" Aksel leaned in, elbows on the counter.

Ricky set aside his sheathed knife with the twelve-inch blade he'd been using improperly to squiggle a whetstone across the countertop. He kept everything boxed inside the stand itself as a safety measure. Before, he kept everything behind him, but thieves were coming up to him, distracting him with idle chitchat, while their friends went behind, pocketing everything they could carry. Took a few times, but Ricky got smart and rebuilt the stand.

"I got some of this," Ricky said, producing a soda can. A plastic bag was attached to its top with a rubber band, the inside dotted with condensation. Ricky gave it a testing shake near Aksel's ear, and some residual carbonation crackled and hissed within.

"Fine." Aksel took a furtive peek about him and saw people across the way watching, trying their best to play the roles of Nonchalant Men #1 and #2. It was best not to reveal where he kept his cache of spots right now. "Put the drink on my tab."

His friend agreed reluctantly and handed the drink over.

Aksel snapped off the plastic bag and drank deeply. It was a lemon-lime flavor, chemically enhanced. His tongue felt like the inside of a banana peel as soon as he swallowed.

Glancing back, he saw Nonchalant Man #1 wave to someone coming up an alleyway between the shanties. The angle was funny, so Aksel couldn't see who it was. Nonchalant Man #2 pointed toward Ricky's stand, and another set of men joined them.

Aksel turned around so it wouldn't be obvious he knew he was being talked about. "Come by my place tonight." He ran his tongue against the edge of his front teeth a few times, spat. "I'll pay you then. I would now, but . . ." He bumped one shoulder to indicate the roughs across the way.

"You mean my new secret admirers?" Ricky smiled sardonically, not a tooth in his head white. His skin was suns ruined, and he was so thin his bones jutted out everywhere to the point that he looked almost thorny.

But Aksel, one eye or none, didn't care about any of that. He knew Ricky was all generosity, big hearted, and so loyal to those he cared about it sometimes made him almost seem a doting nitwit. In short, he was his best friend. Not that he'd ever tell him that. Nah. No need. Mates don't need to spell it out; they just know.

"Been giving you trouble?"

"Some. Haven't given them anything. Keep that close at hand"—he nodded the green beak of his visor toward the knife he'd been busy ruining—"and they usually get the idea."

"Never had this much trouble in Geyser."

"Had the Patrol. Anyone messed with the market, they usually ended up getting Executioner Mallencroix sent after them."

Aksel shivered. "Come on, mate. It's too early for that name."

"Sorry." Ricky laughed. "You don't miss having to blindfold yourself every time there was a Patrol raid when he was after someone?"

"No, I don't."

"Say, are they still looking this way?" Ricky glimpsed

over Aksel's shoulder, cocked an eyebrow.

Aksel glanced to make sure Ricky was indicating the same two men he'd noticed. Sure enough. They were back to feigning they weren't watching them, so Aksel openly stared their way. Getting a better look, he remembered having seen them around. They were similar in build and coloring—big, flaky red with suns-burns, hair cut to stubble, maybe with a piece of broken glass.

However, for as close to brothers as these two sods could've been, one was notably different: bigger, fatter, meaner. Aksel recalled a few of the man's bold displays toward a few of the weaker men around the camp, muscling old and young alike out of their water and toiletry rations. The others always handed them over after one shake of the man's meaty fist. Aksel couldn't deny he would do the same in their position. The terrifying man was made all the more menacing by a jagged pink scar across his neck. It was as if someone had tried to covertly slit his throat but couldn't saw deep enough to penetrate the protective collar of flab. While absently eyeing Aksel as if he were something to eat, Neck Scar scratched at his belly, making the entire mass of his midsection jiggle.

"How is it that he's so fat still?"

"Beats me," Ricky said. "Must have a friend in Adeshka, someone who comes out and passes things through the fence to him. Don't know how anyone could hold on to that much chub any other way." He felt his own flank, his ribs visible through his shirt.

"Ever consider asking him? See if you could cut a deal?" Aksel teased.

"And end up in his pocket? I think not."

"Still," Aksel said, swirling the can to try and get any lingering carbonation to liven up, "we're not going to be here forever. Why not make the most of it while you can? Ask him if he'd share the name of his cookie supplier and go from there? Make a few more bucks, and in another few weeks we'll be out of here, the spots you get out of the deal yours to keep."

Ricky wasn't paying attention. He wasn't looking at the brute, but his hands were poised on the stamped leather of his business protection device: his serrated hunting knife.

"You're such a knucklehead," Ricky said suddenly, lifting his chin so fast a drop of sweat was launched from one of his wispy sideburns. "You really think at some point we're actually going to be let out of here?"

"I have no reason to believe anything else."

"You were in Geyser same time as me. You knew that something was up, too."

"How do you mean?"

"You remember. We were in the square, setting up for the morning, and we saw that bunch of blokes who work down in the mines *aboveground* after their last whistle. They were going to the palace, all hurried like they each had a turd crossways, quiet as if they had some big secret. A week later, boom, here we are."

"The Odium, Rick." They'd gone over this many times already. "Everyone had to leave because the pirates were on their way."

Ricky sighed. "See? You're thick. Listen to me, would you? When those miners were cutting across the square, bound for the palace, they weren't walking with men with bad news to deliver; they were walking like men who had big, full pockets, looking over their shoulders and shite. I'm telling you: they found something down there."

Leaning forward, Aksel lowered his head. The suns beating on his back and this conversation were equally exhausting. "I think you've spent too much time alone with your thoughts. You should take up a hobby, study yodeling or something."

Ricky rolled his eyes. "Listen to me, would you? Don't you know the law in Geyser? Any sudden influx of wealth over a certain amount has to be evenly distributed to all its citizens. It's what keeps everyone there so damn happy. Well, back before all this other shite went down of course."

"Wouldn't matter to us much, would it, though?" Aksel grunted, resting his chin on his folded arms. He kept his back perpendicular to the ground, legs locked. Strangely, it was a comfortable position. His voice was muffled as he dropped his face into the coil of his arms. "We were just there with traders' permits. Quite a difference from being on the citizens' registry."

"No, but we *know* something, which is just as valuable as a wallet full of spots."

A voice, rumbly and terrifying, echoed, "Who's got a wallet full of spots?"

Aksel shot upright so fast he momentarily saw a white haze pass in front of his eye. He tried to turn around with forced calmness, as if Neck Scar and friends were nothing more than a band of biddies brandishing butterscotches.

"Hey, pal," Ricky addressed Neck Scar. "What can I do you for?"

"Shut your face, *madaca'floon*." Neck Scar squinted at Ricky.

Neck Scar was shirtless, as always.

Aksel said, "You know, with a pelt such as yours, Ricky and I could just go into the lamp oil business. Got enough blubber here to light the entire camp for a year, I suspect."

Neck Scar looked dumbstruck, then quickly glared. "What did you say to me, Bullet Eater?"

Behind him, Ricky whispered, "What are you doing?"

Bullet Eater. The blood pumped through Aksel's ears so fast he felt light-headed and could hardly hear Neck Scar's buddies laughing. "I'm not a Bullet Eater. Leave me and my friend—"

"Funny, you got that Rent-a-Killer look to you." Neck Scar flicked Aksel's lapel. "The duds, the coat. You look like an Odium reject if I ever saw one. You got Dreck's mark? Let's see that hand, man."

Aksel raised his right hand. It was said that if you were to be ejected from the Odium, their leader had to cut a perfect square of flesh from your palm, administering the badge of the unworthy. Just in case you wanted to go back to an anonymous life, you couldn't. Upon Aksel's leathery palm, there was no discolored square. It was just a regular, if filthy, hand.

"Doesn't mean you're not some killer." Neck Scar moved forward, his breath hot as if something inside of him boiled, its odor strangely sugary. "Probably means you just go after women, little kids. Yeah, I heard about you, man."

Aksel held his ground. "And what did you hear?"

"I heard you ate a man's heart, psycho."

"What could I do? It was a dare."

Despite their allegiance to Neck Scar, the shirtless men behind their leader gave a braying round of laughter. One glare from Neck Scar snuffed it.

It was the only opening the brute was going to give, Aksel knew, and he took it. He flipped his eye patch up and away, as the cannon hatch on the flank of an old maritime war vessel would be readied. Half a second later, Neck Scar looked back, aghast at the ungainly, yawning hole in Aksel's face.

"What the hell are you doing?" the fat man muttered. When from Aksel's eye socket a telescoping metal shaft slid out, Neck Scar grimaced. Neck Scar and each of his men took a full step back, turned partly from the strange sight. Their resolve began to steel within a moment; their eyebrows dropped, and their fists rose.

"I don't want to do this," Aksel said, the gun barrel ejecting from his right eye socket reaching its maximum length and clicking metallically as it locked into place. The springs inside his neck positioned next, and then came the hollow snap as the round was loaded with a mere flex of his jaw.

"You *are* a Bullet Eater. I knew it."

"Leave me and my friend alone."

"You ain't s-supposed to have g-guns in here. I'm going to get a guard right now and tell him what you got. They'll cut your head open to get that thing out of there, Bullet Eater."

Neck Scar and his friends backed off. Now it was just the departing exchange of barks, promises, threats.

Aksel knew he had won, so he gave no reply, just kept the barrel trained until the men were out of sight. With a twitch of his head, a sideways flick, the barrel shot back in and the springs released in his neck.

He turned back to Ricky, dropping the eye patch with a flick of his finger.

Ricky shook his head. "See what I mean? Knucklehead behavior right there."

"What else could I do? Clearly they weren't going to back down. They heard us talking about money."

"Look in my eyes when I say this, Aksel. You looking? Right here. Okay? Now listen. *You're an idiot.*"

"Yeah, yeah, I know." He turned to watch Neck Scar and his friends make toward the nearest guard tower. He hoisted his soda and drained its dregs. It would probably be the last drink he'd have for some time once the guards got the cuffs on him. Sure, he could try to run and hide, but in a four-hundred-square-foot camp with razor wire fences all around, it'd be only a matter of time. "He called me a Bullet Eater."

"But you are one."

"Yeah, but I'm not a pirate. And to them, it's one and the same."

"Hey, I didn't say it."

"I know. Forget it. Anyway, my place tonight. I'll pay you."

"I know you will," Ricky said. "See you then."

Aksel turned and plodded away. Halfway back to his shack, he pitched the soda can over the fence, just to watch the auto turrets stationed along the guard towers turn precisely and blast it out of the air.

CHAPTER 8

Roadblock

The palace had seventeen bathrooms, twenty-eight bedrooms, three armories, barracks in the basement, and one royal chamber where the king could sleep without worry. The walls were three-feet-thick galvanized steel. The doors, with a simple uttering of the word *secure* could be locked eight times over, air sealed, and filled with a quick-hardening liquid metal that, once cooled, could never be cracked.

This is where Pitka Gorett found he was most comfortable doing his daily duties: keeping an eye on the monitors and watching his men run their circuits about the palace grounds, endlessly training. Of course, the irregularity in the electrical flow of Geyser kept things hair-pullingly vexing. His monitors would die out, come on a moment later, stay lit for a handful of seconds, only to black out again. Gorett had taken to looking out the master chamber's windows instead to watch the men train. He liked seeing them all lined up, in four-by-four squares of armor and guns, ready for anything. They looked like mechanical armadillos from this high up, a funny notion. Just armadillos that were organized, trained, and willing to kill at the drop of a hat. A stalwart army ideally suited to the situation.

Geyser was dead, and there were no citizens to keep in line anymore. The Patrol could work as a genuine army now and keep the city safe not from itself, as a police force would, but from interlopers who would try to knock Gorett's plans off course.

They had put up the walls surrounding the palace grounds, and Gorett liked it better that way. The previous king had been a fool and always kept the front gardens open, like a park for peasants to picnic in, letting their insipid children run, shout, and play.

The guardsmen filed up the ramp and into the back of their armored auto, the massive black thing with six nubby wheels, slot windows, wholly impregnable. The gunner popped out the top through a hatch and gripped the handles of the turret's machine gun. The gates were lowered, and the auto rolled through right on schedule for its morning rounds. The few that remained behind began a game of catch ball, using the forward walls of the fortress as the bouncing board. Normally this would aggravate Gorett, but he had to be honest with himself: things had gotten mundane in Geyser since the populous had been evicted.

Six months ago, there was screaming in the streets, panic roused from toxic gossip about a Blatta infestation: insects the size of large dogs right under everyone's feet, wanting to devour everyone.

Gorett enjoyed the news, as if he were watching broadcasts. Everyone was scared, fleeing to sea level, boarding ships set for the refugee camps, "for your own good," as he'd said in his address to the city. "Let us stay behind to take care of this problem for you, my beloved people," he'd said.

Soon, Geyser was vacant. Of course, none of them knew it was all orchestrated. Certainly, the Blatta would be taken care of, but the deposit of wendal stone could also be dredged up from below and sent off to a moneychanger. Something that couldn't be done with so many still in the citizen registry.

As refugees camped out in and around Adeshka, Geyser's sister city, they'd be temporary citizens of *that* city instead.

Why go to such lengths? That pesky law about any sudden windfall that came to Geyser had to be evenly distributed. Yes, the law could be changed, but the people wouldn't forget it so fast. If they knew about the deposit, they'd all want their even piece, leaving damn near nil for Gorett. Better they were gone so the transaction could be made without them knowing it ever happened.

A few had suggested letting the Odium wipe the city out entirely, but dead men can't work, can't make a city run. Killing them was not an option. A king couldn't be king if there was no one to be a king for, and Gorett liked his title. And while he knew he had an incurable avarice, he didn't want his hands bloody. So long as those who knew the secret of his true intentions—the Stitcher and the Executioner— remained securely detained and gagged, all would be fine. The Stitcher was in no position to talk to anyone; before long, with any luck, her mind would go.

A rapping at the door startled Gorett, and he spun away from the window as well as his daydream. What could possibly be the trouble this early in the morning?

A guardsman stood in his doorway. Pleated armor covered his chest, and ribbed panels of metal protected his shoulders, forearms, and legs. The only spot of flesh visible on the guardsman was his face when he lifted the dark-tinted visor. "Sir, we just got word from the Patrol alpha squad. The south elevator has been broken."

"What do you mean?"

"The car fell sometime in the night."

"All your men were accounted for last night?"

There had been a few deserters at first, but that had tapered off in the first few months. Bandits, sabotage? The machine falling into disrepair on its own seemed most likely. The salty wind from Jagged Bay could rust anything to uselessness. He suggested the possibility.

"No, it appears it was broken when someone tried to use it late last night. The surveillance cameras caught very little, only a couple seconds' worth of footage because of the electrical problems we're having, but it clearly shows a man and an armed Mouflon. But there may've been more."

Gorett turned toward the window and looked south. *Straggling ticks requiring a tweezing.* "Come to Geyser to kick her while she's down and rifle through her pockets, have they?"

"Perhaps we should apprehend them, ask them to work for us." The guard said the word *ask* like the joke it was. Sure, they'd *ask*—with pistol in hand. No sane person would go underground willingly.

"Apprehending them is a must," Gorett stated, "but as far as getting them to work for us, I'm not so sure. Sending them into the mines could be a problem. They could tamper with things and make an even worse mess for us." He took a deep breath and let it out through his considerable nose, the sound like a broken steam valve letting off pressure. The wendal stone deposit was so close yet so far away.

"I agree, sir."

"If the elevator in the south ward is broken, that means they're either dead at the bottom of the shaft or still in the city. Find them and take care of it. We have enough mouths to feed without taking on prisoners as well."

"Sir." The guardsman bowed.

Gorett looked to the geyser. In his high chambers, he was nearly at eye level with its summit. He watched it sometimes during the day, waiting for the top to boil over with a horde of insects. It had never happened, but he never stopped expecting it.

The guardsman cleared his throat courteously. "Anything else, sir?"

Gorett muttered, "Any progress?"

"We lost another three," the guardsman reported gravely. "They don't want us down there."

Gorett chewed on that. "Give it a couple of days, then try again. Send some of the privates, some of the more expendable." He paused. "How many of us do we still have?" He referred to the guardsman as *us*, as if he considered himself one of them, but he didn't.

"Fifty-six men."

"Then send two. Two privates. Yes, that'll do. Leave me."

"Very good, sir," the guardsman replied, clicked his heels together, bowed again but deeper this time, and left the king to his work. The guardsman thumbed the receiver of his radio before he had even left the main chambers, issuing the order. "Look for the bandits if they're still in the city, and start a lottery to choose the privates who'll head underground."

Alone again, Gorett took up a set of antique binoculars. The elevator station was all the way on the other side. He would've seen it if not for the bulwarks around the palace grounds. He spied the top of the skyscrapers in the easterly ward and, of course, the geyser again. He lowered the binoculars and dragged a hand through his silver-streaked hair.

At least this was a different problem from that of the regular workweek morning: managing an abandoned city. Some action—a harrowing chase and a consequent kill for reward—might just keep some of the men on their toes. Even Gorett livened up at the prospect. Getting a foot on the throat of the city had been exciting, but holding it there and waiting had become a bore. Warriors need an enemy, and who better than a corpse-picking set of bandits? For the sake of his men's waning blood thirst, Gorett hoped the bandits remained inside the city so his men could remember how good it felt to drink.

Flam found it suspicious that the pale man didn't ever need to drink anything, eat anything, or, as he'd learned the previous tonight, sleep. He wondered what burned inside the man to keep his gears turning. He watched him move about the haberdashery, reading, looking, delicately picking items up and checking their underside for the price tag. He was childlike in the quiet way he explored and took things in. There were no wrinkles or signs of age upon him anywhere. His attire gave him a stately air, with the tails of his suit coat hanging nearly to the backs of his knees, his shiny black hair always in a neat pile atop his head. He trod about in his scuffed-up loafers that made his feet appear clownish. *Odd duck, this one.*

Flam had just pulled the bedroll blanket over himself and let the ashen man explore the haberdashery as he would. Flam quickly fell asleep and had nightmares of tumbling into the plummets, into the red maw of the geyser.

When he awoke, several parts of his stocky frame

ached as if he had spent the entire night running. He sat up and saw Clyde still up, seated behind the counter, going through a heavy gilt-leafed tome he'd found sometime in the night.

"Still up, huh?"

Clyde kept studying the book. "That I am."

Still sore about last night, apparently. *Maybe I was a little too harsh about his friend,* Flam thought. *Think about how you felt when your uncle Greenspire died. What if someone said mean things about him? You would've knocked their block off.*

But apologizing was tough for Flam. Always had been. So he decided to just be a little nicer to Clyde. "What have you got there?" he asked, getting to his feet and fastening on his segments of armor.

"I'm looking to see if Mr. Wilkshire ever shopped here." Clyde held the book aloft, the cover inscribed by hand with the word *Purchases*. "There are so many signatures, and many of them are illegible. Sadly, I don't see it in here."

"Your friend was a rich bloke, Pasty. I really doubt he ever shopped at this junky place."

Clyde shut the ledger, and a defeated look formed on his face. He spun on the stool and peered through the window shutters. Gingerly, he hopped down, dodged the counter, and approached the front door, fully intending to open it and spring through, when Flam caught him by the crook of his elbow.

Flam shook his horned head. "It's fine to go roaming about in the night, but walking the streets of Geyser during the day is a bad idea. The Patrol has morning routes they take, up and down every boulevard." He checked his multidialed watch, set to various planets' times, focusing on Gleese's, specifically Geyser's. "Surely they'll be by any minute. The elevator across the street is, without a doubt, on their list of places to check. Their interest will be doubly piqued when they see it's been broken."

"So what are we going to do? Wait here?"

"No, we'll go out the back. There are some alleys we can take to the street on the other side of this ward. I have an idea how we can get out of Geyser and be on our way."

"You do? That's fantastic. Did you dream it up in the night? Mr. Wilkshire used to tell me he got his best ideas in dreams. Of course, I wouldn't know anything of that, never having slept a wink in my entire life."

"Okay, okay. Settle down." Flam gazed past Clyde to the windows.

Ducking, he squeezed his fingers between the shutters to get a better look at the street. The suns were bright, the sky cloudless for the first time since he had been in Geyser. The thunderheads appeared to have moved on, Geyser illuminated as if under a spotlight. They were more vulnerable than ever now.

Behind him, Clyde whispered, "What's your idea?"

Across the street, the chain-link gate of the elevator didn't appear to have been disturbed since they'd broken in the night before. The Patrol weren't engineers; most didn't know how to fix anything outside of their autos and firearms. But if they saw it broken, they would throw down pylons and yellow tape and put it on a checklist of places to attend to in the future. They may even post a robot as watchdog, since no Patrol guardsman wasted his day standing about. Especially on a sunny morning when there was plenty of sitting around to accomplish before the day was through . . .

A rigid finger poked Flam's side. "I asked you a question."

Flam straightened, jolted out of his trance. For a big brute, he was still ticklish. He stepped out of arm's reach so Clyde couldn't do that again.

Pulling out his pipe for the first smoke of the day, he said, "In the medical ward hospital there's an elevator that may go out of Geyser, used strictly for emergency care. Of course, that's just a rumor. My uncle was sent there once to tinker with one of the hospital lifts, but that may have just been for the hospital itself and not to go out the bottom of Geyser. Either way, it's worth checking on."

"Certainly is. Are we going right this instant?"

"Don't jump out of your skin. Let me get my things," Flam set to bundling his bedding, bending the sausage-shaped roll in half and stuffing it into his satchel. He fastened its clips to his belt of pouches. He picked up his blunderbuss, which had been at easy reach while he was sleeping, looped its strap over his shoulder, and hopped in place while the strap found a purchase on his armored shoulder. Everything on the shelves clattered and danced as he did.

Clyde looked around, mystified at the small earthquake.

"Don't say a word. I'll go on a diet when I feel like it."

Clyde made no remark but caught the blunderbuss in the sights of his beady black eyes.

It was a rather funny-looking weapon, Flam knew, because it wasn't clean and streamlined like most weapons sold at stores or in vending machines. It was a clunky thing, much like its owner, industrious and nothing more than it needed to be. A sturdy hodgepodge of various mechanical things, the most evident being the brand name of a vacuum cleaner still readable upon the barrel. The stock was made from wood pilfered from an old butter churn. The trigger mechanism was the spring and arm set from a typewriter, the trigger's finger pad the *F* key. *F* for Flam, he always told anyone who dared ask. But it could also mean a great deal of other things, depending on his mood.

"Where did you ever find that thing?"

"My uncle the master tinkerer made it." His eyes were set on Clyde, his smile of pride there one second and then rapidly fading the next, his heart stopping.

Clyde spun to look about the shop.

Flam grabbed him by his jacket sleeve and yanked them both to the floor.

"What? What is it?"

"*Quiet.*" Flam's ears swiveled this way and that inside the coil of his horns. "I think the Patrol just discovered we broke their lift."

Clyde did as he was told and listened as well. His ears weren't as sharp as Flam's, evidently, but over the heartbeats thrumming in his own narrow chest, he could hear it: an engine. A terrible rumbling. The clank and metallic shimmy of mechanized motion. Similar to Flam's auto but a throatier, more aggressive sound. He could barely keep his voice on an even keel. "Is it them?"

"Couldn't be anyone else." Flam regarded the back door of the haberdashery. He nudged the gauzy curtains aside, the view beyond the pane a long alleyway cluttered with waste bins and swollen trash bags.

"What are we going to do?" Clyde turned toward the front windows. Beyond the blinds, shadows moved, giving him a fleeting yet still terrible reminder of the fate of Mr. Wilkshire. The idling engine of the machine purred; doors creaked open and slammed shut. Metallic footfalls on cement. A group of them, Clyde perceived. In a hurry. But thankfully they were moving away, not closer.

Flam slapped a hand over his own mouth and went saucer eyed. Not at one of the windows but at something else.

Clyde saw the same thing and gaped.

On one of the shelves, a glass mermaid figurine teetered. Surely it had been put on the shelf carefully by the shop's proprietor, but during the earthquake Flam had unleashed indoors it must have been knocked askew to the point it was toeing—or finning—the edge. The translucent mermaid, smirking a dead-eyed sneer of pure mischief, seemed to playfully scrutinize them. *Shall I fall? Would that make a loud noise and alert the men pursuing you? Oh my, that'd cause quite a lot of trouble, now, wouldn't it?*

"Don't you dare do it, Fish Lady," Flam hissed. He couldn't move quickly without the figurine teetering even more. He could tiptoe to it and push it back from the edge.

Apparently, however, the dastardly thing deduced that now would be the right time to make its plunge to the floor, splintering into pieces. Loudly.

The shadows outside the window returned. They gathered by the windows closest to the front door, flanking it on either side. In silhouette, one figure raised a hand, as if to perform shadow puppets, all five fingers fanned.

Then only four fingers.

Three.

"They're coming inside," Flam hissed, taking a wad of Clyde's shirt and pulling him toward the back door.

Two.

One.

Flam kicked a hoof backwards, breaking the back door.

The front door opened at the same moment, the squadron of guardsmen filing in. They were ghastly, all made inhuman by their head-to-toe armor, their faces masked behind dark glass. All four raised automatic rifles to their shoulders and fired in unison.

Clyde heard the bullets whiz past his head as he was yanked into the alleyway, the glass of the open back door shattering some more. Flam pitched Clyde aside and slammed what remained of the door closed. Into the broken panel, Flam jammed the barrel of his blunderbuss and fired blindly into the shop—a deafening boom.

There was immediate return fire, the rifles screaming in a shrill whine, the bullets spraying apart the remnants of the door. Flam dodged to the safety of the shop's outer wall, dropped the blunderbuss open, and patiently slid in a new brass-jacketed round.

Clyde watched in horror, picking himself up from the trash-strewn floor of the alley.

"Cast down your arms, bandit," one of the guardsmen shouted. "Thievery is not tolerated in Geyser. What happens to you, even you'd know, is justice."

"Drop headfirst into the plummets, drone." Flam snapped the blunderbuss closed again. Without another word, he fired through the door frame.

Clyde couldn't cup his ears fast enough to block the brunt of the gun's riotous discharge. A clink, nearly inaudible to his injured eardrums, was still loud enough for him to detect.

At the mouth of the alleyway, a small cylinder rolled into view.

Clyde got to his feet, his gaze fixated on it, and tugged Flam's leather shoulder pad. The object matched his memory of the one that had fallen in the yard, when he and his master were having tea. Clyde's throat constricted, and his voice came out as a squeak. *"Flam . . ."*

"Lower your weapon now," the guard screamed from inside.

The cylinder spun in place, gaining momentum. Its metal hull shattered, and the space surrounding the grenade became a hanging ball of strange, greenish-gray light, the same as the other had produced. It mesmerized Clyde, though his stomach twisted and his mind lulled heavily in unfiltered gloom.

Flam had heard the noise and raised a hand toward the floating cloud of light to block his view.

He took Clyde by the arm and pulled him along the alleyway, until Clyde could no longer see the torpor-inducing orb. Out of its glare, Clyde felt better at once.

"Come on, Pasty. Up and at 'em." Flam shoved Clyde ahead so he could reload.

"What *was* that?" Clyde managed, rubbing his forehead.

Flam gave him another push with his paw. "Just get going."

Clyde charged ahead, his legs unsure beneath his slight frame. He got to the corner and rounded it to the street beyond, having to stop to let his mind settle. He felt as if at any moment he'd collapse.

Flam jogged to catch up, turning just as the guardsmen exited the shattered haberdashery doorway and brought their rifle stocks to their shoulders again.

Reaching the end of the alley, Flam stopped. He made no move to dodge their attack but smiled as he raised his weapon and cocked the hammer.

The guardsmen leaped to avoid the shot.

Flam fired, and the countless metal beads from the scattershot round ricocheted through the alleyway toward them—pinging off the brick, the cement floor, the trash containers.

When the guardsmen were sure the Mouflon wasn't going to fire on them again, they got to their feet and looked around. The end of the alley was empty. They gave chase, but the two bandits were too far ahead. They turned and cut back through the shop to pile into their armored auto.

Flam led the way. More than once he had to catch his new companion so he wouldn't tumble into the gutter. Clyde's hasty steps were dizzied and off-kilter.

Flam gripped Clyde's collar with one hand and the stock of his blunderbuss with the other. Every few steps, the Mouflon spun in place to check the road behind them. They were now on Third Circle Street, the third ring out from the town square. Many dead autos polluted the street, which was why Flam chose this particular road: the Patrol, in their massive vehicles, would be slowed by the wreckage.

Flam heard their engine choking and struggling, followed by a clash as they rammed their way in. But the farther Flam and Clyde went, the dimmer the sound became. Hopefully they'd soon realize they were blocked with no quick way around.

"What was that thing? My goodness . . . that light." Clyde groaned, gripping his belly. Sweat beaded his chalky forehead and dripped from his brow. "It's just like the one that—" He stopped, the memory of Mr. Wilkshire's demise much too painful to talk about.

"Gray light," Flam answered gravely.

"But what *is* it?"

"A poison for the mind, taken in through the eyes." He gave Clyde a tug, since it seemed he was having difficulty listening and walking at the same time. "Makes you wish you were dead, that stuff. Got hit with it once myself. Didn't feel right for a week."

When Clyde seemed to be coming around, Flam released him. The pale man took a few more crooked steps, braced himself on a bike rack, and then paced along the sidewalk regularly, if a little slowly.

Clyde looked up, the suns glaring in his eyes. All around were signs for shops advertising bread, pies, and the like. "Where are we going? Is this the way to the hospital you mentioned?"

"It's up ahead. We're in the market ward now. The medical district is on the west side of the city. We'll pass through here and be back on track in a minute or two." He broke his stare at the empty street behind them to look at Clyde. The bloke looked positively dour. "At least we have some more suns! All cannot be lost as long as we have them, eh?"

"I suppose," Clyde managed.

Clyde still hadn't seen the end of Geyser. They passed some larger shops, some of which stretched on for blocks. Every once in a while, when an alleyway or a break in trees allowed, he glimpsed the double horizon line: one where Geyser suddenly dropped off and the second where the planet itself looped around and down. It seemed there was no way to venture to the actual end of Geyser. The city was built close to the middle, and occasionally they went over a bridge that crossed a river flowing to the surrounding body of water that encircled the city. But even then, it was hard to see the horizons. The city was packed, every inch occupied, it seemed. Even the sidewalks were cluttered with newspaper machines, signs, and bales of trash.

"Where is he now?" Clyde asked.

"Who's that?" Flam was walking backwards again.

"Your uncle, the engineer. Maybe he can help us."

"That'd be a tall order. My uncle's with Meech now."

"Oh," Clyde said. "I'm sorry to hear that."

"It's fine; it was a while ago. He was sick. Went to work despite it. Had an accident. Died." He turned around to walk on but stopped in his tracks.

Clyde was about to apologize again for having brought it up but froze as well. He followed Flam's gaze. In the distance ahead, where Third Circle Street began to turn west, a parked auto—this one with six wheels, standing head and shoulders above even Flam—billowed exhaust. The engine's rumble could be heard even from three blocks away. It wasn't clean and new like the Patrol vehicle. This one was old, held together with welded patches of mismatched metal.

Flam urged Clyde out of sight. They ducked behind a row of newspaper dispensers. Flam kept his tree trunk of an arm pinned across Clyde to keep him hidden while he peeked his horned head around the machines. Flam's other hand slid to his gun, a practiced motion if Clyde had ever seen one.

"What is it?"

"Hard to say. It's not the Patrol; I know that much."

"How do you know?"

"They don't drive autos like that."

"Then who are they?"

"I don't even know if it's a *they*. I haven't seen anyone yet. Just an auto, idling there in the street. Must not give much of a damn about gas, just letting it sit there and run like that."

"Perhaps they're citizens coming out of hiding?"

Flam peered around the edge, watching and listening. Flam's pointed ears twitched and swiveled in the space allotted by the curl of his horns, trying to pick up any sort of sound. When Clyde quietly exhaled due to the stink of the garbage canisters, the ear closest to him swung his way, then back toward the street.

"They're probably bandits laying a trap for the Patrol. That's what it looks like to me, at any rate. Leave an auto in the middle of the road, have the Patrol come up on it, explode it somehow, grab the guns and ammunition or supplies from the bodies. Worth sacrificing an auto for a few dozen bullets if you're making that kind of livelihood."

"Should we find a way around them?"

The suns were directly above, chasing each other across the sky.

"Afraid not. Morning's nearly over. Since we pissed in the beehive, they'll be coming this way once they find a way through. We should hunker down, hide out until they pass, let the Patrol clear the road, and we'll keep moving along."

"Where? Where should we hide?"

Flam noticed the grocery store behind them. The door was blocked with merchant carts, but it could easily be cleared with Clyde's help. "Here's better than anywhere, especially since we haven't had breakfast yet."

CHAPTER 9

Loyalty Purchased with Cheese

They shoved aside the abandoned merchant carts. Flam paused when he noticed one of them had been Ricky's and his friend Aksel's, but then he pushed Clyde in ahead and pulled the door closed behind them.

It smelled bad inside, stale. Although the produce had all rotted away some time ago, the whiff of decomposition remained. Above the mostly empty aisles, the lights flashed erratically. The front windows had been boarded up to dissuade looters, but some morning sunshine poured in, cutting through the thick, dead air in orange blades of light.

Clyde and Flam made their way to the back shelves, where the canned goods waited. Flam was looking forward to something made from bread or cracker, since he preferred a good carbohydrate boost first thing, but a vast majority of anything boxed—cereal, crisps, cookies, or otherwise—had been pilfered by rodents, most of the boxes themselves now reduced to flakes of cardboard carpeting the shop's checkerboard floors.

Flam removed an opener from his collection of items hanging from his belt and went to work on a can of ardamires, then fished the tiny green florets out of the syrupy, salty broth. He seemed to enjoy them, taking them out one at a time and popping them in his mouth, savoring each one.

Flam noticed Clyde watching him. "Why don't you go look for a suitable weapon? That is, unless you want to tarnish that dagger of Mr. Wilkshire's with blood, if it comes to it."

Clyde decided to look, even though the idea of hurting someone—God forbid, sticking someone with any dagger at all—made his heart hurt.

He went down a few aisles and found the employee entrance to offices and a break room. Through the door and straight across the room, completely unavoidable, was a large cat's face illustrated on the wall with what appeared to be black spray paint applied with a stencil. Circular, with a top hat and tiny triangular ears, one eye winking and the tongue sticking out. It looked out of place here. Stenciled crookedly beneath it were the words *The Odium*.

He paused, staring at the mural, the first bit of hard evidence that the Odium really existed, that it was a true identity floating about in the world like a blood clot in a vein, biding its time to jam in somewhere. It scared him, that cat face, those words.

He sniffed the air in the break room. Through its reek of spoiled food and burnt coffee was something else. Sweat? Blood? It smelled awful, as he assumed the Odium creeps themselves did.

It felt better to look away from the painting. He continued, his hand having found the dagger handle at his side.

He opened a door with a placard labeled Manager. Within, he found a desk, a monthly planner, and a phone. He picked up the receiver, miming what he had seen Mr. Wilkshire do. He held the phone to his ear and heard a low droning. The screen on the phone's base illuminated momentarily, displaying a list of the most recent calls made.

The power went out, and Clyde reluctantly set the receiver on the cradle.

As Flam had suggested, he searched the desk drawers for a weapon of sorts.

Flam ate three cans' worth of ardamires. His blunderbuss ever ready, he traversed the back of the store, walking each aisle, looking for anything else worth taking. Food was tricky. If it wasn't in a can, it could easily spoil during travel or get crushed in his satchel. He took a few cans of items he knew to be tasty and stowed them away.

He spotted a sign, written in human text, signaling the aisle where the cheese was kept. It made him recall his mother, who made a delightful meat pie with a fragrant cheese that smelled terrible but tasted great. He turned the corner and saw a flash of white from the middle of the aisle move underneath a rack. He thought nothing of it, since Geyser was like any city and had its fair share of insects, birds, and other vermin.

He remembered working with his uncle in the sewer and the bugs that lived down there. Massive things, big enough for a human to ride on if the insect would allow a saddle. Pincers and scales, bulging eyes with a million lenses, that screech they made when alarmed. The sound still haunted the Mouflon's nightmares on occasion. Blatta didn't speak, didn't bargain, only killed.

Flam shook the myths aside and sorted through the cheeses, some of which had softened and gone to waste in the inconsistent refrigeration system. He took up some he knew would never actually spoil, pungently fragrant and good. He pushed one block after another into his satchel.

There came a frantic scratching of nails on tile.

Flam whipped around, the blunderbuss at his shoulder. He aimed up the aisle, then down the other way.

No one.

Slowly, he lowered the gun and continued perusing the cheeses, one ear aimed back.

In the next aisle over, the tiny white frisk mouse found its friend. The two settled on a box of crackers, nibbled a corner, and worked the cardboard away until they could get at the prize within. When another mouse came up, the two paused to greet the newcomer. They all nodded to one another, then worked together. Another came. The three paused, nodded in salutation, and the four worked the cardboard with their tiny yellow teeth. The frisk mice weren't entirely rodents, but they were close enough to be categorized that way. They were actually of the wolfish order, tiny rabbits with fleshy tails like a rat. The signal was sent among them, wordless, that something of value had been discovered, and more of the frisk mice came in a flood, the floor temporarily carpeted in a mass of white wherever the pack moved, tiny fingernails scratching on tile . . .

Clyde went into the next office and found another phone in the same useless condition. A few framed photographs sprinkled the assistant manager's desk: smiling children and a beautiful blonde wife. Clyde set a picture down, hoping the family had made it out of Geyser all right. He went to a machine attached to the wall where a red light blinked when the power came on. He timed it, just as Flam had done with the elevator call button, and struck the button when the surge passed. The machine noisily ground a sheet of paper out the underside, printing in jerking pushes when the electricity allowed until the entire sheet was spat out. Clyde turned the page around in his hands and read.

Due to recent events of disruption within our city's supply line, the geyser, we at the offices of King Gorett advise you to continue as best you can to maintain normal commerce within Geyser. Certainly these are trying times, and with rumor of the Odium circling the streets and in the pubs, we need everyone in the service industry to remain vigilant. Goods should still be sold; orders for off-planet items should still be made.

Commerce is the backbone of any civilization, the way by which we feed our children and carry on with normalcy. If any business owner, shopkeeper, or shipping house is seen with its doors closed, a fine will be issued. If you abandon your establishment, an even steeper fine will be issued.

It is of dire importance that we carry on, stay the course, and keep Geyser going through these difficult times.

Clyde read the message three more times, then folded it and deposited it into the trash bin. He felt a little bothered by the vibe the message gave.

He searched the assistant manager's desk for a weapon. All he could come up with was a tiny wooden club, about the length of his forearm. Soft leather wrapped its handle several times. The end was battered and dinged. What purpose it had served, Clyde couldn't even begin to assume. He took it to the next office, deciding to carry it until he could find something better.

Flam stopped loading his satchel with cheeses and walked to the next aisle, his curiosity finally getting the better of him. There they were, thousands of frisk mice struggling with a box of crackers. They moved all over it, chewing together, but stopped when they confronted the plastic bag inside. The mice, all together at once, seemed to take a deep breath and sigh.

Paying no attention to Flam, they piled atop one another until they rapidly formed a rough human shape: two arms, two legs, a torso, even a head. The body stood tall for a moment, as if ensuring everyone was in place, and bent with an outstretched arm. At the end of the wrist shape, several of the frisk mice pointed their tails out like fingers of a hand. The collective creature took what was left of the cracker box in its fleshy tail fingers and tore the packaging. It poured the contents upon its chest, the score quickly distributed all over the body, a million teeth chewing at once. They cast the box aside, every member of the brood sated, and noticed Flam standing motionless at the end of the aisle, eyes wide, blunderbuss in hand.

"Hello there," the mice said together. The manlike thing straightened its posture, clasped its hands behind its back, and looked at him. Two of the frisk mice that were just a touch darker than the others stood in for the eyes.

"What . . . in . . . the . . . blazes?" Snapping to, Flam took aim. Whatever was happening, he was sure these rodents could reduce flesh and bone to nothing, just as they had the crackers. A shoot-first tactic would be preferable.

"Please don't fire upon us," the mice said in unison,

speaking in a calm tone. "If anyone should fire upon anyone, it should be we who fire upon you since, as the saying goes, we were here first and whatever is left in this place is rightfully ours—or, in layman's terms, finders keepers. But since we don't have a firearm, nor do we condone them, if you should so choose it, you can fire upon us simply because you, sir, are actually armed. Please know, though, that it would be immoral. We understand within the bandit law of things it's typically frowned upon to shoot anyone who is unarmed, for that would be considered cowardly, and pride is chief among a bandit's flimsy so-called principles."

"What the plummets *are* you?"

A thousand throats cleared. "We were given individual names, but since there are so many of us, it would take quite a while to list them all for you. But as we work together in such a way, we've adopted a moniker of sorts that we shall tell you, even though it's less of a moniker and more along the lines of an acronym. Would you care to hear it?"

Flam simply stared.

"We are Rodents of Hive Mind, or R.O.H.M. Even simpler than that: Rohm. Which works doubly as a name and an identifier of how we exist, roaming in a nomadic fashion, being without a permanent home as we are."

"I see. One second?" Flam turned his head, not removing his gaze, and shouted, "*Pasty?*"

"Ah, you're accompanied by someone. Makes sense. Four arms are better than two when it comes to looting, I bet. That is, unless your compatriot is a Blatta, and those typically have six arms, yes? Being of the insect persuasion and all. Perhaps only four, since they would have to walk

99

on two of those legs—but still, four arms to carry and two to walk upon is quite the bargain when talking about pillaging, don't you think? We think so."

"Clyde!" Flam was unable to keep the warble of fear from his voice.

Clyde came running, wooden club in hand. He looked at Flam, asked, "What's wrong?" and nearly fell over backwards into the cheese display when the assembled mass of frisk mice turned toward him. "What is *that?*"

"Oh," they said together, "is this Clyde, your friend? It appears he could use some suns."

"Flam?" Clyde gasped.

"They're frisk mice." Flam retained his distance from them, not lowering his blunderbuss. "They just sort of grouped together. I've never seen anything like it."

Rohm added, "Not a lot of people have—Mouflon or otherwise."

Clyde raised the bat in both hands. To Flam he looked more like he was keying up to receive the serve of a tennis ball.

Rohm filled the silence. "We don't suppose the two of you are bandits. Sort of an odd pairing, a human and a Mouflon working together. The best that we know, we've never seen a Mouflon work with anyone besides another Mouflon. And as for you, young man . . . You are a man, yes? Disregard the bluntness of the question, if you don't mind . . . Are you ill? You appear to have something wrong with your eyes . . . and your skin. Perhaps you have what the ancient humans referred to as scurvy. You may want to wander to the produce aisle. There may be an orange or two over there. Those are rumored to be loaded with vitamin C, good for warding off such maladies, if that is, in fact, what you have."

"How can a bunch of mice be so Meech-damned smart?"

Rohm turned their head back to Flam. "How? Consider this. You have the average build of a Mouflon. Which means your brain is eight and a half to nine pounds, roughly. Each one of our brains is approximately point zero five pounds, just a drop in the bucket compared to yours, yes, but we are using them *together,* all one thousand eighty-four of us—no, pardon us, one thousand eighty-nine of us; one of us recently had a litter. Which is fantastic—more the merrier. Once those pups are full-grown, we'll be one-seventy-ninth smarter. But, long story short, the collected weight of our brains is over double that of yours—and unlike Mouflons, frisk mice use 98 percent of our brains."

Clyde whispered, "Should we run?"

"Why?" Rohm retorted, even though the question hadn't been posed to him. "We will not pursue you. In fact, it would be preferable to us if you *did* run, because then we wouldn't have to share the contents of Third Circle Market with you."

"Is this some kind of fabrick?" Flam said.

"No." Rohm's tone was mildly indignant. "All frisk mice can do this."

"You're kidding," Flam grunted.

"I am, actually, yes. You didn't laugh. We're sorry. Humor isn't really our strong suit."

"So it *is* fabrick that's behind this?"

"No, that much was the truth. We were actually an unexpected development of the Geyser scientists. You see, there are some sewer tunnels and water supply lines that are much too narrow for any human. And to dig up the lines would mean tearing up the street, which, if you know anything about Geyser's sediment foundation, could be detrimental; one false move of a jackhammer might lead to a crack. And a crack, my new friends, is a four-letter word in Geyser."

Clyde had to ponder that. *Crack* is a four-letter word? What was the significance of a word being four letters, when it wasn't made up for four letters? He'd have to ask Flam later. Right now, some talking mice were telling a story.

"At first they wanted to use us individually to check the pipes. But frisk mice—others, not like us—are easily distracted. They wanted us to work as a solid team, an affront against the tyranny of clogged pipes." It shook a fist of collected tails. "They made it so we could work together. We were made by an adjustment of the genetics of a typical frisk mouse, our mother, and her offspring, which—poor lady—were all of us. We are able to communicate and work together in perfect, indissoluble harmony."

"Good Meech," Flam said, slapping a hand to his forehead. He regretted coming to Geyser at all. The lockup in the slums of Adeshka was looking better and better.

"So what brings you to the area? We heard Geyser was no longer operational due to its sudden lack of water." Rohm's two brown mice who stood in for pupils faced Flam and then Clyde and back again.

Flam answered, "I'm looking for something worth selling." He jutted a stony thumb toward Clyde. "And this one's on some kind of vengeance trip."

"Vengeance? My word, what's happened to you? Are

you seeking the individual who did that to your eyes? My, come to think of it, they kind of look like ours. Completely black. Perhaps you're a variation of what the scientists were working on as well, half man and half mouse. You're about the right shade as well, except you have no fur."

"I'm not a mouse person, and the individual I'm looking for is none of your business."

"I apologize." Rohm placed a collected hand of mice tails to its chest. "I didn't mean to offend, but rarely does anything so scandalous occur here at Third Circle Market. The most excitement we've encountered was when a cat wandered in a few weeks ago. Naturally, we lost a few numbers that day, regrettably, but Rohm was the victor in the end, let us tell you. Of course, cat bones are incredibly hard to digest."

Flam stepped forward. "You were made in a lab? Did it happen to be in the medical ward, up the street apiece?"

"Unless you know of another medical ward in Geyser."

"We're looking for a way down to sea level. We're trying to get out of here. I heard about an elevator in the medical ward that goes under the platter rim for emergencies only. Do you remember anything like that?"

"We've studied many diagrams of Geyser during our travels. There are elevators in the city: one is for civilian use, another is in the medical ward—although we cannot say where, specifically—and another is near the palace in the government ward."

"We just want to get down to sea level," Flam said. "You say there's an elevator in the medical ward? Great. That's all we need to know: it wasn't just a rumor." He turned to Clyde. "We can get down, get my auto, see if it's in any kind of working order, find a way across the bay, head to Adeshka once we're on the mainland, and get your frigate pilot."

Rohm took one step forward. "Are you this Clyde fellow's employee? A bodyguard of sorts?" Rohm turned its attention to Clyde, looking closer with thousands of tiny eyes littered all over its collected body. "Are you royalty, young sir?"

"No," Clyde answered, "he's helping me because he said he would and he's held to it by Mouflon custom. My master, Albert Wilkshire, was a good man, and someone killed him, and I aim to find out who it was. I think it was a member of the Odium, and I want to get to Adeshka to hire a pilot so I can catch up to the murderer."

"Determination is clear in your voice. We believe you will find what you're looking for, just by the way you answer. Let us join you two gentlemen. We could be of use. There is always a need for someone who has a good lay of the land, as we do."

"Hey now, I have a pretty good idea of what I'm doing. I've gotten us this far." Flam thumbed his own barrel chest.

"And where is it that you started?" Rohm inquired.

"Residential ward is where I found this one," Flam admitted, partly defeated. They had travelled barely two miles.

"Well, we don't suppose you could do much worse, then." Rohm chuckled. "But, naturally, since we are a subspecies with an incredible grasp on how things are done when services are rendered, we have to ask one very particular question."

Flam and Clyde looked at one another, perplexed.

"Yes?" Clyde said hesitantly.

"What do you plan on paying us with?" The mice making up the chest swelled, and sank, mimicking a sigh. "You see, you can offer to give us all your spots, but money is of no value to us."

Clyde looked to Flam. "Well?"

"Why should we even want you to come with us?" Flam snapped. "I mean, we're doing just fine. Once the Patrol comes by and takes care of whatever's going on with that idling auto up the street, we'll be free to get to the medical ward whenever we please."

Rohm blinked, a set of white frisk mice temporarily covering the brown ones. "Here's how we see it. You are bound to Mr. Clyde here, who is on an important mission. Time cannot be spared. You want to get to the medical ward elevator? Let us operate as a scout. We don't always have to be in this communal form, you know." One frisk mouse detached from the foot of the collected form and scampered away, returning to the group a moment later with one of the ardamire florets Flam had dropped. The morsel was dissolved within a heartbeat.

Flam groaned. He reached into his satchel, removed a shrink-wrapped hunk of cheese, and held it out.

Rohm's right hand took the cheese, which absorbed into the wrist and was rapidly spread among the frisk mice. The plastic wrapper rained out in chewed confetti at its feet. "We wondered how long it would take you, Mr. Flam."

CHAPTER 10

Protein

Flam and Clyde waited just inside Third Circle Market's doors and watched as Rohm disintegrated into individual frisk mice, went into the street in one smooth pack, turned the corner, and trekked up the street.

Flam took out his pipe, mold, and matches. "Do you trust them?" Staring out the front windows, he waited for gunfire, screams, the Patrol sirens, Rohm's plan going to pot immediately . . .

"They seem bored to me," Clyde said. "I can relate. I'd understand if they wanted to get out of here and be of some use. I can't imagine how long they've lived here." He surveyed the shelves. They had gone through almost all the crackers and other dry goods. All that remained were canned foodstuffs they had no way of opening.

"Boredom doesn't make someone trustworthy. And who's to say that if one of them decides to turn on us, the rest won't follow? I should've kept my arse home. Coming here was probably the biggest mistake I've ever made. Plenty of ghost towns on Gleese, and I had to choose this Meech-damned one." He puffed on his pipe.

"I believe they know what they're doing." Clyde balanced the wooden bat in his palms, approximated its weight. "If they know the way to the medical ward elevator, all the better."

"I got only so much cheese in my satchel, Pasty. I took merely what could travel, too. Who's to say those things won't gang up on us the minute we get to sea level and rip us apart? Maybe that's what it wants: a meal that will move along on its own two legs, something to snack on to start its own journey on the right foot when it gets down there."

"I don't believe they want to get to sea level," Clyde said. "I doubt they'll accompany us beyond the elevator. They'll probably want to come back here to a place they know." He wondered if he'd ever see the chateau again: Mr. Wilkshire's books and grand staircases and wood-paneled halls. Without Mr. Wilkshire, it all meant nothing now. *Motivation,* he reminded himself. *Use that terribly empty mansion as motivation.*

Something bellowed.

Clyde and Flam instinctively ducked.

Flam eased open the front door and listened. He looked up the south side of the street, where the Patrol should have come from. It was strange; they'd never come by. Perhaps they had passed while they were meeting Rohm.

They listened, Clyde cupping his ears while Flam swiveled his pointed ones, trying to catch any sound on the humid air.

"Do you think they're all right? Should we check on them?"

"Just wait," Flam grunted. "Either way, it was bandits up there. Maybe our furry friends will come back with a little more appreciation for what I know about Geyser's lay of the land."

"We should see if they're hurt."

"Wait a minute. It was only a shout. Surely the Patrol heard that if they were anywhere in the vicinity. Just wait."

Clyde gripped the handle of his club tighter. He listened to the wind blowing over the surface of Geyser, through the streets. No sirens. No drone of a Patrol auto on approach. No flashing lights kicking up on the storefronts across the street. Just silence.

"I'm going to take a peek," Flam said. "You wait here."

Before Clyde could argue, Flam had edged out the front door, staying low. He got to the trash canisters and let the market door close behind him.

Suddenly, Clyde felt very alone. He listened as Flam's hoofed toes scraped the sidewalk along Third Circle Street until he was too far away to be heard. A moment later, Flam was in sight, waving for Clyde to come along.

Clyde exited the shop and ran to catch up.

"Prepare yourself," the horned Mouflon said.

"Why?" Then Clyde saw.

There was the parked, idling auto and what remained of the bandits who had laid the trap: two bloodied skeletons, every ounce of flesh nibbled from their bones. A remotely swollen-looking Rohm stood off to the side, compiled in human shape, looking at their work.

Clyde went a shade paler.

"Is there more?" Flam called.

Rohm noticed the two companions coming up the bend and shook its head.

Flam and Clyde joined Rohm, but Clyde kept his head turned away from the horrible sight.

Flam reached into the cockpit of the dead men's auto and killed the engine. The street was silent again. A strong wind tore down the street, the exhaust washing away.

"Did you . . . eat them?" Clyde asked, hand on his

twisty stomach.

"We did, yes. They were both human, not normally something we have in our diet, but with the amount of protein found within them, we should be sustained for quite some time. We've found it's beneficial on occasion—eating fresh meat."

Clyde frowned.

Flam opened the trunk on the bandit auto, rifling through the collection of junk they had scoured from Geyser—a lot of the same things he himself would opt to steal. Clothing, jewelry, the occasional piece of electronics. But nothing of true value to the mission at hand. He closed the trunk. "Where are their weapons?"

"They weren't armed," Rohm answered.

"Bandits without guns. Now there's a new one. What do you suppose they would've said when we came up on them—'Give us your loot or we'll tell you knock-knocks till you soil yourselves'?"

"They were large for men." Rohm puffed himself up to replicate one bandit's girth. "Even bigger than you, Mr. Flam. Undoubtedly you would've had a struggle with them, especially if Mr. Clyde isn't the type to join you in the exchange of blows."

With their auto off, the smell of the dead men was now reaching Clyde, making him even more nauseated. "How far is the medical ward?" he blurted.

"Just up ahead." Flam turned to Rohm. "Care to lead the way again? I hate to admit it, but that turned out relatively well."

"I'll take that as a compliment." Rohm fell into a heap, dispersed, and scampered en masse up the street.

Flam and Clyde followed, taking their time. They watched as the pack made its way around the corner. A sign welcomed them to the medical ward, and beyond there were no more shops or newspaper dispensers. The buildings were taller and made of glass, reflective in the early afternoon suns. There was still the occasional auto blocking the road, but most were the emergency medical sort. Signs announced medical treatment specialties—diseases, accidents, the morgue—as well as general practitioners' offices. Every building remained dark even when the streetlights flickered.

At the very westernmost side of Geyser, in the heart of the medical ward, was a massive building. Clyde craned his neck to view the top. It was the main hospital facility, where only those of high governmental rank and the most affluent of Geyser's citizenry could be treated.

This was where they found Rohm waiting for them, standing in the collected human form in front of the doors. It appeared to check the time on a wristwatch that wasn't there.

Flam hopped up on the curb and pulled the blunderbuss strap off his shoulder. He gazed in but saw only his reflection in the glass doors. "Should've figured the elevator would be in here."

"It wasn't often that a patient couldn't be treated by any of Geyser's doctors," Rohm said. "Only on occasion did they actually send anyone out of Geyser for treatment. Among those, they were always those who could foot the bill. I spent a lot of time in here. This is where we were given life, up on the research floor."

"So you know the layout of this place pretty well?"

Flam asked.

Through the doors, Clyde spied only the edges of things, as if they were drawn with chalk on a slate.

"Well enough. I know the elevator through the bottom of Geyser's platter is in the fourth subbasement, and to get down that far will require electricity."

"What about stairs?" offered Clyde.

"There aren't any," Rohm said. "Not down to the subbasements. Security was tight here. They couldn't treat the prime minister or anyone in his cabinet aboveground and risk an Odium rocket striking them while they were having their reflexes checked. They were always taken downstairs by elevator, accompanied by Patrol guardsmen, where the platter worked as a natural protective wall."

"Either way, we might as well get inside and see what we got to work with." Flam wedged the barrel of his blunderbuss between the glass panel doors and pried them apart a foot. He wedged one of his hoofed toes between. "We need to get off the street. Rohm, you care to prove yourself indispensable once again and scout ahead for us?"

"Certainly," Rohm said with enthusiasm and tumbled apart, coursing in single file into the opening Flam provided. Flam cringed and looked away as the mice crawled over his foot. The whole collection of rodents got inside, and Flam let the doors ease shut.

Flam and Clyde waited outside while the rodents did a quick survey of the hospital's main floor.

Up the road, the chirrup of the Patrol autos sounded.

Flam's eyes went wide, and he twisted to face the bending avenue.

Clyde spun on his heel and saw on the storefront faces,

up at the street from whence they had just come, the terrible flashing lights of the Patrol on speedy approach. He felt the soul-deadening effect immediately, as he had from the grenade of gray light but not as severely. Still, he had to shake his head to clear the cobwebby nets they tangled his mind with. He turned to Flam, but he was already frantically trying to pry the facility doors open again.

There was a tremendous set of bangs, even louder than that of Flam's blunderbuss. Clyde watched, stunned, seeing the shattered wreckage of the bandit auto spiral aflame above the shop roofs. It twisted at the peak of its ascent and fell in a lazy arc. Shattered and burnt metal boomed onto the street. The Patrol guardsmen cheered.

"Hurry," shouted Clyde.

Flam grunted, struggling with the door. The hydraulics squeaked, holding fast. Another set of dull thumps, and the sidewalk trembled beneath their feet. The Patrol cannons fired a second salvo. Heavy, heart-shaking blasts. The street was curved, but a swatch of the carnage could be seen. The guardsmen fired upon a storefront, glass shattering, black smoke and orange fire blossoming into the sky.

Clyde helped Flam, but the door resisted. The glass cracked, the frame bending.

Sweating, Flam violently tugged. "Well, Pasty, it was nice knowing you."

CHAPTER 11

Morning Suns

Flam wrenched the doors apart and pulled Clyde along behind him, out of sight of the approaching Patrol vehicle. In the shadows off to the side within the hospital lobby, they huddled among a collection of wheelchairs. Clyde listened as the Patrol auto drove by mere feet away. It crawled along, the guardsmen behind the thick, tinted glass searching up and down each building for looters, bandits, possible squatters.

As the vehicle passed the doors, Flam lifted a flattened hand to shield his eyes from their flashing gray light beacons.

Clyde did the same.

They remained in place until they were sure the guardsmen were a good distance down the street.

It took Flam two tries to get the words to cooperate with his parched throat. "That was a close one." He stood and dusted himself off. "They'll be back when they do their rounds in the late evening. But with any luck, we'll be long gone by then." He guided his light stick's blue glow over their new surroundings.

There was a waiting room, a nurse's kiosk, an overturned refreshment dispenser. A few brown dots littered the floor near the entryway to the nurses' station.

Clyde pointed out the mouse droppings.

Flam entered the area behind the kiosk counter, calling for Rohm.

The lights came on and died out again. There was no sign of Rohm, any part of them at all, not even in the long hallway.

Clyde remained behind Flam as they walked a few yards to where the hallway divided in four separate directions.

"Rohm," Flam shouted, his voice bouncing down the lengths of the halls and returning to them a moment later. There was a sound of scurrying, and then a flood of white rodents filtered from under a door labeled Maintenance.

Rohm assembled into their towered form. "We tried to find a way to turn on the power in there, but it's just cleaning supplies."

"It's probably somewhere else, then," Flam said. "Not that it would do us any good to flip the breakers anyway. Not without a steady supply of juice." He grinned at Clyde. "I suppose we could always load up in the elevator, cut the cable, and see where that gets us, eh, Pasty?"

The surge came and went, and in the momentary splash of illumination, a flickering stood out brighter than any others: the fluorescent glow of a refreshment dispenser at the end of the main corridor.

They headed that way, deeper into the hospital, Flam's light stick guiding. They walked the cluttered hospital halls to a surgery waiting room, where they found some seats. Magazines on a coffee table reported old news of Geyser.

Flam dropped the light stick onto the floor and approached the vending machine with hands out, like a boxer squaring up to an opponent. With a grunt and one solid pull, he ripped its plastic face clean off. He piled the prepackaged loot into his arms and then dispersed items to Clyde and Rohm.

Clyde held the plastic-wrapped sandwich with confusion.

Flam took it back from him. "Right. I forgot." He took his own division of the bounty to a corner seat and collapsed into it, letting the candy bars, bags of chips and pretzels, sandwiches, pastries, and cookies shower about his feet.

Rohm tumbled into a pile, and each of its members worked at its share, eating at a polite volume and with closed mouths.

"There are no windows in this place," Flam commented, ripping open his third semi-decomposed submarine sandwich. "Hard to tell what time it is, even. I wonder if we should just crash here and sort out the whole elevator business in the morning."

The rodents that weren't eating answered, "That would probably be advisable. Regain our strength, get a good night's rest, and see if we can tackle the elevator power supply issue in the morning with fresh eyes."

"Isn't that what I just said?" Flam grunted.

"You use too many colloquialisms, and we weren't sure."

Clyde, without anything to do while the others ate, took up one of the magazines and turned it toward the light stick. Inside, pictures displayed what Geyser looked like when the city was populated and functional. Everyone in the pictures smiled, standing at the base of the town square geyser, having ice cream or pushing buggies loaded with chubby babies, who also looked like they were smiling.

He flipped the page to a section about government reform following King Francois Pyne's death. The journalist had articulated the fears of the townsfolk of Geyser, saying that since none of the king's children had been present for the moment of Pyne's death, the passing of the soul and of the ruling torch had gone to the prime minister instead of the heir. It wasn't anything new to him, but seeing a photo of Gorett—his silver hair parted in the middle, his neatly manicured moustache and pointy beard—he could understand why people didn't trust him. Gorett showed a row of long teeth and a pair of cruel brown eyes. He was smiling for the picture, but something about it made Clyde think that beyond the camera, something savage was taking place. He didn't like making eye contact with the man even though it was just a photo, as silly a thing as it was.

"It's cold," Clyde said, closing the magazine.

"True, the winter cycle is a few short weeks away," Rohm said. They had finished eating, and several of the rodents were now slumbering. A handful of new mothers in the brood were nursing their young. A few of the buck rodents were sitting up on hind legs, pulling their whiskers into their tiny mouths with their paws and licking them clean. "Perhaps if we weren't indoors, a fire might be nice."

Flam tossed the wrapper of his last sandwich aside. With a fist, he beat his chest until a belch dislodged from his guts and boiled up through his throat. "I think, and this is just my opinion, but I think that once we get through with all this Odium business and you get what you're after, Clyde, we should retire to a world that doesn't *have* winter. A couple are still inhabitable closer to the suns, where it never gets cold. That'd be a place I'd like to make a home."

Home. Clyde sat up and sighed, remembering Mr. Wilkshire. Skeletal in his own gardens, facedown. He wished he could've done something to protect him. Of all his masters, Mr. Wilkshire was the only one who deserved his undying devotion and dedication. He was the only one who had never taken a lash to him to vent deeper frustrations after a confession.

He cursed his ignorance, especially the fact that he had momentarily thought the gray light grenade's detonation was some sort of birthday surprise. He gritted his teeth. "I wish I knew the Odium were to blame. If only I had some proof."

"I saw the man's body," Flam said. "He was clearly gunned down."

Rohm offered, "We could always return to the scene of the crime, gather some evidence. Perhaps you two missed something we would be more prone to spot, equipped with so many more eyes as we are. We would like to offer our services. Half of us could remain to assist with finding a way to power the elevator, while the other went back to investigate."

"You can do that?"

A thousand little cocksure nods.

"Okay, then. That might be a good idea," Clyde replied.

"Well, there's no point in talking about it now," Flam said. "Not like anyone's going to be traipsing about in the city tonight. Are you all settled in? I'm going to shut the light off if you are. Batteries for this thing don't come cheap, you know." He didn't wait for a reply, took up the light stick, and with one swing through the stale hospital air, shut it off.

As with food, Clyde didn't need sleep. He wished he could just turn himself off for a few hours, even possibly dream, whatever that was like. He assumed it was a lot like zoning out in front of the television, as he saw Miss Selby do without fail every midmorning. Maybe he'd wake up feeling like all the bad stuff was eroded away.

Not so. He spent the entire night with his thoughts, fresh recollections of Mr. Wilkshire's dead body parading around like demonic puppets over and over and over again. He wanted to get away from them.

Clyde assumed it was close to morning. It felt like it'd been a few hours of sitting in the dark, picturing things moving in the shadows, but it was impossible to tell so deep within the hospital. The others were still asleep, so Clyde decided to check outside on his own. He put on his dinner jacket, which he'd been using for a blanket, and stepped into his loafers.

He ventured to find the front doors to take a look outside. Getting lost in the dark hallways only a couple of times, he turned at each intersection that led to a brighter area. Soon he was at the front doors again. Morning was a welcome sight, even though the sky was full of gray. He didn't dare step outside, though, fearing the Patrol could come rumbling past again any moment, so he remained at the cracked glass and peered up one way and then down the other. Apparently it had rained in the night. The street was dark, the asphalt collecting shallow puddles here and there.

When he returned to the waiting room where they had set up camp, Rohm was still a pile of slumbering mice, but in Flam's place was just an outline of food wrappers in the rough shape of a Mouflon.

Would he abandon him so soon? Did the Mouflon custom work like the legend about leprechauns? Did they remain true to their word only so long as you kept them in sight?

His heart pounded. Clyde left the waiting area, going to the intersection of the four hallways. He peered down all the hallways and saw no sign of Flam. He wanted to call out to him but remembered the Patrol morning routines. He swallowed a deep breath, stuffed his cold hands into his slacks pockets, and kept walking.

"Flam?" he whispered, passing door after door. All the rooms were identical, with their adjustable beds and thin curtains. Dead machinery, vases of wilted flowers. He walked along to the end of the corridor and found a stairwell that led upstairs but not down. It was true what Rohm had said: there was no way besides the elevator to go any farther down. Clyde stood at the bottom of the pitch-black stairwell and called up for Flam, his voice reverberating in the boxy space. No answer.

As he turned around, though, he did hear something. A voice, female, calling out a single warbling note. He listened, holding his breath for as long as he could, his ears aching for the sound to repeat itself. It came just as he was going to give up, but this time it didn't sound so much like singing. It was a groan, like that of someone in pain or some sort of distress. Clyde found a ventilation duct on the ceiling and got on tiptoes, turning his ear toward the grate. The sound didn't come again. He'd read a book about ghosts once and wasn't the least bit eager to meet one.

He returned to the waiting area and found Rohm partly awake—about halfway, by quick estimation. Some were sitting up, stretching, yawning mouthfuls of sharp teeth that almost looked scary—especially since they were so cute otherwise.

Clyde swallowed. "Have any of you seen Flam?"

At once, the rest all perked up, tiny ears rising and eyes bolting open.

"We haven't," they said in unison. "I'm sorry. Have you checked outside? It's rumor that Mouflons adore the first morning light and will be grumpy all day unless they get to see the sky at least once."

"It's overcast. I don't think there's any point in looking for morning suns in that weather."

"Well, best to check regardless. Oh, by the way, give us the address of Mr. Wilkshire's residence. We'll leave at once to investigate."

"It is 4970 Wilkshire Lane."

A few of the mice smiled. "Should be easy enough to remember. Well, off we go."

Half of the pack went with Clyde to the front doors of the hospital, needing his help with the doors. He struggled to open them, and the frisk mice started down the street.

Clyde remained in front of the facility on the damp sidewalk, looking for Flam. He looked up and down the street, as far as the bend in the road would allow. In the morning gloom, he could make out the shadowy shape of the geyser standing tall over the entire city. It blinked its arrangement of lights, then darkened—as if acknowledging Clyde: *Yes, here I am.*

He returned inside. Just as he passed through the nurses' center, he saw the broad-shouldered silhouette in the corridor. "Flam!"

"Yeah, what do you want?"

"Something wrong?"

"No morning light. Went up to the roof to see if there might be any way to get a glimmer of it, but no dice. Guess you'll have to pardon me, but I'm afraid you'll be dealing with a rather unpleasant Mouflon the remainder of the day."

Clyde chuckled. "That's quite all right." He felt a touch bad for even considering the notion that Flam would abandon him.

"Where were you, by the way?" Flam said. "I woke up, and you were gone."

"I decided to take a look outside as well."

"Sad as the foamy bottom of a beer glass out there, isn't it?" Flam sighed. "Where'd the mice get off to?"

"Some of them are still here." Clyde indicated the occasional white streak that slipped along the walls, easy to miss when expecting to see Rohm in his compiled shape. "And some went back to Mr. Wilkshire's home to gather evidence."

"Reckon they'll be gone awhile?"

The frisk mice interjected, "Our other half will try to make our investigation as expedient as possible." They were harder to hear when not speaking with so many voices.

"All right," Flam said, looking around as if he weren't sure which mouse in particular to answer. "Well, either way, it seems we've got some time to kill if we want to stick together." He jutted a thumb over his massive shoulder. "Why don't we go back up, Pasty? We'll tackle this elevator power supply problem straightaway once we get some suns on our faces and the other mice things return."

Clyde agreed it would be a good idea, especially if Flam would be dour the whole day if he didn't get the suns he needed—but that last part he kept to himself.

High atop the hospital facility, crunching through the

gravel on the roof, Clyde carefully sidled the edge and saw beyond the limits of the Geyser platter to the second, genuine horizon. It took a considerable amount of time to get any thought to pass through his head. There it was: the planet stretching in all directions. The island that the spire city was based upon, the ocean beyond Geyser's lakes. The clouds were thick and dark, the mountain ranges hazy and seemingly a lifetime away.

Flam walked to the rim of the roof and gripped the legs of a communication tower to lean out safely. Seeing Clyde gawking, he couldn't resist a smile. "Quite a sight from up here, isn't it?"

"It's beautiful."

"Hmm. I suppose it is." Flam turned to look in the same rough direction Clyde was peering. Clyde was seeing Gleese for the first time from a bird's-eye view, whereas Flam had first come to the planet after a ten-day interplanetary trip riding coach with a bunch of folks who'd apparently had a falling-out with soap. He was so used to dealing with it— Gleese and all its stunted highs and plunging lows from the ground level, out in the wastes and deserts and jungles, where it seemed everything that sucked breath aimed to kill every other thing. But up here, none of that desperation and violence could be seen. It seemed pure, as if the planet were a quiet place where not a single bad thing ever happened.

The breathtaking sight of Gleese was deceitful. Bad things did happen. Frequently. But it was appropriate, Flam supposed, for someone so new to things to see the good before the bad and not the other way around. Perhaps.

Clyde would have to see the bad eventually.

Flam kept his back to the alabaster-skinned man, just a touch of suns warming his face. "What do you aim to do when you find the person responsible?"

Clyde carefully moved closer to the edge of the facility to stand next to Flam. He adjusted the collar of his coat to shield his neck from the cold wind. "I'm not sure."

"You do have Mr. Wilkshire's citizen dagger. I suppose that could be a suitable way to dispense justice. Poetic."

"I wouldn't want to tarnish his memory with that. I suppose I'll think of something when the time comes."

Flam leaned against the metal legs of the tower and slid down to sit. He reached up and plucked one of the looser quills from the back of his head, brought it to his lips, and pricked his tongue to get a dab of black blood upon its point. He took a couple of sheets of parchment from his satchel and poised the quill to write. "I don't suppose you know much in the way of fighting, do you?"

Clyde took hold of a strut of the tower when another blast of wind struck his back. "No, I don't."

Flam wrote in the Mouflon language, with its columns of tight symbols and shapes, and sometimes—if you were a fancy bloke and took that lesson in school—certain three-dimensional shapes that could communicate entire paragraphs of information with a singular expert jot.

"To my uncle," Flam said in response to Clyde's quizzical look. "Of course, the post doesn't run in this city, so I have quite the backlog of correspondence. But it's sort of a tradition among Mouflons. Morning suns on our faces make us grateful for a new day while also making us nostalgic. We're supposed to reflect on those in our lives we hold dear and remind them of the impact they've made in our lives. I write to him every morning I can." He released a frustrated sigh. "Of course, he hasn't gotten a single one of my letters. When I get to a postbox, I'll probably just drop them in, knowing they won't actually go anywhere, the old codger being dead and all . . ."

Flam felt a hand pat his back, nearly so softly it may've never happened at all.

"I'm sorry for your loss," Clyde said. "Do you have any other relatives?"

He grinned. "A brother."

"Did he live here in Geyser?"

"He repairs autos on another world. A few planets over, on a mountainous rock called Aura. The terrain is difficult, and my brother had the stroke of genius to set up shop there. He's the only mechanic on the entire planet and can charge as much as he likes. They'll either pay or travel by foot, which is inadvisable: lots of acid stone."

Clyde nodded. "Do you think you can train me?"

"Afraid not. Fixing autos isn't exactly my area of expertise."

"I mean to fight."

Flam lowered his quill. "I knew what you meant." He looked at Clyde, whose eyes were just above his own eye level even though Flam was sitting down. "You're pretty serious about this, aren't you?"

"I am. My master deserves to be avenged."

"It surprises me, Pasty."

"Why's that?"

"You refer to this fellow of yours as your master. You're no longer in his service, but you feel the need to seek out his killers as if he were your kin. I mean, I gave my word;

I intend to go with you as far as it takes to get you to a pilot—which, if you remember correctly, is the end of our agreement—but shouldn't you be happy to no longer be in servitude?"

Clyde looked toward the town square to the stony spire. Steam puffed out of the geyser's summit, followed by a creak of the turbines deep beneath the streets.

"He was better than all the masters I served before. The others took out their frustrations for their own wrong-doings on me. Not just by confessing but . . . venting in all manner of ways. Mr. Wilkshire was patient. He knew his offenses were the fault of no one but himself."

"And you honor him simply because he didn't beat you? You should honor me, then; I never laid a hand on you. And Rohm, with all those tiny hands; not one of *them* ever put a blow to you. Shouldn't you worship the ground all their tiny feet have traversed as well?"

"Mr. Wilkshire was my friend," Clyde said firmly. "I suppose calling him master isn't right, but that's what the others demanded I call them. I called him master only a few times. He always corrected me, asked me to call him sir instead. He was a great man, very intelligent and kind. I don't understand why anyone would want to do him harm. "

"He was loaded," Flam said bluntly, finishing the parchment page and then flipping it over, pricking his tongue again and beginning on the reverse side. "I imagine he got that way by having hardworking employees. And it doesn't matter how well you pay a bloke, there will always be someone who thinks it insufficient."

"Mr. Wilkshire was good to his employees most of the time."

"Ah, you see? You admit it. 'Most of the time.' There must've been a select few he wasn't good to. Seems to me whoever killed him lived here in Geyser and got rounded up with the other citizens and carted off to the refugee camp. Maybe you should start there."

"I believe the Odium did it, if they are as dastardly as you make them out to be."

"Dastardly." Flam laughed. "Yes, well, they are a cruel lot, but don't jump to conclusions, even if the Odium do indeed deserve your hatred."

"Well, half of Rohm's numbers are going to the chateau. We'll see what they uncover."

"They're probably going through the pantries, finishing off what I left behind."

Clyde's face was marked with frustration.

"I apologize, Pasty. That was wrong of me to say. I'm sure Rohm is doing a bang-up job looking for evidence." He looked at the parchment, both sides of the page filled. "There." He folded the letter three times and tucked it into the satchel. With some difficulty, he got to his feet.

"So, what will it take?"

"For?"

"For you to teach me to fight."

Flam dusted himself off, swatting down his legs and the backs of his arms, three smacks each. It was something he did often, though most of the grime would never come off. "I won't teach you anything right now, but I *will* impart to you this little nugget of information. Before you plan an attack, it's good to know whom you're up against. This is chief among your arsenal. And never underestimate them—any of them. When we find out who is responsible, if it is the Odium or one of Mr. Wilkshire's employees, we'll discuss lessons."

"Why not now, while we're waiting?"

"Because I need to know which lessons you need to fit the situation."

Clyde was clearly perplexed.

"Imagine we only have time for dagger lessons. Fat lot of good that'd do against the Odium. Sods who like guns as much as an arse likes pants, I might add, were the ones that got to your master or friend or sir or whatever you want to call him."

"I called him sir because that's what he asked—"

"Just listen, Pasty, okay? So here's lesson one. Know what you're up against, and use this"—he touched Clyde's forehead—"what good Meech gave ya, and not just this"—then his chest—"because this isn't where your smarts are. If anything, it's where your anti-smarts are. Know whom you're up against, use what Meech gave ya—and, well, yeah. That's it."

"Sage advice."

"Go ahead. Joke. But you'll thank me later." Flam pulled open the door. "I may not be pretty, but I know some shite."

CHAPTER 12

Someone He Thought He Knew

The frisk mice raced to the elevator, where Flam was using the blunderbuss again to open the doors. The mice, standing in an accumulated figure the height of a small child—since the other half of their numbers hadn't yet returned—quavered with excitement.

Before Clyde could ask what was wrong, the mice burst in unison, "Mr. Clyde, we've discovered something quite troubling at the chateau."

Flam steered his attention from the elevator doors, his ears upraised.

Clyde took to one knee before Rohm's short stature. "What is it?"

"Some of us have discovered a journal of sorts within your master's study. We're reading the pages now. I will narrate what their eyes see." The mice cleared their throats in unison. "'I, Mr. Albert Wilkshire of Geyser, hereby record the transgressions of my life for those in my family who will know after my death that I was not the honorable man I tried so very hard to appear to be. I have done terrible things to many, many good people.

"'As you know, I was a mine owner. I owned several branches of the Kobbal Mines beneath Geyser, and despite being informed of a possible Blatta infestation, I sent my men in. My avarice was great, I will admit. Many of them were killed. Being a man who only thought of the bottom line at those times, I took this news as strictly a loss of employee numbers that I would have to struggle to refill. I apologize to the families of those men for this sort of thinking; I should've done more to see to it that they were taken care of, that their losses of loved ones were made easier. I did nothing to serve them except refute my knowledge of the presence of Blatta in my mines. For that, I am sorry. I have received a great many threats upon my life for this.

"'The Odium is rumored to be returning to Geyser for another attack soon, and I wish to get this admission off my chest. My dear Clyde. I tell him all my secrets, but this one I fear is much too great to tell him. The repercussions of having him ease a troubled mind with his generally innocuous hexing this time would probably do me in for good. And to him, I apologize as well. He thinks me to be a good man, and I'm afraid he is wrong.

"'Nonetheless, with Geyser rapidly falling apart and many of my employees joining the Odium in this kill-or-be-killed world, I fear when they return, they'll have me in their crosshairs. If they do kill me, if they do end my life, I will not fight it. They deserve reprisal for what I put them through.

"'For all who read this, know I am deeply sorry. I have never been so sorry for anything in my life.

"'Sincerely, Albert Wilkshire.'"

Rohm's voice returned to its usual, bounding cadence. "I'm so sorry, Mr. Clyde."

Clyde could summon no words. His mind raced. He opened his mouth, then closed it. No, there was nothing to say. Nothing.

He stood, spun away from Rohm and Flam, and trudged toward the front of the hospital.

Rohm was about to follow, but Flam stopped them.

Clyde heard the Mouflon's throaty voice far behind. "Let him go. He needs time to stew with that for a while."

"Should we call back the others? Or do you suppose there is further investigation to be made at the chateau?"

"Call them back. There's nothing else to be learned there, I believe."

Clyde went behind the nurses' station kiosk and collapsed into a seat.

Outside the glass doors, the big rain droplets collided with collected puddles, a small trickle forming in the gutters, rushing in brown torrents where they terminated, vanishing through storm drains.

Clyde thought about the innocent lives his master had allowed to be sacrificed. Clyde had not one but two partners in this journey whose time he was wasting. His master wasn't worth it. He was a greedy man who had countless innocents killed in exchange for a precious metal or whatever was to be found within those mines. No matter what it was, Clyde decided, it wasn't worth people dying over.

If his master's ex-employees joined the Odium, returned, and killed Mr. Wilkshire, they had earned that right. He pictured a widow of one of the miners being the one to pull the trigger on the old man. Regardless, all had been tidied up and scores settled. Clyde's going after the people responsible wouldn't be justice; it would be self-centered retaliation.

When it began to rain again, he returned inside the hospital. He lingered in the lobby, far from where the others were scrounging for supplies in the various closets and exam rooms. He thought about standing out in the rain, because it'd match the dourness that had flopped itself atop him, but he didn't want to risk getting sick. The old man, he now regrettably knew, wasn't worth that.

Clyde wished Mr. Wilkshire had tried to ease his mind of the burden of guilt to him, just so Clyde could know what sort of man employed him. It made his stomach turn. He pounded his fist on the receptionist's counter and cursed.

As if in reply, the patient registry processor flashed on, the diagram of the hospital displayed in a three-dimensional framework representation of all the floors and sublevels. One of the rooms below ground level was marked in a deep red, but then the screen died.

Clyde sat and waited for the surge to pass again, but it didn't come for a full ten minutes. Regardless, he waited. He wanted something to busy his mind so he wouldn't be giving Mr. Wilkshire any more thought than he deserved.

The screen sprang to life. Quickly Clyde zeroed in on the flashing red room within the diagram. He read the label: Patient Eleven. Next to the name a heart rate display blinked in a somber pattern.

The screen winked out. He was about to call out to Rohm and Flam when half of Rohm came in through the crack in the front doors. They moved along, all working together under the gilt-edged journal of Mr. Wilkshire. Clyde had hoped they wouldn't bring it to him, but there he saw it scooting across the hospital lobby floor as if on its own.

The frisk mice climbed the side of the nurses' station counter and set the volume before Clyde. "We understand you had a strong attachment to Mr. Wilkshire and that humans are prone to keeping mementos of their fallen. Do not despair, Mr. Clyde. We are all fallible and imperfect. Remember Mr. Wilkshire as the man you knew him to be."

"Thank you, Rohm." Clyde held the small book.

Rohm moved down the desk. "We are glad to have been of help."

Clyde saw the owner's name embossed on the journal's aged leather cover, and it suddenly felt heavier. He tucked it into the interior pocket of his tuxedo coat and got up to follow Rohm.

The pack of rodents convened with its other members at the far end of the corridor. The tiny mice hugged one another and gathered into a standing adult human form again.

Flam was at work trying to wedge the elevator open, huffing and puffing.

"Don't bother," Clyde said.

"What?"

"Stop. It's not worth it."

Easing into a standing position—with some help of the wall and a hand firmly latched to the small of his back—Flam took a break, tossing aside a tool he'd apparently found in one of the supply closets. Far better than going around beating everything into operation with his blunderbuss.

"What do you mean?" Flam asked, forcing his spine straight. "What's not worth it?"

Clyde wondered how the Mouflon would react when he told him his services were no longer required. "He wasn't worth it. Mr. Wilkshire."

But Flam gave his reply fast, as if he'd been thinking the whole time something like this might come up. "Sorry to hear that. But we still need to get out of here, Pasty, and my word's my word. We'll get you to Adeshka. We'll get you somewhere safe. We may not need to go after a pilot anymore, but I'll see you to a new place where you can start over at least." He gestured at the doors. "I'm going this way regardless."

"Thank you." Clyde wanted to think about what Adeshka would look like, what this new life of his might entail, but couldn't. He was still hung up on what Mr. Wilkshire's journal had said. The words echoed in his mind, not in the voice of Rohm, as he'd heard them, but from Wilkshire himself. Deep tones, slowly speaking as if each word were chosen carefully.

Here he was, giving him thought, feeling sad about him. He changed subjects, telling Flam and Rohm what he'd seen, the active heart monitor for someone who was listed in the hospital basement as Patient Eleven.

"There's someone down there?" Flam grimaced. "Alive? But the evacuation was *months* ago. How could anyone be alive—still in their room?"

"Well, *I* was alone for weeks. Perhaps they're like me and don't require food." That singsong moaning coming through the vents again, what he had thought was a ghost.

"Or like us," Rohm put in, "living off what was left behind."

Flam grunted. "Can't imagine there'd be a lot to scavenge in a hospital subbasement. Which level did you say they were on?"

"The bottom one, the third subbasement. They're still alive; their pulse was on display. They seemed calm enough, but that doesn't mean they want to be in there."

"Maybe it does. Maybe they like it here," Flam said, his pitch a little raised.

Clyde knew the Mouflon well enough by now to tell when he was afraid. "We should try to help if we can."

"We agree. Captivity, voluntary or involuntary, is no way to live," Rohm added. "We can attest to that."

Flam rammed the blunt, bladed tool between the elevator doors again. "I just don't think we should be picking up every stranger we come across, but since we have to go that way anyway to catch the elevator to sea level . . ." Again and again, he partly drowned out his own voice with the great metallic pounds on the stubborn doors.

If anyone was down there, they heard it.

CHAPTER 13

A Proposition

I t took the better part of a day for them to remove the weapon from Aksel's head and neck. The refugee camp infirmary medics told him they'd be unable to provide him with any painkillers. Aksel heard their smiles through their paper masks. They just wanted him to suffer. Which was fine. He didn't mind pain that much. Especially after the accident that had freed up that half of his head for the weapon to be installed. What a weekend that had been.

He was able to block out most of it, but the sounds of drills and pneumatic wrenches were hard to ignore. A few times their tools were too much for their users, it seemed, and they nearly stripped the head off one of the protein bolts fastening the trigger mechanism to his cheekbone.

"Come on. Be careful. I would like to have *some* of a face when you're through."

"Pipe down." After the grisly work of getting the base of the head cannon screwed out, the metal coils were next. After the bracing mechanism was pulled up out of his neck, the anchoring slab that used his collarbone and shoulder blade as moorings came next. More tools were required, and of course they had to go have lunch. They left him there gaping for forty-five minutes in the chemical-smelling room under the hot surgical lamps. When they returned, they finished up and dropped the wet heap of biomechanics onto a tray. While snapping off her elbow-length latex gloves, one surgeon commented that they'd leave the head cannon there in the room with Aksel. It had been requested by the head security officer, so he could use it as a visual aid when speaking to their recently flayed Bullet Eater. Again, with that word . . .

With a few nasty glares, the surgeons left him again. The locking bolt from the opposite side was nice and loud so he wouldn't even feel compelled to leave. He'd come along willingly when they came to collect him at his shack. Why prove himself a bad guest now?

Besides, if they wanted him dead or expelled from the camp, they would've just made it so. Rendering him harmless by removing his cannon meant someone of import was going to be brought in here. No such lengths would be taken for just anybody. They had mentioned the head security officer. What could this be about? Was Adeshka going to recruit Aksel, make him some kind of involuntary frontline man? Rumor 'round the ration lines, after all, was that they were planning to send troops after the Odium. Not because it was the right thing to do but because after Geyser was nothing but a smoldering smudge on the map, where would they come next? Adeshka was nothing if not a city full of calculating procrastinators, only acting when it meant death not to.

With the lamps off, at least now he could actually finally feel the air-conditioning. It didn't provide much comfort, though.

As soon as Aksel sat up, the pain began soaking in. It was like a bad toothache nesting within the itchy burn one felt when a bad fever came on. Thankfully, he experienced pain differently on the right side of his head—which now hung sad and empty, like a half-rotten jack-o-lantern. The initial injury had seared more than a few nerve endings. The bolt shot from that wayfarer's rifle had close to six hundred thousand volts to it, and when a few of those streams of angry electricity back-fed through the rest of him, it rendered more than three-quarters of his pain receptors to mush. This now he could take, no problem. He'd already had his head cracked like a walnut once. Having it done again today, well, *c'est la vie.*

He stared at the biomechanical pile on the tray, still dripping both blood and organic lubricant. The head cannon—the premium edition DeadEye—looked like a bifurcated face staring back at him. There was the jaw, with the teeth and everything; the top part of the skull, which housed all the inner workings and aiming systems; the eye socket itself, which looped the barrel and operated as a hidey-hole for the weapon; and even half a nose made of the same rubber replacement that robot's hands and feet were made of. All in all, it was well worth the eighty thousand spots he'd paid for it, both as a means of threatening self-defense and as a sort of prosthetic. Yes, the half of his face they cloned and stapled on was a few hues off from the olive tone of the rest of him. But as far as these things went, it was close enough. Better than going around with half a face, right?

The door banged open, and two figures entered.

One was tall, thin, and hooded with a black cloak, and the second was a burly fellow who could've very well been Neck Scar's older brother. That is, if Neck Scar's older brother knew how to stand up straight, properly shave, and dressed himself in a regal red surcoat, immaculately creased trousers, boots that gleamed like new oil, and gloves so white they could've been stitched from clouds instead of burlap rags. Not that Aksel could judge a person based on apparel; he too was in the regulation camp fashion of pota-to-sack tunic and knickers.

"My name is Karl Gonn," Neck Scar's long-lost brother said, pulling up one sleeve, then the next of his fine surcoat to show white shirtsleeves underneath.

What is this guy doing here dressed like this? Aksel thought. *Are you trying to make us all feel bad, jerk? We get it: you're rich, and we're temporarily homeless.*

"And this is Moira. Your name is Aksel Cooper, yes?" His voice was buttery, deep.

"Yesh, but it's said like excel, not whatever it is you jush said." Aksel slurred due to having only half a lower mandible now. He wasn't all that well restrained, but he didn't feel like springing to his feet and attacking these two.

While Karl seemed nice, he was wealthy enough that clearly no true violence had entered his life. The woman behind him, Moira, looked like she could snap off Aksel's fingers and feed them to him. She seemed like Karl's puppeteer.

Aksel almost laughed at the thought. "Whash thish abow?"

"This is about you," Karl said sternly.

"Why? I'm nobody."

"True. Aksel Cooper is nobody. Merchant, traveler, buyer and seller of goods. Some late fees for taxes on importing off-world goods, but that's pretty tame compared to *another* Aksel I've heard about."

Aksel's neck grew warm. "I had it changed."

Karl continued. "But—and this might just be me—I would've thought the first name would be the thing someone would change when trying to hide, especially with a name as unique as Aksel."

"I washn't trying to hide. I was trying to start a new—"

Karl kept right on. "Once we heard Aksel Cooper was here, we thought, why not go and see if this man might know of another Aksel in the system somewhere. Aksel Browne. Aksel 'Eagle Eyes' Browne. *Captain* Aksel Browne. So now that we've gotten a chance to sit down with you, could you, Mr. Cooper, tell us if you know this man, this other Aksel we're seeking?"

"Okay, enough," Aksel grunted and clunked his head back onto the table. "You got me, okay?"

But he didn't. He just kept quoting himself, talking in that pompous way that only some Northie Adeshkian could. "And then I thought it'd be a shame if the Aksel we were seeking couldn't be found. Because we could give a man like that, someone of such precise skills, a chance to do something other than waste their time hiding away on third-rate moons and planetoids, hocking guns and stolen goods."

"Stop already."

Aksel looked at all the tools the medics had left strewn everywhere: various bladed instruments and things with moving parts that could cause a great deal of harm in the right hands. He hoped it wouldn't come to that, honestly. Really, with how this Adeshkian was going on and on, he was halfway looking around for something to use on himself. But one well-timed plunge with that bone saw into Karl's barrel chest—

He wanted Karl to see him looking, sort of send a silent

message of his intentions. So he took his time sizing up his options, as one would scan a menu.

"I'd recommend not doing that," Moira said sincerely in one of the most intriguing voices Aksel had ever heard: sweet yet weighty, airy but kissed with the faintest bit of Eastern Embaclawe. Now if she would just take down that hood and let him see if she had a face to match . . .

"I washn't," Aksel said. "I wouldn't."

"You were. And you would."

"Some accent. Dovetail, if I'm not mishtaken, right? Dovetail, Eastern Embaclawe? Yeah, definitely Dovetail. Long way from home, aren't you, girlie? But, then again, I'd forgive speaking to shomeone from that pretentious continent shince, best as I remember, all those Dovetail gals were all gorgeous. Like shomething had been introduced into the water. Caramel skin, blue eyes, hair as blonde as threads of shunshine . . ."

Aksel was nearly spilling off the table leaning in his restraints so far. If only Karl would move to one side a little. "Let me shee your face," he said, giving the best roguish grin he could with a half-gone skull.

Moira shrank back behind Karl. Three of her could hide back there. "Let us get this over with," she said from the other side of the mountainous man. "We haven't a lot of time."

"One peek?" Aksel pressed. "Pretty pleash? Just let me shee your face."

"Enough," Karl said. "All right? We've seen this act before. First you'll come off like some kind of drunken buffoon, trying to get us to drop our guard, and the next thing we know you'll have a knife buried in our necks, classic Bullet

Eater bait and switch. It's not going to work on us."

"Shorry," Aksel said. He brought up a hand to support his face so that the words came out a little smoother. "I think it's the air-conditioning. I haven't been somewhere that wasn't a million degrees day and night for going on seven months."

"We understand," Karl said impatiently, "but, as my companion already said, we're not exactly made of time."

"And . . . who are you and your companion, again?"

"Karl. Moira."

"Got your names just fine, just not who you *are*."

Moira spoke. "We're in the business of insurance."

"That's swell. Because do you *see* my face? I would really like to find the prick who did this to me originally and sue the pants off him."

Karl was clearly through with Aksel's runaround. He moved forward to give Aksel a thrashing, but Moira took a quick step around him and put herself between the two men, a boot heel clicking on the sanitized white floor. Like a trained dog, Karl halted, but his expression remained a scowl.

With Moira one step closer, Aksel could see into the dark recesses of her hood a fraction better. She appeared to be wearing extensive pancake makeup or to have some kind of horrible skin condition that rendered her skin pale as bone. Not from Embaclawe.

Moira shifted and pinched her hood together to envelop her face fully in shadow. From inside the black silk, "Not that kind of insurance, although once you've done what we want you to do, we may be able to work something out."

"Forget about it. A friend of mine got him already. I

was just testing you." Aksel regarded Karl, looming nearby still, ready to plunge in if his companion seemed at all in danger. With him standing so close, Aksel could smell him even over the disinfectant. "You mind?"

Karl kept his eyes on Aksel. "Moira?"

Moira, undoubtedly blind inside her hood, nodded. "It's fine."

Grunting, Karl gave them space but not too much.

Aksel returned his gaze to Moira. "All right. You want something out of me. First, let's get down to the brass tacks. Two questions. What's in it for me? And why me at all? Otherwise, you can just turn right around and—"

"Twenty years ago, at fourteen, you lied about your age and joined the Fifty-Eighth. Am I right? The Adeshka militia outfit? Better known as the Battalion of the Weird, a small army that ran around playing soldiers under the claim they were all fabrick weavers—except one actually was. Susanne Clover.

"I assume you spread this rumor about the rest of yourselves to make your outfit seem even more daunting, even though you were all just ex-gang members, reformed con men, sell slugs, peddlers of all kinds, which in turn sullied the general opinion of the woven for years, something we still haven't completely recovered from . . ."

So that was it. These two were fabrick weavers. Woven. But how did they know so much, specifically about Susanne?

Aksel hated it when people knew more about him than he had told them and gave them nothing in his eye to show them they'd surprised him. He folded his arms and nodded. He didn't feel like talking anymore or holding his face up to get his voice to sound decent. His bravado melted away in a blink, and Karl made it clear he noticed by a wry grin. *Jerk*.

"Yeah, fine, I'm not a weaver, and neither were hardly any of them. What of it?"

"You accepted false information from a freelance battlefield scout that misled your squad and made your battalion destroy a small village occupied by two thousand innocent men and women—"

"Yeah, we all know the shtory."

But Moira persisted, her hand not pulling her hood shut but held out rigidly, fingers spread. She wore a black glove with two white dots painted in the palm that reminded Aksel of a domino. On second glance, he realized it wasn't paint but her actual skin showing through these two round holes. Strangely, he became transfixed upon her hand as she talked. It was as if he had no choice but to listen. Puzzling this out, he suddenly realized how talkative he'd been till this point. Though he hadn't said a lot, even that much was more than he really wanted. Something was going on here.

"I feel shtrange," he said, meaning to just think it. "Are you doing thish?"

"Your position was disclosed when you released said salvo, resulting in all but ten soldiers of your battalion being wiped out. Of them, only three were able to walk again unaided. Susanne, as you know, went on to bigger and better things. Another, who also went to Geyser to start over, has to rely completely on a wheelchair and a bird assistant to perform his job as a miner with any sort of normalcy—"

Aksel interrupted again. "Okay, okay, okay, okay. I get it. You made your point: you know me. Susanne married a prince and ended up dead, and last I heard Nigel is just fine living in Geyser. Well, was fine . . . before, you know, Geyser found itself in its current condition—and that, I assure you, I had *nothing* to do with."

"Susanne Clover died giving birth to someone who should've gone on to become a princess," Moira hissed from beneath her cowl.

"So is thish about Gorett and that rumor about him stealing the throne?"

Moira sputtered, "She—he—"

Karl cleared his throat.

Moira continued after a moment, with less fury choking her voice. "My point is, she was the lucky one. Think about the other members of the Fifty-Eighth."

As much as Aksel didn't want to, he did. He thought about his old cocaptain, Nigel Wigglesby, who was rumored to live in Geyser driving drillers, of all things. Aksel rarely spent more than a day there in town, hocking goods, out of fear he'd run into the man. Now trapped in the camp, he was doubly afraid. After the first few months of not seeing Nigel in the ration line or walking the fences as most of the Geyser refugees did each morning, Aksel concluded Nigel had died in the attack. Which made Aksel feel better, seeing as how he wouldn't have that awkward run-in, but then worse when realizing he'd just thought that about a man he'd once considered a friend.

Clearly Moira had more to say, but she took a deep breath and paused. When she spoke again, it was in that smooth, almost whispering tone. "And if you want to make up for that indiscretion, you can. We have ties to the prime minister of Adeshka, who has agreed to allow us to extend you a deal of sorts."

"Well, since Adeshka has been *so* hospitable to Geyser, how could I refuse? All the dirt I could ever eat. Every day someone else trying to kill me. It's paradise, and I really can't thank you enough."

"Listen," Karl cut in, "we know about everything after your battalion fell apart, too. The sudden . . . entrepreneurial attitude you developed when you got out of the hospital. This thing"—he gestured at the DeadEye—"you paid for by selling your services as a Bullet Eater."

"Adeshka screwed me over, and it screwed Geyser over. Why should I even lift a finger for a city that doesn't give two craps about me or anyone else who isn't on its registry? I mean, what happened was an *accident*."

"Accident?" Karl huffed. "You accepted the word of a freelance scout: people who basically are paid by one side of the fence to hop over and spread lies to the other! You have no one to blame but yourself. And as far as Geyser goes, with the trouble they're having right now, you're lucky they've given your people this much. And you're also lucky they haven't figured out that you and your buddy Ricky are just carrying merchant cards; they could've expelled you both a long time ago without warning."

Moira piped up. "We're getting off topic. Do you want to help us or not, Mr. Browne? Otherwise, we can just call one of the heads of security in here and have you explain you're not worthy of even temporary status as a refugee, a man who snuck in with—"

"I didn't have any choice *but* to come here."

"But you *do* have a choice to help us," Moira said loudly but evenly.

Aksel mulled it over.

Karl said, "We don't have a lot of—"

"Time, yesh, I'm well aware. I'm thinking, okay?" He cleared his throat; it came up gummy with biolubricant. "You shtill haven't gotten to the part of what I get out of it, helping you with . . . whatever it is you haven't mentioned yet."

"True," Karl said. "We're willing to consider granting you citizenship in any of the five major cities you wish. Or a pass off-world, if that's what you prefer."

"A lot of good that'll do me. I've got warrants in pretty much every town under the suns . . ."

Moira added, "With yet another new name to go with it, a clean slate, *and* free pick."

"You're willing to consider granting me—?"

"Yes," Karl said impatiently.

"And how can I trust either of you?"

"You know as well as we do that a man with half a face won't last long in the wastes," Moira said. "With no head cannon, no guns, no spots, no friend to watch your back—"

"Speaking of which," Karl cut in, "don't forget your chum Ricky out there. I don't think he'd fare much better. How much does he weigh? A sparrow could carry him off, for crying out loud. Can't imagine he could take the Lake-bed, stripped of his shoes and that knife of his."

"Fine, okay? What do you want me to do? Or would it be more appropriate to ashk who do you want me to do?"

Karl leaned in. "There's a man in the camp. You may know him. He goes by a nickname: Neck Scar."

Aksel laughed. "You want me to kill *him?* Hell, if you'd started with that, I would've agreed to do it for nothing."

"On the contrary," Moira said. Her black hood had fallen open a little, and a peek of raven hair reflected the fluorescent lights in blue sunbursts. "We want you to become his new best friend."

Aksel had one more question. He watched Moira's hand, looking for a twitch, when he asked, "You guys are weavers, woven—whatever you want to call it. Fabrick people. Am I right?"

She didn't speak. Her hand didn't move but remained half balled into a fist.

Karl's chin lifted. "That's not important."

Taking a deep breath and cupping the boneless side of his head again, he said, "It is if you want me to listen. There's a reason you picked me. And I haven't heard about anyone else around the camp getting one of these little job interviews. I must've been on the top of your list, which means you know what I can do. And all I'm asking is one little thing. I don't even want to know your real names. Seriously, don't try explaining. I can pick out a fake name a mile off, and there's no doubt in my mind your folks didn't name you Karl and Moira. So what do you say? Was I right? You I'm not so sure about, but her—"

Moira stepped out from around Karl and lowered her hand, her sleeve falling past her wrist to drape it. "Agree, or it's off to the Lakebed. Simple as that."

Aksel pretended he was weighing his options just to irritate them for a bit longer. He pictured Ricky padding across the Lakebed wastes with his face sunburnt to cinder and birds carrying off pieces of him even as he walked. A thousand miles of dead landscape, twenty hours of constant suns a day. The image of Ricky, though. That was the deciding factor. His yearning to chase fights had died long ago, but for Ricky . . .

He nodded. "Where do you want me to shign?"

CHAPTER 14

Patient Eleven

"Meech. I can't see a blasted thing," Flam said once all three of them were atop the elevator car. He removed his light stick from his belt and gave it a swing. The light shined to the greasy gears and mechanical parts that made the elevator work. He noticed the hatch, then pulled it open and peered inside.

Before dropping in, he looked to Rohm. "So we can't just take this one all the way down to sea level?"

"Unfortunately, no. Once we get to the third subbasement, another elevator goes to sea level beneath Geyser. This one moves only between the facility's ground level and the sublevels."

"Of course. Nothing can ever be easy, can it?" Flam dropped into the elevator car.

Clyde and Rohm followed.

Inside, Flam beat his blunderbuss against the closed doors, trying to mash a dent deep into the gap. Working together, the three managed to get the doors open, revealing more corridors. This level was darker and reeked of stagnant water and mildew.

They stepped out into an inch of water. Flam's light stick shined cobalt upon narrow columns of water trickling from the ceiling.

By its smell, Flam could tell it was sediment-rich

water from the geyser. This knee-deep stuff carried the reek of sulfur, like bad eggs. Geyser water had gotten in here, into the city; there'd been a break somewhere. A break like that, to the point that basements were flooding, wasn't a good thing at all. It meant the geyser was backed up, and before long one of its little puffs would be a big one—enough to bust the city up even worse than the Odium already had.

Flam trudged on. The smell, as menacing as it was, took him back to fond memories. He knew it well, having worked with his uncle in the depths of the city's underbelly, in cramped sewer lines: patching pipes with clay, spending weeks in impenetrable darkness with the stink of wastewater and stagnant runoff from Geyser's streets, feeling bugs crawling all over him. What was worse was picking the bugs out of his fur weeks after a trip down into the sub works. All in all, not fun in the least. But at least he'd been able to hear all of Uncle Greenspire's stories.

"Ugh, it stinks," Clyde said, clamping a hand over his nose.

"It appears there's a leak somewhere," Rohm said, stating the obvious.

Flam guffawed. The mice were just as dim to the real world as Clyde was. If anything got hairy at any point on their trip, without a doubt he'd be the one who'd have to protect them. Flam the babysitter. He sighed and took the lead, guiding his troop of sheltered chowderheads into the hospital subbasement, the footsteps of his sentient burdens splashing along not far behind.

Angling the light stick toward the ceiling, Flam saw the dark patches above. He pictured the first and second subbasement flooded from floor to ceiling. With a single prick of the ceiling, thousands of gallons of muddy water could come rolling upon them. "Don't touch anything."

Clyde asked Rohm, "Where do we go from here?"

"Best I can remember, the elevator to sea level is straight ahead on the westernmost wall."

"Are we still going to check on this Patient Eleven of yours?" Flam shined a light on the room directory on the wall. "Should be down this way."

"What will we do with the patient if he's hurt?" Rohm asked.

Flam chuckled. "Just lay him out front of the facility doors, fire a shot to get the Patrol's attention, and turn tail. We're wasting enough time." He checked the security alert device on his belt. "We need to get off this island as quick as possible, and I'm sure my auto's going to need a bit more than a simple tune-up. I refuse to cross the mainland on foot."

"Who knows?" Clyde answered, ignoring Flam's comment. "The patient might be of use. Perhaps it'll be someone with electrical fabrick, if there is such a thing. Is there, Flam?"

"I certainly hope not."

They passed room number five.

Rohm said, "A fabrick weaver that can manipulate and fabricate electricity? How beneficial that would be! He could lay his hands on the elevator and power it for us."

"Well, let's pray that Meech is smiling on us today. Even if it is another weaver, that'd be fine with me, as long as we can get the plummets out of here in my lifetime."

They sloshed past room eight.

"Surprised the Patrol guardsmen left anyone down

here," Clyde said. "It seems they were pretty thorough clearing everyone else out."

"Maybe they forgot this one on purpose," Rohm suggested darkly.

Flam stopped in his tracks. Without turning back, he took up the blunderbuss and walked on.

"I didn't mean it like that," Clyde said.

At door number eleven, Flam reached for the handle and turned back to Clyde and Rohm. "Well, I'd rather poke myself in the eye than be surprised by anything."

Both of them were backpedaling, eyes wide. He didn't realize what the commotion was until he looked down. Reaching from underneath the door were what appeared to be dozens of black, headless snakes.

Flam lifted his blunderbuss and fired.

Clyde's hands slapped to his ears.

The blast blew a chunk out the bottom of the door. The black cords that didn't get ripped apart propelled as a thick twisted cable into the hallway.

With shaking hands, Flam broke the blunderbuss open, tossed the empty casing out, and reloaded it. He raised the gun to his shoulder, but the trunk-sized tentacle reached back and swung, smacking the barrel away just as Flam pulled the trigger. The blast pounded a hole through a nearby wall.

Rohm disintegrated into individual mice to charge faster up the hallway to the elevator car.

Clyde joined them, trying his best not to step on any of Rohm's members.

Flam brought up the rear, scrambling to reload the blunderbuss. He cursed to Meech as he dropped bullets he could not afford to waste. A reload successful, he spun and blasted again.

The tentacle wavered. A deep gouging bite had been made in its body. Only momentarily stunned, it continued to chase them, snaking through the flooded hallway.

"Get in," Flam shouted.

Clyde and Rohm fell into the elevator.

Flam turned with the gun and was about to shoot another time when, much to his chagrin, it was *right there,* springing headlong not unlike a Lakebed python. The tentacle wrapped itself around the barrel of the gun, spiraled up its length, and bound Flam's hands, arms, and neck. With one mighty tug, it yanked him off his feet to skid back up the length of the hallway with a wall of white water pitching behind him.

"Flam," Clyde shouted. He took the small wooden bat he had procured at Third Circle Market and chased after his friend.

Rohm assembled into a standing form and raced down as well. It pitched an arm out, throwing dozens of frisk mice at the tentacle. They landed, sprinkling along the tentacle's length and wrathfully chewed.

Flam gripped the edges of the broken door of room eleven, shouting as the tentacle pulled him in.

Clyde unsheathed Mr. Wilkshire's citizen dagger and cut at the cords around Flam's wrist.

All at once, Flam was released and dropped to the watery floor. He scrambled away.

Rohm's numbers combined.

Clyde backed up, dagger in one hand, club in the other. They all stood agape before room eleven. Neither the tentacle nor what controlled it could be seen. When the surge passed, the light was still dim and insufficient save for a few blinking reds and greens of electronics within the room. Clyde took them to be the beady eyes of whatever the tentacle was attached to and raised his dagger like a squash racquet, hand trembling.

A voice came, soft and feminine. "*Tell* me the guardsmen have changed their minds. *Tell* me Gorett has come to his senses. *Tell* me you wish to utilize my talents. Tell me *that*, and I will kill you, because I have been down here without food or water for longer than I care to fathom."

"We saw you were here through the hospital's monitoring system," Clyde shouted. "Why would you try to hurt us? We were trying to save you."

Flam threw an arm against Clyde's chest and shook his horned head. "It's a trick if I ever saw one. The Blatta. They can scream for help like people, and when you come, they launch their attack."

The thing within room eleven must've had keen hearing. "Blatta. Do you know of a single Blatta that can do what I just did? They're dumb beasts, simple insects from the depths with only food on their minds. If anyone should be compared to the Blatta, it is you three dolts."

"Then what are you?" Flam shouted. He reached to reload his blunderbuss, but the barrel had been bent at a severe angle; it would explode if he fired it. He cast it aside and reached into his satchel, removing what appeared to be the handle of a screwdriver. With a flick of a switch on its side, a blade telescoped out, roughly a meter in length with a hooked tip. Certainly no blunderbuss, but it was better than nothing.

Someone edged to the door's threshold, looking ghostly

in the undulating blue glow of Flam's drowned light stick, her gaunt face littered with shadows. "I am the king's Royal Stitcher. Well, I was, before that deceitful shite Gorett doomed me here. Regardless, if you three are in his service, as I believe you are, I'd advise you to steel yourselves for a rather lengthy bout of unpleasantness. I have been down here with nothing but time to dream up an entire compendium of horrors to put to him and any of his pitiable little cronies."

CHAPTER 15

The Stitcher

"Stitcher or no, come any closer and I'll stick you with this thing." Flam shook the telescoping blade in his hand, which to Clyde looked more like a tool for clearing clogged pipes than an actual weapon.

The Stitcher came closer, inadvertently revealing herself in the shattered door frame of her prison, where the light stick's blue found her. She was lithe and malnourished, every visible inch of her skin covered in gouges tracing in every direction. Cuts crossed the bridge of her nose, over one of her eyes, up into her dark auburn hairline. None of the wounds looked remotely fresh or clean; irritated redness ran parallel with the miles of intersecting cuts. Her clothes were tatty beyond repair, basically stained ribbons.

"What did they do to you?" Clyde muttered, aghast.

She continued, "Not just a Stitcher, mind. The Stitcher."

"Hey, I don't care which you are. You broke my blunderbuss, lady."

"You can't possibly be anything but a Mouflon," she said dreamily, squinting past the light, seemingly bright to her even though its illumination was barely equal to that of a match's flame.

"Yeah, and what of it?" Flam snapped, taking a step back as she dared one forward.

"You are not one of them. No way in hell he'd consider hiring one of you. He'd barely tolerate me." She laughed—a big, bright sound incongruous to her appearance. "I guess he wouldn't tolerate me at all, seeing as how he left me to rot here."

Clyde wondered if she was all there.

"Stay back." Flam waved his knife. "I'll jib you."

"I won't hurt you if you'll promise the same to me," she said, sounding almost amused. "Shall we play nice, be neighborly with one another?"

"How do I know you won't try anything?"

"Because I'd be able to live comfortably with myself knowing I killed only one man. Killing anyone else but him would make me feel absolutely wretched." She moved an inch or two farther out. "And I assure you, the state of my mental peace is very important to me," she said, shielding her eyes.

Clyde wanted to see her face, the entire thing, but was also a little afraid to. He stole glimpses of it through the outstretched fingers of her threaded palm. Every time even a flicker of light snuck through, she'd turn her face away and squint painfully. But for a moment, he did manage to catch a glimpse of beautiful amber-colored eyes in that patchwork face.

"If you tell me you're not in cahoots with *him*," she said, her tentacle still coiled and poised to strike, "I'll stop. I promise."

"Fine," Flam said, lowering his blade slowly and unsurely. "You can trust us when we say we're not one of the Odium."

"Good to know, but what about Gorett?"

Flam grimaced, clearly perplexed. "Him either."

"Put the knife away?"

"Yeah, sure." Flam did so.

"There. Isn't that better?" The tentacle unbounded slowly from its tight spring and unraveled, like a fist loosening. To Clyde's wide-eyed disbelief, it wove itself into her skin.

Each cut on her body laced up and cinched tight. Across her face, her chest, her stomach, the threads zigzagged until every cut was bound. Her eyes were closed during this process, a slight twinge of pain written on her face as it occurred.

Complete, her expression softened. She gazed at her onlookers, seemingly relieved. She lowered her hand, apparently having adjusted to the light.

"Nice trick, but you still owe me," Flam said, holding the blunderbuss by its bent barrel for the woman to see.

She silently dismissed it, turning her attention to Clyde and then Rohm. She looked the pile of mice up and down but didn't seem at all troubled or confused by the sight. Finally, she returned her gaze to Flam.

She took a sharp breath and, sounding somewhat bored, said, "If you're not of the Patrol, who are you?"

"We're just a handful of fools who came down here to rescue you when, obviously, you're not worth our time or effort." Flam shifted his arm as if his shoulder hurt.

"What happened to you?" Clyde asked her meekly, keeping his distance.

"I was deceived."

"By whom?"

"She's clearly got a beef with somebody," Flam said while rubbing his other arm.

"Who else?" She raised a fingertip, noticing a stitch upon her index finger hadn't sewn itself correctly. As she focused on it, the stitch burst, then sewed itself together, this time properly.

"The Odium?" Clyde asked.

She chortled, a sweet sound despite her ghastly appearance. "I wish it were that easy. No, it was by our delightful and prosperous king himself."

Flam coughed. "I don't know how long you've been down here, lady, but the king's dead. I'm sorry to tell you, but whatever bad blood you had with him, you'll have to take it up with him when you get upstairs with Meech."

"I *know*," she said, blinking slowly, politely illustrating her annoyance. "I was being sarcastic. I don't want to call Gorett the king any more than anyone else does. He's a leech and a liar." As her tone became coarser, the stitches looped in and out of her flesh over her wounds trembled ever so slightly. She took a deep breath, and the stitches went still again. "I worked for him several years. I was even appointed as a delegate to deal with fabrick weaver affairs abroad. I'm sure you've heard of the cruelty weavers have undergone not only in other continents but in Adeshka and here as well." She waved a hand toward herself. "Clearly."

"No," Clyde said. "I haven't. The others might've. I myself spent most of my life locked up in basements, sometimes in chains and . . ." Clyde had to stop himself.

She looked Clyde over again, as one would inspect a horse they weren't sure whether to bet on or not. "You're one as well," she said evenly. "What's your forte, if you don't mind my asking?"

"I've heard it given many names," Clyde mumbled, "but

I always liked conscience sponge the most."

"Conscience sponge, hmm? That's . . . a new one."

Flam interjected, "You should probably explain the whole thing before she apologizes for nearly crushing me, Pasty."

"Why?" Her brows furrowed. "What's its double edge? Tell me. What can you do? I thought I knew them all."

Clyde explained the best he could, taking nearly ten minutes.

She was patient and said nothing until he was through and even for a while after. "The fabrick is ingrained in us in so many ways," she said finally. "I've lived with my ability for close to twenty years this coming summer, and still I haven't heard of all the different facets of fabrick. Yours, I must say, is the most unusual I've heard of. Better than being able to control plants or make someone sneeze on command or some other blasé thing like that."

"Thank you," Clyde said, unsure. "What is it that you do?"

"My fabrick? Well, as I just showed your friend here"—she patted Flam's flinching shoulder—"I can control thread and string. I'm similar to the Pied Piper in that way." She walked behind Rohm and leaned in to get a look at each mouse that made up its head. She spotted one tiny frisk mouse, a newborn, and wiggled a finger at it in greeting. She looked at Clyde and continued, "Cords of plastic, metal, or stone? Gathering those would be like trying to collect a handful of air. But I can make cotton and silk and other fibers dance and move any way I please."

Unlike Clyde, who felt somewhat ashamed of his fabrick, she seemed proud of hers. It made him like her—or at least admire her. He felt like he could stand a little taller.

She pulled the threadbare sleeve up from her arm, showing Clyde the terrible state of her flesh. "But, as with yours and every other weaver's, my fabrick is double edged. I could make a thousand coats in a flash, mend an entire army's trousers in an afternoon, or even give the king an entire new wardrobe while he had his afternoon tea, but unfortunately I cannot keep myself together as easily."

Her upheld arm trembled, and the stitches broke and pulled out of the wounds. The flesh open and fresh, it became like a new sleeve around her arm. The wounds did not bleed, but Clyde could see within some of the divots in her skin all the way down to the muscle and bone. The sight made his legs go a little numb, especially when one panel of skin was slipping from her flesh and the stitches lunged to grab it up and pull it tight again.

"What is your name?" Clyde asked quietly, daunted by this woman's . . . everything.

"I believe in fresh starts," she said, coming around to the front of the pack of travelers. "And I don't want to be known by my old name. That was the name of someone naive who fell victim to the silver-tongued dignitaries, and I don't care to be known by it any longer."

She faced the room she'd been in for countless days and nights. There, marked next to the hospital door was the number eleven.

"Nevele," she chimed.

"Neh-vel-ee?" Flam echoed, confused.

"The word eleven, reversed: *Nevele*," she enunciated, gesturing at the hospital room's placard.

Flam chuckled. "That's rather good. Nevele. I like that."

Clyde nodded, as did Rohm.

"Fine," she said. "Nevele it is. And I believe a new name should come with a new wardrobe. Pardon me, gentlemen. And ladies—if there are any of you in there." She leaned, looking into Rohm.

She dodged into her hospital room, ripped the sheet from the mattress, and returned to the hall with it. She held it out, one big banner of white fabric with yellow soiled patches.

She closed her eyes.

The sheet threw off its stains in one billowy shudder. The material was suddenly untarnished. With a flick of her wrist, it shifted on her body, the material punctured by thread and reassembled, drawing about her.

She turned around in a long-sleeved tunic, a hooded vest, a pair of slacks—all in the same snowy shade. She looked at her bare feet in the inch of water. She eyed Flam's leather armor.

"Mind?" she asked, but before Flam understood, she reached out with a tendril of her stitches and unlatched the hard leather panel covering his right shin. The stitches held the piece of leather out, working quickly as they broke it down and reassembled it into a pair of midthigh, brown boiled-leather boots. She lifted her left foot from the water, shook it, slipped on a boot, and did the same with the right.

"There. Much better."

She seemed troubled by something on Clyde's shoulder. Her stitches shot out and quickly repaired the rip sustained to his tuxedo in the initial encounter with her tentacle.

"Sorry. Force of habit," she admitted with a smile.

A nice smile, Clyde couldn't help but note.

"Hold on a second," Flam said. "Care to tell me why

you're getting dressed up like you're intending to go some-place, making shoes for yourself and whatnot?"

"I *plan* on getting to that deceitful bastard Gorett. No one deserves to be stashed away in some dank basement like an unwanted piece of furniture."

At that, Clyde felt the journal of Mr. Wilkshire gain a few ounces in his repaired tuxedo jacket.

"And I assume that's what you three are up to, yes? Out for revenge on the prime minister?"

"Out for revenge, yes, but I can't say we're looking for the same bloke you are," Flam said. "Me and the stack o' mice here are helping Pasty track down who killed his friend. But you came at kind of an odd time; our mission statement is in the middle of an amendment, as it were."

"Who are you looking to kill, Pasty?"

"My name's Clyde, actually, and I don't know. I'm not sure I'm going to seek revenge, honestly. I wouldn't use the word *kill*, either."

Nevele took a deep breath, the sutures across her chest creaking. "Right. So here we have a dapper fabrick weaver without a goal, a Mouflon he must've conned into giving his word to help him, and a pile of talking mice."

"*Frisk* mice," Rohm corrected.

"Right. Apologies." Nevele sniffed. "Looks like I got rescued by exactly the *wrong* bunch of bawdy buccaneers. Here I was going to offer you my services for freeing me, but I'm not sure I want to help if there's no true goal in sight."

"Preaching to the choir, lady," Flam said, folding his arms.

"Well, you were down here for a reason other than to free me, yes? Perhaps I can help with that and we can part company afterward. You know, return the favor?"

"We were looking for the elevator to sea level," Rohm said.

"Okay, that I can help with." She pointed. "This way. The westernmost wall."

"We know that much," Flam said, watching her go. "It's the electricity we're having a time with."

"Let's just see what we're up against first and get into the details later," Nevele said, splashing ahead in her new custom footwear. "You Mouflons, always such defeatists."

Clyde took up the rear again and walked with his head low and his hands buried in his pockets. He truly felt he was wasting everyone's time, but he hoped he could make himself useful.

Nevele looked like a somewhat experienced individual. Worldly, even. Perhaps she'd like to get something off her chest—even if it meant a jinxing of a week of stubbed toes and tumbles down flights of stairs. But maybe after they got out of there . . .

CHAPTER 16

Vidurkis Mallencroix

Pitka Gorett looked over the shoulders of his security officers as they sat patiently waiting at their dark monitors. A flash on each display showed junk-laden streets, abandoned shops, innumerable vacant homes. One of the security officers at the far end of the row thrust his arm up and swiveled in his chair, calling for the king's immediate attention.

"Sir, it looks like something has happened at the hospital."

Gorett swept his cloak aside and walked behind the security officer. Ignoring the officer's narration of what he'd just spotted, Gorett bent toward the glass monitor, but all he could see was his own reflection, looking haggard. He glimpsed the security officer in the reflection as well, looking stressed.

The officer sighed when the infrastructure of the hospital facility came on screen for a moment. In the third sub-basement, one room was illuminated differently, a bright cautionary red. Room eleven. Gorett had sequestered someone specific there, and now, if the readings were correct, that occupant was no longer hooked to the heart rate monitors. Either she had died—the preferable outcome—or she had ripped out the diodes. He had warned her how important remaining attached to the machine was; each diode was keeping her alive with a steady supply of artificial nutrients. The minute she wasn't, well, that would be when her slow death by starvation would begin.

Gorett pinched the bridge of his nose, raked a hand through his hair. "Any reading on where she might be now?"

The officer made a few keystrokes, but the screen went dark again. They'd have to wait for another surge to come. "I'm sorry, sir, but . . ."

"Forget it."

Gorett didn't bother to wait but simply walked to a guardsman at the security chamber's doors. He whispered, "Has the keep been compromised?" It was a question he asked often. After securing the stores of food and water, the underside of the palace came next. They couldn't exactly keep hold on a city with those horrid . . . *things* coming in through the floorboards.

The guardsman stared straight ahead. "All layers of the palace are perfectly stable, sir. I saw to it myself this morn that every level is secure. No Blatta can get through our walls, I assure you." Same thing he always said.

"Yes, but the *lowest* of the keep, the prisoner cells. Have *they* been compromised?"

"They are not our highest priority, sir." He dared to make eye contact with Gorett. "You said so yourself, sir: prisoners are an expendable lot."

"Go ensure it's secure. I want to visit someone."

"As you command, sir."

They had to take the stairs since the lift from the palace wasn't cooperating. Gorett marched to the stockade, accompanied by ten of his royal guard. Five walked ahead of him in the narrow spiral stairwell, and five kept watch behind them. They had reverted to firelight long before the power problems. The old man who held the title before Gorett was old-fashioned in that way—annoyingly so.

The guards were armed with rifles and the gray light lanterns that could immobilize any human or beast. Gorett requested a gray light lantern for himself and carried it along, the tiny pearl floating in a viscous fluid within. He rested his thumb on the switch. One flick, and a prisoner would get a shot of its nullifying glare.

When they reached the bottom of the keep, five guardsmen walked ahead to make sure all was safe. Gorett waited, listening to the walls moan with pressurized metal, the occasional splintering of rock making a heart-stopping pop. He considered himself a rather stalwart man, but still he jumped every single time. His city was in agony, and now all around him, underground, it was so much more palpable. The echoes didn't help. Especially the other voices mixing in with them, the other prisoners.

"Oh, Lord Gorett. You're here. Thank the heavens." Reaching hands came from between rusty bars on either side of him. He recoiled, remaining smack-dab in the middle of his mob of guards. "Please have mercy. The city has fallen. Let us at least escape with our lives. I promise you, I'll never return to Geyser for as long as I live."

"Shut it," a guard shouted and banged on the bars. The hands retracted, but the begging continued, albeit at a more subdued volume. All at once, Gorett noticed, they gave up on pleading for their release and began chanting. Prayers, mostly.

All that could be overlooked if it didn't smell so awful

in here. What was impossible to ignore was the city's laborious moaning. It bothered Gorett deeply, but none of the prisoners seemed to notice. He guessed they'd spent so much time here that none of them heard it anymore. He remembered setting up his wares on the sidewalks of East Town, not six miles from this spot, begging for people to buy his mother's crafts and charms. And how he'd gotten so used to the passersby rejecting him or telling him not to touch them that he began to not hear no at all anymore. Only when someone said yes—when they'd buy something and put money into his grubby hands—did his ears work.

Of course, then came the day when his mother approached the wrong man on the wrong day. How he turned and, without even so much as a second thought, cursed all beggars and began hitting her. Splitting her lip, putting these little notches into her cheek where his ring had struck and dug in. From that day forward, he swore he'd find some way, any way, to cocoon himself with enough money to never beg or ask anyone for anything again. He'd form himself into a powerful enough entity that if anyone dared raise a hand to him, they'd find themselves dead within minutes.

Still, the dry whispers from behind the cell walls punched through that armor he'd hammered and bolted onto himself. They'd cut through like a knife, finding the soft spot with such ease. He didn't let his face change, didn't give the memories purchase to climb his soul another solitary rung.

That was a lifetime ago, he reminded himself. *You're a different man now. You're the one who hands out the pittances.* Still, he wished he could flip on a deafness to the agonized cries of his city and of the jailed men.

He was here for a reason. He needed someone to stop not only the Mouflon and the man—if she hadn't killed her releasers—but now Patient Eleven as well.

Gorett watched his guards edge down the row of cells. Maybe when they apprehended the three, Gorett would put them to work—send them into the Blatta-choked mines, clear up Geyser's floodway, and allow safe passage for the retrieval mission with men he couldn't spare . . .

The lead guardsman returned, lifting his visor. "Sir?"

Had he been trying to get his attention?

"What is it?" Gorett said, frowning.

"It's all safe, sir. The walls are holding. The cells as well." The young guard removed a ring of keys. "Which one would you like opened?"

"Executioner Mallencroix's cell, if you would, please."

The ten guardsmen heard it, and as if the gray light were cast upon them, all froze openmouthed. The lead guardsman finally nodded and turned to walk to the end of the hall.

The cell door swung open, revealing the emaciated figure seated within. Gorett pulled his cloak tighter, protecting its luxurious fabric from touching anything, and stepped into the cramped enclosure. He remained standing, for every inch of the space was horribly filthy. For a beat, he lamented that he'd have to pitch his shoes after this.

Vidurkis Mallencroix's beard hung to his knees, and he looked through his matted black hair at the visitor. "Hello." His voice was like a dented bell being rung, a bent sound.

"Vidurkis," Gorett said and gazed at his pearl-like

eyes, his stomach going twisty. They were gray, with the occasional flash of red and green when the torchlight hit them just right.

"And to what do I owe this pleasure?" Vidurkis droned, his chains clinking as he sat straighter. "A visit from the new king? My, my—you should've said something, Pitka. I would've tidied up, gotten a trim, run out for lemon bars."

Despite the dirt, Gorett took a seat on the stone bench across from the bound killer. This conversation needed to come off as personable, as if they were old friends, as they used to be. Hard thing to pull off, certainly, one man wearing the raven robes of the King of Geyser and the other naked to the waist and bound in chains manufactured for use on shipping vessels.

"I apologize, my friend, for not retrieving you sooner."

Vidurkis shrugged. "Those who are told they are the most indispensable are often the first forgotten when there's a change in the staff. I knew you'd need me eventually, what with all this hubbub in the city."

"The citizens have been removed, and the Blatta are nearing the surface. We need to get at the deposit before it's lost."

"I'm no miner, Pitka. You want someone to take up a pick and shovel? Go put a job listing on another planet where there are plenty of dumb and poor willing to risk their lives for payment." Bending forward to reach with his chained wrist, the man swept some greasy hair from his face. "I can hear them, you know? That damn scream they make. Right through these walls." He pressed an ear against the stone. "Every passing week, the sound gets a fraction clearer."

The man was spooky. Gorett decided to just get to the

point. "We believe the girl has escaped. If so, I fear she's going to make trouble for us."

"So go kill her." His face remained pressed at the wall, as if he were too transfixed by the faint sound of scuffling insects to commit to the conversation fully.

Even Gorett could hear them in the speck of silence when everyone present was silent and the torches' crackling paused. The scratching pressed him on. "You know as well as I do that her fabrick is strong. None of my men stand a chance against her. You'll have to go after her. We can only assume she's loose somewhere in the city. She knows about the Blatta. She has secrets in her head that need to be kept, Vidurkis. She could ruin us if she gets to the mainland and calls anyone. Anyone at all. She could bring Adeshka against us. They've always had it out for us, taking our citizenry like it was some kind of damned favor."

"If she could so easily pose a threat to you, why did you keep her alive?"

"I thought . . . she could be convinced. Most people have a price. She did not. Even after giving her a few months in seclusion to tally one up. Regardless, if she's loose, we've got to do something."

Vidurkis laughed, a blast of sickly noise. "We? Come now, King Gorett. You know as well as I do that I'm not included in any sort of *we*. Pyne put me down here. You could've said something at my trial, but you didn't." He paused. "You want the girl stopped? You should've thought of that and put a bullet between Margaret's beautiful eyes when you had the opportunity."

"I know, but there wasn't any time . . . I was going to, but then the Odium started their bombing. Besides, if we could avoid killing her, I would prefer it. She's woven in such a way, unlike any other, and I thought if she could be convinced—"

"Us weavers, we're like amusements to you, aren't we? Or in my case, little tools in little drawers."

"I wouldn't ask you if it weren't import—"

"Let her roam Geyser. Let her get off the island and spread the truth about what you did." He waved a hand, the length of chain clanking. "Makes no difference to me. The view never changes in my little drawer. In fact, go ahead and let her bring Adeshka against you. I hope they put your head on the highest pike they can find. On top of the geyser itself, so the steam—if they ever get the damn thing unplugged—can bleach your skull every hour on the hour. It'll be a way for the Blatta to tell how long it's been since Geyser became their city: how white the old king's skull is. Their calendar."

He was nearly yelling now, positioning himself on thin, brittle legs. One of the guardsmen reached a gray light lantern into the cell, thumb poised over the trigger.

Vidurkis looked at the deactivated gray blob hanging inside the fluid, then at the guard holding the lantern. He raised one shackled wrist to point at his own eyes with his fingers held in a V. "Where do you think that shite comes from, boy? Do you really think it'd work on its *source*?"

The guardsman shrank away.

"Moron." Vidurkis's gray eyes regarded Gorett, who was settling onto his seat. "If you release me, I'll find her if she's out there. But when she's dead, I will not return to this pit. Far too long have I been here, counting the days." He looked at the grimy wall again. "And listening."

Gorett bowed his head. "You kill her, and I will grant your freedom." He stopped, looked into Vidurkis's face. "She may not be alone. We understand there's also a man and a Mouflon loose in the city. Dangerous ones, at that. Armed."

"A man and an armed Mouflon." Vidurkis laughed. "Tall order, King. I was an executioner, remember, Pitka?"

"I want them all dealt with. They can't leave Geyser, considering what your sister knows, if they are in fact working together in any capacity at all—"

"Don't call her that. She wouldn't call herself that—my sister. Nor should I address her as anything but a stranger." He looked at his clawlike hands. "That gulf developed a long time ago. Back when I gave myself over to my skills, became better—but worse in her eyes. I was good, though, at what I did. Lost my sister but gained something so much more wondrous. Usefulness. Excellence at something. Skill." He stopped, looking slapped, as if he hadn't meant to let that tirade spill from his lips. He glanced at the crowd of guards at the door, then at Gorett across the cell from him. "Do you remember? How good I was?"

"Yes, I remember."

"Splendid, draped in Executioner blacks. The boots and the rifle and swords. How magnificent an image I cut. Such a pillar of authority."

Gorett made himself nod and remember. "Yes. You were rather remarkable at what you did. And everyone knew it."

"Damn right they did," he replied without joy. He sat back, seemingly sated. He cleared his throat. "I'll do it, but you must keep your word this time, Pitka. You broke my trust once. Just sat there and stared at me, those damned wormy lips saying nothing on my behalf when Pyne banged the gavel." He was getting loud again but reined himself in. He sat forward, chains clinking, one hand reaching out to point at Gorett's heart. "But allow me to just say this. Fool me once, shame on you; fool me twice, I cut your throat."

CHAPTER 17

Fresh Ink

Water poured continually where the floor ended and the open-air elevator shaft began. The stream passed through the grating and fell through the remainder of Geyser's platter to the forest far below. The flow scattered in the wind, reduced to mist. Clyde watched, vertigo hitting him hard.

He stood at the edge. Even from this great distance, he could smell the sea. He looped his hands through the fencing surrounding the elevator shaft, peering at the forest ending and the beach beginning. The ocean looked inviting. Clean, blue water. As one wave after another broke, he could hear it faintly on a delay: rush, rush, rush.

Some daylight snuck through the underside of the city's structure, letting them know it was late afternoon.

Rohm said, "It appears the elevator car is already down there."

Nevele walked to the control panel and absently pressed a few of the darkened buttons on its display. "I remember hearing them leave. They rounded up a few of the cabinet members' elderly mothers and put them in. I remember the last lot of them. When they left, they never sent the car back up. They probably jammed it up good, too, just so no one else could leave."

"Typical," Flam grunted.

"Well," Nevele said, "if we plan to get out of this awful place, we best put our heads together for a solution."

She turned to Rohm, whose thousands of eyes studied the surrounding area: the cables hanging in the middle of the shaft on the other side of the elevator gate, the control panels, the electric wires running to the elevator works. Rohm silently worked it all out, thousands of little brains analyzing cooperatively.

"There hasn't been a surge in a while," Flam said. "I wonder if the geyser finally gave up the ghost."

"Wouldn't be surprised," Nevele said. "Those Blatta sure were hard at work clogging it."

Clyde, Flam, and Rohm faced her.

She raised her eyebrows. "You don't know?"

They shook their heads.

"It was the reason that bastard Gorett trapped me here. I wasn't in his inner circle, by any means, but I lived in the palace, working as the delegate of fabrick weaver affairs like I said—and seamstress when it was called for. And, as service folk do, we got wind of a fair amount of gossip. But one particular strand of rumors was a bit big: what our new king would do about a certain discovery in the Kobbal Mines."

"The Kobbal Mines?" Clyde exclaimed. "Mr. Wilkshire owned part of those."

Nevele's stitch-strewn eyebrows crunched over her eyes. "You knew Mr. Wilkshire?"

"I did. It's who I am—*was*—seeking to avenge."

"Oh, you poor dear. I can't imagine how you felt when he was framed in such a terrible way."

Clyde shook his head. "Framed?"

"The Blatta infestation? How he was blamed for knowing their hive was down there? And how—good gracious, do you know about any of this?" She turned to the other two, who both shook their heads. "I guess I thought if you were still here, it meant you knew."

Clyde forced himself to speak. "What happened?" His voice sounded muddied, sadder than ever.

"The miners discovered a wealth of precious metals inside the mines. By King Pyne's orders, Geyser law states that any major discovery of wealth must be evenly distributed to every man, woman, and child of the city. Of course, when Gorett got word that such a monumental discovery had been made, he wanted it all to himself. Wendal stone is, after all, one of the most valuable materials on this planet."

"Good Meech, wendal stone? On Gleese?"

"Precisely," Nevele said. "And when Gorett heard the deposit wasn't just a small chunk but an entire miles-wide bed of pure wendal stone, he wasn't going to share with everyone. So he used what he knew about the Kobbal Mines. It was in close proximity to a major Blatta hive, and he saw to it that the hive was *accidentally* tapped. Blatta flooded the mines, killing nearly all the miners within a day. And of course, with something so tragic, *someone* had to be blamed. Gorett saw no one better than the owner of those mines, Albert Wilkshire. I met him once," she said as an aside. "He was very nice to me, despite my . . . looks."

Clyde felt like he'd been pinned under a boulder for the last day and a half and someone had mercifully rolled it off him. "He was a kind man indeed."

Nevele placed a hand on his shoulder. "I'm sorry. I had

no idea that's who you were seeking to avenge. I understand now. But I'm not sure why you were so disheartened. Don't you want justice for your friend?"

"He blamed himself. In his journal, he said he'd known about the Blatta hive. That those who survived the attack probably would join up with the Odium and come back to kill him."

"I highly doubt any miners in his employ would've joined the Odium. And the Blatta hive was no secret. It wasn't such a sure thing until a few miners reported seeing droppings and the husks they shed every few months. Gorett made sure to know where the edges of the hive were, though. I saw the diagrams in his office once. They were mining terribly close to it, even before the discovery of the wendal stone deposit. Not by Mr. Wilkshire's choosing—I'm sure of it. Gorett kept a close eye on the mines and commanded their owners to push their diggers hard."

"So Gorett's to blame? He made Mr. Wilkshire believe he was a bad man?" Clyde felt a touch sick. "Mr. Wilkshire died thinking he deserved what happened to him."

"It's a shame indeed," Nevele said. "I think you have the ink to rewrite that mission statement of yours. Your goal and mine are pretty similar. We could write them together, if you wish."

"I think I'd like that."

"Then we'll do this for him as well as all the others Gorett has ruined."

Flam slapped the gate. "Well, that makes all this pretty damn foolish, doesn't it? If we're after Gorett now, what's the point of getting to sea level? Say we get there and throw rocks at Geyser in hopes one knocks him on the head?"

"That's true," Rohm said. "If we want to get closer to Gorett, we should turn ourselves in to the Patrol guardsmen. It's the only way to get through Geyser's north end."

Nevele smiled and shook her head. "You men. Always the same. Charging headlong into a situation, which will only get you run through." She approached the elevator control panel again. "You've heard of *undermining* someone, haven't you? It comes from the act of doing just that. I suggest we go below and get at Gorett that way."

"Go through the sewer system? Are you barmy? Especially now, with this new information you've handed us. I hope you know the mines and sewers run side by side through Geyser's stem. And you say the geyser itself is jammed because of the Blatta? And *still* that's where you're suggesting we go? This woman is off her nut, Pasty. There's no way I'm going into those tunnels again."

Nevele whipped around. "Wait a moment. Again? You've been in there before?"

"As a pup, yeah. Worked in the sewers with my uncle, doing repairs and such."

"Fabulous. You can be our guide."

Flam laughed. He pointed at Clyde but kept his gaze fixed on Nevele. "I gave my Mouflon promise to Pasty here that as soon as we reached a pilot to take him to the Odium, we'd part ways. That was back when we thought they were likely to blame. And now, with the plan all changed, that negates the previous arrangement entirely." He grinned, thumbing the strap of his satchel. But his bluster quickly dissolved when he noticed the others were glaring at him.

"Fine," Nevele said, her finger poised over the elevator call button, waiting for a power surge. "Go ahead and leave. Consider yourself removed from any responsibility. What are you, anyway? Do you have a profession? Dressed like that, you look like some kind of wrestler or pugilistic entertainer."

"I'm a treasure hunter, Zippergirl. And all this, with the plan to go into Blatta-infested caves and then overthrow a corrupt king? None of that—I repeat, *none* of that—is in the thief's code. And I would know. I wrote the Meech-damned thing. You want to go and play revolutionary? Go right ahead. But me? Once we get to sea level, I'm through with all this. I'll get my auto, piece her back together, and I'm gone."

"Suit yourself. But we are going into the Kobbal Mines, and as I said, there was an enormous deposit of wendal stone down there. And, as I left out and will tell you now, Gorett's breaching the Blatta hive wall was ill timed. They never got to the deposits. It's still down there—more wendal stone than a man or Mouflon could carry up in his entire life."

"They never got it?" Flam's eyes widened.

"Nope. Every guardsman Gorett sent was killed. They tried hiring miners from all over to fetch it, but none would. The news had spread far and wide about that Blatta infestation. Whether it were wendal stone or a truckload of beech quartz, no one would be daft enough to go after it."

Flam crossed his arms, bowing his horned head. "They . . . just didn't know what they were doing is all. Not that I'm saying I'm agreeing to go, that is. I'm just saying. They didn't have . . . the same know-how as someone like me would have. That's all."

Clyde hated that Flam had considered giving up. He was just beginning to like him, to the point he actually started thinking of him as a friend.

Flam must've felt Clyde's burning gaze. He looked up, and the two measured one another's stares.

"Fine, I'll help. But just for Pasty here. Don't call me greedy or anything. But look at him, with his bow tie and those damned puppy eyes. How could I say no to that?" He took Clyde's white cheeks in his stony hands. "Just look at that *face*."

Clyde laughed but knew Flam's sudden giddiness was fueled purely by greed. Still, he tried to push that aside for now. Maybe they really were friends.

Nevele harrumphed and faced the control panel. "Whatever helps you sleep at night."

CHAPTER 18

Goddesses and Floods Most Imminent

A few members of Gorett's royal guard escorted Vidurkis to the block housing on the easternmost side of the residential ward, where it was commonly known that the poor folks lived. Before Vidurkis had enlisted—and even after he was offered a room within the Patrol barracks—he kept his own space. It was a small cottage-style home across the cracked street from a delicatessen, a mere hop and a skip from the railroad tracks. Nestled between the garbage collection depot, where it always stunk the worst on Tuesdays when they burned the heap, it was a place for the old and forgotten, who smelled as bad as the flaming trash.

Without the chains, Vidurkis felt light as a feather. He was much more lithe than he had been before. His daily meals had consisted of soggy, overcooked rice and, every other day, a breakfast of strange, sour porridge. His body was weak, but he knew he was now more powerful in the mind than he had ever been as Executioner. Loads of time to think would do that to a man.

But unlike the prisoners around him in the dungeon, Vidurkis hadn't developed a conscience. A lot of them had begun openly chanting to invisible men and women whose names they had trouble pronouncing, begging for forgiveness.

Vidurkis had taken another tack. While he found solace in a religion of sorts, it wasn't one that would cleanse him. He begged for the roll of the dice to turn up in his favor from the Mechanized Goddess, a deity the Odium pirates favored, for she taught self-reliance with only a bit of mumbo jumbo about fate. Kind of a scandal, that. A man of high birth and social standing within a respectable city's security force subscribing to such a . . . brutish belief system.

He liked it because it mostly dealt with philosophies that if you ever engaged in a fight with an opponent, the Mechanized Goddess would provide you the upper hand in some chance way, like remembering the knife in your boot right before you would have been killed. Things like that. Realistic things. A god *worthy* of all those clasped-handed mental pleas.

He'd found the book devoted to her when he was new to the Executioner position. He fell madly in love with it immediately. Rarely did any school of thought thrill him like that, not only permitting his inclinations but encouraging them. Any trace of humanity in him wasn't just stamped out but redacted from his soul entirely and ecstatically after just reading a few verses. Peace is what he found in the blackness.

His home had been ransacked in his time away, which didn't surprise him. He had been a youth once. He knew boredom. Hell, he had even come to this exact street as a youngster with a pail of stones and sharp eyes forever looking for a ripe piece of unbroken windowpane.

Everything of value had been looted, all his furniture stolen or burned or broken into pieces. That was fine. Those were material things, which the Mechanized Goddess taught weren't that important anyway. What she bestowed favor upon were machines, weaponry, nuts and bolts. The first lesson in her divine cog-powered teachings was that she created man so that man could make machine and machine could serve the god and therefore create this loop—a spoke or cog—to keep everything greased and moving effectively. Of course, with that was the accompanying rule that machines were cold and unfeeling and that any believer should try to be the same.

Vidurkis dedicated himself to that. It thrilled him, just the idea of it.

The floor in the living room was so rotten that his weight sank the boards. He backed away and examined the whole space with his pearlescent eyes. The darker spots were obviously where the wood was the most rotten, but it was hard to determine whether they were just pools of shadow. He took a breath and didn't put much more thought into it. He simply hopped forward to a lighter spot and waited for the sound of the wood splintering wetly, but it held fast.

He moved on to another lighter spot, then another, then crossed the living room and entered the kitchen. There, the floors were stone. He'd laid the mortar himself, doubly strong, just for such an occasion—mostly because this floor operated as sort of a second roof over what was beneath. He walked to the icebox, chosen for its weight and theft-proofness, and discovered that the hatch hadn't been disturbed.

He thought it ironic, being released from one hole just to climb into another. But at least this one was roomier and chock-full of interesting things.

The storeroom was just as he'd left it. The ceiling was very low, and when he reached the bottom of the steps, he crouched like a stalking feline. He was used to the dark, so it didn't take long at all for his eyes to adjust. Out of the gloom before him the familiar shapes began to clarify. His tools, his serviceable objects of deference to the Goddess, all. His guns. He smiled.

The gadget Gorett had given him rang in his pocket, disrupting the moment he was having looking over all his beloved instruments. He hadn't even gotten to touch their metal yet or stroke their working parts, the pins and levers and hammers and magnificent firing mechanisms. Vidurkis pulled the communicator from his pocket while taking the first step into the dark hideaway.

"Yes?"

"Are you there yet? Have you found her?"

Vidurkis drew a hunting knife with a ten-inch blade from the collection of others and imagined, with stunning glee, slowly drawing it across Gorett's throat. "Not yet. I had to get my things first."

"What things? The men have plenty of things for you to borrow. They've got all the armaments you could possibly need." He certainly was ballsier over the phone than in person.

Vidurkis thumbed the knife and felt its kiss. Still sharp.

"I have no time for plastic guns made in some off-world two-bit sweatshop, Pitka. I want Gleese craftsmanship." He set the communicator on the corner of a workbench so he could put on a holster belt, then another and another.

He filled each available spot with a gun and slipped bullets into each waiting pocket of his bandolier. The weight of the weapons made all the years wasted in the dim recesses under the palace melt from his mind.

"Fine." Gorett sighed. "Just get there. They've had no power to do anything in a while, but you never know. They might've figured something out."

"My sister's not that bright." Vidurkis tasted the lie. She was sharp—impressively so. Growing up, he had constantly tried to best her. Typically it ended with her crying and Vidurkis doubly mad and making her swear—typically at the end of something sharp—to *never* breathe a word to their parents of the things he had done. She agreed every time, wordless. Just a nod. That in itself was a display of how smart she was.

"Either way, get there as soon as you can. She's not alone. I'm sure they'll think of some way to get out of the city soon enough."

"As you command, my *liege*," Vidurkis drawled and cut the communicator off. "Useless shite."

He filled each chamber of the revolver with a bullet. As the jacketing grated against the metal of the revolving drum, his heart sang a little. Each shhhk and click as he twisted the drum to the next available slot was a short but beautiful hymn to the Goddess, and he was more than happy to accommodate with a refrain.

For hours they waited, no rush of power having come. The water continually flowed around their feet, and the four travelers stood at the lift gate, taking turns waiting with a finger—or tail—poised over the call button.

Flam waited less than five minutes before giving up. Using the panel as a lean-to, he took out his pipe and packed in a black knot of mold. If there was one thing besides garlic that didn't agree with Mouflons, it was boredom.

A drop of water landed in the pit of his pipe, hissing as it boiled among the embers of his smoldering spores. Another knocked his horns, which he didn't feel but heard, then slithered to the curled tip and plummeted into the inner sanctum of his ear. It tickled and made his legs turn to jelly. Working it out with his finger, he looked up the hospital corridor to the elevator that would go up to ground level.

The water seemed to come from there as well, through the hatch in the elevator car. The steady trickles were now more like the results of a sky whale relieving itself. *Umbrella*, he reminded himself. *Need to pick up an umbrella if I'm ever going to the Lakebed again.*

"No power surge in hours," he thought aloud. "We got a slow build of current from a burst pipe somewhere in one of the subbasements above us, I reckon." He pointed at Nevele with his unlit pipe. "But . . ." He removed his finger from his ear and popped it into his mouth. He bent to cup a handful. He sipped it—and promptly spit it out. "Tasting weirder now. Richer. Higher sediment level. You mentioned something about the Blatta doing this, blocking her up?"

"They need water just like any other living thing," said Nevele, who was seated on an overturned bucket. The water level had raised to the point that she was nearly floating away with it. "Last I heard, they were trying to reroute the geyser's flow directly to the hive. They need it to expand the colony and feed their pupae, their babies."

"Ugh, babies. Far shot from a little bundle of joy, I'd bet. Anyway, unless they've finished rerouting it, where does it go?"

Clyde stepped off the filing cabinet he'd been roosting atop. Anxiety made his voice shrill as he said, "It'll get backed up."

Rohm continued, "And build pressure until . . ."

"You see what I'm getting at?" Flam said to Nevele. Not that there was anything wrong with Pasty and the mice, but if there was going to be any real problem, it would be left up to him and Stitches to solve it. "If there's one thing I understand, it's plumbing." He sneered at the beams of water, their white noise not at all comforting.

"This is a very daft place to be." Nevele stood. "Electricity or not, we need to get out of here."

Rohm, who seemed to be vibrating in place, stepped away from the control panel. The frisk mice among Rohm's legs were constantly circulating so that none of them would drown. They began moving quicker, climbing over one another and trading places much more frantically. "We don't do well with water in great amounts, Ms. Nevele. They used to test us, see how long we could hold our breath. It's unfortunate; our very small lungs do not match the capacity of our brains."

"It'll be okay," Nevele said but didn't seem positive.

Flam sized up the lift gate. It was reinforced from inside with a crossbar of considerable steel. The cable hanging inside looked sturdy enough. The spool would most likely hold their weight if they went down one at time.

Somewhere far up the hallway, a pipe shattered, followed by the shush of vastly pressurized water releasing. It made the floor shake and hanging pictures drop. It was as if a giant had stamped its foot on the floor above.

"Whatever we're going to do," Flam said, "we need to make it snappy."

"I'm thinking!" Nevele dropped her hood and rolled up her sleeves. She thrust her arms toward the elevator gate, and from her fingertips plunged arcs of thread. At once the flesh of her face sagged, the interconnected swatches no longer bound by anything. She sent the tendrils toward the four corners of the elevator gate, and they wrapped themselves around the crossbar and wove into the chain-links. She snapped her wrists, and all the twining locked into the gate went cello-string taut.

She leaped backward, snarling, pulling with all her might.

The gate clanged in its frame but didn't budge any farther.

She drooped her shoulders, her cords going slack. "It's tough," she slurred, since the left half of her lip was now where her chin was supposed to be. She seemed to notice the others staring and released one hand long enough to adjust her cowl to conceal her face.

"Can I?" Flam asked, reaching before her dangling threads.

Face partly obscured, she hesitantly nodded.

He took a double handful of her threads and pulled.

"The bottom—it's coming loose!" Clyde wedged the end of his wooden club into the gap and worked it forward and back. A few of the bolts snapped from their holes, their heads popped clean off.

Flam took the opposite corner and did the same with his broken blunderbuss.

Rohm kept watch on the hallway behind them, the individual mice dancing in a frenzy of fear. "Hurry! It's getting worse!"

The gate came free, and Nevele, Flam, and Clyde fell backwards into the water.

Clyde sprang to his feet, shoved the gate aside, and peered down. He went breathless.

Flam splashed next to him and looked.

The elevator car was halfway down to the forest floor below. Miles of open air.

The sudden drop, with no gate between, made Clyde's head whirl. He took a step back and looked to the others. "What now?" he shouted over the rushing noise.

Nevele's focus darted all around. She gripped the wrist-thick elevator cable and leaned over the edge. She hesitated there, as if taking a second to say a quick prayer, and then let her feet fall from the ledge. She hugged the cable with all four limbs and suspended.

"Does it feel secure?" Flam asked.

"Strong enough to hold me, but I'm not sure about you."

Individual tiles on the ceiling popped out of sockets and joined the flow, washing over the edge past Nevele and thousands of feet to the world far below.

"Meech! We need to do something."

Clyde watched a tile drop, spinning end over end, almost graceful in its two-mile descent. If he were to fall, he knew it wouldn't be so pretty and quiet—falling, thinking about it all, trying to suddenly develop the ability to fly. Vertigo made him take a step back.

Flam felt possessed. This was it, the end. He needed to get everything bad he'd ever done off his chest at once.

He looked to Clyde next to him and began rattling off the lengthy list. "When I was a teenager, I cheated on my first girlfriend. Her name was Coot, and she was as ugly as my furry arse . . . When I got my first automobile license, I used to go to the beach when I told Mum I was going to see Grandma . . . Once, when I was sick, I threw up out the window of my bedroom because I was too lazy to go to the bathroom. That rose garden never grew back the same, and Mum never could figure out why."

Clyde looked into Flam's rambling face, eyes wide. "Why are you telling me this now?"

"What in the hell are you *doing*?" Nevele screamed. "You know how it works with him."

"I don't know," Flam cried. "I . . . I can't die with all this on my chest. I just can't . . . And another time, last week actually, when I went into the Mole Hole general store, I thought about screaming, 'Fire!' and just grabbing up everything I could and—"

"Shut up," Nevele shouted. "And you"—she looked at Clyde—"plug your ears or something."

It was too late.

There was a reverberating thud, and a gale pushed Flam and Clyde from behind. Air from inside the hospital was shoved toward them by something big. Like a whole lot of water, for instance.

The Mouflon closed his eyes, unable to bear the end. He felt something hitting him—soft, warm things pelting his whole body. He looked down. Head to toe, he was covered by leaping frisk mice. They screamed in a mismatched cacophony, too scared to think as one at the moment.

Even Clyde let out a scream.

Nevele was saucer eyed. "Now you've done it."

Flam turned back and saw an enormous white fist of water thundering up the hall toward them.

CHAPTER 19

The Gush and Fall

Clyde took Flam's hand and jumped, pulling the mouse-carpeted brute with him. Nevele saw them coming and glided down the line to make room. Once all were on, they slid down, the grease on the cable making their speed involuntary. They skidded a few yards, came to a near stop when their hands painfully hit a dry patch, and then skidded some more.

Nevele pressed her boot heels together to work as a brake and glanced up to make sure she wouldn't get run off the cable.

Countless gallons of sediment water came pouring down after them. They skidded down and down and down. They were far enough that there was no fear of the water knocking them off the cable.

The wind was strong on the underside of Geyser, and a majority of the flow was carried away as a brown mist. They were all soaked head to toe, which made keeping a grip on the cable difficult.

"We'll keep going down," Nevele shouted up to them. "When we reach the car, maybe we can make it swing over to the stem and we'll climb down that way."

Clyde saw the column that supported the platter of Geyser. The rock was made of the same sediment water, just like what was still dribbling on them. It made formations, like stalagmites, smooth and flashing with the occasional sparkle set within the stone. Nearly halfway to the elevator car below, he considered the prospect of trying to climb down such a slick surface, especially with wet footwear. It wouldn't go well. Trying to get the elevator car to swing that way to make the jump would be suicidal. He opted to keep that thought to himself. Now wasn't the time to start crossing things off the list of possibilities.

He couldn't help but notice all the frisk mice nestled within Flam's fur were in some kind of a power surge of their own. They were all looking up, the downy undersides of their little jaws showing. Some pointed, some gasped, and some even swore. None of it could be clearly made out, especially when one of them stepped on Flam's left eye and he began cursing.

With trepidation, Clyde looked. Within the housing of the elevator gears, far up, the cable was splintering. Unraveling, just as Nevele's tentacle of stitches had, the loose end trailing. A small but terrifying jerk in the cable.

"Feel that, Pasty?" Flam murmured.

"I'm afraid so."

"Move it, Zippergirl! This thing's coming down!"

"*What?*" Nevele shrieked.

"The cable—it's breaking! Get a move on! To the car, the car!"

"What good is that going to do us? Get inside and hope for the best? We'll still be a mile off the ground, you fuzzy dolt!"

Having to force himself to look, Clyde saw the cable coming apart in more than one place.

They all felt a shudder in the line just as they reached

the car, still a dizzying distance from the island's green floor. They all stood on the top of the elevator around the cable, holding on as if they were passengers on an autobus sharing a pole. They met one another's gaze as if wordlessly exploring possibilities.

"I hope you can make a parachute jump out your rear, because this thing won't hold much longer," Flam said. He pinched his eyes closed. Without opening them, he addressed Clyde. "This is happening because I told you all that up there, isn't it?"

Clyde frowned, nodded.

"Meech help us."

A loud snap sounded, fierce as a gunshot, and the elevator dropped a foot. A melancholy droning issued out of the cable, the rusted metal's swansong.

Clyde could hear swishing sounds, like Master Tabernathy's testing of the lash before he took it to Clyde's back. He wondered if this was what he had once read about, seeing his life flash before his eyes. If so, he wished whoever was in charge of that replay would fast-forward over the bad parts and play just the happy ones. Then he noticed it. The sound was Nevele coming completely undone.

Every inch of her threads was spiraling out of her fingertips, and she was sending them snaking down around the elevator car, encasing the entire thing as if in a net. When she had it firmly held, she cast her gaze up. Using what remained of the cords within her skin, she began spraying them up against the cable. The others watched as the stitches inched their way up the cable fastidiously, pausing to loop a few times around where the cable was tattered or weakened from rust.

Clyde's hope spiked as he watched the very ends reach the underside of the hospital.

"I'm going to try to let us down easy," Nevele said, the entire right half of her face beginning to slide off from the bright red muscle underneath. With a flick of her chin, she moved the auburn cascade of her hair to cover most of what was happening to her.

Clyde could see by how loose the skin on her arms was becoming that she had nearly every inch of her stitches out. His heart sank when she noticed him staring and pitched her head forward to get her hood up . . . and a slab of her face fell from her skull.

Upon the elevator's roof, at Nevele's feet, was her cheek with a bit of upper lip.

Flam looked positively mortified, apparently having entirely forgotten their dire situation.

In chorus, Rohm asked, "Will your fibers support us? We were able to bite through them, and this elevator car, if it is of the standard manufacture, cannot be any less than three tons' worth of steel. Add our weight and Mr. Flam's, which must be at least another three hundred or so—"

"Hey, now," Flam said, shaking out of his trance. "It's probably that much only because I'm covered in all you mice and your *enormous* brains."

"At any rate, do you think you'll be able to hold on, Ms. Nevele?"

She said nothing, even as another piece of her fell with a heavy slap.

Clyde glanced, despite himself, and saw it was the bit of skin that framed her left eye, the empty socket staring up.

"I'll be fine," she said, barely audibly. "Hang on tight. I

think it's about to—"

A thunderous crack, louder than any that preceded it, and all of them felt the gravity at once.

They screamed. Clyde dropped to all fours and gripped the top of the elevator car. Flam grabbed the cable, and Rohm loosed a yelp. The only one quiet among them was Nevele as she stepped to the central part of the elevator roof and stretched her arms as high as they would go.

Clyde felt the rigid surface beneath him drop out in a moment of panic-inducing weightlessness. The elevator car and cable tumbled. How were they . . . floating?

Then he understood. They were all caught within a net of Nevele's stitches. For a moment he felt like laughing, like screaming just for the joy of being alive—but death wanted to give a curt reminder. The end of the cable snapped against itself like a whip directly next to his head.

It trailed past, following the elevator. The entire thing violently crashed, a triumphant announcement of contact that had undoubtedly been heard far and wide.

Between the net at her feet and the miles of stitching sprouting out of her hands, Nevele was suspended, slowly being pulled apart. She made small, agonized sounds—grunts, the occasional gasp through gritted teeth.

Around them in the suspended net, more of her rained down.

"I'll try to . . . let us down . . . easy. But I can't . . . make any promises, okay?" she said, her words barely comprehensible.

Another piece of her tumbled out from under her hood, and Clyde was quick to reach out of the net to snatch it from the air. It was warm. He didn't dare look at what he now clutched in his fist but just held on to it for her.

Gradually, they touched down among the rubble that remained of the reception platform, down in a clearing among the tall, bent trees of the forest underneath Geyser. As soon as Clyde felt the solid ground, and heard Nevele's boots crunch down onto the tall grass a second later, she let go from above and her miles of threads spooled back into her. She kept herself turned, face concealed. Once her threads were all back together, she took a few limping strides away.

She squatted to pick up pieces from among the tall grass. It was as if someone had taken the open box of a jigsaw puzzle and cast the entire score into the air. Except here each unique piece wasn't a bit of cloud or grass or kitten face. It was Nevele, her skin, the skin of the woman who'd just saved their lives. Still, as mortified as he wanted to be, he figured she wanted herself back together just as much. He gathered what he could find, accumulating a mass that required both hands to carry.

"Look at that," he heard Flam say to Rohm. "Gentleman to the end, him."

Clyde approached Nevele. "Uh, here you go."

Without facing him, Nevele reached behind her and snatched the pieces from his hands. She held one out in front of her, turning it in place to find which way was up. Once it was right, she brought the red side in under her hood. Clyde heard a sound like Miss Selby's big sharp needles through Mr. Wilkshire's leather riding coat—kind of like a tearing but more like a snap.

Dawning on the fact that he was staring, Clyde walked away to let Nevele compose herself.

A short distance away, frisk mice steadily leaped off

Flam and formed Rohm's feet, legs, torso, arms, and head. "That was terrifying," Rohm said when unified once more.

Flam stared upward, fists placed firmly on his hips, as if sizing up the corpse of a giant beast he had just vanquished. Clyde remembered that Flam had vented a great many personal trespasses before their jump and he was probably feeling much better about himself.

Flam laughed, really pulling a good chortle up from his belly, and slapped his knee. "Oh, I can't wait to write my uncle about that one! They don't even have thrill rides like that in the amusement parks on Quib. Man, oh, man. I tell you, Nevele, you should charge money for that. I'd hate to see what you'd call a bad time, because that was a Meech-damned hoot and a half right there."

"I am truly glad you enjoyed it, Flam." Nevele knelt to fetch an ear. "Really."

CHAPTER 20

Two Different Reflections

The suns set, and the group made their way into a comfortable clearing in the forest. After some flint pried free of Flam's blunderbuss, which he was now referring to as "an expensive paperweight" with a glare at Nevele, they managed to start a small fire.

All the while, Clyde couldn't help but look into the canopy above. He could not recall seeing a forest of such dense and undisturbed quality since looking at the pictures of a book on forestry services Mr. Wilkshire had given him. The photos of the lumberjacks also came to mind. They were all the grizzled sort, with beards and coated in a fine patina of earth. *Kind of like how we must look now,* he thought. But as much dirt as they'd accumulated on themselves, it still didn't feel like any hard work had actually been accomplished. Really, it was more like the grand version of stumbling about blindly and falling into mud puddles. Still, he wasn't used to living like this: being dirty and tired all the time. But, for as much danger as they seemed to be in now and were jumping into voluntarily soon, he had to admit it was kind of a fun change of pace from life at the chateau.

Finding a comfortable seat on a log, Flam opened his satchel and dispersed some of the food remaining from the market. He threw a hunk of cheese to Rohm, who dissolved around it and ravenously tore it to crumbs. "Your payment for the day's service," he said.

He tossed a can of sprouts to Nevele, and they took turns using the can opener. She sat by the fire and dropped her hood, revealing her face. She looked to Clyde, who offered her the warmest smile he could muster. She held out the opened can of sprouts.

He shook his head.

Before he could say anything, Flam informed her, "He doesn't eat."

"Ever?" Nevele gaped.

"Nope," Clyde said cheerfully.

"Don't you get tired, though?"

"Actually, I feel pretty good at the moment."

"Must be part of your fabrick." Nevele pulled free a soggy sprout from the syrup and let it drip into the can before eating it. "You must gain nourishment from confessions, if I had to guess. And I'm willing to bet you're pretty full at the moment." She glared at Flam across the fire. "By the way, Flam, I heard what you said. You threw up out a window because you were too fat and lazy to get up and go to the bathroom?"

Flam shrugged and continued eating.

"I don't suppose you've heard of anyone quite like me before," Clyde said to Nevele. He removed his tuxedo coat and laid it out flat near the fire. Sediment water was drying on its fine black material in muddy patches.

"Yeah, you're quite the unique one. I thought I knew all the basic types of weavers, but one that looks like you and does what you can do? That's fresh to my ears." She absently touched one of her ears then, as if making sure it was even with the other.

"Where does it come from?" Clyde asked, looking at his narrow arms, the veins beneath the snow-white skin. "Does it come from our parents—in the blood?"

"That's like asking how, when you choose to watch a certain television program that you rarely ever watch, it's always the same episode. Or how, when the birds migrate, they know which way is south." She shot another glare across the fire. "Or why the Mouflons are a bunch of slobs."

Flam was clearly too invested in eating to allow any brainpower for a comeback. He merely picked some crumbs out of the fur on his chest and shrugged.

"My parents weren't like this," Nevele said, picking another sprout out of the tin. "I can assure you of that. Kind of an indignity where I come from, a couple of well-to-do business folk giving birth to a couple of . . . well, a fabrick weaver child."

"What sort of company do they run?" Flam asked.

"They were in freight, moving cargo from one rock to another, eighty thousand vessels in their fleet altogether," she said with a touch of pride. "You don't suppose these cans of sprouts got to Gleese on their own, do you? These things don't grow anywhere in this system."

"Well, I didn't know that, but I know they sure are tasty," Flam said, upending his can and drinking the syrup. He tossed it, once emptied, to Rohm, who took turns scurrying within it, lapping up residue.

"Do you still see them? Your parents?" Clyde asked Nevele.

"Not really. Actually, that's a lie. Forgive me. I haven't seen or spoken to them in years." She hugged her knees.

"We got along pretty well up until my talent started to become kind of hard to ignore. I was just a kid, and—"

"Careful. Choose thy words carefully," Flam warned, adopting a ye-olde accent.

Nevele grinned. "It's fine, Flam. I'm not confessing anything." She looked at Clyde. "I remember I was at the playground on the monkey bars. My hand slipped, and I skinned my knee. Well, actually, I cut it. It bled and bled. Went home and told my mother, and we went to the doctor to get it looked at. He patched it up—but it didn't heal, even after several weeks. It didn't bleed anymore, but the wound wouldn't close. He decided to try stitches, and that's when things got kind of . . . out of hand. That night I was picking at it, as any child would do, and I saw that just by thinking about it, I could make the end of the stitch move. I became fascinated by it. I wondered if it was just on my knee that I could do this."

She stopped herself for a moment, broke eye contact with Clyde, looking into the fire. "Where I'm from, just the mention of fabrick is frowned upon. So, naturally, I kept it to myself. I gave myself another knick playing outside a week later and didn't tell my mother about this one. I got her sewing kit and stitched it up myself—here." She pulled up her sleeve, and there was the mark, with some brown twine running back and forth over the inch-long gouge. "And I decided to leave it alone. Summer ended, and back to school I went, afraid of anyone learning my secret. Either way, as it happens, it didn't take long for the girls to begin pestering me why I was wearing long-sleeved clothes all the time. One day they got bold and ganged up on me after school, tore the sleeves off my sweater, and saw. I could tell it scared them, but still they made fun of me. Having grown up with a cruel arse for a brother, I knew how to fight back before it got worse.

"And as anyone does when they stand up for themselves, I got in trouble, naturally. They believed in lashing there, at my school." She shook her head. "It took only that one time, and they—as well as I—got to learn what I could *really* do . . ." She continued, a slight hitch in her throat, "Since I don't want to confess much more than that to save myself the jinxing, I'll leave it at this: the third time I was brought in to the counselor's office for standing up for myself, I accepted that lash."

Clyde looked at her stitches on her arm and banding around her knees. Most of the visible stitching was the same color, a warm brown shade like tanned leather. "It's all . . ."

"Most of it, yeah. I've replaced a lot of it over the years, added some, taken some out that's started to fray. Put this one in because I liked the color." She thumbed a strip of sky-blue twine and pulled it out to show them. When she let it go, it cinched back up tight again.

Flam took another can from his satchel and began working the opener around its lid. "Now isn't *that* the happy story?"

Nevele glared at the Mouflon. "Again, at least I didn't vomit out of any windows."

Clyde interjected before their argument could get stirred up again. "Did they whip your face, too?" Clyde said, wincing. "I can't imagine, even at a boarding school, that they'd do something as cruel as that."

"These came later, unfortunately," she said, tracing one line that ran the length of her cheek from earlobe to chin.

"But that's a story for another fire. What about you? Do you have parents? Have a delightful upbringing like me?"

Clyde shook his head, listened to the crickets chirp for a moment. "If I had parents, I don't remember them. I recall my first master. I assume he was here, in Geyser, but I cannot say for certain. I was kept inside, behind closed doors with no windows, all the way up until Mr. Wilkshire. And even there, I wasn't allowed in the front gardens. I was permitted aboveground in the house only when his children weren't home. We used to stroll around the back gardens and discuss all sorts of things. Not just confessions but about life. He often said he wanted to let me go one day, after he had said all he needed to. Having met you, Nevele, it makes me happy to learn there are fabrick weavers who live by their own accord."

"Not so fast there," she said icily. "Some of us get employment, of sorts. Like me, working at the palace and all. But, really, when you have a specific talent and men who wish to utilize it, they may offer you a wage but you're still owned, by one definition or another. I've heard of others who were kept like you, squirreled away in basements under lock and key. I never heard of any that changed hands like you, though. How many men have claimed to be your masters?"

"Too many to count."

"How old are you?"

Clyde shrugged, staring into the fire. He wasn't feeling as cheerful anymore.

"Truly one for the record books." Nevele finished the can of sprouts and handed it to Rohm. "But that's fabrick for you. It works in weird and wonderful ways. Never the same for any two gifted with it. I heard they were studying it somewhere, trying to see what made it develop so suddenly after no sign of it in generations of families."

"Toxic rays from the suns." Flam giggled.

"Do you ever say anything useful?"

"I have my moments—when necessary."

"How about now? Care to tell us *your* story?" Nevele snapped. "You sure have a comment on everything. Why don't you open up a little so we can poke fun?"

"Not much to say," Flam said, straightening. He crossed his arms and cleared his throat, and when he spoke again, his tone was noticeably more rigid. "I was a normal pup, like any other Mouflon. I was taught right and wrong, learned to herd and farm and all that boring business. Was left to set off on my own, see what I could make of myself. Traveled from one world to the next when I could afford passage." He waved his hand about, lazily indicating different planets in the various systems he'd traveled. "I'd buy a new auto and start all over again, just roving around, getting into scrapes and weaseling my way out of them."

Nevele interrupted. "Never interested in making any of the many worlds you laid your hooves upon a better place? Never gave a squat about anything besides yourself?" She took up a fresh log and cast it into the fire, embers spraying. "Typical Mouflon."

"And what's that supposed to mean? Because I can tolerate a lot of shite, girl, but when it comes to bigotry—bigotry against my people, well . . . I'm easy to upset then."

"There's no bigotry about it. Simple fact: you're all the same," Nevele spat, backhanding the air in his direction. "You all think you're the biggest and toughest things on the planet. Why should you get involved in anything be-sides tracking down your next meal or trying to pull a fast one on someone? You know, I got a couple of marks on me that are thanks to your kind."

"So you're going to make a sweeping generalization of my species just because of a few bad apples?"

"Well, you're certainly not doing much to prove the bushel otherwise."

Clyde sat up. "Hey, let's not fight, okay?"

"Get a load of the Stitcher. Thinks she knows every-thing just because she had a rough upbringing. You go ahead and tell me about tough childhoods after you see your father murdered, okay? You tell me what it's like when you watch the most honest, hardworking, fun-loving chap you've ever known in your whole life gunned down right in front of your eight-year-old eyes."

Nevele appeared struck. "I . . . didn't know."

"No, you *didn't* know. Just keep running your mouth, lady." He folded his arms and turned away.

Rohm finished eating and reassembled. "I couldn't help but overhear. I apologize for your tumultuous experi-ences, but it appears a squabble has broken out among our party. Perhaps it'd be a good time to get some rest. We're all very tired. Having several grumpy individuals among myself at the moment, I know we could use the sleep."

Nevele twisted around and lay down, pulling her cloak up over herself as a blanket. "Good idea," she huffed.

"Yeah, splendid," Flam grunted and rolled over in the other direction.

Clyde watched the mice litter the ground and give way all at once to a heap of slumbering frisk mice. Again, as on the previous night, he was alone.

Within the hour, all their breathing had slowed and even Nevele was softly snoring.

For a few hours, Clyde fed the fire, watching the last bit of moisture in his coat steam away. With that task done, he put it back on, the coat nice and warm on his back and arms. But as he tugged it by the lapels to get it straight on his narrow shoulders, Mr. Wilkshire's citizen dagger dropped from the pocket. It made a loud clatter, but no one in their various heaps of coats around the fire stirred.

As quietly as he could, he removed the blade from the scabbard. Past the inscription on the metal, he looked at his reflection. He could see sadness in his eyes, and that was sufficient to make him turn the blade away. He angled it so he was looking at the fire, then at Flam, then Nevele, then up above. He looked to the stars he could see in the open spaces in the canopy that changed with the wind as the leaves rustled and shook, and he wondered if there was another fabrick weaver as pale and sleepless as he doing the same thing at the same moment.

He hoped so.

CHAPTER 21

The Bullet Eater Details His Summons

They sat in Aksel's shack, nearly knee to knee in the narrow pressboard hut, a lantern glowing between them. They kept their voices low, not knowing who was listening next door. With so much time to fill during the day, the refugee camp was a great place for gossip to spread like wildfire. Ricky was more curious than even Aksel had been about Karl and Moira's proposition, posing more questions in the span of ten minutes than Aksel had the entire time he'd been in the infirmary with them. A good number he could answer, but many more he could not.

Ricky passed the can of beer—actual beer!—to Aksel. "Why do they want you to get chummy with Neck Scar?"

"Turns out his name is Steve, oddly enough, and even though ol' Stevie Boy likes to act as if he hates the Odium, he's actually a member."

"What? Are you *serious?*"

"That's what they said. Apparently he says all that crap about them so no one will skin him alive." Aksel pressed the flat of his hand against his face so he could drink the beer without spilling it all over his lap. They'd had his DeadEye taken out just so they could talk to him without fear, but they'd since reinstalled it after he'd agreed to help them. He was still feeling the effects from the injections of numbing wonder drugs. "Steve was living in Geyser as a spy. Actually helped let the Odium in."

"How'd he do that?"

Aksel passed the can back. "They didn't say, really. Just said he took down a few key security measures the city had in place, and, well, with enough of the sky not being watched, they could sneak right up before Geyser even had a chance to get ready."

Ricky took a quick sip. "So they want you to get buddy-buddy with Scar Steve and . . . join the Odium?"

"Not so loud," Aksel said, eyeing the seam in the wall where the two warped panels of wood didn't quite meet. "You and I are already on thin ice."

"What do you mean?"

Aksel finally looked at him. "They know we're not actually citizens."

"Did you roll on me?" Ricky asked a little louder.

"How could I have rolled on you? They knew."

"All right. Sorry."

"Either way, I mean, I kind of had to agree. Otherwise, we'd both be out on our butts."

Ricky patted his knee. "Thanks, buddy."

"Hey, what are friends for, right?"

Since there was only one can of beer, they had to take turns holding it up in cheers and taking a drink.

"So they knew about you, huh?" Ricky asked quietly.

A while back, Aksel had imparted his entire history to his friend one night. Ricky didn't talk to him for a day, chose to park his cart on the other side of the square, but had returned the following afternoon saying he'd had to just let it digest. Ricky didn't claim to be a saint and said as much, and he promised he'd never hold Aksel to any standard he wouldn't hold himself to. But Aksel had to admit that it was, after all, quite a thing he was asking Ricky to accept about him, what he'd done in the militia. Having him come back and say he was all right with it, all of Aksel's past, meant a lot. Askel had wondered if they were just acquaintances before, two men doing a similar job in a shared space, talking only to pass the time, but it turned out they were actually friends. Aksel was glad; he didn't exactly have people warm up to him all that often. Rarely, actually. When they'd been swept up to be brought to the refugee camp a few months later, they'd looked out for each other. Watched each other's backs, took turns sleeping in the early days when everyone was sleeping on the ground, not a single shack built yet. Sometimes Ricky slipped and called Aksel his brother. Aksel would cuff him on the shoulder and laugh, but yeah, it did warm his heart. Not that he'd ever tell the goof as much.

"They knew everything," Aksel said. "Every flipping bit of it."

"Who do you suppose they are?"

Aksel passed on the final sip so Ricky could have it. He shook his shaggy head, feeling the tiniest of buzzes developing. This was the question he'd agonized over the most since Karl and Moira had rereleased him into the camp. He shared what he knew with his friend.

"The big guy, Karl? I take him to be ex-military. Moira? I have no idea. She looked like . . . you know when they pull someone up out of the water that's been dead down there for a long time?"

"She was all fat and bloated?"

"Not at all. Skinny as a twig, but she was pale as that. I didn't get a real good look at her face, but I could tell she didn't like being stared at. And on top of that, the two of them kept referring to Adeshka as . . . I don't know, like a place they apparently pledge fealty to or something."

"It is a big city, after all. Hell, even you're from there, aren't you?"

"I wasn't born there, but yeah, I consider it home." A bleak flash crossed his mind. Aksel studied his friend's pockmarked face. When Ricky gave something consideration, he nodded, as if his thoughts were all loose dice inside his head that he had to keep shaking until he got the desired arrangement. He shook it many times, leading Aksel to consider perhaps the beer was working for him as well, making his thoughts uncooperative.

"Well," Ricky said suddenly with a smack of his lips, "I don't really know what kind of jam you've gotten yourself into, brother, but it appears to be quite the kicker. You've been tasked to join the most feared entity on the planet, get in with them, and . . . what, exactly?"

"Find out what they know about something called the Sequestered Son."

"*Sun*, as in the suns?" Ricky pointed skyward. "Or *son*, as in male child?"

"Son, as in child. I had to ask the same thing."

"What in the hootenanny do you suppose the Sequestered Son is?"

"No clue," Aksel said. "Not only that, but I have to sabotage their plans to attack Geyser again if possible. Not if it means my life, especially if I learn something about this Sequestered Son business. That's my top priority, I guess.

And after that, I'm to look into why they're so adamant about attacking Geyser when there are so many other cities that'd be a hell of a lot easier to get at."

"Good gracious, that's a lot for one man."

"Tell me about it." Aksel looked at the empty can in Ricky's hand. "Do you happen to know where we can score a few more of those? I have a feeling I should enjoy life tonight while I still can."

Ricky smiled. "I'll see what I can do." He bobbed his head as he walked out of the shack, shaking his thought dice again, Aksel figured. Trying to make up his mind on whom to approach first for the brews among the reliable handful of smugglers around camp.

Aksel, despite the grim assignment he'd been given, couldn't help but smirk. Ricky was a good pal. At least he had him.

CHAPTER 22

Pursuit

Vidurkis stood before the broken door of room number eleven, scanning everywhere with his pearlescent eyes for details that might tell him something, *anything*. There were definitely signs of a scuffle. She had truly given someone a run for their money—whoever had been stupid enough to break the seal on her chamber door. She'd always been a spirited one. Belligerent. Easy to provoke but not easy to trick. Feisty.

Laid into the metal in a scattershot of tiny holes was evidence that buckshot had been fired. Not a lot of people used buckshot anymore. Everyone in the Patrol used silicone bullets. Judging by the human carrion he'd seen, the Odium were supplied with expensive weapons with rounds that burned hotter than the suns and tore through the air so quickly they scorched the very oxygen. No, the buckshot was a crude weapon—something a Mouflon would use.

He regarded the guardsmen waiting around for him to give his next order. The closest one had his visor pulled up. He was young, plainly new to the Royal Patrol, the sole private in his platoon of sergeants and grizzled veterans.

"What do you make of all this, boy?"

The private stammered incomprehensibly. He wore a few badges: some markings on his helm and breastplate indicating that he'd seen things, done things, but still he was clearly scared of Vidurkis.

That was more than fine with Vidurkis. It'd worry him if he came across someone who wasn't.

"Well?" Vidurkis stepped closer.

"It would appear to me, sir, that Patient Eleven was disturbed. The sea-level elevator at the end of the hall had its gate ripped off. It appears likely that Patient Eleven was released, turned on her saviors, killed them, and escaped to sea level."

Patient Eleven, Vidurkis scoffed. The code name for her that Gorett had chosen. Vidurkis could only think of her by her real name, Margaret. But he played along for the time being, referring to her as they did. It wasn't the time to ruffle feathers.

"The elevator car is down there," Vidurkis said, pointing through the open air shaft. "Shattered upon the reception platform. Do you suppose Patient Eleven was in the car when its cable snapped? Tell me what you think, what you see, Private." His tone was even, silky, each word bleeding into the next.

"I assume she found a way to use the elevator, yes. And the cable broke, and she fell."

"And if she killed her saviors, where are the bodies?"

The private shifted. Splosh. "They . . . fell with the car? There is evidence that a water main broke within the facility, after all. Perhaps they got washed out of the gate and fell below." Splish. "I'm sorry, sir, but I don't have your ability to size up a crime scene. Sir." It was tacked on, quick. He winced.

Vidurkis watched a bead of sweat roll down the boy's

forehead until it fell from the outcropping of his heavy brow and vanished with the brown water around their feet, all of it racing for the hole in the floor up the hall.

He left him there, holding him in his gaze one more painful second before approaching the edge. Dropping his chin to stare at the open space beneath Geyser, he let his mind relax. It was the only way he could use one of the aspects of his fabrick—the far look.

Below, appearing almost like a model set painstakingly detailed, the trees looked like tiny sprouts, the oxygen in the air creating a natural haze that made the world look ethereal, as if heaven was actually below rather than above. But never mind that drivel. The Mechanized Goddess said there was no heaven or hell—or plummets or insufferable pit or whatever you wanted to call it. No, the only insufferable pit was the agony one felt when they dared cross the Goddess's followers, made themselves into wrenches in the works that needed to be excised.

He blinked, reminding himself he was on the hunt for more details . . . The elevator's reception platform was shattered; the car itself looked like a crushed tin can. He followed the undulating slope of the landscape and glimpsed the forest floor through the canopy when the wind blew just right. It was morning, and the suns were shining in from the west and northwest respectively. Leaning just right and using his eyes just so, he could focus a bit farther. He'd been blessed; his fabrick was multifaceted.

When the limbs of the taller trees rustled, he could see a flash of something in a small clearing.

Focusing a bit harder . . .

A flicker of yellow?

He waited for the sea wind to cooperate, to move the elephant-ear leaves just right.

And then he saw it clearly. A flame.

He spun on his heel. "Unless it's bandits, it might be her. Send a transmission to the palace. Tell Gorett we're saddling up and heading to sea level."

The Mouflon stood on the edge of the dense stand of trees, looking out over the ocean to the west. He basked in the suns, letting their rays spatter over him and warm his spirit. He sat, removed a fresh quill from the back of his neck, and went to writing his uncle the umpteenth letter. He wasn't sure what to tell him but decided to record his feelings about the new member of the group.

Nevele kind of gives this Mouflon the creeps—but what she can do with her fabrick is really something extraordinary. You should see her, Uncle Greenspire—how she can create nets and ensnare things with the strings from her skin. I know it's against our custom to admire those unnatural folk, but I think even you, a dyed-in-the-wool despiser of fabrick, would have to say you were impressed. Maybe with her help, we can get Pasty where he needs to be. I know I was certainly having my doubts in myself, when the burden was entirely on my shoulders. She and I don't get along, no, but in her company, I feel the least bit more sure we'll get Pasty where he needs to be. Even though I might be impressed by a weaver, I still do not trust her. I'll trust in Meech to guide my trust where it belongs. That is all for now.

Your troublesome nephew,
Flam

He looked up, tucking the letter into his satchel with the bundle of others. Clyde had appeared nearby with his hands in his pockets, looking out over the sun-drenched ocean glistening all the way to the horizon.

"Morning," Clyde said.

"Aye and a good one, too, isn't it? The suns are out, not a cloud in the sky. You will find I'll be in a better mood today than I was yesterday." Flam struggled to his feet, kicking the dirt upon which he had been sitting. Another Mouflon custom: never leave butt-prints upon any planet. Bad manners.

Clyde glanced back at the camp, where Nevele was snuffing the fire. She emptied seawater from one of the sprout tins on it, then dropped dead limbs over it to thoroughly disguise it. Clyde caught Nevele's gaze for a strange moment. She broke contact first, turning so her hood was hiding her face once more as she threw a final branch on the dead campfire.

Flam watched the whole exchange. Turning toward the suns, he said quietly, "I believe she's up to something."

"I thought you said you'd be in a good mood today."

"That I am, but a good mood and a healthy suspicion aren't mutually exclusive. I think there was a reason the Patrol kept her where she was. She's not telling us everything. She tells us sob stories about being an awkward youth to try to win us over, but I wouldn't be the least bit surprised if she used those strings of hers to tie us to a tree and go after the wendal stone herself." He took out his telescoping knife and made the blade go out. He used the nasty bent end of it to pick at his teeth. "I just don't trust her."

Flam watched Clyde out of the corner of his eye to gauge the young man's reaction. Clyde glanced back at

Nevele, who reached into a low-hanging branch to a cluster of berries. She pulled them down, didn't take any for herself, but threw them to Rohm. While the mice quickly devoured them, Nevele watched and smiled.

"She wants to get back at the prime minister, and I'm all for that," Clyde said. "The man is cruel and framed Mr. Wilkshire for the deaths of all those miners. Our goals are the same."

"Don't be so trusting. It's like the fortune-tellers do. They take a little about you, just a hint, make a good guess about it, and start unraveling a story. Then whatever you seem to go along with and nod to, that's what they'll prattle on about until you believe, without a doubt, that they're on board with you. Give her a moment's notice, and just like those Meech-damned so-called mystics, she'll have a dagger in your back with one hand while the other is fishing out the spots in your wallet."

"But I don't have any spots."

"It's a figure of speech. What I mean is this: She might be using us. She knows what's in the mine, how valuable it is . . . And I'm not saying any of this for certain. I just want you to be on your toes. You're new to dealing with folks. And not all of them are worth your time."

"Fine," Clyde said, throwing up his hands and walking away. "I'll keep it in mind that someone who saved our lives might actually be trying to kill us." He walked back toward the camp.

With a bite of anger, Flam watched Clyde approach Nevele and wish her a good morning. They carried on like they were the best friends in the world. Flam couldn't make out exactly what they were saying, but he clearly saw the stitched-up girl put a hand on Pasty's arm when she spoke to him. She said something about tending to some morning ritual of her own and walked off.

Flam's blood boiled as he was forced to witness Clyde stand there, hands in his pockets, watching her stroll off. He could practically see the cartoon hearts drifting out of the top of his head.

Flam grunted. "Daft stooge."

Once everything was packed, they wordlessly fell into loose formation and began their trek. There wasn't a clear trail to follow through the dense woods. They would have to keep Geyser's stem in sight to keep to the right track. Not that it was hard. The city was so considerably sized that unless they were under a thick canopy of trees, it could be seen from anywhere on the island.

"So long as we keep it on our left, it means we're going the right way," Nevele had said.

Clyde liked that she knew which way they were heading.

"And around to the south side," Flam added his two cents, "where we can get to my auto and see if there's anything of use left." He took a few lurching steps so he was matching Nevele's stride.

Nevele bit her lip, seemingly patiently waiting for him to finish.

"If the auto didn't get completely destroyed," Flam went on, talking big, "there will be food, some extra clothing, and a couple of guns in the hold. I know that *I*, for one, could use a new firearm since *my* blunderbuss got damaged in a scrape with a certain someone."

Nevele took a quick breath. "Who gave you the captain's hat, huh? We should take this day and get as much distance as possible, get to the mines before dark. Surely the Blatta, if they're like any other insect, mostly come out at night. They probably roam all over the mine entrance and even in the forests. We should get in while they're asleep, go as deep as we can so we can prepare for their awake hours, find supplies as we go—not traipse all over the landscape way the hell out of our way for some knock-off weaponry and a few tatty blankets."

"*Oh*," Flam bellowed, charging up with a stomp of his hooves to the front of the group alongside Nevele, "and I suppose there's going to be all kinds of shops and places to get supplies en route, huh? Look around, Rag Doll. We're in the Geyser underside forests. There's nothing down here at all except maybe the occasional bandit or hawk turd. Meech almighty, you're just like any other city dweller— think everything will be just hunky-dory, even in the wilds."

"I don't think everything will be *hunky-dory*; I just believe that whatever your junker auto has in it isn't worth going out of our way to retrieve. We don't need guns, you have your knife, I have my fabrick, Rohm has countless teeth, Clyde has his club—we'll be fine. That is, as long as I can remain at point and keep us going in the right bloody direction."

"*You* take point? A *lady* point man—point girl? Hardly!"

Rohm leaned toward Clyde. "Perhaps the grumpiness couldn't be subsided with a night's rest, after all. Perhaps it's terminal."

Clyde covered a grin.

"Look, Mouflon, we do things my way. You may pride yourself on being this great and seasoned explorer, but I have traveled countless worlds. I have traversed the un-mapped oceans of moons you've never *heard* of and could probably never even begin to spell! I've seen . . ." She stopped, cocked her head.

Clyde listened, seeing that Flam's ears had pricked up too. Next to him, Rohm's numbers trembled. They all stopped in their tracks, Nevele's hand shooting up, signaling them to halt.

Far away, a low chant of several engines could be heard, whirring.

"What is that?"

"Is it the Blatta?" Rohm said.

Nevele looked toward the sound. The trees were thick; nothing could be seen beyond them. But between the sturdy trunks could be seen the darting glare of gray light.

"It's the Patrol. *Run*."

All at once, they ended their argument and bolted away from the ominous noise. They cut through the forest, bounding over fallen trees and dodging reaching limbs.

Nevele was the quickest among the group, throwing her stitches out to wrap around a tree and then fling her forward. Flam tromped along, his breath huffing and puffing. Clyde and Rohm rounded up the back, moving as fast as they could.

The forest came to a slight dip, leading into a valley. Several trees had been cut down and heaped in neat pyramids.

Nevele walked to the piles and ducked behind them, the group following. She frantically showed them how to take up lengths of loose, mossy bark for camouflage. "Stay quiet until they've passed," she whispered, unable to hide the warble of fear in her voice.

Flam had to brace a hand over his mouth to quiet his labored breathing.

Clyde let a few of Rohm's more terrified members climb inside his pockets.

Within minutes, the Patrol came.

Clyde dared a look through a knothole in a piece of bark.

The forest at the top of the valley was occupied by several slow-moving Patrol guardsmen, some on foot and some saddled upon walkers. The vehicles looked like insects, roughly the size of a large dog or a small lion, six robotic legs crunching through the undergrowth.

"Cover your eyes," Nevele whispered.

The command was perfectly timed, for it was then that the Patrol switched on their gray light lanterns at full power. They swung them, showering the surrounding area in steady, sick pulses.

Clyde was too scared to close his eyes completely, so instead he kept them fixed on Nevele.

Peeking from behind her strip of bark, she squinted directly into the light.

Clyde could see its reflection in the wetness of her eyes—some of its effect reaching him.

Her heavily sutured face hardened in bottomless woe.

He had to ask. "Are they coming?"

When she didn't answer, he stole a peek.

At the head of the pack was a man who was clearly the leader, perhaps because of his hair pulled back into a severe pitch-black bun or his armor just a touch shinier than the other men's. He just had the look about him of someone who told others what to do, who estimated situations and made decisions. His face was gaunt, thin as a skull. He wore a frown Clyde guessed was the man's standard expression. He imagined his voice had a haunting timbre to it, throaty, flat, and without a scrap of emotion. He was just turning his head to scan along the valley, and Clyde couldn't help but stare. Those eyes . . .

"Look away," Nevele whispered, ashen.

But for whatever reason, Clyde could not. The man was too fearsome, commanding his attention. If he looked away, Clyde felt the man would somehow materialize wherever he turned his gaze next.

The Patrol platoon came to a stop. The man at the lead sat atop the walker, holding its reins and scanning the valley, one hand up in the same gesture Nevele had used to halt their group. Glance passing right over them, the man sat up in his saddle, bent forward, and sent out a flash of gray light directly at a pile of fallen trees a few yards beyond them.

The gray light only minutely stung Clyde's spirit, it being an indirect hit. Nonetheless, it sent shivers to his core, stirring memories and awfulness in him like a disrupted stagnant creek bed, muddiness charging downstream, polluting all. It was then and only then that Clyde forced his eyes closed. He felt if he didn't, he risked his very soul becoming permanently tarnished.

The bearded man snapped his reins and led the guardsmen along around the corner of the Geyser stem, into the next patch of forest. They fell out of sight, and soon thereafter the low drone of their mechanical insects was gone.

Nevele pitched the plank of bark off and shook her head till her hood dropped. She brought a hand to her face, covering half. The visible corner of her mouth was drawn down, her brow crinkled, and she appeared to be nearly in tears. Beyond the sound of Flam's labored breathing and the clicking of Rohm's innumerable teeth chattering, her soft sob could be heard.

"Lord, no," she said. "Not him. Not him."

Flam stood and made sure the coast was clear before saying anything, since his voice was naturally loud and carried better than the rest of theirs. "Who is he?"

"We've never seen a guardsman who can do that," Rohm said. A few of the frisk mice rubbed their eyes with their pink, balled fists.

Nevele glared back at each in turn: Flam, Clyde, Rohm. She took a breath to say something but then didn't speak. She spun and strode through the knee-high grass into the center of the valley.

"Well, that sure doesn't answer my question," Flam said.

Clyde followed her.

At the center of the valley, there was a small creek-fed basin that looked good and clear, free of sediment. Nevele sat on her knees at its edge, drowning the canteen Flam had given her. Clyde approached but kept a respectful distance. Canteen filled, she tipped it back and drank a few swallows before plunging it in again. Clyde couldn't see her face entirely from this angle, only her shimmery reflection in the pool's surface, but her body language spoke volumes. Her shoulders jerked, and her hands shook as she capped the canteen.

"It's all right, Nevele. They didn't see us," he said, trying to stay positive.

"We just need to get to the mines," she murmured as if she hadn't understood him. "We can probably avoid dealing with him at all if we go down there, get to the surface, and find a way to cut power to the elevators and trap him here." She paused, her breathing sounding wet and ragged. "They must know what we're up to. They must've seen us on security cameras or realized I wasn't in my room. The Patrol *never* comes down to the island unless they're after someone." She moaned, thumped her knee with a fist. "We should've stayed in the city."

"We should rest," Clyde said, sitting beside her. "We all got kind of a startle. We should save our energy. We'll let them search the woods, and when they don't find anything, they'll probably go back."

She looked at him finally. "He's my brother."

"The Patrol leader? He's your—?"

After just one glance at the terrifying man, it didn't seem possible that Nevele could even exist in the same world as him, let alone be his sister.

"His name is Vidurkis. He was one of King Pyne's security officers." She rolled her sleeves down until they covered her wrists, her hands. "He was cruel, even as a boy. Later, a murderer. He was in the keep beneath the palace last I had heard, sentenced to death sometime this cycle. A day, as ashamed as I am of it, I personally was looking forward to . . ." She looked down a moment. "Never mind. Of course, that was before Gorett took over. Now, he's out here with us." She sounded as if she could scarcely believe it herself. "Of course Gorett would send *him*."

Her tone was panicked. Her look of fear reminded Clyde of Mr. Wilkshire, on his back, proudly facing death. That look, Clyde now knew, could burn itself into his mind. He looked away.

With a throttled sigh, she continued, "We'll just have

to deal with it, I guess. No other option."

"He didn't see us," Clyde said, trying again to reassure her.

"Oh, but he'll make sure he changes that." Nevele chortled sardonically. "We used to work together in the palace, and every other day he was pursuing someone new. He has fabrick as well: double sight. The gray lights? That's where they come from. They took samples of his eyes and duplicated them. He can see for miles; he can flash gray light with them too. He was given a gift and didn't even consider using it for anything but—"

"What's the double edge to it? What's his weakness?" He felt bad for interrupting, but it had to be done. She wasn't saying anything that would help them. "You said all fabrick weavers have two sides to their abilities, so what's his?"

"Unfortunately for us, his fabrick doesn't come with a curse that'd bother a person like him. It is a curse, certainly, but it would only be one to someone with a heart."

Clyde was afraid to ask. "What is it?"

"If he wants to keep his gray light and the ability to see at all, whatever he lays the gray light upon, whoever he glares at with it, he has to kill. If he doesn't, in three days, his vision will cloud to the point he cannot see at all. It's never happened, since he's always gotten the person he's after, but we assume he'll go blind if it goes much past that third day. It's what made him so good at his job, having a deadline such as that to work by. Not that he ever needed the additional motivation. It'd be a curse to anyone else, having to choose between sight and murdering someone, but to him . . ."

She looked up, toward the city shadowing them from high above, a circle spiked on a stone needle. "Gorett must know you and Flam are in the city, or at least that I've escaped. He wouldn't send anyone else otherwise . . ." She pressed her lips so hard together they paled to a ghostly white. "Gorett knows; he must. This won't be a surprise attack anymore. He'll be prepared. With just *him* out here, it shows Gorett's ready for us."

Clyde had no response. It was all too much, too big and new for him to wrap his mind around. He was still reeling at the fact that their trip from the city to the mines and up to the palace wasn't going to be a pleasant go-as-we-will sort of occasion. They were being *chased*. And ahead of them, the enemy was waiting, prepared. But being pursued by Nevele's brother, a fabrick weaver who enjoyed killing, scared Clyde most of all.

She corrected her hood. "Please don't look at me like that. I don't like being stared at."

"I apologize; I didn't mean to," he said, even though he hadn't realized he was looking at her. But once it was brought to his attention that someone might stare, he found himself doing just that for a second. He tried to see beyond the stitches and imagine what she would look like with whole skin, without all the different panels.

It was easy for him. He prided himself on his imagination. He saw her healed and beautiful. But even with the sutures running every which way upon her face, a splendor was concealed within. To others, he imagined, it would be hard to see, but it was quite plain to him, shining through the roping stitches, how striking she really was.

"You shouldn't be uncomfortable with people looking at you. You don't have anything to be ashamed of, Nevele. Nothing at all," he tried, feeling that it was the right thing to say.

She stood and stepped past him. "Let's go. We've wasted enough time."

CHAPTER 23

Broken Auto and Carrion

Vidurkis stared at the sleek body of the ruined auto. Among the broken trees it had landed upon, a good score of stolen merchandise had spilled out. He dismounted his walker and dropped to the ground. He gestured, and the guardsmen set to scouting the area. Vidurkis knelt before the broken machine and sifted through the goods. Plenty of ammunition, parts for various mechanical things, spoiled food, a few treasures—antique candleholders and a bundle of gold flatware bound in a length of twine. The final item he focused on most. He took up the twine and let the ornate spoons and forks clatter to the ground. He held the ratty hank of string and pinched it by one end, the loose strand dancing and coiling in the salty wind.

He thought aloud, a nasty habit that had begun in his cell. "She hasn't been by here. She would've taken this for sure, my little string collector." He turned toward the ocean, surveyed the surrounding woods, shot his vision out, and scanned the beach on the south rim of the island. Nothing. The footprints there were small and sharp, those of seafaring birds and nothing other. "That fall must've cost you quite a bit, Sister. You need your string to keep your pieces together, lest you tumble apart." He wrapped the twine around his hand and made a fist.

"Executioner Mallencroix?"

His concentration was shattered.

"There's no sign that anyone has been by here. Perhaps we should circle the island again. There's no way she could've left. King Gorett ordered all ferries and aircrafts to avoid Geyser."

"I know that," Vidurkis rumbled, stepping among the disgorged flood of loot from the auto's wreckage. The Mechanized Goddess hated uselessness. Anything without function, her teachings said, should not exist. "And I think the search would probably go a bit more expediently if I weren't so weighed down. Seems a trimming of the fat might be in order."

The other guardsmen, poking at what might be tracks in the mud, all heard this and faced him, lowering their binoculars. Everyone stood stock-still.

The wind whistled, grave and cold.

They made the first move, collectively, reaching up to clamp down their visors, but Vidurkis was quicker.

A slap of light hit them all, sending them dancing and fumbling backwards, gripping their ruined eyes and screaming. He had made it a hefty blow, with particularly incommodious images.

Guns fell from hands rendered useless. A few men dropped to the ground and brayed wildly, like tortured animals.

Vidurkis took his time, going from one to the next and sticking his dagger into the weak spots between the panels of armor. None seemed aware that the others were being slaughtered, too overcome by their plagued minds to notice.

One after another, the screams died out.

One guardsman, despite being blind, tried to run down

the cliff face, tumbling as he did and dropping a few feet until landing on a rocky patch of sharp rocks. Vidurkis went to the outcropping and watched the man in his clunky armor struggle to find footing on the slanted earth.

The Executioner extended his arm over the edge, gripping his dagger with two fingers directly over the Patrol flunky's head. Vidurkis whistled to bring his attention upward, freeing the blade at the same moment.

The man looked, swinging up his unseeing stare as the blade connected with an eye, making a soft wet sound. He crumpled noisily; armor slapping against rock and helmet knocking on the stones like a plastic bowl on cobblestones, his body vacant of a spirit before his short, awkward roll down the hill even came to a stop.

All was quiet then. Vidurkis sighed. He could think more clearly without them buzzing around him, trying to best one another, each hungrier for promotion and Gorett's praise than the other. A massive burden had been lifted, indeed.

He went to his diligently waiting walker and took a canister of fuel from its saddlebag. He doused the auto, the goods, the bodies, and lit it all on fire. He shouldered his rifle, mounted his walker, and continued. The metal feet of the robot insect expertly gripped the rock face, descending with ease. He would circle the island again, working at his own speed, unhindered.

The twine he kept knotted around his hand, fingering it when he needed to coax his mind on to the next tactic. He breathed easily working alone, as he had as Executioner, back when finishing the hunt was all that mattered.

In the shadow of the city, it was nearly as cold as the wine cellar in the chateau, the air heavy and fragrant with mold. The four came upon a stream and took a break to refill some of Flam's plastic bottles. Rohm even took a quick bath, each mouse diving in and popping out in turn, shaking off, and joining the others.

Clyde went downstream a bit, stepped into the water, and plodded around, trying to free some of the dirt that had been deeply driven into the tread of his shoes. He glared at the loafers at the end of his narrow ankles—shoes not intended for walking on anything but marble, mahogany floors, or plush carpet. He was taking to the adventure better than his shoes were. He liked being out here in all this, making progress with each step in his unenthusiastic footwear.

As for Flam and Nevele? Well, they seemed to be in the same category as his shoes. They looked tired and browbeaten. Especially Nevele.

He was about to ask her how she was doing, but before he could even get her name out, she was waving, telling everyone to move on.

He kicked the last bit of moisture out of his loafers and carried on.

Much to everyone's relief, Flam and Nevele had decided to put aside the squabbling and take turns leading. Since the valley, Nevele didn't seem to want to argue anymore. When she agreed to let the Mouflon lead, even Flam himself looked surprised.

Flam led the four around the base of Geyser's stem, using his bent blunderbuss as a walking stick, maneuvering around and over boulders.

Clyde slowed to let the others go ahead so he could walk beside Nevele. "Are you all right?"

"I'm fine," she said, watching where she walked, bounding over a rock elegantly. "I don't think we should talk. They might still be nearby."

"But I just wanted to make sure you're all right."

Nevele stopped and looked him in the eyes. "What's with you? Why are you so doting? Has a lifetime of service made you into mush? Show some backbone. I said I'm fine; now leave me alone." She went on, leaving Clyde in a cloud of confusion.

"If you want to get something off your chest," he called after her, "I assure you, the jinx won't be bad, as long as you didn't do anything that despicable."

"I don't have anything on my chest," she returned flatly, maneuvering around a sharp rock, then ducking under the mossy bole of a fallen tree.

Clyde followed, swerved and ducked just as she had. "We're in this together. Even if your brother is an awful person, we'll get what we're after. We're a good group. Everyone has something to offer. Flam and his brawn and mechanically inclined brain. Rohm and their mathematics and being able to scout ahead undetected. Your fabrick—I don't even need to tell you how *that's* so great. And me, the conscience sponge for whenever anyone needs to confess something to feel better. It's like it was meant to be or—"

Nevele's boots crunched on the loose pebbles as she spun around. "You're such a dolt. You talk about this whole thing like it's some kind of game, like we're just out on a stroll in the woods for a good ol' time. Do you have any idea how many people are displaced because of Gorett? I can tell you for a *fact* that the refugee camp they got sent to isn't exactly a tropical resort. Think about how many people lost their homes and their livelihoods because of his greed. Your Mr. Wilkshire, the poor man, died believing he was to blame for all this. I'm beginning to think you were dropped on your head when you were little."

"I have to stay positive, though. It's the only way to get through all this. If I start thinking about the death and despair, I get too anxious to think about the task at hand."

Nevele sighed and continued on. Her voice echoed weirdly among the rocks, weeds, and dark puddles of water collecting here and there. "Is that the reverse side of your fabrick, how you're personally afflicted, then? You're optimistic to a fault?"

Clyde's expression flattened. "Not exactly . . ."

"Because you should consider yourself pretty lucky to not have been cursed to a worse degree by your fabrick." In the cold air, Nevele's scoffs came out illustrated in loose puffs of steam, trailing up and around her hood's hem as she picked her way ahead of Clyde and up a tall heap of fallen sediment rock.

His patience was bested. As much as he tried to hold it back, he felt a wall crumble between him and his temper.

"I'm cursed, all right?"

Cursed, all right? came the echo.

"Oh yeah? Sad story time, everyone. Gather 'round. Clyde is going to tell us how it's so hard having to listen to rich old men tell him how they cheated someone out of their retirement funds and how they feel *so* damned bad about it."

Clyde stopped in his tracks.

Nevele took one more stride, stopped, and turned around. She sighed. "Clyde, I'm sorry. With all this with my brother and us out here in the open and no visors between us and his gray light, it's just—"

"I have a reverse side to my fabrick, okay? One that I personally suffer from. And even though it hasn't really been an issue in the past, because of the masters I had before, it was quite . . . the plummets, as Flam would say, when I was living with Mr. Wilkshire."

Nevele said nothing, merely stood and listened.

Ahead, Flam and Rohm had also turned around.

"I can't tell anyone how much I care about them or how much they mean to me. I can't ever do it. I don't remember my parents, because I must have told them I loved them once. I might have living parents, perhaps even siblings. I'm not sure. But I know if I ever express feeling love for someone, I won't be able to hold on to their memory the second they're out of my sight."

"And Mr. Wilkshire?"

"I never got to tell him how much I cared about him. I tried to explain it to him, to tell him that I wanted to tell him how much I liked walking with him around the gardens and talking with him hour after hour about everything in the world, and how great it was that he always brought me books—but I could never tell him that I was thankful for letting me live with him, that I cared for him like he was my own father, and that I loved him, because I knew I'd forget him the moment he was out of the room. Nearly slipped once, too. The day he told me what would happen if I did."

"That's terrible."

Clyde marched on, brushing past Nevele without another word. He drove his hands into his pockets. "I know the double-edged way of fabrick, Nevele."

He caught up to Flam and Rohm, where they were posted on the rim of a boulder, overlooking the landscape to the south. As he approached, Clyde noticed something trailing up the smooth rock stem: a column of black smoke. "What is it?" he whispered.

Flam pointed toward a rocky clearing close to the stem base. Several things were still smoldering, most of which Clyde couldn't make out. Just black and sooty marks among the smattering of red stone.

Flam stared ahead. "I reckon they found my auto."

Clyde followed his focus to the thing smoking most exuberantly. It looked like a big fish at first glance, but Clyde realized it was the husk of a vehicle. Flam's auto, smashed to the point it had folded itself in half.

"Do you suppose they're waiting there for us?" The pack of frisk mice posed this question to Nevele, who came up last to join them, standing farthest from Clyde.

She stared, chewing her bottom lip. "I can't say for certain. But Vidurkis is restless. I doubt he would want to wait. He's probably moved on to circle the island again." She glanced over her shoulder, a gesture that appeared wholly involuntary.

Clyde leaned forward to peer at the distant scene. "What is that all over the ground? It doesn't look like just charred auto. It looks like giant bugs, sort of. On their backs with their legs in the air."

Rohm trembled. "The Blatta."

Nevele looked closer. "You mean those things by the

tree line there?"

"Yeah. What are those?"

Nevele stepped back, realizing. "They're the Patrol walkers, all burned up. When they passed us in the valley, there were ten of them altogether. And I count only . . . nine walkers there." Her shoulders sank. "They were slowing him down. He's moving on his own, just as he used to when he was in King Pyne's security detail." She sighed. "He killed them."

Flam turned, a grimace on his furry face. "Your brother killed his own men? What kind of Meech-damned bastard *is* he?"

"A bastard of the worst degree. Let's get up there and check if there's anything left of use. We'll go toward the beach and set up camp for the night. The mines aren't that far off. We should be able to reach them no later than by the suns' highest tomorrow. Hopefully we'll be able to stay ahead of him." She checked over her shoulder again and caught Clyde's gaze. He looked away first, stepping to join Flam and Rohm as they descended toward the horrible vista.

A hand alighted on his wrist. He turned.

Nevele hiked in a deep breath and met his gaze. "I'm sorry."

He smiled, patted her hand. "It's okay." Their touch gave his heart the same feeling—a better one—than anyone's confession could. His heart didn't just feel sated; it sang.

She gently took her hand back and walked on ahead.

He was sad to let the moment end, but it wasn't like they could remain like that forever, sadly. They had things to do.

As he walked, a sensation slithered in slowly—the awareness of being around the bodies of murdered people.

Nine charred skeletons. The metal had gone weak in the fires and melted around the blackened bones. No one deserved to leave the world that way, even if they served a man as bad as Gorett. Clyde remained at the fringes of it all, keeping his back to the sight and trying to not breathe through his nose. It felt as if the very place had been stained by the evil perpetrated here, as if he were suffering a different bout of gray light, one that wasn't so direct.

Clyde hurried to join the rest of them at what they were doing but kept his eyes averted from the smoldering dead men.

Flam's auto had cooled enough for Rohm to scour within. The frisk mice emerged and recompiled. "Mr. Flam, I'm afraid everything was ruined."

Flam groaned. "I had a lot of good stuff in there, too. Guns, some decent clothes. Even stuff that wouldn't be of any use during this journey; I still would've liked it back . . . There was a picture of my uncle in there. Only one I had of the old sod."

There was now nothing to look at but the bodies. Clyde forced himself not to stare. Nonetheless, a question bobbed against the roof of his mind until it couldn't go unsaid another moment. "Why would he do it?"

"He likes to work alone." Nevele kicked over a ruined walker, the legs snapping off.

She tried to stop it from rolling since they were still trying to keep it quiet, but it picked up momentum quickly and tumbled down the hill, spraying nuts and bolts off with each flip. It reached the edge and spiraled off, everyone wincing at the noise she'd accidentally set in motion. After a slight delay, it hit the hard terrain below in a crash.

Nevele cringed. "I'm kind of surprised he bothered working with them as long as he did, actually."

Clyde approached the edge to see where the walker had fallen. He immediately regretted it, having noticed a corpse on the rocks below. Unlike the others, he hadn't been burned at all. The sight of the body, with the left eye stabbed into a gory slit, made Clyde's stomach lurch. He turned away and walked up the hill, choking. There was no good place to look here. So much death.

"What is it, Mr. Clyde?" Rohm asked.

Clyde crooked a thumb over his shoulder. "Another one, over the hill."

Nevele went first, carefully slipping down the grade of the hill in a seated position until she reached the edge. Her boots hit with a couple of thuds. *She just goes right down there,* Clyde thought, *as if the sight of death is nothing at all to her.*

The others remained as she rooted through the guardsman's pockets. She glanced up at them watching her but returned to work unbothered, pulling the flap off the guardsman's holster and removing his sidearm. She broke it open and saw that not one of the twenty rounds within its magazine had been spent.

"Patrol issue," Flam remarked. "Good find."

Nevele held the gun for a moment, unsure where to stow it. She closed her eyes, and the material of her belt rearranged, flipped around, and shaped a hip holster for her. She slipped the gun into it, a perfect fit. Next she removed the guardsman's helmet and donned it. She nodded sharply, and the visor flipped down. Nothing of her face could be seen. Muffled, she said, "They wear these to protect themselves from the gray light."

"I just thought it was a spooky fashion statement," Flam said.

"Nope." She rapped a knuckle against the visor. "We can definitely make use of this if he catches up to us."

"That's just dandy," Flam said, "but did you bring enough for the rest of the class?"

Nevele removed the helmet and tossed it to him. "We'll have to take turns." She smirked and negotiated the remainder of stony grade to the tree line at the foot of the hill.

The rest followed, dropping down in turn. Clyde still tried not to look at the dead man but failed. Part of him wanted to see—a part of him he didn't much like.

The Patrol guardsman was pale, and his head was turned in such a way that when Clyde glanced, it was as if the man knew and had already begun staring in Clyde's direction. While one eye was just a gaping red hole, the other was open wide, terror in its frozen stare. Clyde moved on, resisting a tremor.

They were a few yards down when they realized one of them was missing.

Behind, Rohm looked at the corpse forlornly. "Shame to let it go to waste."

"Good Meech."

Clyde was speechless.

"Go ahead." Nevele sighed.

But not a one among them stuck around to witness the resourceful display.

CHAPTER 24

One of the Gang

The following morning, Aksel lay in his holey cot and looked at the shafts of daylight that managed to steal through the rust-rimmed holes in his shack's roof. They didn't help his hangover much. He now regretted having tasked Ricky to go out with Aksel's last few spots, freed from his boot heel, in search of more beer. Regardless, he had a job to do. He sat up, the invisible clamp on his head spinning tighter as he did so. He strapped on his eye patch, got dressed, bade farewell to his humble abode, crossed the mud alleys cutting this way and that through the shantytown, and reached the square.

Ricky was already there, at his usual spot, and they exchanged nods. Ricky always wore his emotions like little flags that popped up over his head. The one he flew now read, *Be careful, brother.*

Aksel tipped an invisible hat and walked on, cutting across the littered agora to the other side of town, where he seldom dared to tread, where Neck Scar Steve lived. He found his shack and ducked in to ensure it was empty. It was, not surprisingly, seeing as how the Odium spy probably kept a full schedule; the old men and women weren't going to bully themselves, after all. Aksel treaded in quietly.

His shack wasn't much better than Aksel's own, but it had more than one room and its own private bathroom of three walls set up around a hole in the floor. He had a bed, which was made from the hood of an old automobile with some frayed linens piled into it, and a lantern that worked on batteries. Aksel knelt on one knee and felt the blankets. Cold.

It wouldn't take much to find someone in the camp. All you had to do was walk and keep your eyes open. The guards had set up a lot of the shacks themselves and had made it in the style of a panopticon, every shack and alleyway easily observed from the watchtower at its central point. Unable to help being observed, Aksel continued to stride the perimeter clockwise, then counterclockwise.

Finally, without having spotted Neck Scar Steve or any of his buddies, Aksel returned to the agora.

He hadn't had breakfast yet and was already drenched in sweat. He sidled up to Ricky's stand and leaned under its meager patch of shade, his elbows on the counter.

Ricky got up from his lawn chair and looked around. "How'd it go?"

"It didn't. I can't find him."

"The place is only so big, man."

"I know. I looked all over."

"Did you ask anyone?"

Aksel took a second to scan the area as well. "And let word spread that I was asking about him? I kind of think that'd be a bad idea." He turned back toward Ricky. "I wonder if I scared him more than I thought with the . . . you know." He indicated his eye patch and what lay beneath it.

"Well, the first time seeing that thing bust out isn't exactly a comforting experience." He lifted the counter, levering Aksel's elbows off, and produced a bottle of water. It looked clean enough. "Rehydrate. You're leaving a puddle."

Aksel uncapped it, took a sip, and gave the bottle back to his friend. "We really tied it on last night, didn't we?" He jammed his finger under the band of his eye patch to massage his temple.

"You drink too much. Especially when something's eating at you."

"Well, what if I can't find him? Of course it's eating at me."

"Then you'll be out there." Ricky indicated the wasteland beyond the fences, the dead limitless Lakebed that the camp butted against. "Along with the handsome son of a bitch who'll never stop reminding you that you got him thrown out there with you." He winked. "No pressure or anything."

Aksel looked through the links of the fence to the wasteland. How long would they last? No water. No means of quick travel. No defense against the Odium if they happened to swing by overhead and use them as target practice. Not to mention all the other life-forms, both sentient and not, that could easily kill a man if even accidentally provoked.

He flexed his jaw, the metal inside it creaking and a spring giving a musical twang.

"I'd get back to it if I were you," Ricky said. "Before Neck Scar buys more friends."

It was no secret that Neck Scar had money, most likely from selling whatever provisions didn't go down his own throat, considering the paunch about his middle. Somehow his pirate friends were getting things to him, possibly through a hole in the fence or by some covert midnight airdrop.

Aksel took another sip of water, swished it in his mouth before swallowing, and handed the bottle to Ricky again.

"Got any chow?" he asked, mopping sweat from the back of his neck with his sleeve.

"Afraid not. Gonna have to hold off until tomorrow, chief, when they roll out the goody truck." On Mondays, the camp guards brought out boxes of food, water, and toiletries that had to last the refugees the week.

"Eh, that's all right. I think I got something back at the mansion." Aksel used his name for his one-room shack.

He had dug a shallow hole under his bunk one night and buried some plastic-wrapped bread. It was calling his name. He slapped the counter as he turned to walk away. "See ya when I see ya."

Aksel had company. He could see them, clear as day, rifling through his things, since he had no front door. He kept his distance before they noticed him, took a deep dusty breath, held it, then let it go. He reached behind his right ear and pressed into a soft spot in the bone. He felt the vibration of the DeadEye switching on, the aiming system computer taking a minute to warm up. He flexed his jaw, the set of three bullets in a stacking hopper in his cheek clicking as the clip was snapped up and into the breach.

Originally the name Bullet Eater had come from what bodyguards did—ate, or caught, bullets for those they were hired to protect. Later, it switched to mean mercenary, since head cannons were preferred among their kind. Aksel never considered himself a Bullet Eater by either definition, except in the sense that he loaded the DeadEye by literally feeding himself bullets to get them slotted into the magazine in his jaw.

He didn't want to resort to that, so instead, he freed a

length of wood from a pile of rubble, shook off the clinging scraps of trash—and a dirty diaper—and weighed it in his hands. It made an effective club. He just hoped Neck Scar and friends hadn't come equipped with something better.

He didn't step inside. That could only lead to disaster. Just outside the door, he shouted for Steve in a singsong voice. "Can he come out and play, Miss Neck Scar?"

The shuffling and rifling within immediately stopped. Three men filed out, all playing tough, lips pursed, heads cocked, eyes narrowed. For whatever reason, they were all shirtless. Since there were no options of gang colors in the camp, Aksel assumed that for them, skins it was.

Neck Scar Steve came out last, ducking out the shack door, looking at Aksel with stilled hostility. "Just checking in on our resident Bullet Eater, seeing if he's been sitting on any other secrets me and my boys might find useful."

Neck Scar Steve's resolve flattened as his gaze shifted to something behind Aksel.

Peripheral vision wasn't Aksel's strong suit, especially on that side. He had to turn his whole head to see what Neck Scar Steve was looking at. Springs creaked as he twisted that way and saw a camp guard waltz by.

There was no way the man could miss the standoff going on, but he kept on walking, polished black club in hand, eyeing each of them in turn, Aksel last. At him, he stared. Any hint that he knew what was going on, a wink or a smile or a nod, would have been seen by Neck Scar and the rest. He addressed them all with a tip of the hat. "Keep it clean. Any of you get killed, the ones still standing know where to put the bodies." He walked on and fell out of sight behind the next row of shacks.

Aksel turned back to Neck Scar, who was lunging forward. Aksel considered batting him aside with the length of wood in his hand but fought his instincts fast enough to throw the wood aside, backpedal, and raise his hands. "Whoa, man, I don't want any trouble."

"Why? Because the screw just gave us the okay to kill each other, and now you're pissing yourself?" Neck Scar chortled.

His friends joined in.

Aksel wasn't sure if just Neck Scar was with the Odium or if all of them were. The others didn't really look it, nor were they as well fed. Perhaps he would try to get him alone, where they could talk things over.

"Not scared," Aksel said. "Just . . . wondering if a *mutual friend* of ours might not find it so hospitable if two *mutual friends* got into a tussle. Might make that *other* friend upset." It was plain to see that Neck Scar was thick, but he seemed to glom on to this subtlety with surprising speed. His face softened, and he regarded his fellow no-shirts with a backhanded swipe. "Take off. All of you."

"You sure?" one called, but Neck Scar didn't even dignify it with an answer.

Reluctantly, the other men walked on—with some of Aksel's things, he couldn't help but notice.

When they were securely out of earshot, Steve dropped the Neck Scar routine. In a strange display Aksel had never witnessed, he seemed to melt into another person entirely. His posture and demeanor changed. He donned fear like an ill-fitting coat. "May the Mechanized Goddess keep thee." Even his voice was different.

Karl and Moira had mentioned he might say something like this. Aksel gave the expected reply. "And may she keep you, too, brother."

Steve laughed openly. "Man, I never thought you would be one of us. Why didn't you say something when we first got here, dude?"

Dude? Aksel almost liked him better as Neck Scar. "I apologize, but I wasn't sure about you. You hid your allegiance well."

Steve ran a hand over his shaved head. "Thanks. I kind of practiced at it, playing this whole . . . badass thing." He sighed. "Kind of tiring, to be honest with you." He seemed to remember something suddenly. "Dude, I'm so sorry about your house. I swear we didn't take anything. Well, *I* didn't take anything and . . . you know what? I'm gonna run and get a plastic bag right now to clean up what Fripp did."

"What did—? Forget it. I don't even want to know." He had to step in front of Steve to keep him from running off. "Just wait a second. I don't care about that right now. I want to know what the plan is. I kind of lost contact with everyone after we got here." Karl and Moira had told him a detail, which he used now. "I left my radio behind, and I didn't catch the last communiqué from Javelin."

Steve brightened. He was downright jubilant, something Aksel hadn't thought the man capable of. "We're going home, dude. Tomorrow night, we're getting sprung."

"They're coming here?" Aksel tried to sound enthused and not at all terrified that the Odium were planning to raid the camp.

"You know it, man. I hope you got a warm coat."

"I think I do," he said at once.

According to Karl and Moira, the last known location of the Odium's movable base of operations was in the polar ice cap, hundreds of miles north of any civilization, way beyond radar range and with such heavy cloud cover after centuries of blizzards that no satellite imagery could be achieved.

Aksel grinned. "This is good news. We're going home. I'm excited . . . dude."

CHAPTER 25

Fireside Dreaming

Vidurkis had gone all the way around the island, ending back at the wreckage of the elevator reception platform beneath the hospital. He had decided that it would be a suitable place for camp.

He started a cook fire. He sat staring into the blaze. From within the pile of armor he'd removed, a soft bleep emitted. He sighed, slid a hand into the heap, found the communicator, and silenced it.

Vidurkis had received ten calls from Gorett and answered not a one of them. During a spell of downtime, Vidurkis had reprogrammed King Gorett's caller ID to Prime Minister.

Try as he might to think about other things, alas, now his thoughts were on the fool.

Worst of what burned Vidurkis about Gorett was that he didn't deserve the title of king. Just a clever bureaucrat who had unearthed a loophole in the Commencement ritual before anyone else could and exploited it, stacking the deck for himself. He thought he could usher everyone out of the gates to refugee camps in the muddy plains of other continents and get all the wendal stone to himself, sidestepping a second decree, the bit about the fair distribution of wealth. Conniving arse.

Vidurkis threw another fistful of dead leaves onto the

fire just because he liked the sound when they burned.

He had to smile. It had backfired on Gorett pretty well—the Blatta standing watch over the wendal stone like that.

But until he was dead, the idiot would continue to grate at Vidurkis. Gorett feared weavers, thought them insane witches and warlocks. Vidurkis had overheard him say that all of them would one day overthrow the planet and claim Gleese as their own. "Imagine that." Gorett had chortled drunkenly. "A world of nothing but fabrick weavers! They'd tear themselves apart, cursing and killing to oblivion, turning each other to stone or trees until they were all plagued into extinction." Then after a pause, he'd laughed like a fool again. "Perhaps that's not such a bad idea; perhaps we should hand the planet over to them and come back after they've done all the heavy lifting!"

Ever since then, the only thing Vidurkis could picture when looking at Gorett was his head stomped flat beneath his boot, reduced to pulp from bullets, peeled bare and sunk in a salt pit, or . . .

Vidurkis removed his boots one at a time and set them by the fire to dry, the leather creaking as it warmed. He wondered what Gorett would pay him, beyond granting his freedom, if he were to not only dispatch his sister but continue on her likely plan: go up into the mines, help the Blatta out, hold the city hostage. The metal laid down on the platter during the city's construction was only so thick. With a handful of sticks of explosives and perhaps a few days with a torch, a sizeable hole could be made. She was certainly patient and creative enough. The places she used to find to hide in when they were children . . . *Ingenious* didn't begin to describe her.

With the fire burning hot enough now, he set to preparing to roast the pheasant he'd shot earlier. As the blade traveled the length of the bird's gut, he imagined it to be Gorett's.

Only the Goddess knew if the man would follow through with his promises or if he'd find some other way to finagle out of his debt. It bothered Vidurkis that the Odium had slipped in so easily. They were pirates. Well armed and well manned, certainly, but they were still tactless savages. How had they gotten past the Patrol? *Something stinks*, Vidurkis determined.

He plunged a sharpened twig through the pheasant and set it on top of the two Y-shaped branches flanking the spit.

Gorett is up to something.

He gave the bird a few turns.

"I shouldn't trust him," he muttered, watching the meat sizzling almost at once. "He'll surely fold the whole thing to his favor. Find some way to kill me off or put me away again, only to come down and barter with me when he needs me."

He quieted himself. He was thinking aloud again.

The bird hissed and sputtered, hot grease spilling out between the cords of pink muscle and white connective tissue.

But his mind was on a roll, as hot as the fire whose warmth stroked his face, and he couldn't help but think out loud. "I'll do as he asks, to a point. Find my sister, remove that niggling tick from Gorett's hair, and after that, before he even has a chance to turn on me, be ready with my own strike."

Anything that was without a true use, whether inside a machine or in nature, would eventually meet its excision.

Either by engineering: removing what didn't work or have a purpose. Or by nature: slowly removing something that didn't fight or provide nourishment for something bigger.

Gorett had found a way to clamber to the top of the dung heap. But once there, serving no purpose and needing nothing from anyone else, he would find himself rendered an ineffectual member of his environment, something obscenely unnatural.

Life was a struggle. Struggle was the whole driving piston work behind being alive. There was no destination to be staked. There was no finish line, no shining golden cup to grab and put on display. The chase was the purpose; the pursuit had no end, because that was the way things needed to be.

Vidurkis pictured Gorett as the strip of wire in the Grand Clockwork—what the Goddess referred to as the universe—disconnected at either end, just taking up space, flaccid and ineffectual.

Vidurkis took a bite out of the bird's flank, twisting his jaw side to side to rip a hunk away. To the jagged divot in the pheasant, he spoke with his mouth full. "I will gladly be the shears for that strip of wire."

The Mouflon frowned at the empty bag. He was completely out of mold to smoke. He sucked at the pipe nonetheless, in a casual way, sending a sharp few notes whistling out. Promptly remembering they were being pursued, he stopped.

He lay with his head propped against one of the smooth beach stones, listening to the tide falling upon the sand and rolling out again and crashing once more. It made him think of a rumbling stomach, and he soon remembered, hand halfway dug into his satchel, that they had eaten the last of his bounty from Third Circle Market. He blamed Rohm. He was about to call him a gluttonous sod but noticed the frisk mice were already fast asleep, dug into a shallow nest they made for themselves in the sand. He'd save the insult for the morning.

Maybe if Nevele were within earshot, he'd call her a gluttonous sod, just for the fun of it. But turning his head this way and that, looking up and down the beach, he didn't see her or Pasty.

He shrugged. They couldn't have gotten far. Besides, even if they did encounter any trouble, she could obviously take care of the two of them. He canted back, put up his hooves, and rested his eyes, deciding he'd let the insult go unspoken. Stitches didn't exactly seem the type that excelled at restraint. Flam sniffed. "I'm one to talk." He reached absently into the satchel for the umpteenth time for a snack, only for his fingertips to feel the leather bottom, cold from the sand.

"Point taken, Meech." He sighed. "Point taken."

He let the image of chunks of wendal stone dance in his head like ephemeral ballerinas gliding across his tired mindscape in ice skates with diamond blades, silver rings for grommets, and strands of pearls for laces.

He smiled. *Oh, what a proper, fat Mouflon I will be: rich as the day is long and never with another care in the world! No more chasing rumors, no more following in the Odium's wake for scraps, no more headaches sorting out unreliable autos, and never another begged favor from my brother.* He smiled at the prospect of buying a house in Geyser once all was said and done and being the one his brother came calling upon when times were tight.

"What a day that'll be," he snorted.

Nevele tossed in another log. The fire took to the limb with enthusiasm, soaking it in flames immediately. Nevele and Clyde sat on a bigger length of driftwood, and he stared out to the northern horizon. The suns had gone down, and now the moon was high, a fierce disk suspended stubbornly. It was always there but faded to a faint ghostly silhouette when the suns came out, only visible through squinting eyes. Clyde marveled at its alabaster beauty.

"I read your book," he finally said.

"You did?"

Clyde nodded. "I don't think I understood a lot of it, and what I did learn I couldn't really use since Miss Selby did all the alterations and mending around the house. I did use a couple of tricks when fixing my own things, though." He showed her a seam of his suit coat's cuff, which he'd fixed with needle and thread.

Of course, now the garment was irreparably dirty. She had to move closer to pick some dirt free with a fingernail, which Clyde liked. Her moving closer, that is. The dirt being picked away, sure, that was also nice, but the former much more so.

Nevele peered at it with a smile. "You did a good job."

"What can I say? I had a good teacher."

Sadly, she sat back. Their distance was still minimal but more than he'd like. Her smile faded after a moment. "Didn't sell all that great in Geyser, but I heard it was a big hit on Debroscoe. Makes sense. A lot of silk is grown there, and you could go into any town in the countryside, throw a rock, and hit twenty seamstresses and tailors." She casually pointed out a star.

Clyde looked but didn't know which one she had pointed to exactly. He found himself staring at the sky. A few stars slowly trekked the darkness, most likely aircrafts in low orbit, but he disregarded them in favor of looking upon the winking, unmoving ones. One was particularly large and had a pale blue tint to its pointy-tipped flare. "Have you ever been there?"

"Where? Oh, up there? Nothing on that rock, I'm afraid. Pretty place but just not really suitable for people, unless you have the spots to buy a breather kit every other day."

Clyde pondered that a moment: living day to day taking each breath through a hose and your head encased in a glass bubble. Sounded unpleasant. He redirected his gaze straight out, across the black waters of the bay to the mainland, their immediate surroundings. "How about out there? Straight across the way."

"Not a lot there, either, unless you keep going across Angler's Lake, which they might as well rename Angler's Desert."

"Why's that?"

"It's all dried up. Most just call it the Lakebed now."

Clyde nodded and proceeded to picture it. "Is that how this entire place is?"

"This entire rock? Yeah, more or less. Geyser's a hub of sorts, a point of interest . . . a place they'd bother to put on a map, let's just say. And as for the remainder, well, there's Adeshka."

"Where all the people of Geyser were taken."

"Yes," she said, her tone heavy for a moment. "And then there's the Necropolis, to the northwest."

Clyde had read enough to know *necro-* meant dead and *-polis* meant city, so it was . . . a city of the dead? For the dead? A city that was dead?

"It's a wasteland. Has been for decades. Once called Nessapolis, as bustling and populated as Geyser is . . . was, I mean . . . and not much else there. It's rumored that's where Ernest Höwerglaz sits and waits. Apparently. If you believe the stories, that is."

"Höwerglaz," Clyde said, trying it out. "That's quite the odd name."

Nevele smirked. "It suits him if the stories are any indication." She took a deep breath. "Allegedly one of the most powerful weavers who ever lived. His specialty was that he could take the years off anything and put them upon himself. Give him an antique clock that was broken with age and rust, and with one bat of the codger's eyelids, he'd be double decades older while the clock would look brand-new. And vice versa: it's said he once turned himself into a young boy while a brand-new barn fell in on itself with rot even though the last nail hammered into it was still warm from the carpenter's lip. How I heard it, Höwerglaz had this bear cat he was nursing back to health; it was shot by the farmer who owned that barn. Höwerglaz decided to return the favor by turning the wood, fresh off the lathe, to nothing but ash."

"That's amazing."

Nevele nodded, her face solemn. "It would be if only it were true. Some say he was a real man; others say the weavers dreamed him up as a stand-in for us to regard as a role model, a Goody Two-shoes who uses his fabrick for only noble purposes. And *then* there's the moronic folks who think he's something the *weavers* made up to scare the normaloids." She loosed a soft laugh. "Not my term. I just use it when . . . you know, I'm feeling salty. Anyway, there are loads of stories about Höwerglaz, how he took the years off an entire planet once and reversed it back to how it was before when it had trees and birds and what have you. Some say he was . . . well, you get the picture. It's just a story."

"Perhaps one day we'll meet him. It's probably lonely living in a place called the Necropolis," Clyde said hopefully.

"Perhaps," she answered, as if she were trying to sound as hopeful as Clyde but had disappointed herself halfway through the word. She turned to Clyde and edged her hood back. "I'm sorry if I was hard on you earlier today. I really . . . didn't know." She flattened her frizzy hair, smoothing back fly aways.

"It's okay," Clyde said, his gaze fixed on his twiddling thumbs.

"I'm also sorry I scolded you for looking at me. It's just that I'm so used to people staring. You can't even imagine the gawks I got when I was working in the palace. Some people, I swear, just really don't care. They'll even point and talk about you, not even whispering, right in front of you."

"I didn't mean to stare. But it's hard not to seem like I am, with eyes like mine." He knew his smile probably appeared as frail as it felt.

"It's quite all right," Nevele replied quietly.

After a moment, Clyde said, "If you want to tell me anything, to ease your mind, I'll try my very best to not let you get jinxed. I'll cross my fingers as you say it. Perhaps that'll help."

"Thank you, but I think I'm good for now. Just sitting

here pretending we're not dead set on some harrowing task is sufficiently relaxing for the time being." She let her gaze connect with his, and Clyde realized she did this seldom in conversation, as if she were just as afraid to look at someone as she was of them looking at her, as if in every face she saw a pane of freshly wiped looking glass.

"We'll make this place better."

Her warm hand found his and patted it. "Never lose that."

"Lose what?"

She stared northward, in the direction of the dry Lakebed, the awful place called Necropolis, the refugee camp at Adeshka. "Just that."

CHAPTER 26

Betwixt a Rock . . .

The following morning was misty and cold. Clyde had been up all night, as always, and had seen it come on. He felt the sand's temperature drop beneath him. The morning light came, and the suns broke out over the horizon, and when they did, all was gray. The fog peeling in off the bay and over the beach and threading itself into the forest was dense—so dense that the mainland was even harder to see than the moon in the sky on a clear day.

Without anything for breakfast, the group decided to strike out at once and find something to eat along the way.

Flam was haphazardly folding his morning writing to his uncle. Becoming frustrated with the uncooperative parchment, he crumpled the letter, pounded it into the opening of his satchel, and grunted. "That's just great. We'll be going into the mines with nothing but acorns and handfuls of turf for rations. You expect me to climb all the way up that thing"—he swept his arm toward Geyser's stone stem towering beside them—"with nothing on my stomach but the owl pellets we come across down here?" He kicked a rock, sending it careening down the beach, bouncing like a cannonball across the sand.

"It's the only option," Nevele stated, fixing the holster's straps to her hip again.

"Only time I envy you, Pasty. Never have to rely on meals to raise your spirits. Of course, it doesn't seem like a lot *could* dampen them anyway."

Buttoning his coat, Clyde shrugged and took the slight as a compliment. He carried on behind Nevele.

They moved from the beach into the copse of trees at its inward edge as the terrain petered out, gradually giving out to a stonier landscape. Here and there was a piece of forsaken mining equipment, each stooped in a brown ring on the rocks where it had fallen to disuse and rusted in place.

At midday Flam took the lead, using his bent blunderbuss as a walking stick again to negotiate the larger rocks. Rohm had found it easier to break down and scurry along the stony path. Clyde and Nevele walked together, careful not to tread on any of the frisk mice as they followed Flam.

The mist burned off, and suddenly they found it obnoxiously warm. At their early afternoon break, they lunched on pears and apples found at a long-forgotten orchard bursting out of its fences.

To combat the heat, Flam stripped himself to the waist and collected his panels of armor like nesting dolls, wrapped up the whole collection, and carried it at his side as a schoolgirl would do with a belted stack of textbooks.

Clyde walked with his suit coat hooked on a finger over his shoulder.

The collar of Nevele's cloak was soaked with sweat. Clyde was going to ask if she wouldn't be more comfortable taking it off, since she was heaped in so many layers, but he thought better of it. She'd take it off if she wanted to.

After Rohm's members finished passing through a puddle in single file, they hid the spoor of their lunch in a shallow crack between two rocks and moved on.

Flam called over his shoulder, "So you're *sure* none of the bugs will be out during the day?"

"They're nocturnal," Nevele said. "They come out to forage during the night and return to the hive to feed their young and sleep during the day. I highly doubt we'll come across a single one until we're deep inside. They've probably abandoned the original hive and moved into Geyser's stem and sewer system by now."

They came to another abandoned machine. Clyde had to strain his neck to see all the way to its top. There was a cockpit with the door hanging open, the hot wind knocking it forward and back. The blade at the front was dented and covered in a thick patina of dust from broken rock, enormous jagged teeth set into the blade every few feet, each one as tall as Clyde and as wide as Flam's shoulders. The wheels were bigger than he had known existed. He could easily get inside one and stand upright without hitting his head.

Once around the rusted metal beast, they spotted the opening to the mine ahead, an enormous hole in the hill face like a giant's yawning, toothless maw.

"Is that it?" Clyde asked, breathless.

"It is," Nevele answered. "The Kobbal Mines, the most prosperous on all of Gleese. I bet Mr. Wilkshire would be astonished to think his little friend had made it all the way to his former workplace."

Clyde smiled. "I'm sure you're right."

Flam scoffed. "Why don't you two just get some of these rocks and build yourselves a cottage. Your lovey-dovey talk is making my guts ache." He grinned as he turned around, giving away an insult he had in store.

Clyde steeled himself for it, for as much as he knew Flam meant well, some of his jibes still stung. But when Flam turned around to expel it, the Mouflon's smile dropped. Flam wasn't looking at Clyde and Nevele but at something *behind* them . . .

Nevele noticed this too, and together they whipped around.

At the far end of the beach, a man atop a gunmetal-gray insect approached rapidly, kicking up clots of dirt and stone. The driver sat up in the saddle, let the reins loose, and brought a rifle to his shoulder with both hands. His black hair was a torrent around his head, framing a bearded, smiling face.

They all moved as one, putting the mining vehicle between them and him.

The shot rang out and ricocheted off the rocks where their feet had been seconds before.

Clyde's heart felt like it had sprung up and lodged between his back teeth. "*It's him,*" he choked.

Nevele nodded gravely, removing the pistol from her makeshift holster.

Flam frantically went through his satchel looking for his knife.

Rohm's members scampered up the side of the vehicle to the top, the last few to go whispering that they'd keep an eye out and do what they could as the group's eyes and ears.

"Thank you, Rohm," Nevele sputtered. It seemed she had more to request of the mice, but the frantic metal footfalls stopped just on the other side of the mining machine.

"Oh, Margaret Mallencroix"—the voice to Clyde's

ears was like an out-of-tune horn, a battered sound, as if it came from deep inside a well with moldy walls and rotten mortar—"how ever did it come to be that you found yourself so far from your room?"

He clanked from his mount to the craggy soil, his boots crunching into the stones. A steady, predatory series of careful steps came next . . . each one closer than the last. Advancing the bolt on his rifle to push up the next round, he droned, "Let's take the fuss out of this. Just line up for me. I swear I'll do it quick—one shot apiece."

Clyde's blood ran cold. He gripped the citizen dagger in two hands, a leathery squeak sounding as he throttled the handle.

"What's he paying you, Vidurkis?" Nevele shouted from behind the cover of an enormous tire. "Gorett doesn't cough up spots easily. I'm sure he's promised you something he doesn't even have in hand. He hasn't gotten an ounce of the stone yet—"

"He doesn't want you alive, Margaret." He sounded giddy.

A nudge. Clyde turned and saw that Flam was holding out the guardsman's helmet to him. Clyde took it and put the terrifically heavy thing on his head. Flam gestured for him to flip down the visor, and he did. The Mouflon mouthed with furry lips, "Keep it down."

Nevele whispered to the others, "I'll keep him busy. The rest of you get to the mine and go as far in as you can. His gray light doesn't work on me. Flam," she began, a steely tone in her voice, "stay with Clyde."

One of the few of Rohm that remained on the ground stared blankly ahead as they saw with the eyes of their others up top. "Miss Nevele. He's coming around the front . . ."

The hand in which she held the pistol went white knuckled.

Rohm chimed in, "We will do what we can."

"Wait," Nevele urged.

But the last two mice scampered up the side of the machine and, in a flash, were over the top and gone.

Vidurkis took another slow step forward, approaching the front corner of the three-story-tall machine. He swept a strand of hair out of his face while the forefinger of his other hand found the trigger guard and a finger slipped into it. Keeping watch ahead, trained on the edge of the machine from which the Mouflon, the pale man, or his sister might spring at any moment. He was about to charge, spring into their cover, and open fire when he felt something softly impact his shoulder. He ignored it, taking it for the first droplet of oncoming rain, but then another hit, heavier. Then another and another.

He took another step. Not important. Not now. He was so close to having them. He could *smell* the Mouflon.

He felt a painful pinch on the back of his wrist and saw the frisk mouse, paws set where it had pushed away the glove. He swatted at it, but the rodent was quick and had jumped up his shoulder and sunk its teeth into his earlobe in less than a second. He shouted and thrashed to scatter the mice off, enraged. Soon, a steady trickle of them showered on him. He could feel them working their way through the hem of his tunic under his armor, into the cusp of his boots, even up his sleeves. When they all had access to the Executioner's soft tissue, they bit at once, as if on a cue.

"Go now," his sister shouted.

The Mouflon and the pale man charged the entrance of the mine.

Firing from the hip, Vidurkis hit nothing but air.

The cracking shot seemed to speed the two up. They reached the opening and disappeared, running down the ramp where it steeply curved into pitch darkness beyond. They were not the target. They could run in there if they wanted, get devoured. That was fine.

Margaret was still out here with him. That was the objective. That was what the Mechanized Goddess had set for him—his step one, so to speak. Sending up a quick prayer to her, he immediately reaped a gifted celerity. He caught one of the frisk mice and squeezed it to death, its bones crunching pleasantly. He cast the limp thing aside, wiped the blood off on his pant leg, and continued on to the other side of the dozer.

Clyde, still wearing the visor, could barely see anything in this dark place.

Flam stood ahead of him, one arm reaching back to shield Clyde. He held the ruined blunderbuss by its barrel, ready to fling it up the ramp out of the cave if the pearl-eyed slaughterer dared to appear.

Clyde blurted, "Where's—?"

The gunshot sounded. Then another. Then screaming—but from Vidurkis only.

Clyde tried to step forward, to run out and help in any way he could, but Flam clutched a twisted ball of Clyde's shirt.

Nevele appeared at the top of the cave's ramp and charged down, her hood flapping. At her feet, frisk mice flooded in, terror on all their little faces. Once in, she turned and stood between the opening and Flam and Clyde, shoving them back. She aimed her pistol up the ramp, as the remainder of Rohm scurried down to collect with the others. The last one hobbled along as fast as it could go, one broken leg dragging behind. Clyde was going to jump out just long enough to fetch the poor thing, but Flam pushed him back and lunged for the mouse, directly in Nevele's sights.

"Get out of the way," she hissed. "He's right outside."

Mouse successfully fetched, Flam cupped it in his hands and spun to return it to the others.

Vidurkis appeared at the top of the ramp, his face torn to ribbons. The only thing that seemed to be unharmed were his eyes. The rest was a mask of red with tiny bites sprinkled liberally throughout. He glanced at his sister for one second, then switched onto the next available target.

"*Flam*," Clyde cried, his voice bouncing within the helmet. He stood helplessly as Flam looked at precisely the wrong moment. Even though his own eyes were protected, Clyde turned away as the red mask of Vidurkis's face shifted into a cruel rictus unleashing the gray light.

Nevele shoved the stock-still Flam out of the way. The frisk mouse had climbed to his shoulder and was poking his cheek, trying to get the Mouflon to move even farther from danger.

One of Vidurkis's hands showed gory evidence of having been chewed into disuse by mice teeth. He raised the rifle and attempted to aim with the other hand.

With Flam clear of possible harm, Nevele raised her pistol. No stare down, no pithy comebacks, nothing at all like Clyde had read two enemies should engage in during a fight—they seemed ready to kill one another right now, satisfied with the burden that'd follow, almost inviting it.

They both fired at the same time, the dual cracks resounding deep into the caves and coming back a moment later.

Both had missed.

Vidurkis awkwardly advanced the next round.

Nevele thumbed back the hammer.

They squared up to fire again.

A deafening thunderclap sounded. The entire ceiling of the crevasse was awash with white smoke.

Glancing up, Nevele saw the top jaw of the cave's opening crumble, bright blasts of sparks between the rocks. Just as the first large pieces fell, she took a backpedaling leap.

Clyde was now tasked with moving the dull-gazed Flam out of the way. He dug his heels in and pushed the Mouflon to take a single step. Rohm compiled and promptly assisted as boulders the size of autos broke away from the passageway. They struck the ground with such violent force it seemed they would split the planet.

A safe distance away, the group stopped. Choking on the dust, they looked at the cave's blocked exit.

Flam came to his senses, his pupils rapidly dilating. He focused and blinked furiously as if trying to shake off the effects from a nasty thump to the head. "What the plummets happened?"

Clyde lifted the visor on the helmet. "I think maybe the gunshots caused an avalanche or something."

But then, among the debris, Clyde spotted some wire. Some of the rocks had sooty asterisks smudged on by explosions. He pointed this out to Nevele.

"We must've set off a detonator of some kind. There was an explosion. I heard it." She sniffed. "Black powder, by the smell of it."

A voice sounded from behind them, gruff and gravelly. "Actually, love, it's one-quarter beech quartz, a couple of pellets of guano, and just a *dash* of black powder—but, yeah, that black powder smell really stands out, doesn't it?"

The group whipped around.

Out of the shadows came a man in an electric wheelchair. He had a grand handlebar moustache, curled at the ends into sharp points that stuck out at least six inches from either side of his face. He wore a sweat-stained bandanna, a tattered sleeveless tunic revealing muscled arms covered from shoulder to wrist with tattoos, and a pair of workman's breeches tucked into the biggest pair of boots Clyde had ever seen. Upon one shoulder perched a bird that appeared to be molting, its only feathers on its wings. The man stared at them with disarming, caramel-colored eyes. He controlled the wheelchair with one hand on a joystick; the other hand pointed a three-barreled blunderbuss directly at Nevele's chest.

"What do ye say ye all throw down your weapons for me? Looking at the business end of a pistol always makes me a wee bit nervous." He smiled, showing crystal teeth from one side of his broad grin to the other.

Flam, despite his flooding nausea, managed to look at Nevele. "Oh, yeah, this is much better than out there with him."

CHAPTER 27

And a Hard Place

To Vidurkis's enormous disappointment, one glimpse of them after another was blocked as more and more of the entrance cascaded in. In no time at all the entire mountainside seemed to have slid over the spot, leaving not a solitary opening. It was as if it had always looked this way, just a bare rock wall that had never seen a single throw of a pick. He watched it all, shaking his head, his mind reeling. The final rock fell—clok—and tumbled off the heap. When it came to a stop, all was silent.

Dropping to his knees, blood dripping from the countless bites all over his face and neck, he cursed his arrogance. He had gotten the Mouflon—a direct hit of gray light—since he was sure it was mere seconds before they'd all be dead at his feet. But now the Mouflon was in there and Vidurkis was out here, tons of rock between.

His lips moved. "Three days," he told himself, too overcome to stop thinking aloud. "Three *blasted* days." After that, the world would forever be black to him. He'd be blind as something that lived deep in the earth, hapless and dumb. He'd just be another man then. He wouldn't be able to call himself a weaver of fabrick anymore. He'd be damned if he'd go around saying he was an ex-weaver. No, absolutely not.

Three days. Unless that scavenger was dead by then,

Vidurkis would go blind. He'd come close before. It was how he came to learn that's what would happen. A purse snatcher once got the grays from him, tried to run, and managed to stay hidden in a family member's pantry for two and a half days. Vidurkis, still ignorant of how he'd degrade without the claimed kill, took his time. Sure enough, there it was. On the second day's morn, he could barely read newsprint. By that afternoon, he was struggling to reload his weapon; everything was dull and fuzzy about the edges. Luckily, the thief's aunt got paranoid about what might happen to her if she didn't run her nephew in, and he received a tip. The moment the man had the last breath dragged from him, Vidurkis's vision cleared. He learned to treat his gift with a little more respect from that point on, recalling one of the decrees of the Goddess: take care of one's tools, physical or no.

But there would be no family member to turn in the Mouflon, no anonymous phone call for Vidurkis to idly wait for. He'd have to tend to this himself.

That Mouflon had to die.

"Now," the man said, steering his wheelchair up to the group once they had all surrendered their weapons to the earthen floor. "What in the name of all that is good are you—a Mouflon, a whole slew of frisk mice, a lady who's apparently been through the meat grinder, and a bloke I can only assume has never seen a second's worth of sunshine in his life—doing down here in my bloody mine?"

"This isn't your mine. It's Mr. Wilkshire's," Clyde spat, forgetting his manners as well as his wits: they were all in his gun's range.

The man abruptly halted in his meandering glide and pulled back on his joystick to throw the wheelchair into reverse. Angling it nimbly forward with a flick of his wrist, he stopped before Clyde, the blunderbuss now trained on his face.

"Excuse me, lad," he said with a chuckle devoid of humor. "I didn't catch that. I'm a bit deaf after that blast, ye see. Say that again if ye wouldn't mind. Go ahead. Lean right in here to me *left* ear—me good one—and tell me what ye just said one more again."

Nevele sidled forward. "Pardon my friend, sir. We're kind of on a task, and we just want to get up into the waterworks so we can get back up to the city."

"*Ha*," the man's haughty voice echoed through the enormous chamber. "Ye can *say* that ye and ye friends are trying to get to Geyser all ye want. Ye could even *say* ye mean to enter this one here into a beauty contest"—he waved a fingerless-gloved hand at Flam—"but I know what ye're up to. Ye're down here lookin' for the deposit. Word finally got out, did it? That Gorett found the only source of wendal stone on Gleese, and yer band of ninnies thought ye'd just *stroll right* in and take it. Didn't ye? Well, I guess ye didn't count on any of the miners sticking around, did ye? Sorry to burst yer bubble, but Nigel Wigglesby will *not* be chased off from his post quite so easily!"

Hands still raised, Clyde noticed at the back of the cave another set of the mining machines, one of which had its blade sunk into the cave wall, blocking the way to the deeper passages. But as far as accommodations, there seemed to be precious little. No bed, no store of food, nothing. Just the shadows, the stalagmites like a chamber of pointless columns clogging up the fringes of the space, and a whole lot of dirt.

Hands up and not looking the least bit happy about it, Nevele said, "We just want to pass through. I assure you we don't give a damn about your wendal stone."

At this, Flam shifted, the words *speak for yourself* plainly on the tip of his tongue.

"Mr. Wilkshire hired me to prevent anyone from entering the mine without proper paperwork. He told me, straight to me mug, that if anyone were to come down here day or night without their sheets in order, I was to report them posthaste, no questions asked. And since I'm sure ye're aware that not even the authorities can be trusted any longer, this here"— he indicated his blunderbuss with a nod and a smile—"is the *only* means of reporting that I trust."

It was then that Clyde noticed the stock of the gun had several shallow notches carved into it; this man wasn't going to take any guff. He stammered, "I w-was also an employee of Mr. Wilkshire."

"Fantastic," Nigel said with sarcasm, his wheelchair in front of Clyde once again. "Let me see yer paperwork, and I'll be more than obliged to lift that blade out of the passage so ye can get your arse chewed three ways to Sunday by the Blatta. Come on, then. Where is it? Make with the forms, lad."

"*Forms*," his diseased-looking bird called.

"I don't have any," Clyde said first to the bird, then to this man who called himself Nigel.

"No?" he said, the corners of his mouth pulling down in faux sorrow. "That's really too bad. Maybe we should break down the wall there, see if that mad-lookin' fella that was chasing ye has any paperwork. I got plenty of sticks to do it, too. All it would take is one little pop, and I could bring him right in here."

"No," Flam exclaimed. "Don't. Please."

Nigel showed his crystal teeth, apparently amused at inciting Flam's reaction. He settled in his wheelchair and slid his hand off the handle of his blunderbuss. He chewed his lip, his crystal teeth flashing when they caught the meager, diluted light.

After what felt like hours of apparent deliberation with himself, the man turned his head slightly to confer with the thing on his shoulder. "What do you make of all this?"

The bird made a few strange clucks, flapped its wings against its flanks with fleshy slaps, and let out a long screech.

Apparently Nigel found it absolutely hilarious. He belly laughed, slapping the armrest of his wheelchair. Then he became very serious very quickly. It was as if the man's emotions were on some kind of board game spinner, the flicks it received coming at unpredictable intervals. His gaze was on Nevele. "Ye two were shooting at each other."

"Yes, we were."

"Just standing there, facing one another. Like people do when they really want someone dead. Not even *tryin'* to dodge the other's bullets."

Nevele's head sank a little, but she kept her hands up. "Yes."

"And he was dressed in a Royal Patrol guardsman uniform, of the Executioner rank, if I'm not mistaken. Two bronze axes on the lapel." He fingered his own stained collar. "That is what that means, right?"

"It is," she said quietly.

"And so, if ye aren't bandits who mean to filch Mr. Wilkshire's wendal stone and ye're down here out of honesty and the joyful spreading of goodness . . . why in the blazes was a member of the Patrol shooting at ye?"

"Well . . ." Nevele began at length.

"Gorett is corrupt," Clyde said. "He made everyone leave Geyser so he could have the wendal stone to himself. He framed Mr. Wilkshire for the Blatta invasion. Someone murdered him. We're just trying to get back into Geyser to make things right."

"Make things *right*, ye say? My, my, my. Intrepid warriors on a grand adventure looking to set things right. Gracious! That is one for the storybooks, don't ye think, Scooter?"

The bird slapped its wings excitedly and pealed, "*Gracious!*"

"I agree. I believe they *are* pulling our chain."

Clyde slowly lowered his hands.

Nigel's grip was quick to find the stock of his blunderbuss. He turned to Clyde and closed the gap between them with a tweak on the joystick. "What's that ye're doing there, boy? Looking to draw steel on me, are ye? Let's take a look, see what was so dire that ye didn't toss it on the ground like I told ye to before." He reached out and moved Clyde's suit coat aside to look. Clipped onto the belt loop was the citizen dagger.

Nigel's hand faltered, fingers outstretched but hesitating. After a moment, he seemed to remember what he was doing and snatched the blade from the scabbard. The grating sound alarmed Scooter, and it flapped and screamed until Nigel soothed it with a stroke of its yellow, hooked beak.

Nigel studied the blade in his hands for a moment, paying particular attention to the engraving. He peered at Clyde with one eye narrowed. "This really his?"

Clyde nodded.

Nigel let out a long whistling breath through his nostrils. He seemed to melt into the chair, sinking forward, elbows resting on his knees. He stared into the peerless blade, which he held reverently in his palms.

"Guess that means he really is dead." Nigel's bottom lip trembled ever so slightly. "I had heard he was being blamed for all of it, but I figured it would work itself out. News travels slow through two miles of rock, as you can imagine."

He raised his head, his sorrow visible, his moustache an upside-down V on his face. "I'll tell you one thing. There's no way in hell Mr. Wilkshire would let his men die like that." He glanced at the dagger again, turned it around so he pinched the blade between thumb and index finger. He allowed Clyde to grip the handle and return it to its scabbard.

Nigel pushed the butt of the mounted blunderbuss aside, swinging the barrels away so they were no longer pointed at the group.

Everyone seemed to relax.

"Any idea who could've done it?" Nigel asked, resting his hands on the thighs of his stunted, atrophied legs.

Clyde shook his head.

Nigel did too and added a groan.

"That really is quite a shame. I know in my heart that Mr. Wilkshire didn't have anything to do with that. Where we were mining, it was a good half mile from the Blatta hive. The wall got tapped after hours, when we weren't even here. Figured it was a cave-in. I imagined the evidence would make it to the right people before . . ." He frowned. "Forgive me. I just can't believe old man Wilkshire's dead."

"I apologize, but is there a way through there?" Nevele asked, gesturing at the massive, sunken blade of the mining machine.

Beyond it, faintly, the screeches of the Blatta could be heard. All the commotion and explosions must have rattled them.

The sound drove a chill into Clyde, and he involuntarily placed a hand on his chest to quell the sensation.

"Aye, but it's rather shite at the moment. I work on it when I can, but as ye can clearly see, I'm not exactly the rock climber sort. Been tinkering with a few concoctions of my own to make some kind of poison to gas the nasty things out. So far, nothing's worked." He steered his wheelchair away, rubber wheels leaving a set of trails in the dirt toward the machine blocking the path.

The others picked up their weapons from the ground and replaced them on their persons. They followed Nigel beyond the reach of the meager fluorescent lights mounted to the cavern ceiling.

"Come on in. I got the kettle on," Nigel said, sadness still straining his voice.

The group paused before the wall of darkness that had effectively absorbed Nigel. The soft crunch of his wheels in the dirt led them, but there was no telling if Nigel was leading them off a cliff while he took a narrow bridge only he knew about. The group paused when the sound of Nigel's wheels halted.

Then came the clap of gloved hands. A series of lights thumped on in sequence and illuminated a beautiful house—right inside the cavern.

A full wraparound porch, a turreted foyer, dormered windows on the second floor, just like a home one would see in the ward Mr. Wilkshire had lived in. Atop the turret was a rooster weather vane, which didn't make much sense here but made the house's inviting visage complete.

"Beg your pardon, Mr. Wigglesby, but how is it that you have electricity?" Rohm asked. "I thought the Geyser turbines weren't running anymore, the floodway being as blocked up as it is."

"Ah, yeah—that was kind of a headache, but I got the whole house wired to the digger out there. The battery on that thing could power Geyser for a month if it had to. A good use of the old noggin on my part, if I say so myself."

Clyde spotted the thick cables, like big black vines, running from the digger to the house.

"Impressive," Flam remarked.

Using the ramp, Nigel bypassed the porch's stairs. With a casual wave of his hand, the front doors swung open. The bird on his shoulder took flight and shot out ahead of him to a perch in the roomy, wood-paneled living room.

The others followed.

Clyde marveled at the beautiful furnishings: varnished dark wood, leather wingback chairs, elegant spider-silk sofas. Moving along behind Nigel, Clyde was treated to the sight of marble kitchen countertops and an army of pots hanging from a rack suspended from the hammered tin ceiling. In the large dining room, stretching from one end to the opposite, was a grand table that could accommodate dozens.

Nigel pulled open the icebox and called over his shoulder, "Anyone care for something besides tea? It is quitting time, after all, and by the looks of it, you've earned it."

"What is this place?" Flam asked. "Did they build this for visiting rich folk or what?"

"It was ours—the miners'." He said it as if a grand home inside a cavern were the most normal thing in the world. "Mr. Wilkshire didn't want us sleeping on cots and working in bad conditions. If we wanted to live here full-time, we could. Some men did. He had the place built shortly after he bought the mine. You should see the shack that was here before—just a can and three walls of clapboard. But this, yeah, I don't mind living here one bit. Of course . . . it has been a bit quiet as of late."

"You're the only one left?" Clyde said.

"That I am." The pride in his voice was mostly unconvincing. "Out of a crew of eighty employees in the Kobbal Mines, I am the last one."

He cleared his throat, and when he spoke again it was with a levity that sounded anything but sturdy. "So beers all around, or what'll it be? I got some sandwiches in here that are only partly expired. Some bread. Eggs. We could fry them up and see what happens."

He spun around from the open icebox door. "Come on, now. Don't be shy. Place your orders. Ol' Nigel can cook just about anything!"

CHAPTER 28

Vacancy

After dinner, with everyone seated around the long dinner table and a majority of the travelers' tale told, Nigel studied his guests.

He blinked at Rohm. "Don't take no offense, little mice, but I typically fight to keep your kind out of this place, and here ye are, eating off the good china, no less." He chuckled, as did most of the mice.

Next, Nigel studied Nevele and Clyde, who sat side by side. "You two weavers I have figured out. You mean to set things right. Makes sense to me, given how Geyser—and the whole damn planet—has treated the lot of ye in the past few years. That much I can wrap my head around."

He bobbed a finger at Flam, who was finishing his third helping of stew. "But what about ye, fella? What's *yer* story? Thought all Mouflons skedaddled from this rock ages ago."

Flam tapped his spoon on his bowl. "There's a few of us left kicking around," he said with a grin. "I would've done just that—skedaddled—if it weren't for Pasty here making me give my word. Not sure if you know, but if a Mouflon gives his word—"

"He has to keep it. Yeah, I've known quite a few Mouflons in my day. Had a few work down here for a while. This one big galoot named Greenspire used to be a real good drinking buddy of mine—"

"Greenspire?" Flam's spoon crashed against the edge of his bowl. "Greenspire Flam?"

Nigel smiled. "Knew him, did ye?"

"Greenspire Flam was my uncle!" Flam nearly overturned his chair with excitement.

"Well, dress me up in lace and send me to the debutante ball—I had no idea that grumpy jerk had any relatives. I figured that old coot would likely eat any young in his family. Makes sense, given the surname, now that I think about it. I should've known. Ye two have very similar . . . horns."

"He was a swell guy. The best."

"I agree. He ranked high among my best mates." Nigel raised his wooden cup in salute, but his smile faded and he stared at the pot of stew, then at all the other chairs at the big table, empty.

He's lost so much, Clyde thought.

"Wait a second," Nevele said. "Flam is your *last* name? Then what's your first?"

Flam cleared his throat and murmured something.

Nevele smirked. "Sorry. I didn't catch that. It sounded like *tinkle.*"

"Tiddle," Flam shouted. "My first name is Tiddle, all right? Everyone have a good laugh. My name is Tiddle Flam."

They all chuckled, even Rohm, but Clyde tried to be at least a little polite by covering his own smile and turning away to pass his laugh off as a cough.

Nigel continued, "Remarkable bloke, he was. What ever happened to the big lug?"

Flam sank a little in his chair. "He was lost while on the job, in the city sub works. They assume he came to a cross tunnel and fell in." Barely audibly, he said, "They never found his body."

Nigel looked at his place setting, his brow wrinkled. "Those cursed tunnels . . . I always *said* they should spray something in there to reduce that algae. It can get slick. Heard of quite a few fellas meeting their end that way." Solemnly, he lifted his glass of beer again, this time much higher. "For Greenspire Flam."

Flam lifted his stein. "Greenspire Flam."

They clinked, finished their drinks, and set the glasses down.

After some lighter conversation, Nigel clapped his hands together. "I suppose it's bedtime for this particular bloke. Do I need to show ye to yer rooms, or do ye think ye can manage? I don't get upstairs a lot, and if ye wouldn't mind finding the way by yer own ingenuity . . ."

"Sure," Flam said, "we'll figure it out. Thank you for your hospitality."

"Yes," Clyde said, "thank you."

Nevele added, "We really appreciate the semblance of normalcy after all we've been through. The eggs were delicious."

"Ah, well, ye can tell Scooter in the morning," Nigel said, heading through the kitchen. "She drops about ten a day, and it's good to have someone else around here to eat them so they don't go to waste. At any rate, good night."

The others echoed, "Good night."

Vidurkis watched the walker take one rock at a time, as he'd programmed it to, and move it away from the pile in front of the cave. Slowly. So slowly. He sat atop the mining machine, legs dangling out of the cockpit, watching the walker work in the darkness. He couldn't believe his luck, giving the Mouflon the gray light just as the wall came down. He drove his fist into the steering wheel, and it issued a long bleat.

He dropped to the ground and watched the walker as it pushed a boulder out of the pile with its hind legs in the fashion of a dung beetle. Working so hard, trying and trying to finish its task in a timely manner, beeping occasionally as it processed how much farther it had to go and which rock would be best to move next . . .

He couldn't take it another second.

Vidurkis kicked it out of the way, overturning it onto its back. He took the boulder it had been working on and pressed his shoulder against it. He succeeded at rolling it a few feet, but if he pushed for another solitary second, he might peel the skin right off his shoulder.

He slouched against it and withdrew his pipe. He struck a match and held it before the pipe's end but didn't touch it to the waiting fragrant green mold.

He looked up and felt as if he were, at that moment, the dumbest person on Gleese. There was the mining machine all along, built for exactly his predicament. He had even been sitting in the cockpit but never thought to give it a try. He threw the pipe aside and climbed back in, frantically searching for the ignition. He pressed it, and the mighty machine gave one heave. The blade made one rotation, then stopped. He looked at the instrument panel. No gas. He realized he was not the dumbest person on Gleese but perhaps the unluckiest.

He dropped out and gave the walker a thorough trashing until all six of its legs had broken off and its metal exoskeleton was flattened. He wiped the sweat from his brow and sighed, feeling a touch better. He canted his head back to really suck in some deep breaths of the cold night air. He caught himself staring up the hillside to where the stem reached out of the ground—and higher up, where Geyser stood like a gigantic stone mushroom. The well-oiled cogs of his mind spun full steam ahead.

"I'm going about this all wrong," he muttered.

Chasing them, dodging all the obstacles they threw over their shoulders for him, would waste too much time. Perhaps going in through the geyser and meeting them halfway would be the best approach. They'd gone into the mines voluntarily. Whatever they were up to, he assumed their goal was to get back up into the city. To what end, he didn't know. His sister was crafty and undoubtedly vengeful. She had been thrown out of the palace and caged in that hospital. She probably wanted the same fate for Gorett that Vidurkis did. Surely she was going in there to try to steer the Blatta to the man who'd released them in the first place, to make certain the puller of the floodgate switch was among the drowned. He had to hand it to Margaret. She may have gone about things arse backwards, but she still had the Mallencroix cruelty to her.

He would help his sister, if only to get at her Mouflon companion. After that, he'd kill her, the others, Gorett too if Margaret couldn't manage it, and then . . . well, that was up to what the Goddess wanted of him, wasn't it? Better left unknown. "Having all the answers, like Gorett," he muttered to himself, breath steaming, "would lead only to complacency."

After packing up, he began his long trek north to

the palace elevator. Doing some quick arithmetic along the way, he decided he would return to his cell under the palace, one of the lowest places in Geyser's platter, and begin his own tunneling there. He'd take to the task smartly, though: long after Gorett had laid down his head in his heavily fortified private chambers, where the so-called king would be none the wiser to the digging just ten floors beneath him. Even if he dared wake and storm down there and say something—well, with the Goddess on his side, Vidurkis knew he'd just have to kill Gorett and continue as a functional cog, a good cog, a man of purpose who sought not only a Mouflon but everything he could lay his hands on beyond it.

He marched through the dark. Rain pelted him, and his boots squished in the mud. One foot, then the next, one turn of the cogs after another.

Flam found a workbench in the basement of the house and decided to repair his blunderbuss since he was almost sure sleep would not come to him easily this night.

His head still felt abuzz after the Executioner had hit him with the gray light; traces of the gloom were still in the peripheral of his mind, like resonances of a scream from inside a well that refused to degrade to silence, ringing and ringing forever. He kept seeing flashes of possible outcomes, horrid ones.

Nevele in a heap, all her threads unspooled from her body and collected around her like beach-washed seaweed. Immobile and sprawled in a pool of red. Her face devoid of its flesh patches, raw and leering, lidless and dead.

Then there was Clyde and the foreboding flash he had

about him. That citizen dagger he carried now jammed deep in his belly. His mouth sewn shut and his ears blasted deaf, unable to take any confession or utter any plea to receive a new one.

Rohm. Every single frisk mouse stamped to smears, ground under a hoof.

Flam wasn't sure if these images were the result of his own morbid imagination or if they had been what Vidurkis had wanted. Either way, Flam found busying his hands the best way to shake the images loose. He hummed a familiar ditty to himself as he doused the barrel of his gun with the torch to make the metal pliable for straightening.

The hum transitioned into soft singing. Then muttered lyrics became clear. Each word deliberately sung loud, and off-key despite his best efforts, to drown out any more waking nightmares.

Nestled deep into a richly upholstered love seat, Clyde and Nevele sat together in the study.

She slouched and stared at Rohm, still at the dining room table, poring over one of the leather-bound volumes on the maintenance of mining equipment with a particular attention paid to the proper care for drill tips. In a complicated process of timing and precision, like a trapeze act, the mice lifted, caught, and turned the pages.

"I wonder if they all made it," Nevele said.

"The miners?"

"Well, them too—but I mean Rohm. There's so many of them. I wonder if they'd know if one or two of them got killed."

Clyde watched the studious mice and contemplated

this. "It's hard to say." He hated the idea that some of the matron mice were doing head counts before tucking their children in for the night and coming up hand-to-heart short.

Not wanting to think about any of that, he turned away and stared out the front windows. Outside, all was dark in the cavern at first glance. Here and there, pools of light from the house gained purchase on a few towering stalactites. His gaze found the new wall that was an opening just a few hours before.

With the living room's amber glow, the faint shape of the rocks that had made the blockade in front of the entrance stood stalwart, unmovable. Still, he knew what was beyond those rocks—*who* was beyond those rocks. Deciding he didn't want to think about that, either, he noticed Nevele.

She took a deep breath, the sutures across her chest creaking. She picked at a rogue strand lacing her hand to her wrist, the threads splitting, knotting, and resetting. But seeming discontent with the completed look of it, she redid it again and again until the knot lay flush.

"What's on your mind?" Clyde finally said.

She answered at once, as if she had been waiting for him to simply ask, the plug pulled free. "My brother won't give up. Ever. I saw him throw the gray light on Flam. Now my brother has to hunt us." She blinked slowly. "I can picture him pulling himself through there, forcing his bones out of socket and slithering out of the mess to come and kill us in our sleep." She looked at Clyde. "Sorry."

Attempting to lighten the mood, Clyde took the guardsman helmet from the arm of the love seat and flipped the visor down. He turned this way and that, looking about the room. "I don't know how they see anything through this thing."

She snickered. She flipped the visor up and cradled his cheeks in her hands. The sutures mapping her palms were surprisingly soft, like waxed cotton strips and not rough twine or leather at all.

"If you're going to confess something," Clyde said, "I might ask you to wait until after we get to the surface. We have kind of a harrowing day ahead of us tomorrow."

She stopped, a slightly annoyed expression on her face. "I was going to kiss you."

"Oh . . . in that case . . . well, I suppose . . . never mind, then." He closed his eyes, for that is how he had read people prepared to be kissed. He often wondered why, but he supposed kissing was one of those things too beautiful in life to witness up close, an art meant to be witnessed blind.

It felt like an eternity packed into a moment, that lingering silent time before she actually pressed her lips against his. When she did, a song erupted in his heart—a bright tingling that ran the length of his body, down the backs of his arms, and across his knees.

Her hands moved off his cheeks and onto his shoulders, the kiss developing into a deeper contact, her arms looping his neck in a full embrace. Her hands, so warm. Unsure what to do with his own hands, he kept them at his sides.

But when he tried to lift them, he couldn't.

"What's wrong?" she whispered, her breath sweet and tickling his ear, which he didn't mind whatsoever. "Don't tell me kissing someone will curse you to forget them."

"No, it's not that. I can't . . . move."

They looked down and saw her threads were cocooning

them both from head to toe. He brought his gaze back to meet hers and saw mild humiliation marking her face. Just as it started to slip, her left eyelid drooped and her nose went crooked.

"Whoops," she said with a slur.

Clyde smiled, correcting his bow tie to busy his hands.

She stood and pulled herself together again. The last of the dark bindings uncoiled from Clyde's arms and legs and leaped back to her, some of them cracking like a tape measure in their speedy retraction.

"Quite the grip you got there. Yes, a kiss is admitting feelings, but since my fabrick works on words, I think we're safe." He looked at his fidgeting hands. "I want to tell you that I care about you, Nevele." He met her eyes. "But I won't. And I'm not, right now, for whatever persnickety fabrick weaver fates are listening right now. I could, I want to, but I won't." It felt like tempting fate even saying that much.

She leaned in and patted his cheek, gave him another small kiss. Her face was back to its normal state, everything in its place. "It's fine. I know how you feel." She gathered her things and headed upstairs but stopped halfway. "Do you want me to bring you a blanket or a book or something? I can't imagine it's going to be really fun staying up by yourself all night."

"It's fine. I think I might go check on Flam anyway."

"All right. Well, good night." Nevele gave a brief smile and clunked up the remainder of the stairs.

"Good night."

For a while Clyde was content just listening to her above, the click-clock of her boots, the two squeaks of bedsprings, and the silence that followed. He hoped she had pleasant dreams. Perhaps even ones that could be considered fun and good, and not at all about their present reality: sleeping in a house flanked on one side by an army of hundred-pound bloodthirsty insects and on the other by a murderous sibling. To Meech or whoever might listen, he prayed for her to dream about flying, his own favorite imagination.

Heading toward the basement, Clyde found himself smiling. He wouldn't be able to stop thinking about their kiss for quite some time. The smile remained glued in place his entire way down the narrow basement passageway. He felt as if he were floating, the buzz singing in his chest and making him feel like nothing bad had happened to anyone ever. He knew it wasn't true, but for the time being, in this glowing little bubble, it felt like it.

He did a quick rewind of his entire life. Nope, in spite of the looming circumstances, he'd never felt as good as he did right now.

Downstairs, Flam was envelopcd in his task, running a blue flame up and down the flared barrel of his blunderbuss.

"How are you doing?" Clyde asked.

The Mouflon twitched. It wasn't as if Clyde had snuck up on him, but maybe he was just deep in thought. Clyde's concern was abruptly cleared when Flam said, "What in the plummets has got you grinning like a fool?"

Clyde took a seat on the floor and hugged his knees. "Oh, nothing." He tried not to sound like a dopey, dreamy victim of Cupid's sharpshooting, but it was impossible.

Hammer in hand, Flam paused before giving the blunderbuss another blow. It was nearly straight. He stared at the hammer's head and weighed the tool in his hand with a loose grip. His face went serene, his eyes glassy.

Clyde didn't particularly like the look in his eye . . . "Everything okay?"

Flam snapped out of his stupor. His answer was a grunt, a shrug, and a quick return to his job, giving the blunderbuss one high swing after another—bang, bang, bang. Somewhere in the cacophony, Clyde thought Flam answered, "I've been better."

CHAPTER 29

Rewired and Rekindled

An unnerved guardsman private bowed at the main chamber doors, and Gorett waved him in.

The private removed his helmet and put it under his arm, busying his hands. "My lord," he said at last, "I want to suggest something that may be of use."

Gorett rolled a limp hand. "Go on."

"I believe if we use one of our fleet's autos, I can rewire it to supply electricity to the palace. Of course, we'd need to select which electronics would be of priority since we can spare merely one auto and a single machine can supply only so much power."

Gorett brightened, lifted his chin. "Do it at once. Splendid thinking. Once this is all resolved, consider yourself at the front of the line for a promotion." He feigned making a note of the guardsman's name.

The private smiled, replaced his helmet, and left the chambers with a slight skip in his step.

Alone again, Gorett tossed the scribbled sheet in the bin. On the next clean sheet, he decided to make a list of electricity priorities. He looked out the windows lining his main chambers, then at the spire sprouting out of the town square. No steam had shot from the geyser for days, and it had been nearly as long since the lights on its stone flesh had flickered. It was almost impossible to see it against the night sky, the stone blending in with the starless expanse beyond it. He told the dead power source, "Seems I've found a way around you, after all."

Returning to the sheet of parchment, he dipped his quill into ink. Below the list, he began the first draft of a letter. A letter that would be immediately handed off to the communications department, the first department to receive electricity once it was resupplied. Otherwise, it would be impossible to send a wire to the Odium requesting a temporary treaty.

Gorett scratched out three drafts. Each time he sounded like he was begging, he'd ball the sheet and throw it away. He hated doing this, but this was the point they were at. The Executioner wasn't answering any calls—hadn't in hours—and was now most likely dead. This was necessary, Gorett kept telling himself. It wasn't surrender; it was a strategic maneuver, a tactic. Yes, Gorett thought, signing his name in big, black, darting swirls, *a tactic*.

As much wendal stone as the heathens could carry if only they'd allow him safe passage off-world. He would return when it was all settled, repay his debts. Putting forth this request had been on his mind for the past few weeks, an option forever hanging in the back corner of his mind, nailed in place by more than a few factors.

The Blatta, for example, would eventually make their way to the surface. It was inevitable. Also, if Patient Eleven got anywhere near him, she wouldn't hesitate to end his life. And then there was the matter of having released the Executioner, the equivalent of loosing a rabid dog and asking it to ever so politely do as it was told and not rip the throat out of anyone it came across.

The sheet was full by the time he was done. The proposition was clear; what he was offering was precise. More than once, he reassured the recipients that none of this should be thought of as a trick. The Odium were nothing if not paranoid. But distrust could be curbed if money was involved. Working in the palace as long as he had had taught him that lesson.

The Odium pirates were more than suitable candidates. He certainly wouldn't trust any of the figureheads in Adeshka. But word would get to them eventually. It'd be impossible to keep his alliance with the Odium secret forever. But all he'd lose were the citizens waiting clueless in the camps, really. Expendable.

No one could take the throne from him, even if he were voluntarily applying the label of defector and war criminal to himself. Geyser could become whatever it became after all this was over, just as long as he could get the stone out of the ground by some means. And, he assumed, if the rumor of the Odium was true about living in man-made caves carved into the permafrost at the ice caps, they'd have to be skilled miners. Maybe they'd be impetuous enough to volunteer to go after the stone.

Gorett wouldn't mind sharing the profits with them, so long as it meant his protection. The girl could have the city—what was left of it. The Executioner and the Stitcher could fight for it the rest of their lives. Gorett snorted. He imagined her expression as he came back, aligned with dozens of pirates and their ships and weaponry—how dumbfounded she'd be. If she were, after all, the victor. If it were the Executioner, well, then, Gorett wouldn't even give him the time to be dumbfounded. He'd take up a rifle and put the mad dog down himself.

It was close: the means to the end. It was like building a house: one had to lay the foundation before anything else. And with the Odium, Gorett could practically smell the fresh mortar, hear the grind of flagstones, the bite of a shovel making that first exploratory divot into the earth. Things would shape up. Even if he had to force them to.

Two miles almost straight down, through a labyrinth of winding tunnels and damp warrens, rubber wheels rolled over the hardwood floors of the miners' house. Clyde looked from the pages of the journal in his lap to Nigel, who was easing into the living room. Clyde closed the leather cover on Mr. Wilkshire's journal and met Nigel's gaze. The man had parked at the far end of the room, as if he were avoiding a bad smell. With a few flipped switches, he engaged the brakes, never removing his focus from Clyde. He shimmied down in the seat to become comfortable. He gave Clyde a long stare, the gears in his head nearly visibly turning.

"I've got plenty of supplies for yer road ahead," Nigel said finally, voice thin. "I couldn't find sleep tonight, with all this excitement and the damned Blatta screeching out there." He referred to the digger outside. The only thing keeping the Blatta from flooding the entryway cavern to the mines was the machine's heavy, notched blade. "That and whoever's banging away down in the cellar."

"Flam," said Clyde.

Nigel nodded. "Like his uncle in yet another way. Restless." He looked over his shoulder to survey the front windows. He scowled toward the far wall of the cavern outside, peering toward the source of the hissing and chattering of the insects once more. "And like them as well."

"They do make a lot of racket."

When he looked back, Clyde noticed Nigel wasn't staring outside anymore but was eyeing him carefully, really looking into his face and eyes. The miner sucked on his lower lip, bit it with his shining quartz teeth. He blinked, tired, and took a deep breath, ready to say what he had to.

Clyde steeled himself for the worst.

"I saw these on ye." He pointed to his own wrist, then at Clyde. Clyde looked at the cuff of his jacket and saw nothing terribly exceptional or out of the ordinary there, except the cuff links with the ornate *P* set into them. "And I didn't want to say this in front of the others," he went on. "I wasn't sure if you'd want them to know . . ."

Clyde set the journal aside. "I'm sorry. I don't follow. Know what?"

Nigel's eyes danced. After two false starts, an irritated groan, and a sigh, he got it out in one push. "After I left my previous . . . place of work, I moved to Geyser. I wasn't always in this chair, and I was new to it and didn't really know any kind of work besides what you do on two feet. I applied, on a whim, to be a digger operator, since . . . I thought, well, there's a job a man can do whilst sitting down, and I won't be in any sort of office pushing papers.

"Met the boss man, Albert Wilkshire, on my first day. He didn't care what it was I used to do. He and I hit it off—as close as two men can be when one is an employee of the other, I suppose. A few months in, with maybe a wee bit too much brandy in his coffee one Friday night, he told me about ye. A lot, actually. As much as he cared for ye, he always thought it was such a shame that he had to keep ye locked away. But since he knew I was a man of good character and could keep a secret, he told me something he probably shouldn't have been telling a man of such low standing as myself. But, as it were, I think he'd been sitting on it too long and had to tell someone. It really had nothing to do with me. I just happened to be the one present when he spilled the beans . . ."

"Please continue."

"It was right in there, in the dining room, long after the other men had gone to sleep. It was just he and I. He told me about the fraternity he was a part of, a secret group assembled by King Pyne himself. And about ye and his guilt in being yer keeper—when the roles should've been reversed."

"What do you mean?"

Nigel pushed with his elbows and sat up in his chair. "Wilkshire was a close friend of King Pyne, which was why he was part of his secret fraternity. They grew up together, went to war in the Territorial Skirmish with Embaclawe together. They lived big lives before returning to Geyser. Saw many worlds, many battles, many terrible things as well as good.

"They wanted to maintain Geyser as a good place of permanent peace. When it was time for Pyne to take up the throne at his father's death, he went to Mr. Wilkshire and devised a plot to ensure that the goodness of Geyser would never be tainted—a safety protocol of sorts."

Clyde sat up on the couch, his tiredness releasing him. "I had no idea Mr. Wilkshire and King Pyne knew one another. He never had him over as a guest. Not that I recall." Clyde would've certainly remembered royalty in the chateau. Miss Shelby would've been polishing everything in sight for weeks leading up to the occasion, certainly.

"Aye, but to maintain the ruse, they sadly had to end their friendship. No one could know. Really, it made their friendship more meaningful by seemingly ending it. It'd become less about being chums and more about dedicating themselves to something bigger, more important than having another feller as a close mate. That sacrifice had to be made in direct reply to a new threat.

"Angry folks believed the path to total parity on this planet could be found only in having a constant state of turmoil, unrest, one leader always replacing the last. They believed machinery and bits and pieces of metal were not the product of a man's hands but the work of his soul made manifest. That metal, the constant hammering, always adopting the better model, ceaselessly making draft after draft in a product line—that was mankind's purpose. To them, machinery and engineering and tinkering weren't just livelihoods but divine influence pressing its way into reality . . ."

"The Odium," Clyde managed, the name like dirt in his mouth.

"Yes. And with their numbers growing, something had to be done. When Lady Pyne was with child, they decided their firstborn son would have to be kept safe. They knew the Odium may attempt to take the throne from him. So upon his birth, it had already been decided he'd be put into hiding."

Nigel paused and raised a finger. "But they never guessed in a thousand years that the child would be born a fabrick weaver."

Perplexed, Clyde opened his mouth for another question, but Nigel raised a hand. Tears rimmed his tired eyes. "Let me finish it, lad. I got to get through it fast; otherwise, I don't think I'll be able to do the story justice. Gots to get it on the first swing or we'll be here all night."

Clyde nodded, fighting his impatience. "All right." His heart was hammering.

Nigel cleared his throat. "He saw the curse of yer fabrick early on. Ye would tell one of yer nannies—or even yer mother and father on a few occasions—that ye cared about them, and when they left the room and came back, ye'd have no memory of them at all, having to meet them all over again. If ye spoke of yer love for anyone at all, they'd become total strangers to ye.

"Yer father used that when he began to suspect treachery within his cabinet. Prime Minister Gorett was determined to usurp yer father by any means necessary and wasn't secretive at all about it. He *wanted* your father worried. But yer father also knew Gorett was timid at heart, and to make up for it he would be patient in his planning. Without any solid grounds to discharge him, yer father kept Gorett close—as ye should with enemies—and learned that Gorett planned to arrange accidents with yer siblings and ye, so that when it was time for the Commencement, when your king father's soul passed to the next heir, Gorett would be the only one present to inherit it. And so Lord Pyne and Lady Pyne decided to fake your death."

"Wait. I'm—?"

"What'd I say, lad? Let me finish."

"Sorry, sorry."

"I apologize, Clyde. It's just that this is difficult for me. I've sat on this for quite some time, and seeing ye here now really gives me . . . hope. Somethin' I haven't had in quite a while. Anyway, he sat ye down on his knee and asked ye to tell him how much ye cared about him, even though he knew it would wipe yer memory of him completely. Unaware of what it'd do, ye told yer pa ye loved him. He set ye down, left the room, and came back. He said ye smiled at him and said hello and introduced yerself—being the polite little shite ye always were—and as much as it killed him, he had ye put in an auto and sent off.

"An hour later, he was out on the balcony making the public announcement, lying for the first time to his people ever, that ye were dead. To him, it wasn't so much of a lie. He had lost ye, in a way. He'd never see ye again, he knew. Gorett was well on his way to getting his plan set in action already.

"Grief, and the outpouring sympathy from Geyser to the Pyne family would be the cloak that'd operate as a way to get ye away. In the hubbub, he appointed Mr. Wilkshire to the task to move ye from place to place. Ye were always hooded and bound, to protect them not only from ye but from those who may have been privy to the colossal secret of *who* ye were. Ye changed hands, kept under lock and key, with your extraordinary ability exploited left and right. Ye see, Mr. Wilkshire had to rely on his business partners to house ye, and not all of them were good men, were they?"

Clyde shook his head. "No, they weren't."

"But, sadly, it was to be done. Ye couldn't be kept in one place, and only Albert himself ever really knew where ye were at any given time. Mr. Wilkshire decided to keep ye himself, the last of the line of caretakers. By the time ye were twenty years old, he figured that would be when he'd start training ye to be a good leader. He planned on letting ye know everything about yer royal blood, about who ye really are. But he had to also maintain an outward image of normalcy. And that was about the time my team found the deposit of stone, and . . . well, I had no idea it'd put so much pain and treachery in motion.

"Gorett played at accepting the throne humbly, as if it were his duty to accept it. People speculated he'd kept yer siblings busy elsewhere or had them murdered outright, and for a while people let that gossip go by the wayside since, really, for the most part, Geyser was in all right shape. People felt safe, protected against the Odium—who, by then, were making announcements and broadcasting threats against the city. No one cared. Geyser's people were confident the city was safe and their new king would keep them that way."

Nigel sighed. "Then word began to spread about the deposit, and then the Blatta infestation was discovered . . ." He sounded exhausted suddenly. "And I lost ten of my best men in one week and . . . well, everything plumb went to shite. I holed up and prayed for the best, that yer father and Mr. Wilkshire's plan wasn't ruined, that maybe the Sequestered Son made it out . . .

"And as luck would have it, ye survived and, well, now—there's hope."

His smile was tired but there.

Clyde lowered his head, shook it. It was all so much to take in. His head swam, as it had after Nevele's kiss but different; it wasn't a swelling of the heart, a blossoming of good feelings inside of him but a crushing that kept driving him further down. It wouldn't have felt much different if the cavern ceiling gave out right then on top of the house.

Nigel gripped Clyde's wrist. "Geyser can be great again. The citizens can be brought back. The water will flow again once the Blatta are pushed back and Gorett is relieved of his duty." He gave Clyde's wrist a shake as if testing his attention. Clyde looked at him and nodded, although solemnly.

"This is big," said Clyde, breathless.

"That it is. And I don't mean to lay such a heavy burden on ye, lad, but Gleese depends on this. The fall of Geyser means the fall of the rest of the rock. We're pretty much all that's left besides Adeshka and, well, they're a bunch of money-grubbing sods. The Odium will return when they know they can easily raze the city. Gorett must be stopped."

"But what about the others? My siblings? My mother? What about them? I had heard that King Pyne, my . . ." He wanted to say father but couldn't bring himself to—not yet. It still felt too fresh and alien to him. "He had other children, didn't he? Where are they?"

"Gorett was successful in displacing them. They're scattered among the stars, lad."

"Dead?" Clyde grimaced. *Can this get any worse?*

"No, but conveniently out of communication range when yer father's days became numbered. Maybe when word spreads far enough of what has happened, they'll come back. Bad news travels fast, for certain, but not fast enough in some cases. Either way, ye were born first and, as the fates would have it, also a fabrick weaver. They were good people, yer two younger brothers and little sister—"

"What were their names? Were they like me?"

Nigel blinked. "Lad, there will be time for all that later."

"But what about my mother? Where is she? Was *she* like me?"

"Yer mum, Susanne—bless her heart—she was a *wondrous* woman. She was a commoner, like any of us, but if anyone was ever to be destined to be a leader's wife, it was her. And to tell ye true of it, Clyde, behind every great man there's always a woman."

"But was she like me?" Clyde pressed.

Nigel continued on dreamily as if he hadn't heard Clyde's question at all. "I knew her, back before she and yer father were ever acquainted." He scratched at his arm, and Clyde focused on one of the tattoos: a faded 58th encircled with chark thorns. "Big heart in that lady."

"But where is she now? She's my last connection, if my brothers and sisters are really that far out of reach . . ."

Nigel's hesitation confirmed to Clyde the worst was true even before he said, "She passed away giving birth to yer little sister, I'm afraid . . . I really wish I had more good news to impart to ye in this story, but the whole thing is rife with tragedy and there's no two ways about it. If anything, I hope it gives ye the mettle, a fire under yer arse, to want to make things even more right."

Nigel sighed. "Forgive me, lad, but I wanted to get what I knew in yer ears before ye set off. Perhaps it was cruel of me to lay this all on ye before the trip ahead, but Mr. Wilkshire trusted me with this. He knew that when he was running out of time and Gorett was seeking to have him killed for what he knew, ye would survive and possibly come this way. It was to be my job, if all else failed in the fraternity, to hide ye down here." He gestured at the house around them.

"I apologize for pointing the gun at ye before, when ye first arrived, but consider it some impromptu acting. I couldn't let the others become aware that I knew who ye were, if they were holding ye against yer will. Of course, I can see now that those others ye travel with are mighty great friends."

Clyde brightened. "They really are. And I understand. There's a lot to be wary of now. I probably would've reacted the same way."

"No." Nigel showed his crystal teeth in a wide smile. "You wouldn't have. A good bloke, ye are. And that's why, when the time comes, ye'll make a great leader. Always true, like yer father, saying what ye mean and what ye intend regardless of who may be around. Stubborn but in a good way."

Clyde stared at the cracked leather cover of Mr. Wilkshire's journal. Nothing of what Nigel was telling him had been within its pages. Besides mention of a burdening thought, it had all been figures and tabulations, reportage on the day's progress, and some sheets used as scratch paper for mathematics with the occasional doodle, poem, or grocery list. He looked up at Nigel. "What if I don't want to be king?"

The miner cocked his eyebrows and sat back. "Well, I can't say I'm surprised to hear ye say that; I just figured it would've taken a while." He struck a match on the underside of his armrest and brought it to his pipe. "It's like anything in life: ye take it as it comes. Being the new employee of anything is hard—learning the ropes, knowing what to do and, more importantly, what not to do. I remember when I started down here in the mines. Mr. Wilkshire taught me how to use the diggers and how to properly wedge wendal stone out of its surrounding rock without damaging any of it. Back before, ye know, we were getting bits and pieces and not wholly intact deposits the size of a house. He was patient, understood that people fresh to a new task will make mistakes.

"And that's what ye'll have to be: patient. With yerself. It'll take time. But ye know Gorett *must* be stopped. On that task, ye cannot allow room for error whatsoever." He sat forward, pointed the burning end of his pipe at Clyde. "Ye have managed to gather a good circle of people around you, and that is most fortunate. I will help ye in any way I can.

"I apologize for laying such a hefty load on ye like this, but it's up to ye, Clyde. Ye have to be present when Gorett is slain so ye can inherit the throne."

"Slain? But I don't want to . . . *kill* anyone." That word, like *the Odium*, tasted bad.

Clyde put his face in his hands. Here he was, feeling as if he were simply trying to scrape by. He relied on his friends to do a majority of the work, and he figured it would be Nevele in the end to kill Gorett, since she seemed to have just as much, if not more, of a reason to see the corrupt prime minister dead. And now, he himself had to take charge of their task—to quell the bumps in the road, steer them proper.

"Ye can tell the others or keep it to yerself. I wouldn't blame ye either way. But, as it stands, yer survival means everything to Geyser. The citizens will support ye once they know the truth. They will take up arms against the Odium if they know they have someone at the lead who will stay sturdy. It's a damned tragedy that ye cannot remember yer father, because he would be such a great example for ye. But this way, it can be something new and exciting. Ye will do great things that are all yer own, learn as ye go, and be yer own man."

Clyde was a shade more okay with all this than he had been a minute ago. Perhaps Nigel was right: all it would take was time to get used to it. "Thank you for telling me this. And I'm sorry if your telling me this might result in a jinxing coming your way."

Nigel sniffed a tiny laugh. "I'd only be jinxed, Clyde, if what I told ye was something I felt bad about. Yer secret is one I'm happy to part with."

"I'm glad to hear that. But if you'll excuse me, I believe I have to step outside for a moment. I need to be alone, take the remainder of the night to think this over."

Nigel's smile soured into a grimace. "I'm sorry, lad. It had to be said. I couldn't very well send ye into the mines without telling ye. I know ye will do what needs to be done, but if I didn't tell ye and—fates forbid—ye were killed . . . well, I just don't know what would've come of me. I'd probably do myself in if ye died not knowing. And it may sound selfish, but I had to tell ye before ye left in the morning."

"I understand," Clyde said and got to his feet, his head a bit whirly. "Thank you for telling me. I mean it. But I need to take as much time as I can to mull this over before the others wake up."

Without another word, he stepped away, out the front door, and gently closed it behind him. He couldn't get to the porch swing fast enough. He dropped into it and rested his head in both hands. *Too much, too much, too much* was all he could think.

CHAPTER 30

The Plea, the Demand, the Order

Night was nearly over by the time the Executioner returned to the palace. The elevator platform locked in place, and the three guardsmen appointed to watch it were plainly perplexed.

One stepped forward. "Where are the others? Was there some sort of mishap?"

Vidurkis shoved past him. "One side, boy."

He crossed the palace courtyard and took to the front steps. Navigating this place would be easy even with his eyes closed. The blond stone steps, the echoing halls, and even the iron rings on each of the palace's doors were like old friends to the Executioner.

Besides the lack of people in the courtyard, something else was different. There was the low drone of a single Patrol auto, and long cables ran from its open engine compartment to the courtyard stairs and in through the open door.

He paid it little mind. He left the path of wires crossing into the communications room and took to the second and third staircases, walking in total darkness for a few spells, passing the countless busts and statues of kings and queens drenched in shadow. Without knocking, he entered Pitka Gorett's private chambers in the palace's stronghold.

Gorett, looking as if he'd aged about twenty years since Vidurkis had last seen him, sat up at his desk, setting aside his radio. He goggled at the Executioner, then his desk.

The radio squawked, "Sir, he didn't come back with any of the men. Do you want us to apprehend him? Sir?"

"Mallencroix. You're back. What a relief." Gorett sprang out of his seat, stopped, and stacked a few sheets of blank parchment on his work, covering the typewriter, as if Vidurkis were some sort of ape and wouldn't notice.

He turned down the radio as the guardsman was saying, "I believe he went into the palace. Should we do something, or do you wish him to remain alive? Sir?"

He flapped around the desk toward Vidurkis, frantic, smiling, waving his hands about. He urged the Executioner, "Speak, man! Tell me what happened. Did you kill her? Let me get you a drink of water." He was halfway to the sideboard, where a carafe of water and some glasses waited.

Vidurkis said nothing, merely took a seat. He liked being able to ruffle Gorett so easily. He was sure he looked frightful, filthy from head to toe and covered in all of those mouse bites. He hadn't bothered washing any of the blood off. He'd left it to dry into a brown, crackly sheet on his face and hands.

"She's not alone." Vidurkis accepted the glass of water from Gorett but didn't take a sip—didn't *dare* take a sip, no matter how tempting the purified water was. He set it on Gorett's desk. "She has an entire band with her: a pack of mice under some kind of fabrick, a pale man in a butler's uniform, a Mouflon as well."

"We already know that. But did you kill her?"

Vidurkis caught Gorett's expression before he'd turned himself away to hide it. Ashamed of his fear, possibly. Vidurkis savored the idea that it wasn't just little

Margaret that Gorett feared but Vidurkis himself as well. The Executioner allowed himself a little smile, hearing the sheets of dried blood on his cheeks crack.

Gorett turned away with his hands clasped behind his back. He looked out his giant windows toward the southern wards.

Vidurkis gave his bad news without an ounce of care. "She's gone back in."

Gorett's beard did a little flip when he turned his head over his shoulder. "What?"

"She's gone into the mines."

Gorett's snowy white beard flexed as he clenched his jaw. He turned again to, Vidurkis assumed, hide his panic, but his reflection still allowed the Executioner to view it. "What the hell is she up to? She could've left the island, built a raft or something, gone to the mainland, to Adeshka, told them what we're doing here. But . . . she went back inside. To what end?"

His tone was strange, as if he were heavily distracted by another project, as if he were feigning concern for what Margaret was up to. It was as if, given a few hours, the problem would resolve itself by some other means.

Vidurkis didn't like playing second fiddle. But so long as he was here and expected to give answers and updates, he played along. He couldn't very well tell him nothing. He thought of Gorett as an infant in that moment, wrestling and wailing and in need of the teat. He indulged but kept it brief.

"I chased them into the Kobbal Mines. My way was blocked. They might have some friends in there. They seemed prepared for it, at least. I couldn't get through. I got the Mouflon with my gray light, a heavy dose of it. The effects should slow them down, but I'm afraid unless I get to him in the next two days, my usefulness will be drastically reduced." Now Vidurkis was acting. He wasn't worried at all about getting to the Mouflon. He just wanted Gorett to be scared he might soon be down a man, his most useful one.

Gorett faced him, brow furrowed. "What do you mean?"

"Come off it, Pitka." The chair creaked beneath Vidurkis as he sat up, as much as it hurt his tired legs to do so. "You know how it works. He wanted to add, *Leave me to it, fool. I know what I'm doing*, and nearly did let the thought fall out from his lips. He prepared for Gorett's next salvo of questions.

Gorett merely grunted, took his seat behind his desk, the lush leather grunting under him, and folded his hands. He leaned forward until his forehead was pressing upon his thumbs. "Fabrick and its endless rules and backwards curses," he said, muffled.

"I need to kill the Mouflon," Vidurkis stated, pulling his leg up to cross it at the knee. He had to deliberately keep himself from picking up the glass of water and downing it. "They're in the mines, the entrance blocked. They are undoubtedly halfway up into Geyser's stem by now. If I could go down to them, meet them halfway . . ."

Gorett looked up, pink thumbprints in his forehead fading away. "Perhaps they've already met their end?" he suggested excitedly. "Maybe the Blatta have done the job for us? Do you think that could be the case?"

"The clouds in the corners of my eyes say otherwise." Vidurkis sighed. "I have no choice. I'll have to go in after them."

"Can't we just give you some of the others?" Gorett gestured at his personal gray light lantern on the edge of his desk. The shielding was up, and the dark thing in the fluid bobbed, waiting for the electrical charge that'd make it blast its own, less powerful gray light. Vidurkis sneered at it.

"I don't want your duplicates. I have my gift. I want to keep it as is."

Gorett spied the lantern, silent for a while. "Very well. Take your men down with some explosives." He slid the shielding onto the glass shaft of the lantern. "Do what you must."

Vidurkis sat forward. "Chasing where they've already been would be a waste of time. I'll go where they aim to come out—cut them off at the pass."

Gorett frowned, then went saucer eyed. "What are you suggesting, exactly?"

Vidurkis stared back, blinked.

"No." Gorett shook his head, his hair swinging in silver banners in front of his face.

A smell found its way over the desk to Vidurkis's nostrils. The king hadn't been bathing, apparently.

Gorett slammed his hands on his desk. "Absolutely not. You expect me to allow you to open a hole in the platter, possibly let the Blatta in here with us, just so you can go after the Mouflon? Take your curse like a man, Vidurkis. Let the Blatta execute them. You'll be taken care of after all this is resolved. I'll grant your freedom. Once I have the wendal stone, I'll ensure you have a great home in the best end of the residential ward, where you'll never be bothered again."

Looking at the glass of water staring him in the face, Vidurkis swept it off the desk onto the floor. He'd kill Gorett, certainly, but not now. "He has to die," he said slowly, grabbing Gorett's attention from the mess he'd just made. "I won't allow some filthy Mouflon to rob me of my gift. You don't understand my sister. She will get them up here. Either way, the Blatta will breach the surface. If you let me go down after them, we'll be able to control the situation. I'll make one hole instead of several, as they undoubtedly plan to do."

Gorett looked at Vidurkis as if he were about to say something, but then he looked past him.

Vidurkis listened, half expecting to hear a firearm's hammer being thumbed.

But Gorett's expression wasn't that of smug relief— the face he'd most likely develop if he ever managed to get one up on Vidurkis—but one of red-faced shame. Vidurkis savored Gorett's slapped look for a second, then twisted in his chair to see who'd interrupted their talk.

In the open doorway stood a single guardsman private.

Gorett waved him in, cut his eyes at Vidurkis to silence his mad plans. "What is it?"

The guardsman clicked his heels, bowed. "My lord, the communications array is up. Do you have the message prepared?"

Vidurkis watched Gorett, who eyed the covered type-writer.

"Message?" Vidurkis asked with a smirk, sitting up. "Who are you summoning here now, Pitka?"

"No one." Gorett shifted the pages and furtively extended a sheet to the private between two fingers. "Formalities. Arranging a supply drop is all."

"My arse." Vidurkis snatched the paper with a snap.

Gorett sighed, allowing the Executioner to read the

note. The private stood by uselessly, gaze darting about the room. No one had told him he could leave, so he remained trapped here.

When Vidurkis finished, he balled the page up and threw it at Gorett. The trash bounced off his beard and landed on the surface of the desk in a tight knot.

"The Odium," Vidurkis said, spittle flying. "You're proposing a treaty with *them*? You call yourself a man of power, a man of action—and yet here you are, begging that degenerate band of pirates for assistance? Have you seen what they did to this city?"

"I thought you'd get along charmingly," Gorett said, bold now with a guardsman nearby, "seeing as how you subscribe to the same delusional faith. The Mechanized Goddess who says that the first screwdriver ever devised is a holy relic to be cherished for all time and that weapons are but tools and we, the gun wielders, but tools for her—"

"It's the first *wrench*. And I'd recommend, when you're in my presence, you leave her out of it."

Gorett sighed and gestured at the guardsman. "Leave us."

As soon as they were alone again, he stepped around the desk, avoiding the broken glass and spilled water, and sat in the chair next to Vidurkis. Together they faced the tall windows behind the desk, the cloudless blue sky. Vidurkis couldn't help but think that at any moment Gorett was going to use that natural tableau of the surrounding galaxy just beyond the atmosphere as a speech to say—

"You can come, too. We can all go. Let the girl and the Mouflon do what they will. They won't be able to get any of that wendal stone out of the ground. And even if they did, the entire island's on quarantine. No one will help them move it off-world. The Odium, once paid, will treat us well. They must. We'll return once the Blatta go back down when their food supply is gone."

"You're promising that wendàl stone to everyone, aren't you, Pitka? There won't be any left by the time you're through. You probably have every square inch of that deposit covered in IOUs. If you allow me to do what I want, none of that haggling with those *animals* will be necessary."

Vidurkis looked to his left. The throne. Black metal, beautifully wrought, with numerous inset gems and spirals of iridescent glass. Then, letting his head drop onto the seat back, Vidurkis saw the mural of King Pyne with Lady Susanne, with the geyser behind them, both clad in heavy-plated armor. Together they cradled a blade of emerald metal, one rumored to be crafted from the tempered marrow of dragons. At their feet, their children. Four little cherubs with their faces obscured by the artist, either with tufts of flowing black hair stirred by an ethereal wind or the hanging spiked branch of a chark bush. Those four, all seemingly ghostly pale in comparison to their parents' rather olive complexions, were the rightful heirs to the Geyser throne who were still, last he heard, missing. Had Gorett had them assassinated? The oldest, if he hadn't died of respiratory problems, couldn't have been older than twenty this year. Making the others eighteen, seventeen, and sixteen respectively. Children. All this—the throne, the painting of the likely dead Pyne offspring—haunted Vidurkis faintly. It wasn't so much the evil Gorett had perpetrated that bothered him but the desperation in the act itself. That he'd do anything to keep the lion's share on his plate and his alone.

When Vidurkis leveled his gaze back to the man next to him, he realized Gorett had been giving him a long stare. His tone was dry, pitiful, and small. "I mean to survive this by any means necessary. As much as I want you to retain your eyesight and your power, I'm afraid I cannot sacrifice my safety and the safety of my men. The Odium will work for us, as long as I promise them payment. I've seen the wendal stone down there. It's an enormous deposit—biggest ever recorded, an entire continent of it right under our heels. And it's mine—and yours, if you just cooperate with me."

Kill him now, the Goddess chimed to Vidurkis in his mind, as she sometimes did. *He is as useless as an auto with no wheels. Treat him as the scrap he is.*

But he resisted. She had a plan, indeed, but he wanted Gorett around a little bit longer. Just as a means to keep things stable up here. Plus, they'd most likely turn on him—Executioner or no—if he slayed the king. And then who would help him dig? Every piece in the clockwork had a purpose.

"I sacrifice my abilities for no payment," Vidurkis said, "whether it be wendal stone or a home in the finest corners of any residential ward. Some dark god deemed me fit to carry this gift, and I will not squander it for material goods I won't even be able to see. You forbid me to tunnel, and I will do it anyway."

"Have you shared this insane plan with your team? What did they say about you getting them killed in the process?" Gorett stood, walked to the window, apparently done trying to appeal to Vidurkis as if they were just a couple of mates.

The Executioner watched Gorett's back, assuming what he saw out there—that among the parked Patrol autos, there'd not be a single mechanical walker returned from the ones they took. And how there might seem to be fewer men than usual running in place for evening drills. As expected, Gorett turned back with horror written on his face.

"You . . ."

"They were slowing me down."

"Has that poison in your eyes seeped into your mind?"

Vidurkis stood and dusted off some dirt clinging to his uniform, hiked the rifle strap higher onto his shoulder—ignoring its plea for use—and said, "Send your men to the keep. We're digging immediately. You tell them to turn on me, and I'll rattle up a mutiny on you, let them know you're planning to abandon them." He marched across the chamber floor.

"But I want them to come with me. In my message, I ask the Odium to bring crafts that have plenty of room for *all* my men."

"All your *luggage*, more like." Vidurkis grunted, facing the doors. "You can come down and watch or not. I'm getting that Mouflon regardless. After that, my sister and the other man if you want, but the Mouflon comes first." He shoved the door open. "Remember our agreement. That is, if your gracious hosts let you live to keep it."

Once he was clear of the chamber, he heard the sounds of Gorett painstakingly unballing his message, frantic and pathetic. Marching down the hall, Vidurkis heard the king summoning the private, desperation in his reedy voice, "It's ready."

"Worm." Vidurkis sighed.

Outside, the dawn soaked its warmth into the brambly thickets of his beard and hair. He surveyed a handful of guardsmen yawning and standing about in armor, sipping tea from earthenware cups. Noticing him, they stiffened and set aside drinks and morning meals and saluted. He looked each up and down and ordered one by one, "Pick. Shovel. Wheelbarrow. Pick." He pointed toward the palace. "Get your tools and go."

So long as they did as he told them, he'd let them live. He felt a burn etch into the back of his neck and wheeled around on his heel. Sure enough, high above was Gorett, framed and set behind a thick windowpane like a worried creature on display. Vidurkis gave the king a salute and a smile.

The king, face twisted in disgust, turned away.

"Run with your tail between your legs," Vidurkis murmured, gray eyes fixed on that window. "Go right ahead."

As the guardsmen moved the equipment into the palace, across the main hall and down the narrow stair to the keep, Vidurkis stood outside on the front balcony overlooking the city's square. He gazed at the stone finger of the geyser. In his mind, he saw the mural of Pyne and his children. Vidurkis recalled the security footage he'd been shown after being freed from his cell and allowed to shower. The Mouflon and the man in the dinner jacket, standing before the elevator. They both had their backs to the camera and what the lens had captured had only been a scant two or three seconds, but it . . . blended together easily, with the mural. The man in the dinner jacket was pale, but he assumed it was just because of the camera's poor quality or an effect of the fluorescent lighting around the elevator station.

Could that be one of the Pyne sons? He had two—one dead, yes, but another two that may or may not still be alive. Maybe Gorett wasn't so ruthless, after all. Maybe one of them had made it back. Or maybe those rumors Vidurkis had heard whispered in the cells were true. That the firstborn had really survived and Pyne had tucked him away into some cache off-world somewhere. What had they referred to him as?

Gray eyes on the geyser, Vidurkis whispered mindlessly to himself, "The Sequestered Son."

He marched up the palace steps, his filthy, torn cloak flapping behind him. He left the speculations of Pyne kids alone; it was useless thinking. The teeth of that thought didn't align with those of his other thoughts. To keep his brain well oiled and moving in the right direction, he had to maintain focus, all frivolous thoughts engineered out at once.

He reached the palace's front doors, found the men waiting with their tools, and pointed toward the stairs to the keep. Still, though, what a thought that'd be. The Sequestered Son to come along and be the thing, instead of him, to broom Gorett off the heap of needless things. It'd be fitting, if nothing else. Almost worth letting him slip by, if that was indeed who he was.

Snagging a brazier off the wall, Vidurkis approached the open cell door—his cell. He shoved the burning end into the dark, cramped room and pointed at the outermost wall. "There." With the men setting in to dig, he stepped aside and returned to the thought of the Mouflon and Margaret. The teeth between the thoughts grabbed at once. "Yes, this is what I should be planning right now."

The men walked around him, paying no mind to what Vidurkis muttered.

"Run. Carry that fat Mouflon body of yours to wherever you think you can hide. Keep digging, chipping away, chasing off the Blatta with torches as long as you can. I will find you. I will tunnel to the center of Gleese if I have to. I'll come out on the other side, chase you to the ends of the world and beyond if it comes to it. Even if my sight leaves me and I have to dog you by smell and sound, I will find you." He blinked, swallowed, a slow smile creeping up.

"The Mouflon wants me to find him. He sees my plans. He sees the future as I intend to have it written," he mumbled, addressing Margaret. When they were just toddlers, they could communicate without words, but that was long before they despised each other. "The Mouflon and I pull to one another, Sister, and my plan will become his. He will be my ally in the darkness with you, even if he doesn't know it. You see, little Margaret, I've had time to shape my skills and tighten my fabrick. I can do things now of which you have not even the foggiest—"

There was a presence near him. Already, his periphery was clouding. He had to turn to see the soldier.

"Executioner. Sorry to, uh, interrupt, but the men are ready to begin. By your command, sir."

He gave a curt nod.

The private nodded. "But, uh, what should we do if we encounter any Blatta, sir?"

"What do you think you should do? Shoot them! Shoot anything that moves down there—unless you see a brown-haired, fat Mouflon. By absolutely no means are you to kill him. Wound him, capture him—but bring him in alive. My sister, the others, those damned mice—fire at will. But that Mouflon is mine, understood? Go! Start digging. But once you reach the catacombs, you're to stop. From there, I'll be going alone."

"Understood."

CHAPTER 31

Dressing for the Occasion

"Have you been out here all night?" Nevele stepped onto the front porch.

Clyde nodded. He was on the swing, knees pulled to his chest. For hours, he had been watching the bats marvelously steer themselves around the stalactites.

She took a seat next to him, careful not to squish any of the sleeping frisk mice who had joined him sometime in the night. She placed a hand on Clyde's knee. "Hey. You okay?"

He met her gaze and feebly grinned. "I'm . . . just nervous about heading into the mines."

"We'll be fine. As long as we stick together, everything will go fine. We'll get up into the stem, work our way through the tunnels, break into the catacombs and the sewers, and then we'll go for the palace. I guess since Flam's uncle used to work in there, he should know the way—if his memory serves him."

"Yes."

The word *memory* triggered a lot for him. He tried to dig through the membranous wall dividing him from his father, King Pyne. The man whom Mr. Wilkshire, Clyde now knew, was very good friends with—probably a lot like how Clyde was friends with Nevele, Flam, Rohm, and Nigel. There was a certain goodness and warmth found in the mere idea of having friends, people he could trust through thick and thin. Clyde thought about how Mr. Wilkshire had lost Pyne. It must've been unbearable to lose someone so dear, but then again, Clyde could relate.

He tried to focus on Pyne for a bit, prying between the mental blocks of stone that divided him from the recollections of his own father. Even if what lay beyond was painful, it was his and he wanted it, good and bad.

There were no two ways about it. He had jinxed himself, and there was simply no breaking that.

"Are you sure you're okay?" Nevele leaned over Rohm to study Clyde. "You look a bit paler than usual."

Clyde forced a smile. "It's just that it's morning, and here I am on a porch swing and there are no suns. It makes me feel strange. Guess Flam's rubbed off on me." He couldn't look at her face and lie, which probably made the falsehood all the more obvious.

Her laced brow creased.

"Really, Nevele, I'm fine. Say, speaking of Flam and suns, what sort of state do you suppose he'll be in today?"

Nevele rolled her eyes. "Gracious, I hate to even think . . . Well, I'm going to get ready. Perhaps you should do the same. Tough day ahead of us." Without another word, she got up and started back inside. Hand on the knob, she said, "As much as I don't want to deal with his sour suns-starved mood, where is Big Fuzzy anyway? I haven't seen him—or heard him—all morning."

"Last I knew, he was downstairs working on his blunderbuss."

Flam had the downstairs barracks to himself. Every bunk

bed in the entire room was vacant, tidily made. He stared at the spring frames on the bottom of the mattress above him, zigzagging. It reminded him of a heart monitor, like the one that had been hooked to Nevele at the facility. A steady beat, a good heart, thumpa-thumpa. He pictured that metal line going flat, the shrill electronic squeal heralding death. He recalled everyone in his life who had died. His mum, pa, one of his older brothers—and, of course, his uncle Greenspire.

He closed his eyes, and a thick tear squeezed out among his bristly lashes, curved down his cheekbone, and dripped off the tip of his ear.

All night, he heard the same thing over and over in an endless circle. It started in the middle of the night, when he finished repairing the blunderbuss and decided to turn in. He tried his best to ignore it, chalking it up to night-before jitters or perhaps a latent case of claustrophobia, but it came as steadily as the pulse in his chest.

Before long it had a voice.

Keep digging, chipping away, chasing off the Blatta with torches as long as you can. I will find you. I will tunnel to the center of Gleese if I have to. I'll come out on the other side, chase you to the ends of the world and beyond if it comes to it. Even if my sight leaves me and I have to dog you by smell and sound, I will find you.

It would end and start its cycle anew but not before he saw a series of images of his friends all monstrously slain.

"Meech help me," Flam said, raising his paws and rubbing his wide forehead. He gripped the ends of his horns and pressed their points into his hands. The stony tips dug into both palms, but he continued to push until he could take the pain not a second longer. He shouted, and the unremitting chant subsided at last.

He laughed. He'd stopped it!

Keep digging, chipping away, chasing off the Blatta with torches as long as you can . . .

He thrashed and kicked the blankets from his legs and pressed a cloth to one palm, then the other. He dressed, gathered his satchel and bandolier, and rushed downstairs, as if it were possible to outrun his poisoned mind.

Flam shoved out through the front door of the miner's house. There they all were, not at all as his bleak imaginings had painted them. They were doing as any group would to raise their spirits for the road ahead.

Clyde and Nigel sparred with sheathed daggers, Nigel propelling his chair around to mimic what a Blatta might do, shooting forward for a rushing attack and then immediately retreating.

Rohm scattered in a dizzying spray in all directions and then retracted into form.

Nevele aimed her guardsman pistol at the blotches of bat guano on the stone walls.

Flam, not wanting to alert the others to what plagued his mind, took the blunderbuss from his shoulder strap and plunked a round into the chamber. He was sure to secure the safety catch before he approached the group, afraid of himself and what his hands might do.

He did some target practice off on his own, returned good mornings when they were sent his way, and tried not to rouse suspicion.

He'd been hit by gray light before. It had gone away, but it was never like this, never so . . . ensnaring. Maybe once they got on the move with a task at hand, he might be able to ignore it. He pulled the trigger, and the scatter-shot went more or less where he wanted it to, snapping the rounded tip of a stalactite from its stone shoulders.

The satisfaction didn't last. The murmur set in louder than before in the fuzzy din in his ringing ears. He reloaded like an automaton, his mind reeling off one prayer after another to Meech on high: *Please. Make this thing let me go.*

Later in the morning, Nigel came outside in his wheelchair with a box on his lap. He checked the time on the pocket watch from his waistcoat and snapped closed its golden lid. "It appears ye are all set to go and yet, at the same time, not at all prepared." He tucked the watch away.

The group stopped their exercises and turned to the mustachioed miner.

Clyde was still new to wielding the dagger, and it took him three tries to get it back into its sheath without jamming the blade into his trouser pocket or through his belt loop.

As Nigel hummed down the ramp of the porch, Scooter on his shoulder, Clyde noticed that the large cardboard box on his lap held several folded garments, buckled straps, and loose clasps that chimed with each bump.

Clyde looked at his own tuxedo, which was becoming threadbare in the knees and elbows—to the point even Nevele could do nothing to salvage it—and was in dire need of a good laundering. It smelled of all the places they'd been.

Nigel threw the brake on his chair. He pulled the bundles out one at a time and tossed them over. Unfolding his pile, Clyde realized it was heavy, industrial overalls with sturdy bands of metal-woven leather crossing the chest and waist, a deep hood with an attached respirator mask, and a boot connected to the end of each pant leg. Out of a pocket, a pair of insulated gloves fell, and Nigel explained that the wearer could grip metal at white-hot temperatures without even feeling so much as a lick of heat. Next Nigel handed out accessories for the suits that could button on or clip to the garments: goggles, extra holsters, canteens, tinned rations that'd never in a million years spoil, and of course ammunition for not only Flam's blunderbuss but Nevele's pistol as well.

Helping one another, they all put on the miners' outfits and did up the complicated series of zippers, flaps, toggles, buttons, and clasps. Rohm was the only one who required no assistance. The frisk mice poured into the open collar, and the suit ballooned like a ghost taking up residence inside a sack.

"It'll be hot as blazes one second and freezing the next," Nigel explained. "That's the give and take of the mine, and ye will have no choice but to deal with it. Ye can unzip vents under the arms of the suits as well as in the gloves and on the hoods. Keep them zipped until ye get so hot ye can't think. Leaving one open by accident and letting a glob of magma drip in there probably wouldn't feel all that delightful."

"*Delightful*," Scooter squawked.

Nevele's and Rohm's suits fit well, but Flam's was a size too small and Clyde's was a size too big. They decided to swap, and yet the same result was found. The others had a nervous bout of laughter.

Nevele took pity on them and sent her stitches out to

repair the suits. The hem was let out of Flam's, and suddenly there was room for his gut as well as the remainder of his girth. She stepped over to Clyde and extended a hand toward him. The stitches moved out and he wiggled through every inch of the suit. She retracted the stitches and patted his shoulder, the suit tailored perfectly. "Good as new." There was a slight quiver to her voice that even her reassuring smile couldn't hide.

Next, Nigel took out a box of flashlights: chrome rods with bulbs netted with metal on the end. He passed them out to the travelers. "A torch for each of ye, plus batteries. A miner's best friend, these."

Once everything was in place, Nigel looked them over, nodded. He held Clyde's gaze, and while the others were doing some last-minute adjusting, Nigel addressed him with a jut of his chin. He reached into the box and stealthily took the last item out.

He presented it to Clyde: a greasy rag cocooning something heavy and oddly shaped.

Clyde unwrapped it: a shiny green, ornate revolver with a very long barrel and highly wrought etchings. The grip displayed the design of a large broadsword between flowing gusts of wind or smoke. Lifting it from the box, he immediately felt its weight. It seemed like some kind of anomaly of physics, as if it should weigh half as much. Clyde ran a thumb over the designs and turned it so Nigel could see.

"Commencement," Nigel said. "The spirits passing, one folding into the other. One passing the sword, the other receiving it. The ceremony and the weapon have the same title . . . Have ye told the others what I told ye last night?"

"Thank you, and no." Clyde tucked the gun,

Commencement, into the hammer holster on his miner suit's hip. The balled rag he held for a moment, wondering if it too was part of the artifact. In the bottom right corner of the stained rag was monogrammed *AW*.

Albert Wilkshire. Always with him.

He carefully folded the handkerchief and slipped it into the pages of the journal.

"I'd offer ye another weapon, but I tore the place top to bottom last night and couldn't find anything besides my own and . . . well, I'm afraid I can't let ye take my own blunderbuss. Kind of need it to keep myself safe, ye understand."

"Yes." Clyde deposited the journal into his pocket. "But I suppose I have to tell them now, don't I?"

Nigel looked grave but nodded. "I was going to give it to ye after all this was said and done, bring it to ye myself, but it's the only weapon I had lying around."

"Will they know it was my father's gun?"

The others came over, their preparations finished. To Clyde and Nigel's chagrin, it didn't take them but a second to notice the new gleaming piece of emerald metal in Clyde's holster.

Flam laughed. "You could probably hock that thing for a pretty penny when this is all over. If you want my help, I know a guy who knows a guy who—"

"That's . . ." Nevele said, aghast. She looked to Nigel. "How do you have that? That thing's been lost for years. Gorett nearly turned the entire city front ways back looking for it."

Nigel took the accusation full-on, said not a word, merely twitched his eyebrows in the direction of Clyde.

"I'm sorry, lad. I think the bear cat's out of the bag."

Nevele was confused but not nearly as much as Flam, who kept looking from one face to another.

"The royal revolver," Rohm added, reaching but not daring to caress the ornate grip of the gun flanking Clyde's hip with their tail fingers.

Clyde felt funny, as if he'd been given a present he liked for one reason but was envied by all the others for entirely different, deeper reasons.

Nevele looked Clyde in the face, her eyes shining but her expression dire, as if she'd been tricked. She had to swallow twice and take a deep, hitching breath before she could muster the words. "I had thought it was like the stories about Höwerglaz. Just made-up things to keep young weavers having hope that there was someone out there who had it worse than us, who was just waiting to . . ." She huffed, going red faced, too astonished to speak for a moment. "I just never thought in a million years that the Sequestered Son was a real thing."

Nigel piped up. "He is, lass. And here he stands: all one hundred pounds of him, shite-stained overalls and all."

"You're really him?" Nevele asked, afraid to be too close to him, it seemed now, as if he were a fragile piece of sculpture too delicate to even so much as look at.

Clyde shrugged and smiled. "I suppose I am."

"How do you like that? Rags to riches in a Meech-damned week and never even had to leave the rock once."

When Clyde looked at the Mouflon, he saw he was smiling with pride, but it was just his style to not let it be too obvious.

Nigel gave Clyde a swat on the butt. "Ye all can talk

about it at the after-battle tea and scones."

The declaration came as a relief to Clyde. He didn't like all this attention on him, especially when it was for undeserved nobility.

"Fall in!" Nigel barked.

The ragtag group did their best to file before the miner.

Nigel circled them in his wheelchair, making sure everyone had the ventilation zippers done up, all boots laced, tools in their proper places.

Even Scooter scrutinized them from head to toe and nodded in a perfect mimicry of his companion.

Nigel drew a deep breath, and Clyde could hear the doubt it was packed with. "There were no maps of the mine," Nigel said after a while. "We miners just knew our way by a few symbols that are pretty easy to understand. An *O* marking means it's a safe tunnel, okay to travel. An *X* means it's not safe. My little trick—ye see an *X* and think of a skull and crossbones. Of course, with all the activity going on in Geyser, the flooding and whatnot, ye may end up having an *X* tunnel that means *O*, as in, *Oh, shite*, instead of, *Oh, okay, it's safe*. So be on the lookout.

"Once ye get through, ye'll head up until ye hit a cavern like this one. It was kind of a base of operations, and there ye'll find the rock crusher and maybe a few supplies if the bugs didn't get them. Beyond that, taking the first *O* tunnel ye come to, ye'll reach the way station at the base of Geyser. That is where the turbine works and sewer systems connect to the mines. Follow the turbine works up until ye hit the catacombs. The sewers will be right above them and the keep above that. Got it?"

They nodded.

"All right, then." Nigel's voice rose to an enthusiastic shout that got Clyde's heart pumping. "Ye got the wardrobe. Ye got the know-how. And if I say so myself, it looks like ye rough-and-tumble nail eaters are ready. Let's take this city back."

Within minutes, from high in the cockpit of the digger, Nigel ducked and shouted to the group, "Ready? There's going to be a whole slew of them, I hope ye know." He took the controls of the massive digging machine and told Scooter on his shoulder, "All this time we've spent trying to keep these blasted things out, old chap, and here we are letting them in."

Scooter picked at his fleshy side, indifferent.

"Here goes nothing." He advanced the lever to activate the digger's blade.

The four travelers faced the entrance, the screeches of the hungry Blatta beyond impossible to ignore. With the digger using its battery for the engines, the miner's house went dark and the lights above flickered out. The whole cavern darkened, but the headlights mounted to the front of the tremendous machine were brilliant, throwing their passageway into luminosity.

Clyde swallowed, and his dry throat clicked from the effort.

Flam removed the light stick from his belt and swung it on. He looked Clyde's way and offered a thumbs-up that would've been encouraging if it weren't for the stream of sweat trickling off his brow.

Beyond Flam, the frisk mice steadied themselves within the sleeves of the miner's overalls and inside the mask, using the goggle lenses as portholes.

To his right, Clyde glimpsed a bright flash. The blade slowly rotated against the wall, gaining speed. Crunched rock poured out, and the air thickened with dust. Beneath the blade, a small gap was made. Bony, yellow arms could be seen already reaching out. The Blatta's heads appeared within the narrow space, pincers chomping and dagger-like teeth gleaming.

Clyde felt like his skeleton might pop right out of his body and run away screaming at any moment. He redirected his focus to Nevele, whose appearance had just the opposite effect. He felt grounded looking at her, as if his soul had suddenly been equipped with lightning rods, safety measures for what storms may come. Sure, there was danger ahead, but it was okay. She was here.

Over the ceaseless noise—the machine, the bursting rock, the screaming army of insects—he shouted to her, "I don't know what to say to you right now. I mean, I should've told you as soon as Nigel told me."

She interrupted him with a smile, blinking away one wave of brown dust after another. He read her lips: "It's okay."

Clyde withdrew his ornate pistol and, with some concerted effort, cocked the hammer. He'd had only a few minutes of training from Nevele as Flam and Nigel had prepped the digger. They couldn't spare any rounds for the unusual weapon, so he hadn't fired it. He didn't want to, anyway. Holding the thing made the rumbling in his stomach double. He was afraid of hurting himself—or, worse, someone else. He kept it pointed toward the ground. Nevele had instructed him to never, ever aim it toward anything he didn't want to see dead. She repeated the warning with unwavering sternness in her voice: "Never, ever."

Letting one hand free of the revolver, he palmed his goggles to suction them onto his face. The dust was unbearable, and he dreaded getting a blinding face full of it right when he needed to see. With his thumb, he cleared the brown patina collecting on each lens.

Abandoning these last-minute distractions, he made himself look at the breach in the cavern wall. Long, jointed legs twisted in the opening, clawing at air. Once and again, an eye or a mandible passed—horrors they would have to fight in a moment.

Above, Nigel screamed to be heard over the digger. "Since counting to three is considered bad luck among miners and ye already got enough of that on yer side, we're going to four. Understand? On four!"

Rohm held out the sleeves of the overalls, ready to spray its numbers out, ready to sacrifice its members. The ones standing as captain and cocaptain in the porthole goggle lenses gave one another a reverent nod.

"*One!*"

Flam cocked his freshly repaired blunderbuss, sweat freely dripping from his waterlogged fur. He blinked some away with his long, bovine eyelashes.

"*Two!*"

Nevele trained her guardsman pistol on the gap. The Blatta could see her; she could see them.

"*Three!*"

Clyde held Commencement with two hands, aimed the sights down, and found the trigger with a fear-numbed finger.

"*Four!*"

The digger's arm lifted, and gunshots rang out in a frenzy.

The Blatta scattered into the cavern in a flood, tripping over their brethren, who were shot down immediately. They scattered up the walls, across the floor, toward the travelers.

Rohm pitched its arms forward one after another, throwing volley after volley of mice. They covered the Blatta closest, going between the plates of the insects' exoskeletons and relentlessly biting.

Flam's blunderbuss released one blast after another, sending scattering buckshot into the insects.

Clyde and Nevele, side by side, slowly backpedaled and fired round after round, covering for one another while each reloaded.

Nigel, in the digger's cockpit, leaned out with his own tribarreled blunderbuss and killed those that climbed his way.

The pandemonium seemed to last for hours.

Soon the deluge tapered off. After a few of the fatter stragglers were put down, the cavern was quiet again.

The travelers were safe and completely unharmed, save for a scratch or two. They collected, carefully trotting through the mess of dead Blatta: broken, bony legs and spilled ichor. The entire place now stunk as if someone had extinguished a smoldering trash fire by getting violently ill upon it.

Nigel was waving his arms and shouting.

Clyde brought a hand to his ear, signing that they couldn't hear him.

The digger's engine still filled the cavern with its roars.

Nigel bellowed, cupping his hands around his mouth, "Go! This thing is running out of gas. It can't hold the arm up forever. You have to go now!"

The four exchanged glances, making sure everyone was ready to go, and charged. They ducked under the swinging blade of the digger, which came within inches of the tops of their heads, and through the tight breach. Flam barely squeezed into the gap last before the digger's engine gave out and the arm slammed earthward, a foul gust chasing them as metal crashed against stone.

Behind them, nearly rendered inaudible from the commotion, came Nigel's last call of encouragement: "Godspeed!"

Inside the cave, the floor was uneven and the walls jumped out in random, sharp outcroppings. It was a place where nature was still listed as owner, and it didn't have any conveniences, such as lights or guardrails. Nothing but darkness lay ahead. And it was cold, Clyde noted, putting the revolver away.

Flam angled his light stick around the group. In the cobalt glow, Clyde saw behind them the digger's blade parked among the rubble, completely blocking their path back. The sheer isolation of this place made him feel as if he'd been swallowed by the planet itself.

Still, on Nevele's face he saw determination, although wavering.

Rohm, spying from behind the goggles, looked resolute, if faintly nervous.

Nevele said, "Well, whether we like it or not, we're on our way." Her voice echoed and returned to them altered. It was a haunting sound, as if there were dozens of women in the impenetrable darkness mocking her.

Clyde clicked his flashlight on, turning it toward the path ahead. The passage became tall but narrow, and the walls smoothed out like that of the Geyser's stem, undoubtedly made up of the same sedimentary rock but covered in a thin membrane of Blatta . . . goo. Each time they stepped forward, the scent ripened. Pungent death polluted the tunnel.

Shining his light at something catching his ankle, Clyde gasped. The others moved up around him to look as well. He was ankle deep in what at first glance looked like a basket but was actually a human rib cage tangled with rotten clothing. Unable to help himself, Clyde yelped and kicked the bones away, sending them scattering.

Rohm pinched a broken rib off the floor, the captain and cocaptain in the portholes peering at the specimen. "They must use acids to break down their food. If they're like their cousin, the cockroach, they reduce their prey to mush. In a crowded, close-knit society, where there's such competition for sustenance, it'd be beneficial to make their meals as soft as possible so as not to risk damaging their teeth, lest they become unable to eat and become dinner for their fellow Blatta."

"Isn't that lovely," Flam grunted.

Clyde took a step up the tunnel. "Let's get moving," he said, the idea of being turned to mush making his stomach flip.

The others followed, clicking on their torches. In single file, they ambled sideways into the first passage, marked with an *O*.

CHAPTER 32

Arrangements

The armory had more weapons than Vidurkis could carry on his back, so he had to prioritize. With a guardsman nearby, he went through the racks of guns: the rifles and pistols, the shotguns and harpoon launchers. He walked on to consider the bladed weapons: the swords, spears, and daggers. He pictured himself trying to get through a tight spot in the tunnels with a heavy sword and getting its cross guard caught on something, only to end up devoured by Blatta.

He kept his supplies to what he was familiar with: two daggers, which he slid into scabbards and clipped to his belt; the trusty rifle he'd carried since his security detail days; plenty of rounds, which filled four pouches on his belt. He added a few necessary items: a pick, a load of block-shattering explosives, a chisel, and a hammer. He went to the end of the line to a display of intriguing weapons behind a locked grate. "Open it."

"Weapons for the Patrol elite guard only, sir."

Vidurkis glared. "Do you see this on my lapel, boy? Executioner. Make with the key. Get this open. *Elite*. Honestly, now."

The guardsman went through his hoop of keys and, with shaking hands, unlocked the grate. He pulled the doors open and gave the Executioner ample room to browse.

Vidurkis picked up what appeared to be a canister the size of a paint can, with a metal hoop stuck into a plug on the top. There were no markings on the black metal housing the device. He turned to the guardsman, holding it in both hands. "What is this thing?"

The guardsman swallowed. "It's a winger grenade, sir."

"A winger grenade?"

"One pulls the pin; out of the top come six dozen mechanical birds. They are used as scouts to report back or, with this switch on the side, can be set to kill on sight. It's mostly used for recon, but it has been tested in the field for lethal purposes, with mixed results. But, sir, I wouldn't recommend—"

"I'm taking it." Vidurkis dropped it into his bag of supplies. He felt the third day niggling, creeping up on him, time running out. The device could be useful as a last resort. Perhaps one metal sparrow could find the Mouflon, dig out his heart, and save Vidurkis his sight as well as his fabrick.

"Any tool in the right hands can be useful," he muttered, quoting the eighteenth decree of the Mechanized Goddess.

"Sir?"

"All right," he said, seeing nothing else of interest within the cache of elite weapons. "Close it up. I'm ready to depart." The guardsman closed and locked the cabinet, and they turned and exited the armory together.

They treaded the three sets of narrow circular stairways to the keep. There, the men were piled tightly into Vidurkis's former cell, chiseling and hacking away at the stone. Many had stripped their armor in the heat. Piles of dirt lay everywhere. Prisoners coughed and sneezed from the dust as one shovel load after another was thrown through their bars so that the walkway wouldn't get dirty.

Vidurkis got to the door of his old cell and peered over the hunched, sweat-slick backs of the toiling guardsmen. They had gotten nearly six feet down already and had just about broken through into the sewer system. Apparently it had been tapped already, perhaps in a single pock from a pick, because a nauseating odor wafted up. It was a smell he found grossly familiar. He'd spent years in this very room, stepping outside its walls only once a month, when they put the hose to it. No, he didn't have an actual bathroom and working commode. The soles of his feet were still waste stained and probably would be to the grave.

The sharp recollection suddenly soured him and made his patience disappear as swiftly as a canary was turned into a handkerchief in a parlor trick. He shoved the men aside, toppling one. Snatching one of their picks, he brought it overhead and drove it into the gap, taking one bite of rock away at a time, as they had been doing but at triple the speed.

The guardsmen shrank out of the cell and watched him but genuinely recoiled, bringing their hands up like spooked maidens when they heard the sole drawling howl of the Blatta inside. Vidurkis ignored it and continued picking in violent swings. When he heard a scuttle of the bony legs of a Blatta pass directly outside his newly made gap, only then did he stop.

He looked over his shoulder. "I hope you protect your king. I hope he takes you all with him, as he says he will. I even hope he pays you. But know this: Once I am in there, I will not hinder the Blatta's desire to get in here with you and him. I have other objectives than His Majesty's safety, whereas you men probably do not. Serve him well, and tell him that I saluted you."

They nodded, readied their rifles.

He said to himself, hacking away at the stone, "Fools. Standing down here with me, with your backs to the man you think you're protecting. All the while he's slipping out the back door to leave you to this nightmare. You deserve what you get."

"Pardon me, sir, but . . . what did you say?" Vidurkis remembered the voice: it belonged to the guardsman who had assisted him in the armory. He had stepped forward when all the others remained back with puzzled looks on their moronic faces.

"He's leaving you all behind. He's siding with the Odium," Vidurkis spat. "Leave me alone." He lifted the pick for another swing at the rock. Sharp bits stung his face. He squinted and continued.

"But surely he's trying to make peace with them to prevent another attack."

Vidurkis was out of breath. He set the pick down and leaned on its handle. He said over his shoulder, "Surely nothing, boy. As if you couldn't tell, Gorett is as greedy as a two-ton sow, and if there's one thing a sod like him understands more than how to finagle and cheat, it's how to keep from getting caught."

"But he's our king," the guardsman said, his voice hitching up at the end of the whine as if he were hearing his own naiveté for the very first time and trying to bite his words before they left his mouth. And then, as if trying to convince himself, "He wouldn't do that. Not with them."

"He will, and he has." Vidurkis glanced at the young man but had to look away. *Had to.* "Don't look so damned surprised. It's frighteningly pathetic to see that look on someone as young as you. You should be in the prime of your rebellious years, traveling the world, doing what you want to do, not taking orders from anyone. But I reckon it was a family trade, was it not? Pop a guardsman, Grand-pop a guardsman, now you. Perhaps you should ask to be relocated in the next life. Somewhere warm, maybe, where independence and free thinking are encouraged instead of frowned upon. But I suppose idiocy runs in your family, too, eh?"

Vidurkis heard a gun pop from a holster. The click of a hammer being cocked. Vidurkis glanced over his shoulder but had to turn to see him clearly through the fog in his eyes. The guardsman was aiming right at him, hands shaking. "You're a liar. They all said you were. I don't know why I'm—why any of us are down here helping you. Just because you outrank us doesn't mean we have to listen to you."

Vidurkis knew the guardsman boy felt as if he were serious and choosing a side. It made him sigh. "Even though I just suggested adopting independent thought, I'd recommend reminding yourself who you're pointing that at. My recommendation: put that steel away, boy."

"Draw and f-face me," the guardsman barked, voice cracking.

Vidurkis estimated him a moment, chuckled, wiped his brow, and lifted the pick to return to his task.

"Face me! Face me and d-draw! In the name of King Gorett, I c-command it."

Boots grated on flagstones. Vidurkis couldn't see them

but knew the other guardsmen were making a slow retreat. At least some of them had sense.

A shot rang out, colliding with the wall of the cell. Vidurkis glanced and was in awe to see how close the boy had dared to shoot. Mere inches away. It was sufficient to get him to wheel about, casting the pick aside and going for his own sidearm.

The guardsman fired a second time and missed again. Vidurkis made no move to dodge and weave. The others made for the staircase, and the prisoners in their cells flanking the carnage let loose the exclamations pouring from minds they had lost long ago.

The boy didn't have it in him to fire again. Vidurkis slapped the gun from his hands, maneuvered the barrel of his own weapon up fast, tucked it under the guardsman's chin, and discharged—all in a singular, swift motion. The man lay dead at his feet, the chorus of prisoners' anguish reaching a crescendo.

Vidurkis pointed his weapon at them until they stopped screaming. They had been his caged neighbors for years. He'd probably spent more time in close proximity to them than his own kin but had never spoken a word to any until now. "Shut up!"

Even in the silence, he didn't feel sated. Knuckles white on his gun at his side, sweat squeezing from every pore, he needed something . . . more. He brought his focus to the guardsman he had just slain and examined his slack face, his still-open eyes. He fired again and again until there wasn't much of a face left. He dropped the empty brass onto the guardsman's chest, reloaded, returned the gun to its holster, and went back to work, mumbling to himself.

Gorett paced the communications room countless times. The message had been sent to the Odium leader, but no word had yet come back. For hours he listened to the endless hammering, drilling, clanging of pick on stone. He cursed the madman. "I should've left him down there to rot," Gorett muttered to himself. "But if he stops the girl and her pack of troublemakers, all the better. One less way the wendal stone has to be divided." He wasn't planning on paying Vidurkis, anyway. Gorett had managed to pull the rug out from under a king before; a strange-eyed psychopath would be no trouble at all.

"Message incoming, sir," one of the communications officers said, pressing the headphone tighter to his ear.

Gorett leaped toward him and yanked the headphones off the guardsman and strapped them to his own ears. A spray of his white hair cut over his eyes. He listened, staring ahead. The screen of the receiver was picking up the signal from eighty thousand kilometers away, in the Gleese ice cap region.

The voice was drawling, words incomplete or slurred, a strange vernacular spoken. Gorett listened intently for his answer.

"Here we are, right after we gave you a thorough bashin', and you, the stinkin' King of Geyser, want to make a deal." Guttural laughter. "You wanna put aside our differences and talk about givin' you a lift outta town? Why's that, Gorett? Got a bit of the bug problem? Can't get an exterminator on the horn? You evacuated the damned city. You know now it'll be all the easier for us to boot you and your men off that footstool you call a city and keep the place to ourselves, don't ya? Mayhaps that's what we'll do."

There was a long pause. Gorett was terrified the message had ended.

The Odium leader smacked his lips and continued. "You say you got wendal stone under that mushroom of yours? Consider me interested. You and your merry band of men can come aboard; we'll go out a few clicks, maybe have a picnic and a sleepover or two, come back and take care of that creeper-crawler problem o' yers, but—listen good now, okay?—we want half of that deposit. We want to be there when it's weighed. We want to see each pebble of that shite pulled out of the ground, and we want to see the math bein' done. You ain't going to cheat us like you did your townsfolk. No, sir. We get half, and if it's as much as you say it is, then we have ourselves a deal. Day after tomorrow, we'll be by to pick your arse up. Be out front, town square, highest suns." The message ended with a mechanical bleat.

Gorett held the headphones to his ear, the drunken and crooked talk of the Odium leader silenced. Half. They wanted half of the deposit. He threw down the headphones and marched away from the communications room. Whether he agreed or not, they'd be there the day after the next—at highest suns. He couldn't imagine how it would go if he went to their waiting ship and told them to forget the whole thing. He saw the slaughter that'd surely follow. They'd probably rig Geyser's stem with explosives and topple the whole city, just for having wasted their time.

A shot rang out from somewhere in the palace.

Gorett rushed into the hall but kept his distance from the staircase.

Up from the stairwell on the north wing rushed a platoon of guardsmen, all too frightened to answer, and the ones who met his gaze had a marked look of disgust in their eyes.

"What's happening?"

As if in answer, the piercing screech of the Blatta echoed through the palace, followed by a bevy of muffled gunfire. Gorett spun. He rushed to his private chambers, threw the security switch, and closed the room up tight.

Hours passed. No one called; no one knocked.

Gorett smoked one pinch of mold after the other, stared out the slits in the windows between the security panels, and watched the town square. He begged time to speed up. He wanted to be gone from Gleese, away from all this trouble. Even if it meant being half as rich as he'd expected. Whatever it meant to avoid being ripped apart by Blatta and having his body used to feed their young.

"Damn you, Vidurkis." He'd said it countless times since locking himself in. He looked at the windows where his reflection, crumpled in the throne, hands shaking, glared back. He had no one to blame but himself, but he would never admit it.

He continued cursing the Executioner, watching the purple sky darken past his own ghostly image, which became clearer with each passing minute. He watched for trailing, blinking starboard lights of an incoming craft, but after an hour he finally locked with his reflection. For the first occasion in time beyond counting, he saw his age: the creases and dour expression he apparently carried all the time now. He still fancied himself straight backed and strong in build, a young buck in the tumultuous world of Geyser public office and, before, on the street with his mum. Not so much anymore. The grief and paranoia had taken their toll patiently, between glances in the looking glass.

"Damn you," he said, not meaning the Executioner this time.

The four didn't encounter any Blatta from the time they left Nigel to when they arrived at the first widening of the cave. As Nigel had said, there was an area where the miners could gather tools and supplies. Everything looked ransacked and broken, as if the Blatta had ruined anything humans had ever touched out of sheer spite. Nestled between two jagged outcroppings at the farthest back wall of this new cavern was a corrugated steel lean-to with a crank-operated water pump. Flam gave it a couple of pushes, but from its spout came only a cough of rusty dirt. Flam sighed and recapped his canteen.

Clyde looked to the far corner of the next set of mine chambers. One was marked with an *X* and a second with an *O*. He considered insisting they press on, but exhaustion gripped him. His knees and back roared, and the bottoms of his feet felt as if they'd been handed over to a carpenter and sandpapered to the bone.

They had been at it for hours, climbing steep inclines of one tunnel after another, wiggling through tight corridors, and negotiating dark passages, always with the fear another wave of Blatta would bottleneck them in. He wasn't sure if it was the worry of being cornered and unceremoniously eaten alive or the trek itself that wore him out so.

He toed the plateau's edge in the miners' rest area,

seeing the infinite crevasse stretching down, down, down to where the light terminated in vast, swallowing darkness. It might take entire minutes to fall, an endless drop of kicking and screaming and tumbling, before the abrupt end. The thought triggered his feet to step back.

He turned and scanned the area. If they stayed away from the edge, used the lean-to as a shelter from the cold, and always had someone on watch, it might make a suitable temporary camp. "I think we should take a rest here."

Flam kept his distance, staying at the opposite edge of the yawning gap. He played with the pump handle some more, filling the chamber with a metallic screech with each pull and push. "Fine by me."

Rohm's overalls crumpled and deflated into a pile, mice filtering out through the sleeves and collar. They seemed happy to be out, the final few bleary eyed and panting from the congested heat in the suit. "Whatever you think, Mr. Clyde," they chimed as they sought out some soggy cave mushrooms and a wispy strand of tree root to nibble.

Nevele pushed back her hood and straightened her hair. Her eyes never rested on any one thing for longer than a heartbeat, Clyde noticed. She'd twitch at every movement, drip of water, or anyone taking a step by her. She blinked and stared past the dripping stalactites at the slumbering bats, hanging inverted high above. "I don't care for this place. Nope. Not one bit." It sounded as if she was attempting to be humorous, but the truth of her joke fell on Clyde's ears.

Flam grunted, picked up a pinch of mold from the wall, and stuck it in his pipe. "I don't think you have any room to talk. It was your idea to go this way. If it was up to me,

I would've sooner stayed down there with Nigel and his bird. At least they had bathrooms."

Nevele turned toward him, put her hands on her hips. "And what? Just wait for all this to blow over? Either way, we were going back to Geyser to get at Gorett. If it were up to you, we would've knocked on the front door, asked if we could allow Clyde in for a moment to get his revenge, had tea, and been off."

"We haven't even gotten through a full day yet, and you two are already fighting?" Clyde lowered his voice. "Either way, let's try to keep it down. Who knows how many more of those things are in here."

Nevele looked down. "You're right."

Flam seemed incapable of looking Clyde in the face, returned to toying with the pump handle, clutching his empty canteen in the opposite hand, hoping for a miracle. Finally, he pitched the canteen away and, leaving a trail of smoke puffs in the air behind him, approached Clyde, face serene, determined. He got halfway to him and stopped and, as if remembering something, turned around. Then he turned back around. He walked toward Clyde again, one hand balling into a fist over and over. He seemed to remember something else and walked in a different direction altogether.

Clyde looked to Nevele.

She shrugged.

They watched Flam mosey around the space awhile, shaking his head and lightly pounding a fist against his forehead.

Clyde took a wide sidestep away from the edge. "Something wrong, Flam?"

Flam muttered a halfhearted apology, faced the wall,

and began picking at his fingernails.

It was only when Nevele spoke again that Clyde's attention was peeled from the Mouflon's back. "To answer you, yes, I too think this would be a fine place to camp for the night. And I agree: the fighting needs to stop." She dropped her bag, which slapped against the stone.

The noise made Flam jump. He shot Nevele a glare over his shoulder and returned to facing the wall, picking his nails.

"A lot stands between us and Gorett," Clyde said. "The Blatta, Vidurkis, Gorett's men. And who knows what the conniving crook himself will have in store for us. So let's keep the quarreling among ourselves to a minimum, yeah? It's the last thing we need." He wasn't sure where it came from, this new take-charge way, but he hoped it would hang around. He didn't like being bossy, but the fighting needed to be addressed, sternly, once and for all.

Flam grunted at some frustration he alone was feeling and returned to the pump handle, raising and lowering it in slow, grating screeches. "Fine," he said after a moment. "Sure thing."

Two of Rohm's members approached and offered Flam a twisty length of root. He shook his head, and the mice brought it next to Nevele. She accepted it, chewed it as if the hairy, kinked brown thing were bubble gum, and thanked them. The two mice, fascinated by her willingness to eat something so ugly, immediately bolted off to find more.

Time was impossible to gauge down here with no suns or clocks. It was dark for as long as it was cold, which was to say those conditions never changed. They rested for what Clyde approximated to be an hour, but he knew he couldn't trust his own internal clock: what felt like three weeks to him was apparently six months.

He was glad to see Nevele get to her feet, brush herself off, and walk to him. At the brink of the plateau overlooking the gap, she kicked a rock into the darkness. There was silence for a frighteningly long stretch and finally a soft crack, then another, then another, as the rock pinballed between the walls until it made one last resounding clack and all was still again.

"I liked what you said."

Clyde looked away from where the rock had gone, still imagining it was himself down there, broken and lost. He slowly stood, knees stiff. "What did I say?"

She stared into the dark but smiled. "Kind of reminding us what we're doing. How he and I"—she thumbed over her shoulder to Flam—"need to cool it with the bickering." She looked at him. "You took charge. Like any prince should."

"Don't call me that."

"Why not? That's what you are, the Sequestered Son, Prince Pyne, Clyde Pyne. A folktale come true, in the flesh right before me. I have to say, I really believed in you about as much as I did Meech, the Great Mouflon from the Mountain." She flicked her eyes toward Flam to see if he caught that slip, but he appeared to be asleep.

Clyde shrugged. "I don't feel any different."

"I can't imagine you would, really. Big changes take time to sink in. But you sure sound different. You did for a moment there, anyway. Like him, your father."

"I did?"

"Yeah. Kind of freaked me out. Clear message in a big voice. Exactly like him, when he wanted something to be known that was important."

"I wasn't *trying* to sound princely, though. I guess I was just fed up with you two tearing into one another all the time." He smiled.

"Well, let me be the first to tell you that you sound the part, even if you don't want to." She kicked another rock over, and this one hit the opposite wall sooner than the first had. It banged back and forth all the way down. She watched, long after it wasn't visible anymore.

"You've certainly come a long way in a matter of days," she said. "From servant to adventurer to prince, all in about a week."

He grunted, simply to let her know he'd heard her. He didn't really want to talk about this much more but was happy to oblige Nevele now that she seemed to be happier since resting. "So you knew my father?" It felt like everyone knew him except Clyde.

Nevele shook her head. "I worked in the palace, sure, but I knew King Pyne about as well as someone gets to know their boss who's ten levels up. On occasion I'd have to bring something to his attention, and when he looked at me, he really . . ." She laughed. "Yes, just like that."

"I'm sorry. Was I making a face?"

"I really can't believe I didn't see it sooner. Take your mother, take your father, put their images together, and then remove all the color, and . . . sure enough, it's you."

"I look like them?" His voice hitched, mimicking his heart. He wished Nevele had a picture or a bit of footage—anything. His imagination could scratch out only so much detail.

Nevele nodded, auburn hair falling from behind her ear and into her eye. She swept the unruly strand back with a pass of her hand, momentarily covering her averted eyes. He wanted to ask her to describe them, but she spoke calmly and quietly before he could ask, her gaze fixed on the shadow-choked abyss. "I want to tell you about them, everything I know and remember, but the memories wouldn't compare to the people they really were. Not at all." She looked at him. "You should feel honored having been among some amazing people, Clyde. Not just your mother and father but Albert Wilkshire too. I barely knew him, but if he raised you—even somewhat—he must've been a great man."

"What were they like, my parents? I mean, I know you didn't know them really well or anything, but . . . for the few times you did see them?"

"Well." Nevele developed a broad smile, looking out to the cavern wall across the way as if they'd appeared to her among the rocks. "They talked to me, looked at me like I didn't have . . . all this." She gestured at her stitched cheeks, her sewn forearms. "Just like you do."

"And my brothers and sister?"

"Now, they I never really got a chance to meet. By the time I was working in the palace, Moira had been sent to Adeshka for school—"

"Sorry to interrupt, but Moira is my sister's name?" He liked the way her name sounded, the way it rolled off the tongue.

"Yes, she was the youngest. And there was Raziel, your younger brother after you, and Tym, your second younger brother."

"And were they like me? Were they woven, too?"

Nevele shrugged. "Sadly, I don't know. If they were, they never had any problems that I was aware of. I dealt only with abuse of weavers, and their names never came up. Which, I suppose is a good thing—even if I never did get to meet them."

"Where do you suppose they are?"

"Well, if they're smart"—she smiled—"unlike us, then they're worlds off, trying to keep a low profile. Gorett, as the rumor went, sent some people after them. Some not-so-nice people."

"To *kill* them?"

"I'm afraid so."

Flam looked up. "To *kill* them?" Clyde was asking, stupidly. *Little lamb, so dumb to this world and how it works. So blissfully ignorant to everything.* At every turn, his idyllic picture of this world was being shattered. Fool.

"I'm afraid so," Zippergirl said.

Flam listened, turning his ears this way and that, catching her words both from her lips and in the echo that played after it. She sounded a lot like her brother sometimes, when her voice reached certain octaves. Certainly a similar cadence, especially when the cavern distorted it. It made Flam wonder, for a flash, if Vidurkis wasn't in here with them now.

With his mind wistful, his body feeling not in the least his own, Flam stood and approached the two who had their backs to him.

It would be easy enough. One hand on each of their backs, a single strong shove toward the ravine. Gone. Simple.

He continued to walk until he caught himself midstep and stopped. There, at his feet, was a single frisk mouse looking up at him. It batted its curiously long lashes at him—reproachfully? A glare from a mouse? It dropped to all fours and scurried off.

It was a sufficient enough break for Flam to think things over, get some clarity. He took a breath, tried his best to think of the most cheerful things he could, and went back to stand near the cavern wall, the only place he could find a shred of solace from his plagued thoughts. They gathered like the mud being pulled in around a sink-hole. But at least he was far away from the others . . .

Nevele patted Clyde on the back. "You're not alone."

The members of Rohm who were close sat on their hind legs, looked up at Clyde, and nodded. "We're with you, Mr. Clyde. We liked Geyser back when it was in working order. We, too, could benefit from some good old humdrum everydayness in Geyser again."

Nevele added quietly, "And Flam, too. He lost someone. Perhaps it was an accident, but if it weren't for the overbearing hours Gorett demanded of the maintenance crews, his uncle probably wouldn't have had an accident at all."

She was speaking confidentially to Clyde, but apparently her voice carried.

Flam muttered, "Leave me out of this. Pasty knows what I'm after." He kept his back to them, his horns pressed against the wall. He throttled the water pump's handle in his grip again, pulling down on it until the metal bar bent with a prolonged creak. "I just wanna get him where he needs to go, and that's it. I'll get my satchel filled with wendal stone and be off." He toyed with the snapped-off handle for a moment, weighing it in his hands before letting it fall to the earthen floor. "My uncle was a drunk. He probably died because he was sloshed to the gills on the job. Don't try to make it into anything poetic, Zippers. My story ain't nothing complicated, and it certainly ain't honorable."

"I was saying something nice about you for a change," Nevele barked at him. She shook her head, visibly reining herself in. She turned back to Clyde. "Look. Never mind him. You and I, we have our reasons. Rohm as well. And everyone else from Geyser who's living off rationed food and sleeping in a shack at that blasted refugee camp. And Mr. Wilkshire and King Pyne. They're all our reason to persevere."

"Yeah, you're right," Clyde said. "Thank you. But let's leave it at that for the night." He was weary from such big talk and massive revelations. He wanted some normalcy. "Let's get a fire going, and we'll get our energy back. We've got quite a ways ahead of us still."

How far, he could not say. All he knew was that he craved things the way they were. He knew they couldn't be the same, ever, not after what he had learned about himself. But he'd go until a new normal could be made, and within that, he'd take comfort. He just knew that the time between now and then would be chock-full of unpleasantness. But it had to be done, and he was willing to do it as much as anyone is willing to face less-than-stellar odds stacked against them. He sat back, tossed a fist-sized stone into the darkness, and listened to it sail. If only it were that easy; if only he could just glide in an endless carefree dive and let things come as they would. He thought of one of Mr. Wilkshire's sayings, usually in reference to microwave dinners when Miss Selby had evenings off: *Easy as falling.*

But of course, anything good—anything truly good— was never obtained as easily as preparing a microwave dinner. Or falling.

CHAPTER 33

The Rumor Mill Gets Inundated

A ksel met with Neck Steve in the man's shack, planning all the details of the escape. It seemed it wouldn't be a pleasant affair. Aksel had pictured the Odium coming overhead with drag hooks and ripping the fencing down, lots of noise and confusion, but the actual strategy was much more covert—like a prison break.

Remaining incognito required Aksel to listen to Neck Steve go on and on about how great the Mechanized Goddess was and nod and smile and even dispense a few expressions Moira and Karl had told him he might need to know: *May your gears always stay greased, brother. May she keep your wiring straight always. May she keep the rust out and the cogs turning.* Things like that.

Seemed like Neck Steve felt the need to inject them constantly into conversation. Maybe he was just relieved having a fellow follower with him here, instant friends just because of what Neck Steve assumed they shared.

By the end of the hour-long talk, Aksel was exhausted from playing his part. Leaving, he grinned and gave a sly wave to his new best friend. "Midnight."

"Midnight," Neck Steve said with a broad smile. "We're going home, brother."

"You might be," Aksel said under his breath, walking off. "I'm jumping headfirst into the badger warren."

It'd gotten dark in the meantime. Flashlight beams cut this way and that, and the general din of the camp settled, as it did every night. Cook fires blazed here and there, and the smell of rations being prepared—a bitter smell of processed soy and artificial flavoring—wafted freely.

Passing through the camp agora, he nearly ran into an old woman hunched at the edge of the muddy creek. By candlelight, she was attempting to filter the brown water through an old cotton tunic. Having only one working eye, Aksel had poor depth perception and nearly bumped her off the trash-strewn bank.

"Excuse me," he said, righting the makeshift water bucket he'd knocked over.

The water absorbed into the thirsty earth within a second. They both stared forlornly as the puddle quickly disappeared.

"Ah well," she said, "looks like Gleese needed it more than I."

"Forgive me," Aksel said, bending to fetch her plastic ladle where the weak current was beginning to drag it away. He handed it to her and looked into her kindly old face. While partly obscured by a faded paisley babushka, her eyes were a brilliant green and her smile was perfect, teeth as white as the ivory keys of a new piano.

Her expression folded, from the mundane smile you'd offer a stranger to wide-eyed panic. One scabby hand latched onto his sleeve. "I've been meaning to find you," she said, almost with a gasp. She leaned in close. "I've heard you're the man to talk to."

Aksel recoiled slightly. "About what?"

Could word have spread so quickly about the DeadEye?

What now? Was he going to be the refugee camp's go-to man for settling scores, a problem solver for hire? He needed to keep a low profile.

"I need to get home," she said.

So that was it. "Shortly, ma'am. Heard it through the grapevine we're all heading back to Geyser in a week or two." The lie stung, especially laying it on such a nice old lady, but right now he felt it necessary.

He tried to walk away, but she grabbed him hard, with both hands this time, around the thick of one arm. Her grip was surprisingly steely. "I need to find him and make sure he's okay. He doesn't know anything about the world. I had to leave him. I didn't want to, but I had to."

"I'm sure your son is fine." He would've said anything at this point if it meant this woman would let him go and stop making such a scene. Dotting the perimeter of the agora, faces lit by campfires were openly gawking. Heated arguments, crying, drama of any sort were crowd makers in a place without a single working TV. And a desperate, begging old biddy ranked up there as prime-time entertainment.

"He's not my son," she said, hysterical. "He's . . . he's . . ."

"Ma'am, whoever he is to you," Aksel said sweetly, patting her hand with his free arm as a gentle cue that he'd appreciate it if she'd let him go now. "I'm sure he's okay—"

"But he doesn't know nothing about anything. He's too innocent to be out on his own. Please, I know you're planning to get out somehow. You have to take me with you." It seemed she had no control over herself. Her eyes seemed to apologize for what her mouth was doing. To Aksel, she looked insane. Too much exposure to the suns coupled with too much worry—it could happen to anyone. Some days, it took Aksel conscious effort to keep it together.

"Please," she shrieked, "he can't be out on his own. He can't."

Soon, a younger woman rushed over. "Miss Selby, please, let this man go. He can't do anything to help us." Like all people from Geyser, she had a lilt to her voice, something Aksel had heard originated from a place called Europe. "I'm terribly sorry," the woman said. "She's upset about her boss's good friend. She was close to him and worries a great deal about him."

"It's quite all right," Aksel said, stepping away. He turned and walked on, feeling every eye on him. He took a corner and dodged down an alley, but still his skin burned as if they watched him through the walls of plywood and scrap tin. Everyone in the town center now knew he meant to escape, and word would spread fast.

He slapped aside the curtain of his shack's doorway and let out a ragged breath, his head spinning. What if Neck Steve heard their plan had leaked? What if every refugee begged them to bring them, even if it meant hitching a ride with the Odium? Would Neck Steve call it off, abandon Aksel entirely? Moira and Karl would get word within a day, and minutes beyond that Aksel and Ricky would be in the Lakebed with nothing but endless desert landscape and the ceaseless beating of the suns on their backs, easy picking to whatever hunted them first.

But the most important question simmering to the top: who had loosed the rumor in the first place? Aksel hadn't spoken to anyone about it except Neck Steve, and while dim, he didn't seem like the type to voluntarily ruin his own plans. Too much of an Odium fanboy to allow that, surely.

The back of Aksel's head thudded on the metal wall. He wracked his mind as to how this had gotten out of hand in less than twenty-four hours. His skull ached, reminding him of his most recent hangover. Seeking some sort of solace, Aksel thought about what had caused that recent hangover.

And just like that, he remembered he *had* told someone about the plan. Over beers.

Ricky.

Aksel was halfway to Ricky's stand, cutting through the alleys, when Neck Steve walked out in front of him.

Aksel steadied himself against the side of a shack.

"What the hell happened? Everyone knows."

"I don't know." Aksel wouldn't dare sell out Ricky. Violence and Neck Steve weren't exactly strangers; he'd kill Ricky at the drop of a hat. Aksel was kind of scared for himself in this cramped alleyway.

"This isn't good. Not good at all, brother."

"No, it's not, but it's fine . . . I mean, it will be. At midnight, right?" He glanced at the sky. Just a few hours. "I don't think anyone knows what time they're coming by."

Neck Steve sized Aksel up, as if he were weighing the possibility of just killing him. Apparently his conscience won out. He put a hand to his forehead and stared at Aksel.

"What?" Aksel murmured.

"I just hope they still let us join."

Aksel nodded, then stopped. "Wait. I thought you were already a member." He lowered his voice. "You were in Geyser, planted as a spy, weren't you?"

Neck Steve waved a hand. "Initiation. Well, part one of it. I mean . . . *you* had to do something to prove your devotion to the Goddess, didn't you?"

Aksel scoffed. "Right, of course. Yeah. I . . . yeah. You know, bad stuff. I do bad stuff all the time. It was like, you know, easy. Cake."

Neck Steve drew in a deep breath and, like a bored horse, let it sputter out from his lips. The pirate-initiate dropped his arms to his sides, palms slapping his legs. With heavy-lidded eyes, he said wearily, "Just be ready."

He shuffled toward his shack, swearing to himself.

Heart pounding, Aksel watched him skulk off. "You got it, brother."

CHAPTER 34

Two Curiosities Unearthed

The meager campfire threw golden light onto the wet cavern walls, making them appear to undulate like a breathing, living thing. It was oppressive to Clyde, but then he felt something alight upon the tip of his nose. He looked up and saw in the highest reaches of the fire's light tiny snowflakes slowly descending, extinguishing the doomed feeling just a smidge.

"Must be an opening somewhere." Wiping the flake away, he saw his fingertips were not only wet but streaked with black. He patted the rest of what he guessed was now smeared across his nose. "But I don't believe I've ever seen black snow before."

Rohm hunched by the fire in their miner suit. "Atmosphere mites, Mr. Clyde. They make the air breathable on Gleese. They suck up the toxic fumes from the geyser's spout and turn it into oxygen. But when they get nervous, they make snow instead of air."

"Does that mean the Blatta are near?" Clyde himself became nervous then, but fortunately for his trousers, he didn't make any snow.

"No." Rohm snickered. "*We* make them nervous."

"Useless," Flam grunted, brushing away the flakes that had collected on his horns. "What sort of defense mechanism is that?" He mumbled something else, but it was too low for anyone to hear.

Nevele took another wooden handle she'd found from the broken assortment of miners' tools and tossed it onto the fire. "We're lucky to have them. Otherwise this trip would have been over hours ago, especially after the cavern closed."

Clyde remembered the man pursuing them, firing at them moments before Nigel had detonated the cavern ceiling, saving their lives. Those fierce pearl eyes, that wicked black beard framing a feral sneer. It was nearly impossible for him to imagine he could, in any way, be related to Nevele. He remembered the man shouting her name: "Margaret Mallencroix." Accidentally, Clyde said it aloud.

"It's strange to hear that name," she said blandly, focused on the fire.

"Why? Isn't it the name you were given when you were born?"

"Yes, but I went simply by Stitcher, or Royal Stitcher, while working for King—er, your father. Apologics; that'll take some time. Anyway, he was big on titles and formality. The only people to ever call me Margaret were my parents and, of course, my brother."

"It's hard to convince myself that you and Vidurkis could possibly have a drop of shared blood."

"I can hardly come to terms with it myself. When he was a kid, he'd lash our ponies raw when they didn't do what he wanted. Mother was always trying to get him to have more patience, to show a little heart toward living things. He never seemed interested in doing anything unless it was hunting, harming, or killing."

"Must be why he decided to join the Patrol."

Nevele watched as the fire took the fresh bit of wood,

lapping around the pickaxe handle's length and then chewing into its grain bit by bit. "Yes, I think he joined the Patrol as an excuse to hurt people. It's the only way someone like him could fetch a regular paycheck without becoming a bandit or bounty hunter. He liked Geyser, oddly enough. Took a lot of pride in living there. Claimed he did what he did to root out anything that would attempt to corrupt the city. Lo and behold, look at who he ended up pledging allegiance to."

Clyde imagined Vidurkis and Gorett having meetings in dark spaces, bent over candlelight and whispering their wicked plots to one another. But, if he was thinking on the timeline right, his father was still king when Vidurkis was Executioner.

"Did my father hire him?" he asked, batting some smoke out of his eyes. "I'd really hate to think that he would. I mean . . . I apologize. He's your brother. I shouldn't—"

Nevele merely shrugged. "It's fine." She poked the fire, rolled one log over onto another to get it to burn. "But you have to understand, Geyser wasn't nice around the middle of your father's kingship. For a spell there, people like my brother were necessary to have around."

Clyde nodded, hoping he understood.

"Vidurkis," she said, appearing almost pained in saying his name, "was an extreme man for an extreme time. And when things evened out and the city was a safe place to live and work and raise families, he became sort of redundant. Hated it. Started seeking out crime, going against Patrol protocol. Some said he even started some of his own, bringing bad men into the city from other places, knowing they'd be up to no good. Give himself something to do."

The fire popped, and both of them flinched.

"Do you suppose he'll find a way through the collapsed entrance?"

Rohm spoke up. "I calculate roughly fifty tons of rock fell. There's no way one man could move all that in time to catch up to us. Besides, Mr. Nigel is still down there keeping watch. He won't let Vidurkis past."

"If I know my brother, and it pains me to admit I do, he'll find a way to get to us that won't involve so much work. He has probably already abandoned the idea of coming in through the collapsed entrance and is trying to find a weak spot above to head us off at the pass."

She watched without joy as the big, dark puffball flakes tumbled down slowly. "I'll take first watch tonight."

"No, you need your rest. I don't sleep, remember?"

She looked at him and forced a smile. "I don't think I'll be able to sleep tonight even if I want to. Knowing he's out there is nearly unbearable. I can work on little sleep; it's fine. Once we hit the sewers, we won't have so much climbing. It'll be pipes we can actually stand in and actual ladders. This will be the hardest part of the ascent." She gestured at a nearby passage.

"But thanks to all the volunteers. Your generous offers don't go unnoticed," she called out, voice ringing off the walls.

Off by himself, Flam grunted, mumbled, and rolled away, pulling his sackcloth blanket tight up around his head and neck.

She looked at Clyde and shrugged. "I'm trying to play nice with him."

"No suns," Clyde mouthed.

Nevele nodded. "Right," she whispered. "I forgot about

that." She smirked. "Explains a lot, actually."

"It's not nice to talk about others as if they aren't present," Flam said. "You've decided who's taking first watch. Fantastic. Now cut the chitchat. Some of us still want to get some shut-eye."

Nevele twisted in her place at the fire and stared at the back of Flam's head. She popped up to her feet and said, "I'll start my watch by going down that tunnel over there, see how far I go down it. I'll shout if I run into anything."

"Okay," Clyde said, watching her enter the tunnel marked with a crudely written *O* that looked more like a *G*.

"Finally, some Meech-damned quiet."

When Clyde was sure Nevele was out of earshot, he flung an empty canteen at Flam's back. It collided noisily off him, and he rolled over, giving his attacker a confused sneer. "What's your problem, Pasty?" He threw the canteen back.

Clyde caught it, the velocity slapping it painfully into his hands. "What's gotten into you? I stood up for you just now, saying it was just a lack of morning suns, but it's not that. You've been nothing but a pain since we got in here."

Flam picked at one of the several knobbles of lint peppering his blanket, stalling. "I don't like confined spaces."

Clearly there was more going on. "Did something happen at Nigel's?"

Flam closed his eyes and shook his head. "It's not that. I just . . . I'm going through something. If I put my mind to it, I can work through it. It's not worth wasting your or anyone's time bellyaching about it."

"Flam, we're friends. Talk to me."

The Mouflon pushed himself up onto one elbow and

finally looked at him. And just as he was about to speak, the entire world shook. Deep within the stem somewhere, a hefty boom signaled what felt like their doom.

Nevele.

Clyde jumped up and was about to charge for the tunnel in which Nevele had gone, but a firm hand grabbed him from behind by the belt banding his waist. He spun and saw Flam staring ahead.

"We have to get Nevele," Clyde shouted, pointing.

"Just wait. It's the backed-up water. Wait a second; let it depressurize. If it breaks when you're in there, you'll be cooked alive."

Clyde wriggled. "Let me go! I have to see if she's all right."

"Mr. Clyde," Rohm added, "please be sensible."

With the final word of that plea, as if on cue, Nevele charged out of the tunnel into the cavern with them, carefully minding the cliff where the plateau terminated into the pit, giving it ample breadth. Behind her, the tunnel lost all its darkness. It wasn't becoming brighter, but the murk seemed to be retreating into the walls. Clyde watched, perplexed. After a moment, the air began to mist, and a long gray tongue of steam gently wafted into the chamber. He understood.

After a few minutes, the rumble faded and then stopped altogether, but the loosed steam seemed as if it might go on for much longer than the quake that had freed it.

The four stood completely enveloped in a bubble of soft white so dense that none of them could see very well. They held on to one another's suit straps to prevent anyone from taking a bad step into the pit. The fog was made doubly worse when the atmosphere mites above contributed their own visible reaction to the shake-up.

Clyde looked at the three others around him and laughed with relief.

"Guess we can consider that way out of the question," Nevele said, staring hard into the gray where she assumed the tunnel was. She shook some mite snow from her hair. "Too bad, too. Looked like it connected with a main shaft. Might've been able to get out of this mess by tomorrow afternoon if it hadn't . . . *exploded* like that," she yelled. She probed a pinkie into her left ear, wiggled it around. "Mercy, that was loud."

"Can I propose a new rule?" Clyde said, still catching his breath. "Can we *please* not split up anymore?"

Nevele grimaced. "Gross. Who spit up?" She eyed Rohm. "It was one of you, wasn't it? I know that was scary and all, but there's no reason to go vomiting all over the place. Where was it? I don't want to step in it."

"Not spit up—*split* up," Clyde said, laughing.

"Yes, and we do not throw up," Rohm said. "Some might say we're incapable; others say we've evolved to genetic superiority."

"Well, you learn something new every day," Nevele said.

Clyde took her new pluckiness to be a direct reaction to her near-death experience. It was a playful side he hadn't seen, and he hoped to see more of it.

As the mist cleared, collecting on the walls and floors, the four let go of one another and returned to their campfire, now just a soggy black smudge on the floor.

Nevele dropped to her knees on her blanket and then spun to sit. In a heartbeat, her movements went from twitchy and excited to languid. "You know, I might take you up on your offer to take first watch. I suddenly find myself very much in need of rest," she announced, still shouting.

Clyde smiled. "Certainly."

"If you don't stop screaming like that," Flam said, "I might be forced to . . . to think of something nasty to say to you once my heart stops pounding so hard." He gave Clyde a wink and bent to rebuild the fire.

"Ha," Nevele said, pulling the blanket up to her chin and staring at the chamber ceiling. "You're a funny one. A real laugh a minute." She looked to Clyde. "My throat hurts. I'm still talking loud, aren't I?"

"It's okay." Clyde sat next to her. He patted her knee, which was trembling.

She met his gaze. She had been really, really scared. Her hand found his, mittened in the wool blanket. She patted it and held on.

Clyde turned his hand around so they were palm to palm. The amber glow swelled upon her face. Soon her smile was gone as she watched the timber take to the fire.

He gave her hand a squeeze and hoped it freed her thoughts from the fearful events. When death was narrowly evaded, he didn't feel plucky. All he felt was thankful.

CHAPTER 35

The Loss of Many,
the Loss of One

Vibrations loosened some cinder blocks, sent them tumbling off the walls and raining around Vidurkis. Pressing one hand to the sewer wall, he brought his opposite arm overhead to block any pavers that might fall his way. The eruption was an immeasurable distance below, but he could feel it in his legs as if the entire island had become dislodged from its groundings and was now floating freely in the bay. In a moment, it was over.

Sitting before his meager fire, he stared into the open sewer tunnel ahead. He had gotten through the catacombs with no difficulty. The Blatta were dumb beasts that attacked impetuously, going at their prey with no tactical foresight. For such notoriously indestructible predators, their bony husks were no match for his guns. Each bullet had found its mark, piercing their shells with remarkable ease, spraying their guts out in satisfactory splats.

He had hollowed a few of them out, wearing their wings on his armor and spreading their green blood on his face. From inside their bodies he pulled slippery organs, things he couldn't identify, and even though he had more than enough rations to spare, he cooked and sampled some. Not one was worth another bite.

He felt like an animal again, in the wild—something

he hadn't had the pleasure of experiencing for quite some time. Sure, in the palace keep, he'd used the gray light on the occasional rat, instilling a desire in it to be found and released from torment with a quick chop, but those were rats. Mouflons were known to be incredibly stubborn creatures. Vidurkis hoped he had an ally of sorts in the band of travelers, steering them wrong so they would cross paths with him quicker, but he couldn't rely on that entirely. He had only himself to be certain of.

The Executioner sat in the dry sewer tunnel, studying the brickwork all around him. The aqueduct ran parallel, taking water out of the geyser floodway up into the city. If he needed drinking water, presumably all he needed to do was tap the stone pipes, canteen ready. But he wasn't sure what sort of pressure had built up, with the Blatta clogging the floodway. Surely a great amount, considering that eruption a minute ago.

He checked his mental time line. Geyser hadn't had a single rotation of its turbines in close to a week. He pictured hitting the wrong tunnel, tapping the wrong rock, laying a single foul step—and meeting his end.

It'd be a shame when he was so close.

Margaret Mallencroix, her doting pale-faced assistant, the mice, the Mouflon—they were all deep in there, beyond his sight, scant hours away from being found.

Anticipation chased away sleepiness, even though Vidurkis's body pled for rest.

He held a hand in front of his face, fanned the fingers out, and brought them together again. It looked like one triangular black flipper in front of his face. Using his flashlight didn't help. His eyes were dying.

Drawing a deep breath, he lowered his hand and stared into the flames, a mercurial blob of orange wiggling in the surrounding darkness. It made him remember what the Goddess said about hope and those who had it, and he got to his feet. He scraped some dried filth off the sewer floor with the edge of his boot, smeared it over the fire, and pressed on.

Rest was for the weak. He would rest when the Mouflon, his sister, and the others were dispatched.

For hours, he walked.

He arrived at a collapsed tunnel and turned around.

Another was flooded a good six paces in.

Distantly, he heard a low screech: Blatta alerting each other. With failing eyes, he had to rely mostly on his hearing. Dropping to a knee, he snatched off a glove, set a palm on the sewer floor, and held it there gently to pick up any vibrations.

Oh, they were in there. Skittering about drunkenly, screaming at one another. He hoped this trick would allow him to pick up on where his sister was, but there were no telltale two-footed steps being made, just those of the frantic six-legged ilk. Stampeding this way, then that, and back again. Getting closer?

He murmured, "Those who have the best tools will always survive to serve the Goddess best; preparedness overcomes skill." He repeated the last bit a few times, each pass rising in volume until he was shouting down the brick tube where he thought the insects would hear it best. In his palm, he felt the vibration of them halting, shifting, and then charging as one. They organized it that way, it seemed. For that, Vidurkis had to give them a scrap of admiration.

He patiently took the rifle from his shoulder, pulled back on the bolt, and loaded the chamber with a round. Rancid breezes blew into his face. There were so many of them approaching that they were moving the dead oxygen out ahead of them in one big, displaced wave of stinking air.

A scuttle, a low buzz of wings, and a thud of six legs hitting dirt. A slight hesitation for the thing to get its bearings, taste the air, and then another scuttle—this time *fast*.

He fired. The sound of the Blatta catching the bullet with its carapace was the same as if someone pitched an earthenware bowl to the street off the top of a house.

More filed in behind, stampeding over their fallen brother. The kill was all they sought.

In a flash of his hand, the rifle bolt was worked and a new round readied. He fired, but the bullet made the sound of striking rock and ricocheted noisily.

A strange thing happened then. The insects seemed to get what was going on, that they were outmatched even though they outnumbered the interloper greatly, and retreated.

Palming the floor, he felt their descent, a quaver that turned one way, then another, as they expertly navigated secret passages. Soon the floor didn't shake and he couldn't hear anything but the calm rhythm of his own inhales and exhales.

He approached the kill. It was a larger Blatta, most likely a male. On its back with all six legs ramrod in the air, it was like an overturned table of Cynoscopian design. Comical.

He knocked on it, as one would a door, the firm thuds demonstrating its thickness. He was surprised he'd punctured such a sturdy carapace. He searched for the bullet hole, feeling the thing's belly. He found the rifle shot had been drilled right into its horrid face, an inch or two above its vertically opening mandibles. Just for curiosity's sake, since this one was different from the others—bigger and sounded *fuller* inside—he jammed his first finger in the entry wound, popped it out once it was slathered with blood, and brought it to his nose.

It smelled worse than the others, too. Like a bucketful of congealed sickness. Probably to prospective mates, it was a smell that sang of the creature's virility and genetic prowess, proving he was an alpha.

It made Vidurkis think. "Evolution is just the Goddess's way of going back to the engineering drawing board for redrafts." He dabbed the blood onto his forehead, drawing glyphs on his cheeks and chin in praise of her: the First Wrench, the Divine Rivet Gun, the Bloody Hammer.

Finished, he wrung his hands to spread the muck out, then dragged the stuff down his beard's length. *He who wears no crown but the blood of the old king is the man in charge,* he thought. Or maybe said aloud. He was losing track of the difference between thinking and speaking now, not caring at all that he was forgetting it.

He kicked the insect over. When it rolled facedown, Vidurkis thought his eyes deceived him.

The Blatta was wearing, squarely on its abdomen, a saddle. It was crudely constructed, seemingly of repurposed Blatta bones and cartilage, but was clearly a saddle. He bent and touched its seat: well worn. The saddle horn showed where four fingers and thumb would rest. It had gotten plenty of use. It wasn't tied around the thing's middle but fastened to the Blatta's shell itself with organic nails hammered in around the edges.

"Is this your work, Stitcher?"

The prospect of being run down by a herd of domesticated Blatta with Margaret as the lead wrangler made his blood boil. Sometimes he felt like he was possessed, and when a thought crossed his mind that made him angry, he dwelled on it until he was positively seething. He did this now, picturing not only Margaret but the Mouflon and that pale-faced thing reducing Vidurkis to pulp under a thousand trained bug feet as they danced him into bloody mush, blind and unable to fight back. Dying disgracefully.

"No," he said, or thought. "No."

He stomped the head of the saddled Blatta flat and moved on. Time was waning.

The sewer wall at the end of the pipe's line was broken. Bricks lay everywhere, Blatta tracks pounded in the mixed soup of mud and waste. Vidurkis ducked in through the narrow opening and saw that the Blatta's tunnels were not for anyone taller than three feet. Feeling a little disgraced by having to do it, he dropped to his hands and knees and shuffled through the tunnel.

He crawled for what felt like days until it came to a wide opening, the air here surprisingly fresh and cool.

Getting to his feet, he turned and was immediately struck with awe.

Moonlight poured in from above into the interior of the geyser floodway—the actual main line where the water passed from deep within Gleese to the surface, like a volcano but with less smoke and no fire at all, just the occasional column of steam. At first, he thought his mind was painting in what his eyes couldn't see. Certainly it wasn't a perfectly crisp, vivid sight before him, but he could still hear the enormity of this space. How the wind moved and how his own shuffling steps echoed.

He squinted and could mostly make out where, far below, the Blatta had meticulously plugged the floodway. He leaned out a little over the edge, staring till he soon developed a headache. Sure enough, it was the geyser itself, dead and dry. He eased back from the edge, amazed. He had grown up staring at this thing and never thought he'd be inside it.

A movement brought him back to business. Something far below had zipped by, causing him to lift his rifle.

One Blatta, apparently too preoccupied with its work to notice him. A moment later, it wedged into some hidden crook in the wall and was gone.

Now instead of the sky, he was marveling at what the insects had been working on. What they'd done to the geyser nearly appeared to be the work of humans in design.

Apparently they had expelled their muck, one at a time, let it dry in a hard shell from one side of the floodway to the other, building off what the last had laid down. They had created bridges from their regurgitated sick that could've passed for stone at first glance. On the walls of the geyser were nest pods, tiny globular eggs nestled among bone-gray honeycomb. He cursed under his breath, truly stunned at the sight. He squinted down and saw that the Blatta had turned the inside of the geyser into a corkscrew, a path circling down to where it reconnected with the tunnels going deeper. It reminded him of the grooves inside a scored gun barrel, the entire geyser one massive passage for an enormous bullet to be shot from.

And that's exactly what would happen, Vidurkis

thought, once the pressure built up enough. Perhaps the bugs weren't so dumb after all. Perhaps that's how they were going to get their numbers up and out, rocketed out of the geyser to rain on the city from above. Landing behind the palace walls would be easy. "Simply incredible," he breathed.

He had to hand it to them: they were, in their own way, on the cusp of serving the Goddess without even knowing it. If the Blatta did invade, kill everyone, and take back Geyser, he couldn't really hate them. They were at least being creative, the first rule of a life of Mechanization.

He was so impressed he'd temporarily forgotten his quest. At once, he straightened his armor. He took a long time to scan the floodway at the corkscrew path below. His dying eyes loosed a flash of gray light in slapping waves but hit nothing. No Blatta, no Mouflon, no Margaret, no pale man. He smirked. No one in sight, at any rate. With the playing field no longer so cramped, he thought it a good time to use some other tools.

He dropped to a knee and fetched the winger grenade from his bag. After a minute of fondling the thing all over, trying to find out how to activate it, his finger caught the pin. It was secure, preventing the user from accidentally tripping it. With a few tugs, it snapped free. The metal cylinder violently shook in his hands. He tossed it away, fearing that if it detonated while he was still clutching it like a fool he might lose his hands. It banged and rolled down the slanted corkscrew walkway a few yards, stopping when it caught on a sharp stone.

The torrent of robotic sparrows shot in a flood from the top of the canister. They became a six-foot tornado spiraling in the geyser floodway in front of Vidurkis.

From it, a monotone voice posed a single query: "Target?"

"A group below in the tunnels. Kill them. Ignore insects, unless the targets are riding them."

"Priority target?"

"The largest one," he said. "But make sure they all die."

"Understood," the robotic sparrows said and scattered for a moment only to snap together into an arrowhead shape and shoot down the open floodway, weaving between the Blatta bridges, flying true until they pounded into the tunnel opening and out of sight.

The tunnel marked with an *O* stretched on forever ahead of Nevele. Clyde had asked her not to volunteer as scout, but since she'd been in there the day before, she said she knew it better than the rest. He'd reluctantly agreed.

He watched, chewing his lip.

She stood just inside the opening, keeping the others in sight as they peeked in behind her.

There was nothing to be heard besides the push and pull of the wind that found its way through the caverns. She looked down, reporting she saw something glimmering among the debris and Blatta droppings. She bent and picked it up, spat upon it, and cleared away the muck with the heel of her palm.

She brought it back to show them. It was shiny like metal but flecked with iridescent sparkles of deep cobalt. The glow from their electronic torches danced on its surface; it seemed to catch it and swirl it around within itself before absorbing it.

"What is it?" Clyde asked, mesmerized.

"I think this is it—what caused all this mess," she said

through gritted teeth.

"That's . . ." Rohm started.

"Yes. A fragment of wendal stone." She weighed it in her hand, bouncing it. "Approximately a pound, maybe a little less."

"It would easily fetch a thousand spots in any prospector camp on Gleese," said Rohm, "if the going rate is what it was a month ago."

She held the stone out to Clyde, as if she couldn't wait to have it out of her hands.

He looked at it with big, curious eyes and gently took it from her. It certainly had an appeal about it. The way it shined—even in weak electronic light through filthy flashlight lenses—was remarkable.

Even so, such a thing shouldn't have displaced people or caused so much death. He suddenly didn't see beauty in the hunk of wendal stone. "So this is it?"

Nevele nodded, solemn. "Yep. That's what it was all about."

"A shiny rock," Clyde scoffed. "All that horribleness for this." He shook the precious stone in his hand. If it could cry, he wouldn't mind hearing it. But he knew it wasn't the rock's fault. It was the people who put a price tag on it, pinning such imaginary value on a silly thing like shiny blue rock. But since he didn't have any of those people around—who were probably long dead anyway—he projected all his disgust onto it.

"I guess I should've just left it where I found it," Nevele said. "I didn't figure it would upset you like this."

"No, I'm fine," Clyde said, even though he felt anything but.

He wheeled around to find Flam, but he wasn't anywhere

near. In fact, he was across the plateau, a frightened look on his face.

"Looks like you might be able to buy a new auto after all," Clyde said, trying to be cheerful. He walked over with the stone, but for each step he took forward, Flam took one back.

"If you wouldn't mind, please throw that in," Flam said, gesturing toward the abyss. "I don't need to see it any clearer than that."

"I'm giving it to you," Clyde said. "Of course, I'd like to. I want to take every bit of this stuff and throw it in there, but this one I think is all right to hold on to. Here."

Flam showed his palms. "Don't give it to me. Throw it in. Please."

"What's the matter with you?"

Clyde was so close now that if Flam took another step back, he'd teeter on the edge.

"Mr. Clyde," Rohm advised, "perhaps you should give him some space."

"I'm just trying to show him my word is good. He's been a big help."

Nevele's face showed she was just as concerned as Rohm sounded. "I think you should do as he says and just throw it in."

The Mouflon's face was cast downward. Blinking fast, he seemed pained.

Clyde whispered, "I'll do it if you really want me to."

Flam nodded.

Clyde looked at Nevele and Rohm and shrugged. He canted back his arm to lob the stone into the darkness. He heard Flam shuffle and dart before he understood what was actually happening.

Nevele shouted.

Rohm screeched disharmoniously, blaring contrasting alarms.

"*Wha—?*"

A hand struck him in the back, twisting a fistful of his suit and wrenching him around. It was Flam, pawing all over Clyde to get to the chunk of wendal stone. Desperation was in his face, his jaw slack and his eyes enormous. He said nothing. Above, the atmosphere mites expelled more and more snow. Clyde wasn't sure if Flam had changed his mind or simply lost it.

"*Careful,*" Nevele screamed.

Perilously close to the edge of the plateau, Flam drove a fist into Clyde's face. A flash of white streaked Clyde's vision, and he fell, releasing the shard of wendal stone. He got to his feet quickly and backpedaled from Flam and the cliff's edge.

He smeared the trickle of blood rolling out of his nostril. The single brushstroke of crimson from wrist to first knuckle didn't make him want to retaliate; it just made him sad.

The Mouflon turned, holding the rock in his hand and hungrily staring into its flecked, craggy surface. He looked up at Clyde, not a trace of apology present. If anything, he looked . . . not himself. "There's got to be more of it around," he said, voice low.

"That's not what we're down here for," Clyde snapped. "If you want that piece, go ahead and keep it. I'm sure it wasn't worth hitting me over, though. What's gotten into you? It's time you said why you've been acting so strange."

"I've been acting strange?" Flam shouted. "You're the one who's gotten us wrapped up in this shite. You. Harboring secrets. Sequestered Son, praise his name. Bah. When this is all over, you've got a throne, the whole city to yourself. I've got to get something out of this, too, don't I? Some sort of payment for giving my word to you, you pathetic little twerp."

"Maybe I'll release you right now," Clyde yelled. "Tell you that your services have been rendered and I'm through with you. Would that make you happy, you greedy . . ." Swearwords failed him. "Look. How about this? We'll keep going and you can stay behind and pick up all the rocks you want. How's that sound to—?"

"Go right the plummets ahead," Flam roared. "Say it. Tell me I'm released. Tell me I'm through being your chaperone. Not that it hasn't been a lovely time, nearly being killed every other Meech-damned minute. You and Miss Patches there can make kissy faces in the dark all you want, then. Me and the mice, we'll go back and do as we please once we're through with you!"

"Uh . . ." Rohm murmured, taking a step back.

"Don't pull Rohm into it. They didn't do anything. They've been nothing but helpful this entire time. You? You don't get enough morning sunshine, and you're nothing but a bag of complaints the rest of the day!"

"Say it, Clyde. Your Highness, Clyde Pyne of Geyser. Tell me I'm released. Say it."

"No, I won't. You know why? Because it'd be too easy. Then you'd get exactly what you want. You consider yourself such a proud Mouflon. I'm going to make you keep your word, all the way until the end."

For a beat, all was quiet while Clyde and Flam stared at one another.

Seemingly spurred by demons unseen, Flam lumbered forward, gaining momentum rapidly. Even though Clyde had little to no fighting experience, he was able to dodge the incoming Mouflon with a quick sidestep. Flam stopped short and spun in place, pitching loose gravel out from under his hooves as he came in with a tree trunk arm raised, the wendal stone wedged in his thick fingers.

Quickly, Clyde's hand trailed his jumpsuit's belt and found Commencement. His fingers grazed the handle, felt the texture of the inlaid images—the streaking souls, the sword they coiled—and stopped. He would not shoot his friend.

Dropping his arms at his sides, he let Flam come up on him, the Mouflon's eyes wide, lips peeled back in a snarl.

Clyde remained standing before him, made no move to dodge the blow. The fist rocketed in, and he took it square across the cheek, his head slung to the side. The wound burned as if a slab of molten rock had struck him.

Facing him, Clyde stood with his hands limply at his sides.

Again, Flam wheeled back and hit him, this time with the arm not clutching the rock.

Knocked off balance, Clyde was thrown down and caught himself on his hands and knees.

He heard a quick scuffling of boots. Nevele, unable to suppress herself any longer, was moving to his aid. Peering up from where he lay in the dirt, Clyde saw her entire body was busy with activity. Beneath each sleeve and pant leg, things were squirming. Her bare hands and the skin of her face and neck were unbinding, her laces pulling out and collecting at her forearms and hands—readying to be deployed.

Through the mask of loose flesh, she met Clyde's gaze, seeking him for permission to lash Flam to pieces.

But he raised a halting hand to her.

With hesitation, she rebound herself and stepped away.

Clyde climbed to his feet, dusted himself off, and faced Flam again. His nose was bleeding even more profusely than before, running down to his chin in a thick trail. He let it drip freely. He wanted Flam to see what he'd done. Perhaps it'd shake him out of whatever had gotten him so wound up.

"Don't eat, don't sleep, but I see you can bleed pretty well."

Clyde ignored it. This wasn't his friend. "I don't know what's come over you. But if we're in this together, then you have to trust us. If you're just after the wendal stone, say something. If that's all you want, I'll release you from your word and you can go. But if there's something else, now is the time to speak up."

Flam gaped at Clyde.

Clyde thought maybe he'd said the right thing and whatever was plaguing his friend had been lifted.

Then an indignant smile crossed Flam's face as if whatever had its hold on him had keyed in the reply it *really* wanted Flam to say. "All hail the new King of Geyser. Look at you, making speeches already." He hocked and spat, the foamy missile smacking above Clyde's left eye.

He didn't wipe that away, either. "If something happened on our way here, if something's going on, say something. Perhaps we can talk it out. Nigel gave us plenty of medicines. Perhaps you got a flu of some kind. Maybe you have a fever or—"

"*Look out*," Flam shouted and reached for Clyde, wrapped him in an arm and, tossing the wendal stone aside, grabbed Nevele and carried them both out of the way.

From what, Clyde wasn't sure, but as he was yanked from his feet and hoisted away, he saw what Flam had seen.

From the *O* tunnel came a wall of metal, buzzing wings and the screech of mechanics announcing a thunderhead of robot birds.

For a moment, the sparrows hovered and scanned the travelers with harmless blue lasers swatting this way and that, apparently measuring each of them several times. It wasn't the way Rohm worked together. They were disorganized and frenzied while sizing up their prey, as if each bird was in direct competition with its neighbor to collect the most data the fastest.

Clyde and the others stared in bewilderment. After the perfunctory scan was complete, the sparrows became a rippling mass, darting like a startled school of fish.

To Clyde's horror, Rohm stepped forward. The frisk mice coordinated to lock their jumpsuit boots into the crunchy earth, preparing for an attack. They ballooned the miner suit as broad as it could be, puffing up the chest and shoulders to exaggerated sizes.

Unable to form words fast enough, Clyde shouted unintelligibly, more scared than he had been on this entire journey. These mechanical birds, with their razor-tipped talons and cruel beaks, could eliminate Rohm in seconds.

The sparrows rearranged into a triangular fist of metal, zeroing the point squarely on Rohm. They shot forward as one, rocketing across the cavern, scattering the inky snowflakes.

Rohm took the strike to the chest of their suit, the birds punching into it as if intending to impale their target clean through. None of the mice were able to hold on to their brethren for long. The suit ripped, and mice spilled out. They tried to collect, but it was a fruitless effort as the sparrows rapidly devoured, pecking and clawing and reducing the suit to ribbons. Gnarled, furry carcasses rained from storming birds.

"*No,*" Clyde shouted, scrambling for his revolver. Flam raised his blunderbuss, firing into the flock of sparrows as it moved away and dove again for another pass at the straggling mice trying to make a break for it.

Nevele swung her arms in overhead circles, laces smashing the sparrows ten at a time.

Clyde fired into the pack again and again. Despite having downed a few with each bullet, he felt there was no hope. They'd never kill them all fast enough.

The birds continued their bloody work, unbothered by the travelers' salvos.

Flam threw the empty shell aside from the blunderbuss, reloaded, and fired again. The final scattershot round ripped through the last handful of the terrible things, the pieces raining into the crevasse in a disjointed, chiming song of spilling bolts, wires, and circuit boards.

Silence then.

Clyde was the first to holster his weapon and approach the tatty remains of Rohm's jumpsuit, the sundered garment dotted throughout with splotches of red. Dropping to his knees, he began gently feeling down the legs and sleeves for a soft lump—for any of the frisk mice that may've survived.

"Please, please," he begged, his voice splintery. "Not *all* of them."

In the left boot, an infant mouse remained, having found shelter within an alcove of the boot's steel toe. It took some coaxing, Clyde telling the poor thing numerous times that it was okay to come out. Its motions were slow, its eyes enormous. It reluctantly stepped into his palm.

It was unavoidable. It saw its dead siblings scattered around, but Clyde lifted the mouse and carried it away as fast as he could anyway. He cupped his hands around it, but the mouse had seen enough. It held a paw clamped to its chest, tiny pouts escaping from its mouth made into shrill, panicked whistles by its big front teeth.

"Are there any others?" Clyde choked. "Can you hear them?"

The frisk mouse looked up at Clyde, nestled in his white palm, and after a second of staring into the misty air, measuring it, slowly shook its head.

Speaking as only one, its voice was nearly inaudible. "Only me."

Clyde pinched his eyes shut. He brought the tiny mouse to his chest and let it climb onto his shoulder. Once there, nestled against his neck in the safety of his suit's high collar, it whimpered and soon wept openly. Clyde wept as well.

He removed his revolver and reloaded it, tossing the empty brass to the stone floor of the plateau. When he looked up, Flam and Nevele were both trying their best to hide the fact that they, too, were crying.

Hands spread, Flam sputtered, "Pasty. Forgive me. I didn't mean a word of what I said, I swear to Meech

I didn't. I think when Vidurkis nabbed me with his gray light . . . I think it's gotten in my head somehow. I've . . . it's been hard, these past few days."

Nevele sniffed, wiped at her eyes with the back of her hand. "What did you say?"

"Your damned brother. He hit me with his eye thing when he chased us in here. I can't stop thinking these really bad things. This whole time, it's been driving me insane."

"But he couldn't do that before," Nevele said, aghast. "He could just stun with it, and now you say you can . . . hear him?"

"Unless you got another explanation for why I hear him talking and talking and talking all the time in my Meech-damned head." He crumpled, doubling over and taking his horns in his hands, wrenching his head side to side as if he were attempting to break his own neck. "He won't shut up," he roared.

Flam searched Clyde's paper-white face. When he caught the frisk mouse's gaze in the shadow of Clyde's collar, Flam lost it. "The poor mice," he screamed at the ceiling. "Those little shites didn't do anything to anybody!"

He continued this way for what felt like several minutes, yelling and yelling as if trying to make himself into a volcano and expel the taint on his spirit, purge it from his body and soul. When he was through, he collapsed, balled up, and remained that way as if he'd been successful in screaming not only the blackness but everything good out of himself, a knotted crust on the ground Flam's residuum now.

In a delayed reaction, the atmosphere mites responded by giving Flam a shroud of snow.

Clyde brushed the flakes from his friend's fur and sat

beside him. Nevele did the same on the other side, and together they became a heap of overlapping limbs with Flam in the center.

Clyde kept trying to think of something good to say, some bit of positivity, but he came up dry. Instead, he hugged Flam harder.

Nevele held the Mouflon just as tightly. The look on her face wasn't that of obligation but genuine sympathy.

Lastly, the sole surviving member of Rohm scurried out from under Clyde's collar, ran the length of his sleeve, hopped over to Flam's horn, and trekked down until it was standing squarely upon his forehead. It stretched down over the outcropping of Flam's heavy brow and said, peering into his left eye upside down, "I'm still here, Mr. Flam. I may not be able to speak as loudly as I used to, but I assure you, I'm still here and willing to help!" He saluted. "At your service."

It was clear Flam wanted to give a smart remark, his lips working and his eyes narrowing, but then he just sighed. "Thank you . . . Would you mind getting off my head? You're standing on my eyelash."

The rodent obliged. It turned and saluted Clyde, bowed deeply. "And at your service, sir, Mr. Clyde! And you, Miss Mallen—"

"Nevele will suffice." She patted its head with the tip of her index finger. "But thank you."

CHAPTER 36

Going Separate Ways

Once Flam was grunting about Nevele having sharp elbows and how she needed to get off his hip with those things *pronto*, the travelers knew they'd gotten themselves together enough to press on. They gathered their things, reloaded, and collected in front of the next passageway.

Flam stumbled and swung about, looking for what had dared to trip him up. There in the pool of light from his torch was the glinting shard of blue rock.

Everyone stopped and watched Flam. He didn't seem to pay any mind to the fact that he was now being very closely observed. He simply picked up the rock, glowered at it for a moment, and then hurled it into the abyss. It sailed soundlessly, struck the wall, and fell. After its noisy descent was over, Flam clapped the dirt off his hands, turned, and saw he was being scrutinized. "The hell are you all staring at? I'm fine."

Clyde was unable to suppress his smile. He knew Flam wasn't that daft, hadn't forgotten about what he'd done or that the wendal stone had been the trigger, but it was now clear how selective his friend's memory was.

They moved on. If he said he was fine, they could only take his word for it.

One open tunnel led into the next. Then a series of

perilous meter-wide ledges flanked yet another fathomless fall into the planet, and then more tunnels, some true to their *O* markings, some not. They found a small pool of standing water in which Flam volunteered to be the appointed taster, claiming his palate was more refined and could detect contamination. When he gave it a slurp and a thumbs-up, they filled their canteens. A few hours later, they stopped midway through a tunnel for something to eat and more water, but then it was right back to it as soon as the canteens were capped.

"Those sparrows," Nevele said as they went up through a tube wider than most, so wide in fact that they could walk abreast for the first time since leaving the plateau. "Vidurkis must've sent them in from above."

"Does the Patrol have things like that?" Clyde asked.

"Looked like one of their winger grenades," Nevele said. "If they came in from the opposite way, there's a clear passage somewhere, even if it's just big enough for those birds to fit through . . . He must be getting nervous." Clyde picked up a bit of giddiness in her tone. "They open that armory cabinet for elite guardsmen only."

"Well, if they came from that direction, it means that's the way through, right?"

Flam sighed. "And it also means he's down here with us, for certain now."

"But those birds—they came from ahead, where we haven't been yet," Clyde put in, pointing where the hurricane of metal sparrows had come from. "He must've gone up to Geyser and back down through the sewers and sub works. I can't imagine he drilled through the side of Geyser's stem that fast, if that rock is strong enough to hold up an entire city."

"Nor could I imagine Gorett would've allowed him to try that anyway," Nevele said. "That is, unless my brother already did the job for us, killed Gorett, and crowned himself."

A stony fist developed in Clyde's stomach. "Do you think he'd really do something like that?"

"I wouldn't put it past him," she said, reaching a section of the tunnel that was halfway blocked from a collapse. "Give me a hand here?"

Clyde and Flam gave her a boost. Once over the top of the pile of rubble, she pulled debris out of the way for the others.

The frisk mouse tugged on Clyde's ear. "Mr. Clyde, do you see that down there?" He pointed.

The group stopped.

Flam followed the tip of the mouse's pink finger. They trained their lights that way.

Along the tunnel wall were markings in some sort of paint, splashes in deep burgundy and brown: a crude estimation of a hunchbacked man, seen in stick figure form and lacking any detail besides jots for hair hanging from its circle head. It appeared to be either seated upon a beetle or to be legless and attached to its back. The figure gripped a spear in one hand, a lasso or an upheld noose in the other. Even though the artwork was unpolished, the insect was unmistakably a Blatta.

"Is that a man *riding* one of those things?" Nevele grimaced.

"You know, I can remember when they used to have rodeos in Mole Hole and they'd give twenty thousand spots to anyone who could stay on a Blatta's back for more than eight seconds," Flam said. "Nobody was ever able to do it.

It's probably where they got the idea to make walkers. A lot easier to saddle up a bug when it's made of metal and full of computer parts, I bet. But this . . . this is something else altogether." He tapped the picture of the man riding beetleback. "He's running that thing hands free."

They angled their flashlight beams down the tunnel. More pictographs were found, faded and old. They sidled down as a group, sifting out the story as one tableau faded into the next. Nevele discovered what they took to be the beginning: a stick figure man approaching what appeared to be a mountain but with a squiggle reaching out of its summit. Everything before this image had been eroded from a constant trickle of water.

Flam pointed at the smoking hill. "That'd be Geyser, I reckon."

The next pictograph showed a stick figure man looking quite alarmed by one of the beetles, the figure's head a frenzy of lines shooting out as if his hair stood on end.

Flam narrated for the bent-backed figure, "Yikes. What is that ugly thing?" He snorted.

They moved on, and soon the pictures evolved in detail and artistry. The subsequent figures were drawn with more patience and care, now including a face with rudimentary features and clothing. The longhaired man bowed before the beetle, presenting something that could've been fruit or a severed head; it wasn't clear which.

The beetle was depicted in even greater detail. It seemed to be taking the offering and bowing to the man.

"You give me thingamabob. I like thingamabob. Now me like you," Flam narrated.

"Stop," Nevele said. "This is interesting."

Clyde said, "Looks to me like the man meets the bug, and at first it's scary; then he brings it a present for whatever reason, befriends it, and then here, where we started before, they become partners."

"What do you suppose happened to them?" the mouse on Clyde's shoulder asked.

"They got hungry," Flam said, "and decided to buck that twerp off and eat him instead of the bruised pineapples they had been getting."

Nevele dragged her finger down one of the stick figures, but it didn't smear. The paint seemed permanently stained upon the rock. "These have been here for some time." She paused. "Kind of explains why people claim that sometimes you can hear them talk, I guess. What they thought was the Blatta copying human speech, anyway."

"Are you suggesting there are still people down here, riding these things?" Flam said. "There's no way. Someone would have seen them. Ain't nothing on Gleese that hasn't been netted and jammed under a microscope, documented, and given a name."

Nevele steadied her flashlight's beam on the image that had been mostly washed away. Jagged circles, colliding or being absorbed by the others. An engulfed one was chased by what looked like an arrow. "There's a lot in the universe we don't know yet," she said, her tone distant. "Mom and Dad told all kinds of stories of stuff they saw while making deliveries to far-flung regions."

Flam's imagination ran wild. "Like what?"

"Weirder than people riding on the backs of bugs, that's for certain," she said. "Come on. We should keep moving. I think I feel a draft. Maybe we're getting close. This way."

Flam took a step back, troubled not only by the pictographs but the reminder that Vidurkis was just on the other side of every wall, under every rock, looming beyond every next turn. He ran a hand through his fur between his horns, trying to push the thoughts out of his skull.

It was getting worse. The images were flooding back again. The red stains on the wall that made up the drawings looked like blood. It made him think about Clyde's bloody nose—the one he'd given him—and his wicked imagination ran amok.

"That's enough," he told his turbulent mind. "That's good. You can stop there. No more, please. Thank you. Please stop."

"Flam?" Clyde turned around. "Are you all right?"

Flam fought with himself. He backed away from the others, becoming panicked that he might hurt them again. He felt his back collide with the cave wall. Snap. He stopped, his heart lurching.

A crack.

"Do not move." Nevele snatched Clyde's arm.

"Where is it?" Clyde said, turning his flashlight beam all around the cave.

They remained stock-still and looked for the jagged black line in the stone where the crack may have started.

"Do you see it?" Flam stammered, hunched with arms out, afraid to move anything but his eyes.

"No," Clyde said, searching.

"Maybe it was just a small one, something harmless. At least, that's what I'm going to hope—"

The wall behind him gave out. Flam scrambled for something to hold as gravity sucked him farther down the opening. The others leaped to grab him by his hands but ended up with fistfuls of his matted fur. He kicked and bellowed—not just from fear but pain. As the ruddy fibers of his fur popped free, he skidded down the rock wall beneath the opening.

He had enough sense to pull out his collapsible pick, swing it around so it unfolded, and smash it down to catch the stone surface. The pick threw off a screech and rained sparks into his face. His fall was temporarily slowed until the pick's tip snapped off with a ping. His hooves made a sound like nails on a chalkboard.

Then nothing.

Just cold air rushing up around him, whooshing past his ears. In the darkness, all he could hear was his yelp. He plummeted, turning end over end, uselessly kicking and fighting his horrible end.

Chasing him even past the thunderous wind was Clyde's scream: "Flam!"

Poor Pasty. Bloke's lost enough already and here I go, dying on him too.

He let the fall take him.

CHAPTER 37

Gas for the Magic Carpet

Now unsure of Ricky, Aksel avoided his friend the remainder of the night. In a camp only so big, this was difficult. He steered clear of his own shack, the agora at the camp's center, and the creek banks. He circled the camp through the alleys, always moving. He adopted a disguise of sorts: he walked around bare chested, took up a limp, and wore a sweat-stained baseball cap he found wedged among some trash. He tied back his hair with some wire and kept the bill low to hide his eye patch.

The moon was directly above him, beaming down benevolently. Normally, it'd be a peaceful thing to gaze up at it, but tonight this signaled that he was to meet Neck Steve at the agreed-upon place. Phase one of their escape. Aksel trudged that way reluctantly. He wanted to complete Moira and Karl's assignment, but he knew the escape wouldn't be pleasant. Somehow, with the plan having been leaked, he knew something would go awry.

Circling to the back of the western guard tower, he got hit by a wall of stink in the hot wind. At night, the bodies of people who passed away in the camp were loaded up, sent through three sets of gates to the exterior fence, and dropped onto a heap to be shuttled to Adeshka for processing and burial. The pile was usually small, except on particularly hot days, when they lost the most elderly, but tonight it reeked as if a thousand bodies were heaped there. Aksel wondered if that particular corner of the camp would be permanently stained with the aroma, even after the surviving refugees had been allowed to return home.

On the pile, an old man, bent as a diseased tree, lay sprawled across another man, this one younger. The second man's torso was polka-dotted with knife wounds; dried blood covered him as if he had been painted with the stuff. Another was a cocoon of stained burlap, the figure beneath it frightfully emaciated. Next to those two lay a fourth man on his stomach, covered in a wadmal cloak. The size of the body—as well as the slow, labored breathing—gave Neck Steve away.

Exhaling through his mouth, Aksel said nothing and dropped to his knees and then onto his stomach alongside Neck Steve. The two lay masked in their stillness, waiting for the guard to come with the three-wheeled tractor and wagon to collect them and the bodies that weren't pretending to be inert.

They lay there for an hour, aware of each other but neither speaking. Geyser's poorest lived in the shacks nearby. Any conversation might give their positions away or, worse, startle the superstitious into thinking the dead were springing to life. Aksel imagined every man, woman, and child of the camp fetching a torch to thrust into the faces of the presumed zombies to send them to their second deaths. Despite the night's humidity and Neck Steve's warm breath spraying him, Aksel shuddered as if he were encased in ice.

He recalled what Neck Steve had said about where they

were going. The ice caps. How long did he have to remain a spy for Moira and Karl? Would he be playing pirate the rest of his life? And how would he escape from them? How was he to report what the Odium knew? Aksel began to doubt he'd ever have a life after this. Was he lying here now, pretending to be a corpse, when that's what he really would be in a week's time?

Finally, the guard and a partner pulled alongside the heap. They lifted Aksel by the wrists and ankles over the bulwark of the wagon, banging his head on its edge. It took him every ounce of control not to scream out.

"Sorry about that." One of them chuckled, his voice muffled beneath a gas mask. The guards loaded Neck Steve, dropping him right on top of Aksel, and then a few others until Aksel—when he dared a peek—could barely breathe and could see nothing but bodies above him. The guards jumped into the tractor, spun it around, and headed toward the gates. Aksel kept his eye closed, just in case anyone decided to hop onto the bumper, peer in at the dead, and find two corpses breathing.

One gate rattled open, then closed, followed by another and another. Outside the camp, the tractor rattled for a few minutes, then came to a stop. The guards unloaded the bodies, once again slamming Aksel's head against the side.

They waited until the wagon's tailgate slammed. Bumping down the road, the sound of the engine petered out into silence. Soon, all Aksel could hear were insects and the rumble of an aircraft taking to the skies over Adeshka far away. He opened his eye. All he saw above were points of light—the moving ones and the comfortingly stationary ones.

He pushed a wadmal-wrapped body off, took a deep

breath through his mouth, and sat up.

On the other side of the mound of corpses, Neck Steve did the same. He pulled his sweat-logged cloak away and looked at Aksel, a broad semi-toothless smile forming. He sprang to his feet, and Aksel did the same.

Again, they didn't speak. The plan was to get out on the other side of the fence, wait until the tractor left, and bolt eastward. With no compass, they relied on the stars. The Odium was going to send one smaller starship, park three miles out into the Lakebed, and wait. They'd have a window of ten minutes. Anything longer, and they'd risk being detected by radar.

The two men charged, kicking up a small cloud of arid dirt. On the far side of the desert, the lights of a solar farm created a beacon, but the ground was hard to see. He prayed he wouldn't step on a scorpion.

One of the stars was growing.

Neck Steve restrained a cheer and redirected their trajectory toward it.

The star grew a halo for a second as it broke atmosphere and hovered through the thin, gray clouds. The starship's undercarriage lights came on, and its landing gear clanked down, its jets tossing up a wall of choking dust.

Pressing an arm to his forehead, Aksel squinted his eye shut and charged on, leaning into the hot gale.

More lights slammed on. Most likely, onboard cameras were sizing them up. There were no cockpit windows; the thing was entirely enclosed from one end to the other. Approximately fifty feet tall and with a wingspan of just as much, the Odium craft bore the standard artistry the pirates subjected each of their stolen crafts to.

This one was painted in elaborate, interlocked patterns of gold, burgundy, and midnight blue. On the tip of each wing was a dotted line of tassels, several of them missing or burnt to black nubs by exhaust.

Soon this strange paint job made sense. Next to the smiling cat face of their Dapper Tom insignia, the ship's name was painted in a curly, exotic font: *Magic Carpet*.

Neck Steve clapped Aksel's shoulder. He took his cheeks in his callused hands and screamed with glee.

Aksel couldn't help but laugh, even though they were about to be picked up by the most fearsome group of disenfranchised kill-happy psychos in the solar system. Neck Steve's enthusiasm was infectious.

The *Magic Carpet* touched down, its landing gear hydraulics squeaking. A strange buzzing sound came next, likely the magnetic locks being set. In one whoosh, all the engines cut off, the desert thrown into deafening silence. Not a second later, the back gate blossomed open and a ramp was lowered. Three men walked out, boots heavy on the diamond-plated metal. It would've been hard to miss that each one of them was . . . lacking something.

For one man, in place of an arm, there was just a smooth field of shiny flesh on his shoulder. The next man was missing his left leg below midthigh and relied on a wooden crutch. The third pirate helped him down the ramp. When the light caught him, Aksel thought he was seeing things, perhaps a rogue shadow or something. But, no, he had a triangular black hole in the middle of his face where his schnoz had been.

"Two o' you, huh?" this man said, his voice sounding like someone with a severe head cold. "I thought we were just picking up one."

"Slim pickings, at that." The one-armed man looked dubious. "I think I should get the captain to estimate this lot. Might be throwing these two back."

The first man agreed, and the one-armed man bolted up the ramp, his stride off-kilter.

The man with one leg sat on the ramp and, with a crusty fingernail, picked at a patch of lichen growing on his crutch. With the engines off, they were steeped in silence. Aksel glanced to Neck Steve and for the first time, saw worry marking the large man's round features.

For a spell, they watched the pirates and the pirates watched them.

Finally, the man with the missing nose ran a gloved hand over his bald head, the leather squeaking. "If I know my captain, he's going to suggest a recruitment rodeo. See if any of them actually got the giblets required for the job."

This got the seated man to look up. Wild eyed and grinning, he flicked the nub of lichen away. "I like the way you think, Proboscis."

"Thanks, Colin." Proboscis's gaze fell on Aksel and Neck Steve. He sniffed, and it made a sound like a squeeze horn. "I do too."

"Even if the captain doesn't think o' it, you should suggest it."

"I just might do that."

"Your name is Proboscis?" Neck Steve asked, his voice small. Not teasing whatsoever, but posing the question with childlike curiosity. Trying to get to know the men who might, hopefully, become his future coworkers.

If Aksel could've kicked him, he would've.

The no-nosed man stared. "It's a nickname." He gestured limply at his own face. "On account o' all this business. Like you'd call a short feller Stretch or . . ."

"A dead tosser Breather," Colin supplied, leering at Aksel.

"Well, Mr. Proboscis, I just want to say how . . . just how honored I am to be here. I found you guys online and sent an e-mail. I'm Steven. From Geyser. And I know you guys don't know me or anything, but I've studied the Mechanized Goddess's decrees from back to front. I know every passage."

"You the spy?" Colin, the man with the crutch, asked.

Neck Steve smiled broadly, happy to be remembered. "I am, sir, yes."

"Fat lot of good that did us," Proboscis said and honked a scoff. "Wasn't a damn bit o' trouble there at all. You spied on a city that had no defenses worthy o' spyin' on!"

"But . . . I did it. Just like you asked."

The one-legged man shrugged. "You got a point?"

"I just want to say I think I'd really be an asset to this team and a good fit is all . . ."

"Fantastic. Another wannabe." Proboscis laughed, the sound more like nasal hiccups, but he abruptly stopped. He drew a gun, its barrel parallel to the ground.

Aksel dodged, pulling Neck Steve with him, but the gun didn't waver. The man was aiming at the dead landscape behind them.

Proboscis shot up to his feet. "Oi, who the shite are you?"

Aksel spun about. Out of the gloom stepped a figure, seemingly materializing at the edge of the starship's rear blue-white lights. It was the cocoon from the corpse pile, now a living human shape wearing the sack like a poncho, but the burlap mummy's face was awash in shadows.

Proboscis brought a hand to his forehead to block the blinding light. "Closer. Let me see your hands."

The figure stepped forward, upraised hands shaking at the end of his twiggy arms.

Ricky. His face was shiny with perspiration. "I'm . . . I'm sorry I'm late."

Aksel nearly screamed with dismay and anger.

"You?" Neck Steve barked. He shot a glare at Aksel.

"You two, quiet. You in the body bag, you had better start talking . . ." Proboscis kept his eyes on Ricky but shouted, "Captain!"

"I can't run," Ricky squeaked. "I just . . . I have a bad knee and . . ."

"Friend o' yours, mates?" Colin, who had also drawn steel, angled his weapon toward Aksel and Neck Steve. He clicked back the hammer. "Well?"

Aksel wasn't sure what to say.

From the ramp, Proboscis hoarsely called, "Screw it; just kill 'em all."

Hands up, Aksel closed his eye. Here it was. Death. He flinched when a sound broke the cool, desert silence.

Not gunshots. It was Colin's and Proboscis's laughter.

When Aksel opened his eye, the guns were being put away.

From within the starship came a cacophony: thuds, slammed doors, creaking metal, one final boom. Proboscis and the man on the ramp stiffened, laughter breaking off. The crutch's tip dug into the ramp's rubber treads, and Colin scrambled to a standing position. The captain of the Odium pirates came down the ramp, his face in a patchwork of shadow and light as he walked into view.

Ragged apparel from head to foot. Every piece of patched garment on his slender frame was battered and oil stained. An underarm holster hugged a sawed-off scatter-gun, and a three-barreled handgun dangled from his hip. His stringy red hair hung from a bandanna that sat low on his brow. He wore various pieces of homemade jewelry, all of which featured nuts, bolts, rivets, washers, tiny plastic toy wrenches, and screwdrivers. Some were woven into his hair, and two washers anchored the ends of his long, blond moustache.

"Evening, fellas." His voice was low and monotone, except when he punched out a syllable with random force.

"Evening, sir, Captain Dreck Javelin, sir," Neck Steve blubbered, saluting.

Dreck got all the way down the ramp, bypassed Aksel and Neck Steve, and cut directly to Ricky. He gave the young, greasy man the once-over, apparently puzzled by the burlap body bag, and made a slow circle to the first two. Like a man with a fat wallet at a cattle auction, he looked them up and down.

He returned to the ramp, his men filing around him. More pirates were coming out now, a similarly ragged bunch. One, Aksel noticed, was dressed in a laughably bad wig with lipstick smeared on a mouth that showed he wasn't the least bit happy about it. This pirate also wore a lei and a hand-painted sign, secured to his belly with shipping tape: Welcome Aboard! A bet lost, no doubt.

"Three o' you." Dreck tilted his head to confer with Proboscis. "I thought we were picking up one."

Proboscis never took his focus off the new recruits. He

shrugged. "I thought so too."

As much as Aksel's arms ached, he didn't dare lower them.

Beside him, Ricky followed suit, while Neck Steve held his crisp salute.

Dreck faced them again, shaking his head to clear the hair from his eyes. "What're we going to do about that, then? As I understand it, our weight limit is pretty much at its max." He smirked. "And if Ludo back there hadn't quit with the nightly binge of creamed ardamires, we might not've been able to pick up anyone tonight."

The group laughed, one larger man in the back markedly less loudly.

"And none of you can go back, not after you've seen our faces. Even if we did let you go back to the camp, I kind of doubt they'd welcome you with open arms. Open fire, possibly." He smirked, brown teeth showing.

The silence seemed to last a month.

Dreck drew a breath. "What'll it be, then, boys?"

"Sir, if I could say something?" Neck Steve inched forward.

Dreck glowered and, after a second, made a small motion with his hand for him to go ahead.

"I'd just like to say how great it is to be here among you. And how much I'm looking forward to this opportunity—"

"Shut it." Dreck sneered at him, as if he were at the edge of vomiting. "Just shut it. Never talk to me like that. Ever. You're embarrassing yourself. Goddess almighty, look at you." He strode forward. "You were my first pick, but I changed my mind. Figured a man with a slice like that across his gizzard would have a greater inventory o' bollocks in his trousers, but I reckon I was *dead* wrong."

A low rumble of laughs emitted from the pirates crowded on the ramp.

"Might I make a suggestion, Captain?" Proboscis called out.

Dreck stared at Ricky, still apparently intrigued by the burlap sack. "Go ahead."

"Perhaps a rousing round o' recruitment rodeo would be the way to go."

Slowly, Dreck nodded, still sizing up the recruits. He paid particular attention to Aksel and his eye patch.

"Recruitment rodeo," Dreck said, drawing the words out. He adopted a radio announcer tone: "Due to an over-abundance o' interest, the Odium will now be taking submissions for consideration only by way o' a . . . recruitment rodeo." He smiled. "Yeah, I like it. A lot."

But then he frowned. He checked a pocket watch dangling on its chain. "But unfortunately, we have a date in Geyser and we're due there in the morning. I guess we'll have to postpone the rodeo for now. Plus, I wouldn't be surprised if the fuzz keeps this place carefully watched." Dreck's gaze flicked toward the horizon and various points in the sky.

"But, Captain, what about the weight?" Ludo piped up.

"We won't be going that far," Dreck answered, keeping his back to his men. "We won't need to break atmosphere. So taking on a few extra pounds won't be much of a concern for the time being. We'll do the rodeo when we stop for supplies." He looked at Aksel and the others. "So, fellas, good news for you: consider yourselves in on a probationary basis. Sound good? Good."

Aksel shot Ricky a look, not a good one. As Dreck handcuffed the three new recruits' wrists, he considered piping up to ask if he could forgo the recruitment rodeo and kill Ricky himself. As they were taken inside the starship and immediately down a flight of stairs to the cramped holds below, Aksel saw red whenever he caught the back of Ricky's stupid head filled with its stupid thoughts about jumping the stupid gun and escaping.

They were brought into a little room that smelled worse than all the bad smells of the camp crammed into one. Several bone-thin men were chained to stationary bicycles, stair-stepping machines, and a few other pieces of indoor exercise equipment. Each one, Aksel noticed, was wired to a central machine the size and shape of a refrigerator on its side, a green light affixed to its top with all the wires converging into it.

"Welcome to the heart of the *Magic Carpet,* where the magic is made, you might say," Dreck narrated. "Kind o' like seeing behind the illusionist's curtain, I bet. Probably thought the Odium used demon hearts and the spleens of orphans to run our crafts." He nodded for Proboscis to show Aksel, Neck Steve, and Ricky to their places. Three spots were open in the rows of wired-up machines. Aksel's hands were chained to the yoke of the stationary bicycle. They pedaled, encouraged by Proboscis's gun and a wiggling of his fingers like a tiny man running.

Dreck stood at the front of their row. "We need eighty-five thousand volts o' good, old-fashioned electricity to keep the reactor's cooling cycler online. If it drops below that, well, there won't be much around for me to scold, let's just say. The room's sealed, so if you attempt any kamikaze missions to try taking us down, forget about it. The engine will stall, but we'll survive while you blokes are cooked alive." He clapped. "Great. Well, enjoy it, lads. The rodeo's on a rain delay, but we'll let you know once we get a new date penciled in. May the Goddess keep your gears greased."

The door slammed, Proboscis remaining with them. He threw a wheel set into the door to lock it fast. Standing in front of the line of new recruits, the noseless man drew back the hammer, the ratcheting sound keeping time with the slow crawl of his smile.

Over the whirring, he shouted into Aksel's face, "Get kicking."

CHAPTER 38

An Impromptu Reunion

Clyde stared into the darkness that had just swallowed his friend. Thankfully, the heartbreak was short lived. A heavy slam and a whooshed "Oof" announced Flam's ungraceful touchdown, followed by a moan, a cough, and then a word not suitable to be quoted here.

Clyde was so relieved, he actually laughed. Shining his flashlight into the chamber, he saw no Blatta scurrying down the walls to eat him or anything else. The darkness seemed to wholly absorb light.

"There he is." Nevele pointed.

Far, far down was the brown dot that was their friend. His light blazed out a white triangle. He had fallen what seemed to be five stories, but it was hard to say. From above, it looked like Flam had landed in some sort of nonplace, as if he had reached the center of Gleese where there was nothing but solid darkness.

"Is anything broken?" Nevele shouted. "Are you hurt?"

"Well, I think my arse has two cracks in it now."

Clyde and Nevele exchanged looks.

"He's just fine," she concluded.

Flam slowly got to his feet and was glad that when he shined his light to and fro, there weren't pieces of his body scattered all about. He could hear Nevele shouting: "Are you *really* okay, or are you just being macho?"

"Yeah, I'm fine." Flam groaned, pushing a knuckle into the small of his back. "Mostly."

Above, into the narrow gap he had fallen through, lights darted this way and that. Undoubtedly the others were trying to figure out some way to get him out. He hoped it wouldn't involve Stitches unraveling herself and using those things to pull him back up. He didn't typically consider himself afraid of germs, but that seemed unsanitary to him.

In the meantime, he decided to get his bearings. Maybe he could find a new route out. The surface he stood upon felt mighty cold, the chill soaking through his hooves and making his leg bones sore. He caught a glimmer on the ground. He waved his torch and saw another, then more.

He bent and picked up some loose debris. Turning it to the light, he saw it gleamed just like . . . wendal stone. With some difficulty, he got his flashlight to shine as brightly as it could.

His jaw dropped.

He was standing directly upon the deposit: the glacier-sized hunk of wendal stone.

He knew he had a mission to fulfill. He knew he had given his word to Clyde. But he set all that aside to savor this moment.

He stood in the boundless glory of the sight, all this stone. If it could be harvested and brought to the surface and taken to the prospectors, his great-great-great-great-grandkids could probably live off it. That is, if he didn't blow every last bit of it on the finest drink, smoking mold, a different auto every day of the week . . . *Plummets, why stop there? One every day of the month—the year!* Not to mention the biggest reward of them all—he could settle down finally. Give up the scavenging, plant some seeds, so to speak, and live out a life that didn't require eyes in the back of his head and a loaded 'buss under his pillow.

More pragmatic uses for the money came to him. He'd have his parents' burial plots remodeled. When his father died, they were too poor to get him a tombstone made out of anything but wood, and his mother's funeral plaque was stamped plastic. He'd change that, get genuine marble— better yet, *crystal*—monuments put in. Something that'd befit the type of elegant, wonderful people they were. Something nice for Greenspire, too, even though his casket was empty. He was still his uncle, after all. Maybe he'd order a tombstone-slash-mailbox, somewhere he could deposit all these letters weighing down his satchel. *That'd be nice.*

His starry-eyed delusion was smacked away when Clyde's voice rained in from above. "We'll come down and get you."

Hands on his hips and nodding for no particular reason, Flam peered from one corner of the beautiful sight to the other. *The possibilities.* "No rush," he called back.

Wondering if his goofy grin would ever go away, he turned around and nearly walked into the arrow trained upon his face.

Standing directly ahead of him was a shrunken young man, wraith thin, his skin stained a putrid green, his eyes eerily milky. At first he thought the man was tall for a human, but then he noticed the man was at eye level with him because he was seated atop a saddled Blatta.

"Well, I'll be damned."

The bug rider growled. *"Chik. Non-Lulomba. Chick-chickity. Bzzzt."*

"Whoa now, fella. I come in peace. Or I fell in peace, rather."

He felt the prick of an arrow at his back and turned to see another emaciated man with a bow drawn. At the edge of his flashlight's glare, another arrived and another and another. Last, beyond the circle of those surrounding him, he heard confident strides, heavier than the rest. Once the figure made a full circle, the man wearing the darkness as a cover moved close enough to be seen. He was enormous.

Flam squinted. It was a Mouflon with a great beard reaching toward his knees, nearly obscuring his face entirely. Not any Mouflon Flam recognized, that much was for certain. But, whoever he was, he'd evidently been down here a long time and had not plucked his quills to write anyone for just as long, as evidenced by a spiky black crown of barbs standing nearly a meter off his head.

Flam's heart raced. He opened his mouth, but words failed him. All he could do was stand agape as the Mouflon stared back over the line of bug riders. His face was hidden by both shadow and wild fur. He could be just about any Mouflon under all that, but something about him—the familiar curl of the horns, perhaps even his smell . . .

"Who are you?" the voice was tired and reedy but familiar. Different from how Flam remembered it.

His uncle had been down here for a very long time indeed.

After trying three separate times to uncoil enough rope of her threads and only ending up in pieces, Nevele drew herself together and crouched at the edge where Flam had tumbled over. He'd wandered out of sight, and now not even the faint sparkle of his flashlight could be seen down there. She stood and faced Clyde.

Rohm was perched on his shoulder, and he fed him a piece of cave moss.

"I hate to say it, but I think we should press on without him," she said.

Clyde grimaced. "What? You can't be serious."

Nevele brushed her knees off. "I don't want to upset you, but my brother apparently can do some pretty bad things with his gray light now. And if that's true, what Flam was saying about my br—*Vidurkis*—being able to somehow make him do things, we can't entirely trust Flam. I mean, look at the way he lashed out at you." She brushed a thumb under the wound on his cheek. "And what about all these cliffs and random drop-offs? It probably wouldn't be a good idea to have someone with us we can't entirely rely on."

Clyde pulled away from her hand.

"Maybe you should lean over the edge and yell down there that you care about him so you can erase him from your mind."

"I can't believe you're saying this."

"Make things easier." Nevele dropped her shoulders. "Wow, forgive me. That was out of line."

Clyde agreed. It was, but he merely nodded.

"Listen, all he cares about is the wendal stone anyway. He said so himself." She gestured at the cliff. "We could hear him down there. He's safe. Maybe he'll get what he's after. We'll come back for him once we stop Vidurkis and Gorett."

"Is that what this is all about to you? Revenge?"

Nevele stared for a moment. "Gorett had Mr. Wilkshire killed. Your Mr. Wilkshire. And your father. Do I need to remind you of that? Besides, if you're heir to the throne, you kind of have to be there when he dies."

She gestured at Commencement, nestled in Clyde's hip holster. "That thing wasn't made entirely for self-defense, you know. It's also intended as an impeachment device for when things get out of control. Back when it was a sword, they'd use it to lop off the heads of bad kings. You know, just like the one we have now."

"I'm not going to kill him. I want him put away in a dark cell, somewhere deep. As I was, all those years—and you. No, murdering him is not the answer. If I'm going to be king, and if I have any say in it, I want a kingdom where bloodshed isn't allowed. It's never made anything better."

"He's corrupt. Irreparably so. If anyone deserves death, it's him."

"No," Clyde shouted. "There has to be a better way. We should try and figure problems out instead of just . . . beating them into resolution."

"So we'll pull down Gorett's bloomers and give him a spanking instead?"

"Don't be like that. You want to be a violent person, fine."

"What are you saying? We split up, go our different routes?"

"Perhaps."

"Don't be a child." Stepping forward, she slipped a hand to Clyde's side and pulled Commencement out of the holster. He tried to snatch it back, but she was too quick. She aimed it out over the open cavern with one eye closed. She spun it around by its trigger guard and somehow managed to shift it as it was still spinning. When she stopped it, she held it by the barrel, the handle pointed out at him. He stared at the grip, the design of the two souls swirling around the embossed image of the sword.

"It's not about revenge or violence anymore," she said. "It's about fighting for something, about taking a stand for what's right and true. We're in short supply here—those of us who know how Geyser is supposed to be. It's just us three and Flam down there—once he's right in the head again, but even then I'm not totally sure."

Clyde said nothing.

"I kid," Nevele said and waved a hand. "But it's just us carrying on what Mr. Wilkshire and your parents stood for. They understood what goodness was, what it meant to be true and earnest and just. We have to keep fighting, if not for them, for the things they believed in."

Clyde took the pistol from her hand. He held it in his palms and looked at the images molded into it, the peaks catching the flashlight glare and the valleys accepting the shadows. Finally, he nodded and replaced Commencement in his holster. He held the craggy wall for stability and peered over the edge. "You really think he'll be fine down there?"

She joined him at the lip of the inky gully. "I swear it. Even if I have to go down after him when all this is said and done, he'll be fine. If anyone can withstand a Blatta bite, it's a Mouflon."

"All right," Clyde said reluctantly. "Let's keep going. We'll find where Vidurkis sent those birds through and hopefully hit the sewers before the end of the day." He sighed. "Of course, getting through that spot's going to prove difficult without our guide."

"You have a point there." She grimaced. "I hadn't thought of that. Think if we threw some parchment down there and a pen he might bc ablc to whip up a map for us real quick?"

Rohm piped up. "I can always scout ahead, Mr. Clyde. Check each sewer tunnel and report back to you."

"I appreciate your dedication. Prepare to be heralded as First Mouse of Geyser when we get through here."

"I like the sound of that very much, Mr. Clyde."

"Sorry, you complainy turd," Nevele spoke toward the gap. "Guess you'll have to go without a few more morning suns." She patted the wall. "I think I'll actually miss him." She walked on, clicking a light on and trudging up the next incline.

"We'll be back." Clyde reassured their displaced friend and patted the same spot Nevele had.

Within just a few steps, Clyde felt awful for abandoning his friend. Fresh air wafted down from the tunnels, giving him some relief. The surface waited ahead.

Greenspire looked his age, which Flam estimated to be roughly a hundred twenty years, which even for a Mouflon was old. Meech himself was said to have reached a hundred ninety when he died. Flam studied his uncle. He showed all the signs of a Mouflon getting close to meeting Meech: the grayness in the eyebrows and the hairs on the tips of his ears, the quills that looked brittle and hollow. His horns had grown unbidden and were now long, giant coils jutting out of the sides of his head like stretched, broken springs of a shattered clock. He was bent and walked with a rod crudely fashioned from stone.

Greenspire cautiously stepped near Flam and, muzzle buried in the fur of Flam's shoulder, sniffed at him with flaring, wet nostrils. "You smell familiar." He moved around to his back and sniffed his neck. Back before the Mouflon race had language, it was said they used smells to describe how they felt, able to shift the aroma this way and that to tell entire stories about themselves.

But Flam didn't feel like speaking with stink right now. Never learned how, anyway. He turned to face his snuffling uncle and took him by the shoulders. "It's me, Uncle. It's Tiddle Flam!"

"Tiddle." Greenspire squinted. "I'm afraid I don't know any Tiddle Flam except for my sorry excuse for a nephew who's probably rotting in a cell in Adeshka. Clickity-chak. Chick-chak. Bzzzt."

Groaning, Flam bellowed, "That's me. I'm your nephew. And it was only a misdemeanor."

Greenspire sniffed. "Pucky. A whole load of bear cat pucky."

"Come on. Listen to me, would you?"

"Well, you may smell like a Mouflon, but you sure as plummets don't talk like one. You use big words—man dialect. *Clickity*. The big, stupid hubbub jibber-jabber of man! *Bzzzt*. No, I don't believe for one second you're a Mouflon. *Chik*." Greenspire turned on his hoof to push through the bug riders.

They parted for him, dipping their chins to their chests reverently as they stepped aside.

"If anyone's not talking like a Mouflon, it's you," Flam shouted after him. "What's with all the nonsense words?

When you fell down here, did you break your fall with your head?"

Arrows were readied.

"Oh, piss off with that," Flam said.

His uncle stopped in his tracks and turned around.

The bug riders waited for his command.

Greenspire walked back through them toward Flam, pushing his face close to his nephew's. "It was a *blessing* I ended up here. A blessing." He let the words sink in before turning once more to leave. It seemed final, this parting comment.

He slowly retreated into the gloom, leaving his minions to do with Flam as they would.

"Dear Uncle Greenspire, it's a glorious morning, and the suns are out. I had a dream last night about working with you in the sewers and that one time when we went under the market district to fix a clogged line. I remember you hit it with your chisel, and suddenly both of us were sprayed with stinky water. It wasn't until later you told me what that stinky water really was. I don't think I've ever screamed like that since. But I remember you laughed and laughed . . ." Flam looked up.

Greenspire hadn't taken another step away but was frozen in his tracks. He wore a big smile, one Flam knew so well. The ancient Mouflon stepped forward and threw his arms around his nephew.

"I remember that." He laughed and laughed.

The bug riders took their cue and lowered their bows and replaced arrows in their quivers.

With an arm around Flam's shoulder, Greenspire led the newcomer across the wendal stone deposit. No one else used torches or flashlights to navigate, but Flam ran his flashlight beam around and saw an entire ramshackle city built at the fringes of the deposit. Their conversation had had an audience of thousands, none of whom he'd known were there. All watched him, and he watched them right back.

With a simple wave and an announcement, "My nephew is here," they all went back to life as normal, blind and hunched and secretive.

CHAPTER 39

A Mole Hole Rodeo

I f Aksel closed his eyes, he could swear his legs fell off hours ago. Something in him persisted nonetheless, and he continued to pedal. Once every three hours, a boy no older than fifteen would come in with a pressurized bottle and squirt stale water in their mouths and down their backs, give them a look both curious and apologetic, and be gone.

Ricky seemed to be doing okay. For an idiot. He was thin, and the heat didn't seem to bother him much. He'd always had energy reserves like no one else.

To Aksel's left, however, Neck Steve wasn't faring well. A chime would sound whenever one of the pedalers slowed too much and the cooling cycler began to overheat, so Aksel never had to give him any encouragement. Not that he would've had the breath to anyway.

A speaker mounted to the ceiling kicked on. "All right, fellas." It was Dreck's voice, tinny and overamplified. "Just a bit farther. We're about a hundred kilometers from our destination, so keep them feet moving. Over and out."

But something happened next that Aksel was sure Dreck hadn't intended.

"Still got ten on the guy with the patch?" Dreck asked.

He'd left the microphone on.

Proboscis's voice was muffled: something about going double or nothing on the fat one.

"Either way, we get to Mole Hole, get fueled up, pick up the warhead, have the rodeo to keep the blokes entertained and morale high, and then it's off to Geyser to pick up our guest."

Aksel's legs fumbled, his feet momentarily losing the pedals. He got them back on and continued pedaling.

Ricky smiled and said between gulps of air, "Good save."

Aksel ignored the compliment.

Another pirate came through on the loudspeaker. "I still can't believe you're going to trust him. All due respect, Captain, but I mean, why bother? Why not just send Gorett down with the rest of the city?"

"Is that the sound of doubt I hear in your lovely voice, Colin?"

"No, perish the thought, Captain. I'd never. But what if they say we kidnapped him? He's a *king*. I just think it might turn out to be more trouble than it's worth."

"Well, I'll do the thinking if you don't mind."

"That's fine . . . but just tell me why. He's a deserter. A king, perhaps, aye, but this will make the second time he's turned his back on his own city, if the rumors are true. Who's to say he won't do the same to us the minute he gets the chance?"

"Would you shut it, mate? You're giving me the brain hurts," Dreck snarled. "Just trust me when I say taking on a king as stowage is necessary. Couldn't have worked out better, really. Rumor goes that the minute you get the crown, they tell you all o' Gleese's secrets. And if that gossip holds water, that means Gorett's one o' the few who knows where Father Time is, as in *precise coordinates*. And you can't exactly buy that kind of information."

Aksel pedaled, sweat dripping from his chin to his knees. *Father Time?*

"Forgive me, Captain, but I just think looking for Höwerglaz is a waste of time."

They're chasing legends? Aksel thought, dismayed. The Odium were rumored to be off their nut, sure, but wasting fuel to scour the planet for urban legends? Even Susanne, despite being woven, used to laugh every time anyone in the Fifty-Eighth asked whether she believed.

"There you go again, thinking."

"Sorry, sir."

"It defies any logic to believe Höwerglaz isn't alive and well. A man with so much potential *function* in this world? The Goddess would never allow him to die. If his gift is as it's said, there's no way the man could ever die, either because of how he's woven or by the Goddess's plan."

Proboscis muttered a line from the Mechanized Goddess's decree.

"Wait. Can you hear me talking right now?" Dreck said. "Didn't I—? Oh, blast it all."

The microphone went dead. Above their heads in the engine room, Aksel heard banging footfalls, things being knocked over, and muffled shouts.

Aksel turned and glanced to either side of him. Ricky and Neck Steve were panting and bent over the handlebars of their machines, their gazes darting.

Ricky looked at Aksel.

"Forward. Just keep going, all right?" Aksel said between huffs. "We'll get through this."

Neck Steve started speaking to someone unseen. Aksel figured he was praying to the Mechanized Goddess, until he reached a particular line in his panting plea, eyes locked on the far wall. "I made a terrible mistake. I'm sorry, Mama, but I think I screwed up again."

When the *Magic Carpet* heaved, rocked backwards, and then rumbled through turbulence, Aksel knew they were descending. The ship came to a rest, and all around him the engines clicked and deactivated. The cooling cycler issued a chirp as its green light blinked a series of times and went dead, signaling that it was okay for them to stop. Aksel couldn't remember the last time he'd eaten anything, but the minute his legs were allowed to stop, he threw up.

The same young man with the water bottles shuffled in, sidestepped Aksel's puddle of foamy sickness, and unchained them. Aksel could see it in Neck Steve's eyes: he wanted to throttle this boy to death but didn't have the energy. They were guided out of the *Magic Carpet* into the gleaming morning light.

"We're in Mole Hole," Ricky hissed through horrifically dry, peeling lips.

The town was so small it could barely be called an outpost. A street with buildings flanked it on either side, nothing taller than two stories. Wood plank sidewalks, awnings, here and there a water collector, and the only sound was the occasional staccato scream.

The pirates had clearly disembarked long before Aksel, Ricky, and Neck Steve and set to their grisly work at once.

A few bodies lay in the street. A group of men chased a young woman through town, shooting at the sky to scare her. A man hung by a noose from the bell tower of a church, his body glowing with flames.

Dreck stood at the bottom of the ramp in a rectangle of shade made by the *Magic Carpet's* wings, too busy to pay any mind to the recruits. He manned the pump that sucked the town's fuel reserves through a spigot in the street. Between glances at the pressure dials, he watched a large bullet-shaped object being wheeled out through the front doors of Mole Hole's armory. The massive, black warhead cut parallel lines in the dust as it was pushed along on a small cart meant for much lighter loads. The pirates guided it along, grunting with the effort of getting it up the ramp and inside the craft. Dreck turned to watch it pass and finally noticed the recruits standing—*barely* standing—behind him.

"Ah, you're here."

A gunshot sounded, and a cheer echoed behind it.

Glancing, Aksel saw the woman that the group of pirates had been pursuing, now slumped and lifeless in the street. The pirates descended upon the body to take anything of value, yanking necklaces and cutting the ribbons binding her shoes to her legs.

Aksel thought perhaps Dreck didn't agree with this display when he drew his gun, stepped out from under the starship's wing, and fired once into the air. But apparently he was merely summoning the pirates.

The men came running and gathered in a circle at the end of the ramp.

Aksel and the others were dragged, stumbling, into the middle with Dreck.

Dreck stuffed the three-barreled gun away. "In

the lawless spirit of Mole Hole, this is where we'll hold the recruitment rodeo."

Excitement boiled up into every pirate face.

Dreck spun on his heel. "For those who've never been to a rodeo—and how sad for you—it works like this: You three will attempt to kill each other, and whoever is left standing will be welcomed aboard. Every man you see here has gone through this. And if the Mechanized Goddess sees potential in you, she will make your tools work to your benefit." He turned to Proboscis. "Give them their means, if you'd be so kind."

"Certainly, Captain," Proboscis wheezed and drew from a holster at the small of his back a set of three switch-blades and a small plastic remote, bundled by a length of twine. He took them all out and handed them to each man in turn, keeping the remote to himself.

Aksel took the proffered switchblade. It was a type he was quite familiar with. He thumbed the button.

"Not yet, friend," Dreck said. "That's not how the rodeo is done."

Proboscis said, "The knives have magnets inside controlled by this." He waved the remote above his head. "Each round, I will press the remote, which will randomize a device inside every knife that may align the magnets to release the blade or keep it locked in place. Understand? One man will stand here and another here, both o' you holding the stabby end of the handle to the other man's neck. When I say go, you will press the button, and if the Goddess is smiling upon you today, your tools will do the same and kill the other man."

Aksel stole a peek at Ricky. He looked ready to fall

apart, either from exhaustion or from the mental turmoil of this game. Over the course of pedaling for what felt like months, Aksel had forgiven Ricky. It made sense that Ricky would follow him. He didn't need to ask him why he'd come. They'd always been partners, always looked out for one another. "Why not here, through this shite as well?" he could almost hear him say.

Aksel felt the switchblade give a small vibration over and over as the magnets wheeled one way and then another, Proboscis testing the remote from a distance. The blade would pop out, then retract, and pop out again randomly. He looked up from the switchblade's brushed chrome handle just as Proboscis pointed at him, then Neck Steve.

"You and you. Right here."

Aksel swallowed, his throat so parched it felt as if boulders were being forced down his esophagus. On jelly legs, he stepped forward to where Proboscis pointed and squared up to face Neck Steve, who took to the position without hesitation, his round face set. Aksel looked at him full-on. If he had lost twenty pounds in sweat from the six-thousand-mile journey from the refugee camp to here, he wouldn't be surprised.

"Knives up."

Neck Steve immediately brought the cold knife handle out and held it to the skin covering Aksel's carotid artery.

With trepidation, Aksel held his switchblade up and pressed its harmless, slotted end to Neck Steve's scarred neck.

"One more for good luck," Proboscis said and issued a few more clicks of the remote so their knives' magnets swapped around a few more times. "And . . . go!"

Aksel closed his eye and pressed the button. It wouldn't

depress all the way. He opened his eye and didn't smell blood, nor did he feel a cold blade harpooning his throat. That round was over, no winner or loser named.

"Next."

Neck Steve and Ricky.

Click.

Click.

No blade.

"Next."

Aksel and Ricky. Friends.

When Proboscis said the word, Ricky closed his eyes.

Click.

Only after hearing Ricky's knife did Aksel press his own.

Click.

"You two again," Dreck ordered, bringing his index and middle fingers together in a scissoring motion toward Aksel and Neck Steve. "We're losing daylight here."

Knives up. "Go."

Click.

Click.

"She's being fickle today, eh, mates?" Neck Steve said hoarsely, but none of the pirates laughed.

Aksel and Neck Steve stepped away from each other, neither acknowledging the other. This was just survival, really. If they had to voluntarily kill each other, Neck Steve wouldn't bat an eye. Each time Aksel was paired with the man, he didn't wait to press the button. He didn't want to kill him, but if there was no way to get away, well . . . he was going to take what he had. He just hoped he had a chance to explain in the afterlife.

"Go."

Click.

Click.

"All right," Dreck grunted. "Enough is enough. Lightning round. Patches and Sack Man. You two, square up. Proboscis, keep hitting that thing. We've got to scoot boots soon." Dreck eyed the horizon with a hand cupping his brow. "I'm sure one o' these Molers called Adeshka when they saw us landing."

It took a lot for Aksel to step forward within Ricky's reach again. They put the knives up. There would be no way to avoid it this time, no hoping they'd just kill Neck Steve on the next round. One of them had to die, or they all would.

He looked into Ricky's eyes. They were rimmed with tears. His mouth was moving, repeating the same phrase over and over. As Proboscis readied the magnets, Aksel had time to study Ricky's chapped lips and pick up on what he was mouthing. "This time, this time, this time."

"Go."

Ricky pulled his knife away just as the blade popped out, giving Aksel just a glancing slice across his neck.

Ricky spun and dove at the pirates with the knife low, ready to come in at Dreck with clearly nothing on his mind but sticking him in the heart with the blade. It was over in a flash. Ricky took only three long strides before a shot rang out and he was sprawling to the ground, the knife dropped from his hand.

Aksel stood staring, the world's sound sucked away.

A smoldering bullet hole burned through Ricky's heart.

Aksel threw himself down to his friend's aid. He didn't care if it blew his cover.

Ricky's voice was scarcely audible. He was gone in a moment, but in that moment Aksel listened intently. "You go ahead. I'm sorry I followed you, but I had to get out of there and . . . just . . . you go ahead. You win. Look at me when I say this next bit, okay?"

Aksel did.

"Keep it up. Keep winning." A weak smile formed on Ricky's bloody lips, and his body went slack.

When Aksel's ears cooperated again and he returned to reality, he heard a chorus of erupting cheers.

Aksel, despite himself and his audience, felt he would weep. Ricky had volunteered his spot so that Aksel could go on with his mission.

He turned toward Dreck. His DeadEye's computer was triggered by Aksel's murderous thoughts, and the barrel prepared to extend from his left eye. One mental command—*Stand down*—was all it took for the computer to deactivate.

"Something to say?" Dreck asked.

"No."

Dreck holstered the gun nonchalantly. "Then . . . next."

With Ricky's corpse not a full stride from his boot, Aksel stepped up to Neck Steve. The big man looked shaken now. It was an honest moment, facing death. Aksel had been there before: with the Fifty-Eighth, as a cart-pushing merchant accused of ripping someone off, even on a few occasions due to misunderstandings at bars. This was altogether different. They were being subjected to it. It was cruel.

"I'm sorry if I win."

Neck Steve's words shocked Aksel, but there was no

time for a reply. Proboscis gave the go, and both men frantically clicked the knives in time with the remote's advancing of the internal magnets.

Click.

Click.

Click.

Click.

Click.

Click.

Something felt different the millisecond that Aksel pressed his switchblade's button this time. If there truly was a Mechanized Goddess—something he didn't believe in—something had been issued, a stroke of luck, a sudden swap of fates. He felt the knife kick the blade out of its handle.

Neck Steve's face showed that he was the loser. He dropped his own switchblade to bring both hands to the knife in his neck. He fumbled to one side, a wet spatter hitting the unpaved road, gurgled, gasped, choked . . .

Aksel looked away and tried not to listen. Steve was gone in a few seconds.

He turned toward the pirates, who wore it plain on their faces that they had wanted the other man to win. Money was exchanged, slapped reluctantly from one filthy palm into the next. Dreck was the only one who seemed remotely pleased. More so when Proboscis next to him gave over a handful of spots, the plastic coins raining into the captain's waiting hand.

Aksel felt sick. If he hadn't thrown up already, he would've now.

He turned away from it all, felt his boots developing a mind of their own. *Just run.*

Behind him, a revolver was cocked. "You look like a man who's changed his mind," Dreck droned.

True, he didn't want this. His friend was dead. His mission—to find the Sequestered Son, to find out when the Odium intended to attack Geyser again, if that was their plan—didn't matter anymore. He had a hard time drawing the words into his throat, some curse that would provoke Dreck to shoot.

Neck Steve weakly twisted on the ground, kicking a leg, reaching with a bloody hand toward the sky. Dreck temporarily moved the gun barrel from Aksel to fire three rounds toward the interruption.

"What say you, Patches?" Dreck said. "Climbing aboard with us or no?"

Back still to Dreck, Aksel looked to the sky. What if this mission operated as some sort of retribution, that once complete would wash all his shame from him? What if finding the Sequestered Son meant loosing himself from everything before, so he could float up toward a better life? He didn't care about having a new name, the pick of the cities, or all the spots that could fill his wallet. He didn't want to be the man to do these jobs anymore. He didn't want to have a reputation hanging on him like a stain. He didn't want to die under these circumstances, unfulfilled, a man incomplete. All this passed through his mind in the span of a heartbeat, while a dozen murderous pirates stood behind him. His various thoughts compiled into one.

He had to keep going.

"May the Goddess keep your gears greased, brothers." He turned.

Dreck smiled and lowered his gun. "Glad to hear it. Now get on board, all of you. We got a king in need of a lift."

CHAPTER 40

Dangerous Accommodations

Pitka Gorett had ordered his men to gather in the palace's front lawns at precisely one hour till highest suns. Once they were in formation, he exited onto the balcony and looked over them all, a sorry sight compared to how they'd looked at the onset of this mess.

The formerly strapping men were malnourished and visibly exhausted. They all had their visor-equipped helmets off and tucked under their right arms uniformly, but it seemed done out of habit, as if they were going through the motions, waiting for him to be done just so they could go sit down.

The king drew in a deep breath, a deliberate three-second pause for effect. "My men. This is a wearisome time for Geyser. In the entire history of this great city, we have never encountered so much tragedy. Our enemies surround us, coming up from the earth and down from the skies to claim our lives. Everywhere we turn, there is peril and challenge." He surveyed their faces, seeing concern and doubt.

He continued after a sigh. "But you must stay vigilant. You must see to it that Geyser remains as a prevailing outpost for mankind on this planet. While I may be gone, know that all your efforts will not go unnoticed."

At that, some of them shifted; some glowered.

"All of you have fought hard, seen to it that law and order can remain steadfast in this glorious place. But I must realign my focus to see to it that I face my own challenges as well. I must keep the crown safe. I must fight my own fight to ensure that the kingdom of Geyser continues to draw breath. Upon my return, all of you will be granted many treasures, your pick of the houses in the residential ward, and a generous share of the deposit's earnings."

"You're leaving us?" one of the men called out.

"No," Gorett shouted to keep them in line. "I am not leaving you. Do not make it sound like abandonment, guardsman. I will not forsake you. I simply see that we need further numbers. I mean to forge an alliance with an outside force, perhaps quell one enemy's desires so that we can live to fight another equally powerful foe, one that has infested the geyser herself." He gestured grandly at the towering visual aid in the middle of the city.

"But the Odium killed my sister!"

"They burned down my father's church."

"This is a perfect example of why King Pyne was a much better leader."

In moments, they all had broken into a choir of anger.

Gorett had to shout several times to regain their silent attention. "You must stay true to the cause. You must see to it that your individual deaths are not merely empty sacrifices but a means to an end in a fight that will come to an end as long as we persevere!" And since it seemed the time to put his foot down, he shouted, "I will not tolerate a mutiny, and any man who abandons his post will be killed!"

"By whom?" one of the communications officers shouted. "Who will enforce it? You? You won't be anywhere near here. You warn us about abandoning our posts. What are you doing? You're the deserter here if anyone is to be called such a thing."

They all cheered at that. As one, they broke file and were now becoming a mob of soldiers, cutting across the courtyard and picking their way up the palace stairs to the balcony, shouting their disgust.

Gorett knew this would be his sole opportunity to get away unharmed. He went down the other side of the stairs lining the front of the palace and bolted as fast as his legs could carry him to the main gates, picking up his cloak in the front so he wouldn't trip. He couldn't remember the last time he actually ran.

Even though they were weary, the guardsmen gave immediate chase.

Gorett shoved through the gates and tumbled out into the city square. He had grown up here, knew the city like the back of his hand. He had requested they pick him up in the square, but since there was still no sign of a ship, he had to lure the guardsmen away from the landing zone if he was going to make it out with his life. He quelled his fear and turned it into a burst of energy. *Soon I'll be through with this place.*

He made the loop through the alleys, across First Circle Street. He evaded the men who had once hung on his every word and cheered at the climax of every rousing speech he'd given.

He was slathered in sweat when he returned to the square, pleased to see it was clear of his former men-at-arms. Against the glare of the suns, he spotted the telltale blossom in the sky, whiter than any cloud. His heart sang.

The obnoxiously painted craft glided down like a swollen bumblebee. Among the colorful blotches of paint, a big, round cat face had been stenciled onto its side. That damned winking cat with the top hat and its tongue protruding. Nearly every building in his city was marred with it. But Gorett's opinion of the Odium's mascot, the Dapper Tom, changed at once. If it meant his safety, he'd have the image tattooed onto his forehead. *Fine. Whatever. Just get me away from this mess I've gotten myself into.*

The engine gurgled and clanked, and when it changed over from forward thrust to hovering, employing six smaller jets along its belly, it spewed a black cloud and clanked and wheezed even louder.

Behind him: "There! There he goes!"

The guardsmen spilled into the square, took up pieces of trash and broken rock, and opened fire at their king as well as the Odium craft. Gorett pounded at the underside of the hovering craft, screaming for them to open up. The hatch depressurized with a loud hiss, spewing steam, and the rear of the craft split open, a long metal plank ejecting.

Clambering up it, Gorett used the handles and dug his fingers into the slats of the plank, dishonorable on his hands and knees. He didn't care. He was nearly free. He'd made it here unharmed. If he weren't breathing so hard right now, he may have laughed.

Once inside, he didn't even take a look at who was there. With any luck, it would be empty, sent down on autopilot to fetch him.

But no, he confirmed, as he collapsed among the myriad filthy boots. He was yanked up to his feet, his cloak tearing. Even this he didn't care about—the manhandling or his garments being ruined.

The hatch slammed, followed by a prolonged screech

and thud as the cabin pressurized again. The lurch in his belly told him they were no longer hovering. They were moving now—and fast. He fumbled backwards, tried to grab one of the pirates but they let him go ahead and fall into the bulkhead and back onto the floor.

Over him, one of them stood. He recognized him from the wanted posters that he, as king, had often been asked to review and estimate a reward for. Small, wicked eyes over a dark triangle in the center of his face where a nose should have been. Hard to forget a face like that.

"I'd like to offer you my most humble thanks and—"

"Save it," the pirate said, picking him up again and shoving him harshly into a jump seat bolted to the wall. "The captain will be out in a minute. He's in the head at the moment."

Fixing his robe, Gorett noticed how awful it smelled in there, like old onion-tinged sweat and the cloying odor of engine grease. Strangely, it brought to mind the mini jewelry factory his mother had set up in their apartment kitchen. Odd, getting nostalgic at a time like this . . .

After a few minutes of travel, Gorett noticed all the others as they came and went throughout the ship, tending to different tasks. They were all filthy as this first one, dressed in mismatched panels of armor, some of which he recognized to be lifted from the corpses of Patrol guardsmen. All were unkempt; all had either very long, gnarled hair or skulls shaved to stubble.

One thing stood out at once that they all shared. Each man was missing one part of himself or another: an arm, a leg, an eye, or some teeth. One sat strapped in at the gunnery controls, and as he spun to shoot Gorett a malignant wink, he revealed he had no lower jaw. At first, Gorett thought it was a trick of his eyes. He stared openly and unapologetically, figuring the man was used to this.

"Like anything you see?" the man hissed with the aid of a robotic-voiced speaker box bolted to his chest.

Gorett reeled and stared at the wall, the floor, horror-struck.

They laughed.

Outside one of the smeared portholes, he could see Geyser: just a tiny toadstool far, far below. Jagged Bay surrounding the island was clear and shimmering. He wished he was leaving under better circumstances, but it was better to be a breathing coward than a dead hero. Or, in his case, better to be a breathing coward than a dead traitor. His conscience gave a tiny click of activity, but all he had to do was remind himself about the deposit and that part of his mind was hushed once more.

A door opened, creaking obnoxiously on ungreased hinges.

A man approached.

All the others made way, crushing themselves against the walls of the craft's hull to give him suitable breadth.

The first thing Gorett noticed was the captain's headwear, clearly an Adeshka army captain's tri-corner, although it'd been spray painted a fluorescent green over the Adeshka maroon. He removed a set of aviator sunglasses and sauntered to Gorett, yanking a fingerless glove off and thrusting a hand toward him.

Gorett recalled the man with no nose informing him that Dreck was in the head, which he knew to be the lavatory, and wondered if this man had washed his hands. Either way, he accepted his handshake, which nearly dislocated his shoulder.

"Pitka Gorett," Dreck droned. "Tell me, should I have the boys prepare the goose down comforter for your chambers? Or would you like to have some quiche and croquet before your midday nap?"

Uproarious laughter filled the craft.

Gorett snickered and smiled politely.

"Just a bit of humor. My apologies." Dreck took a seat across the narrow hold of the starship and put his right ankle to his left knee, his leather trousers creaking. From seemingly out of nowhere, he produced a double-barreled scattergun.

For a moment, Gorett thought it was the end for him—so soon, too—but was relieved as Dreck used the spiked pommel on the end of the gun's grip to pick under a thumbnail.

Gorett folded his arms into his billowing sleeves.

With their boss present, the other men were no longer throwing morbid looks at Gorett, but in fact all seemed a bit on edge. It reminded Gorett of the bit of stage acting he'd done for spots in his youth with the other children born of vendor parents. These pirate underlings looked to him like his fellow street performers who hadn't studied their lines and were hoping those to the right and left knew their cue.

Dreck spoke, still working at something under his purpled thumbnail. "And how long are we goin' to have you accompanying us, Your Majesty?" he asked, chin to chest. When Gorett didn't answer straightaway, his jaundiced yellow eyes peered up. "Because I got me a quarter-ton drill-head off-planet in layaway I've been making payments on, and I shouldn't leave the shopkeeper waiting."

Gorett cleared his throat to summon his kingly voice. "We stay clear of Geyser for some time, and when we return, all the bloodshed will be over. I have my men standing guard. Whatever happens, when we get there, there won't be anyone to contend with, I assure you."

The pirate wiped a strand of grease-mottled hair out of his eyes. "Funny. My eyes—they aren't so good. Correct me if I'm wrong, but your men didn't look one bit too pleased about you leaving them behind. And the funny thing about men—they don't tend to have that same fightin' spirit when their boss man has scooted on them."

Apparently satisfied with the state of his nails now, he tucked the scattergun away. "Be a shame if we come back and that deposit was already dragged outta the ground, wouldn't it? I would be mighty sad about that. And there's a bit of a funny thing 'bout me, Pitka. You see, boo-hoos are contagious. When I'm not happy"—he leaned forward—"nobody's happy."

"You'll keep your hands off me."

The entire group, Dreck included, broke into a fresh peal of laughter. They all mimicked Gorett with yippy voices and commenced with further howling and doubling over, slapping knees. Even the man missing his jaw let loose a robotic ha-ha-ha from his speaker box.

"Okay, boys. That's enough," Dreck said, chuckling. "We all knew he was going to be this way, so let's just . . . let him get it out of his system now, all right?"

The man with no nose suggested, "Let's give him the rules."

Dreck shouted at the top of his lungs, "Simply *stupendous*

idea." He clapped his hands in time, and the others joined in. Dreck watched them like a proud parent would watch a performing child as they called out in a singsong chant: "You cheat, you bleed! You cheat, you bleed!"

Soon, Dreck joined in the song, and all of them began to dance, shouting their mantra: "You cheat, you bleed! You cheat, you bleed!"

He turned away, pulled his robe tighter, and stared absently at the aircraft's grimy bulkhead. "At least I'm not in the company of any blasted fabrick weavers."

He didn't mean it to be so loud, and he didn't think he could've been heard, not over the engines of this rust bucket, but the dancing stopped at once, save for the man who had only one leg, who hopped for a few more steps until finding a grip on a wall-mounted handle.

In one fluid motion, Dreck lifted Gorett by his cloak and slammed him against the opposite wall of the aircraft. He pointed into his face, gritted his teeth, chuckled low, then caught Gorett's stare, ready to talk with his temper momentarily dammed.

"Apologies, mate. But would you possibly care to repeat that?"

"Let go of—"

"No, no, no. I *asked* you to repeat what you said about weavers just now. And I asked it nice. I did."

Gorett could scarcely breathe with Dreck's forearm pressed against his throat. "I was only expressing that I'm glad none of you are fabrick weavers." He choked. "You're just salt-of-the-earth men"—he indicated the others with a strained bob of his head—"and not practitioners of fabrication."

Holding Gorett in place, Dreck lifted his opposite hand in front of the king and opened and closed his fist a couple of times.

Gorett watched calmly at first and was about to ask what the meaning of all this was, then his scalp began to tingle. The flesh of Dreck's outstretched arm developed marks, like the latitude and longitude lines of a map. Then, in one silent burst, the entire arm divided into individual dices of flesh suspended like an exploded-view diagram of a machine.

All the while, Dreck remained perfectly calm—as if this didn't hurt an ounce at all. His brow twitched, and the dices of flesh tumbled and moved around atop one another in a puzzle of dizzying complexity. No longer did the man have fingers or an arm, just a chaos of cubes chasing one another, turning, flipping, folding, compressing, de-compressing—all while Dreck watched, seemingly bored.

"You see, Gorett, even the most blue collar of Gleese's children can be granted fabrick, if the fates choose it. I happen to be a Fractioner. Yep. Anything mechanical, anything with working parts or elements that move I can take apart and put together any way I please. Even you, for example. I could take you apart, Pitka, make it so your head is coming out your arse, perhaps put two arms on one side—or, hell, I could just make you into a mess that looks somethin' akin to my mum's Sunday haggis. And the best part about it: you wouldn't feel a thing. Not unless I wanted you to, of course."

The men with their missing parts. That was how it was done.

Dreck must've seen him looking at them. "Aye. I fix 'em when I can. I do my best with what they bring back in a bag." He indicated the man with half a head. "Stewart is a particular achievement. Ain't that right?"

The man without a lower mandible droned a fuzzy, "Yes, sir."

"Bone worms," Dreck said. "Pretty nasty things. Did what I could, but you can see with your own eyes Stewart's still alive and well, in one definition or another."

Gorett watched the dice of Dreck's hand move around, rearrange, and then come back into shape. Dreck released the stasis, and he opened and closed his hand again. He paused, flipped his hand around for Gorett to see, the limb complete.

"Another example might be in order." Dreck turned to one of his nearby men, this one with only one ear. "Get our little friend Aksel out here, would you?"

The pirate dutifully sprang to his feet and marched off.

Dreck pulled away the arm pinning Gorett to the wall, but he kept the king in his fixed stare. The faintest of smiles curled on Dreck's flaking lips.

A young man with long, ratty hair and an eye patch was brought out into the aircraft's holds. Two of the other pirates had to restrain him. Gorett got a look at the writhing man, bearded and generally disheveled, naked above the waist and dotted with deep bruises. His eye patch banding his head had been knocked askew so it now was more like a nose patch, and below it, a snarl of fear and anger stretched his pale lips wide. Dreck broke his gaze from the king to face the captive, narrating for Gorett's benefit.

"We got a rule among us, Pitka. One that's kind of important when dealing with aeronautics. Weight is something of an issue, as you probably know. Can't fly straight with a lot of excess worthlessness in your trunk." He looped an arm around the bound man. "Isn't that right, Aksel?"

Gorett glanced at the porthole. An endless blur of yellow screamed past below. They were no longer over Jagged Bay but over the dead Lakebed to the north of Geyser's island, the mainland.

Gorett had never seen this man and didn't really like the look of him, though he wasn't as ghastly as the others. For whatever reason, he felt a sympathetic fear for him. Holding on to the strap dangling from the ceiling even harder now, he said, "You're going to throw this man out?"

"That I am."

After grabbing the chain binding the man's wrists, Dreck pulled so his palm was clearly displayed. For a moment, nothing happened, but then the man screamed. Dreck looked over his shoulder at Gorett as he removed a square from the victim's palm without even touching it.

"Let's say a year, then. Will that be sufficient enough of a wait?"

Dreck's question was nearly drowned out by the man's scream ringing off the metal walls.

Gorett nearly covered his ears. "Why are you doing this to him?" he cried, unable to stomach it a moment more.

"*Answer me.*" Dreck eyed Gorett. "It's rude not to answer when someone asks you a question."

"Yes, yes, a year. That's fine!" Gorett snapped, as if this would end the suffering of the man in Dreck's grasp. Instead, the screaming continued, even doubled, when Dreck motioned for one of the others to reopen the rear compartment hatch.

"So why am I doing this?" Dreck said, grunting with his near inability to restrain the man. "Because, like the boys told you in their informative serenade, you cheat, you bleed."

Gorett winced at the spray of fierce noontime sunshine. Wind pounded inside, and trash and debris were ripped out. It felt like his hand would break if he clutched the strap any harder. Gorett's beard became alive, twisting this way and that.

Again, the man with the eye patch made fleeting eye contact with him. But the man was too woozy—either from pain or blood loss—to sustain it.

"And when trying to keep the weight down, who better to give the flying lesson to than one of the cheats?" Dreck cocked an eyebrow while turning the profusely bleeding man around so he was squared up with the open hatch. The injured man kicked weakly, but it was pointless.

"Any last words?" Dreck asked, his mouth pressed against the man's ear.

He clutched his hand, blood pouring between the fingers. His gaze was loose, his remaining eye rolling. "Yeah," he managed, "I've got one."

"Oh?" Dreck said, feigning pleasant surprise. "Go on, then. Do tell."

"Bang."

The eyelid surrounded in a deep tan-line popped open, and a telescoping shaft emerged from the socket in a flash.

Dreck recoiled as if slapped, shouted in surprise—and anger at being surprised—and kicked the man in the chest, sending him tumbling toward the open hatch. Just as his boots were skidding across the precipice of his doom, a blast sounded—and a spattering of warmth hit Gorett's face.

The man fell out of sight silently. Clutching his arm, Dreck slammed the button next to the hatch to raise the ramp.

It sealed once more, and Gorett's beard settled down. He touched at his face and looked at his fingers. Red.

Dreck collapsed into a seat, a bullet hole in his left shoulder. "Why didn't anyone check him for one of those?" he screamed at his men.

They mumbled apologies and went back to their tasks with a little bit more of a skip in their step than before, all fighting to keep out of the captain's sight.

Gorett also kept quiet and watched as Dreck held up his trembling, bleeding arm, made it splinter apart again. When it was a cloud of cubes floating in the air, the bullet—the breadth of Gorett's thumb—hit the floor with a thud. Dreck reassembled his arm and it was once again whole, not a single mar in the suns-leathered flesh whatsoever. Dreck hocked and spat on the closed hatch. "Good riddance."

"Who was he?" Gorett said, unable to keep his voice from quavering.

"You cheat, you bleed. Remember? Or, in his case, you take on the recruit, toy with him, and make him kill someone to prove he'll go the whole nine yards. And *then* you run a check on him to see if he's a spy. Here. Catch."

Something landed on Gorett's lap. He stared at it: the bloody tile of flesh nestled among the white hills of his robe between his knees. As much as he wanted it off him, he couldn't bring himself to touch it. "A spy?" Perhaps someone had heard about him aligning with the Odium and planted a spy to covertly dispatch him.

Dreck glanced out a porthole, as if afraid the man he just threw out might be hanging on to the tail fin. "He used to run with a militia based out of Adeshka. I will never trust a man with military experience save for what

I teach him. Shame, too. We just picked him up the other day. Really went for it. He killed another man just to make us believe he was one of us."

He looked at Gorett briefly, then back outside the *Magic Carpet's* porthole once more. With a fingertip, he squeaked a drop of blood off the glass that was obstructing his view. "Probably would've been fine keeping him on, even with his history, if I hadn't opened my big mouth about who we were picking up next. Just couldn't take the chance."

Gorett wasn't sure whether to be flattered or scared by the pirate's forward thinking. Clearly Dreck had some sort of plan. He thought it best not to respond at all.

Dreck shrugged and stepped away from the porthole. "Listen, we'll reach the ice caps by sundown. I'd suggest you get comfortable. It's going to take a while, and we don't stop for anything." He cuffed Gorett on the knee as he passed him. "Chin up. As captain of the Odium, I'd like to welcome you aboard, King Gorett."

"Thank you," Gorett replied numbly.

"Roll out the welcome wagon for our guest," Dreck muttered on his way out the door. His laughter boomed throughout the ship.

A man in women's makeup and clothes appeared, adjusted his coconut bra, and made sure his lei was straight. He danced in front of Gorett, a look of misery on his face. "Welcome aboard, Mister Prime Minister. Welcome aboard," he sang dryly.

Gorett ignored the man as well as he could. Looking down, he caught sight of the swatch of skin. It made it rather impossible to ignore the mistake he had made.

A year with these people.

CHAPTER 41

A Ceremonious Occasion

Flam saw where his uncle had been living for countless cycles: in a dark hole in the wall with makeshift tents of animal skins and collected exoskeletons of Blatta. The bugs seemed completely docile now, and not a one attacked or even made noise. Unlike their riders, they could see in the dark and heeded hand gestures and understood several vocal commands. The humans themselves were a strange group, though. They walked around with no clothes on at all and seemed to be either painted or tattooed with splotches of green and black in intricate designs all over their bodies. The men wore unruly beards and hair that hung to their shoulders. The women uniformly wore their hair forward, swept from back to front in a veil in front of their faces. Everyone walked in a hunched manner, even the children. It seemed their bodies had adapted to maneuvering narrow passages, and even when the space allowed for an upright walk, they continued to bend at the middle.

Greenspire gestured at a seat by the fire. On the spit, they were roasting what appeared to be a giant maggot skewered end to end. He poked the grub with his finger and gave it a few more rotations over the fire. He leaned over the roasting maggot, gave it a long sniff, and turned toward Flam.

"I know it's not typical Mouflon eating, but you have to remember I've been down here for a very long time.

Chik-clickity. Of course, Mouflons are famous for adapting. Legend says some of us developed gills like the Cynoscion just to eke out a living."

"Why didn't you ever yell for help or something? So many people were looking for you. You know Nigel Wigglesby, from the Kobbal Mines? I had to tell him you fell, and now he thinks you're dead. Makes me an awful liar."

Perhaps, when it was all said and done, he could tell Nigel the truth and then go to Clyde for a conscience sponging. He hoped the pasty-faced dolt was doing all right.

Greenspire folded his hands at the top of his walking stick. "I suppose if Nigel Wigglesby fell into where the sewer maintenance shaft and the mines connected, I'd probably think he was dead too, being just a man. A man with two bum legs, at that. I most certainly would've died if I hadn't been found by this fine group of people. *Chik.*"

Flam looked over the tribe, moving around in circles on the wendal stone deposit. They were all muttering and making that buzzing sound on occasion, bent and chasing one another in a never-ending circle. In the middle, a Blatta was on its side, groaning and limply kicking at the air with three legs on its higher side.

"They're people? Human people?" Flam asked, watching their strange dizzying dance that picked up speed and slowed at intervals he couldn't decipher.

"Aye, that they are but not just that. Before I could understand them, they kept taking me to their wall of stories to explain."

"What good are pictures if they can't see?"

"You don't need to be able to see to understand a picture," Greenspire explained. "The paint they use has these granulations in it, a powder they make from the ashes following a funeral pyre for one of their own. Their family members become the stories."

"We saw some of those," Flam said. "I didn't think to touch them." He wondered if it would clarify the stories. He doubted it. He recalled what they'd been able to understand. "The man and the Blatta, making peace."

"Not just that," Greenspire said, "and I know which one you're referring to. That first drawing is how all their stories begin. The discovery of Geyser, back before there was the platter or homes upon it or banks and stores and all that rubbish. If you were to read some of the others"— he gestured into the darkness—"you'd learn that the pilgrims went inside between bursts of steam and traveled in here. They changed the future forever when they met their partners in symbiosis, what you know as the Blatta. Other tales, more detailed, tell an even earlier story than that. There were two tribes: one that went into the geyser and one that feared to and eventually went to other lands. And then there's yet another story, going back even *further* about how they got here in the first place, landing on Gleese when it was just Mouflons and Cynoscions and Blatta populating it."

"Wait a minute. What?"

Greenspire chortled. "Oh, you must forgive me. If you remember, Flam, I get kind of excitable about stories of yore."

"I remember," Flam said fondly. "But just one thing at a time, and take it slow, okay? I'm not as smart as you. Never was, never will be. You got to give it to me in bite-size chunks."

"All right. So man landed on Gleese, arriving here by way

of a great chase, and struck themselves of all they knew."

"What were they chasing?"

"I'll get to that. Man arrived on Gleese. All language was gone from them. The means by which they got here—rocket, aircraft, space-faring arc, whatever you'd prefer to call it—they didn't have the foggiest on how to operate the thing, and it went to rust. They were stranded but fine with it. Soon, conflict split them into two tribes. One tribe wanted to go into the geyser and the second wanted to stay outside, harness it, use it as a power source. And so"—Greenspire swept a hand toward the dancing group of bug riders—"here you have the Lulomba, the group that went inside the geyser."

"And the other group," Flam muttered to himself, piecing it together, "ended up building the platter, the palace, all that up there? Right?"

"That's correct."

"But let's go back for a minute. What were they chasing back before?"

Greenspire smiled. "The answer to that is in plain sight!"

"The deposit. They were chasing the deposit? With a starship?"

"Back when it was a meteorite, yes. Apparently where men were originally, they got word or a message from on high that this thing was hurtling through space. They knew it was worth chasing and went after it, pursuing it until it landed hard enough to end its rudderless travel. And they caught up to it, too, just a bit too enthusiastically"—he laughed big—"and knocked themselves silly in the process." He grew solemn. "Of course, the Lulomba have come a long way since. Better off now than they were before or that other group, if you ask me."

"That's what these people call themselves? Lulomba?"

"It is. From what I can understand, it means something like keepers of equilibrium. And since that equilibrium has been unsettled, well—you come at an exciting time. The Lulomba are planning to do just as their namesake implies and begin the reset of that equilibrium. If you're lucky, you'll be put upon the walls with their other leaders. It'll be—"

"Hold the phone. How exactly are they planning to perform this little reset?"

Greenspire stared, fingers intertwined atop the well-worn horn of his cane. He looked very old, the furless rims circling both rheumy eyes pressed deep with wrinkles. It was then that Flam realized that just because someone was old didn't necessarily make them wise.

"How else do you think an entire populous of misguided people adjust for equilibrium?"

"Uncle . . ."

Greenspire cut his attention away suddenly, gazing absently in the direction of the tribe encircling the one listing, moaning Blatta. "You see them dancing over there? The female in the middle is pregnant, and she'll be the first of her kind to give live birth. Normally they come from eggs, like this." He indicated a maggot. "They saw the change coming into the old girl a few months ago, but unfortunately that offspring was stillborn. Still, it was a remarkable sign of things to come. She has not produced eggs, like the others, by the week. Something is in there, something new. A Blatta born like the babies of man. As soon as her placenta hits the wendal stone, that's when they will set off. An omen."

"But there are good people in Geyser, too, you know. They're just trying to live their lives."

"The walls have been quiet. We know a lot of them have left. We understand that in every encampment of killers and thieves, there are the innocent wives and children with not a fiber of hate in their hearts. But we know from the sound of the boot heels above that not a one of them making that noise is innocent. They wear the armor, carry the guns, shoot that unholy brain-ache light upon us."

"Okay," Flam said, with outstretched hands, "settle down, Uncle. It's good you've broken bread with the locals and you've decided to take an interest in something bigger than yourself, *but* I have a friend on his way up there as we speak, and he's the heir to the throne."

"They dare call themselves kings. Bah!"

"Listen to me, Uncle. This guy is good. Whatever happens from this point on will be different, I swear to you. He's on his way to make Geyser a better place."

"And what is this prince's name?"

"Clyde."

"King *Clyde*?" Greenspire choked. "That is a treacherous lie if I ever heard one! Who's ever heard of a king named Clyde?"

"It's his name. He can't help it. What matters is that he's going to kill Gorett, do the whole soul Commencement thing, and turn Geyser around. I'm sure if you wanted to have some kind of negotiations about leaving the deposits alone, he'd listen. He's a good bloke like that, always willing to listen to anyone."

Even if it means the speaker has to trip over his own feet for a week, Flam thought but decided to omit that detail.

Greenspire continued as if he hadn't heard his nephew at all. "We've blocked the floodway of the geyser, cut off their water. They'll have to drink the stuff they pour down here for a while. We're letting it build beneath the honeycomb, and when we're ready, we will seat ourselves upon the cork and break the seal—pouring down all over the city for our great invasion."

"You can't kill them—not after a couple of days from now. You'll be killing good people then. Just show me the way, and I'll catch up to my friends and ask Clyde to come. You guys can have your powwow and discuss what'll happen after he—"

"I worked in the sewers thirty years before I fell in here. Thirty years, Tiddle. And there was a patch of rock that was weak. I sent in a repair request ten whole times to my supervisor. One day I walked across that patch, confident they would've taken care of it, and I fell through. How long do you think they looked for me? A week? A month? *One day.* I heard them with their ropes and their mechanical sparrows looking for me for one measly day. They went back up, patched the hole I had made, and that was it. I lived up there, in that city, Tiddle.

"These folks around me right now may be crude and may not wear clothes, but they know how to live right."

He hushed himself, for the Blatta in the middle of the chanting circle was beginning to screech and growl with agony. "It comes. The new generation comes." He stood. "We launch the attack tonight!"

All the Lulomba stood as well and began their unintelligible chatter.

His uncle walked across the planks of refuse wood to the top of the deposit, where everyone else was.

"Shouldn't be surprised," Flam said to himself. "I suddenly remember you weren't a very good listener even back then."

The way station was where Nigel Wigglesby said it would be, but it wasn't as Clyde pictured it. Instead of a warm and inviting place, they came upon a dark, shuttered, two-story shack. Inside was a stove for metalworking that clearly hadn't seen a flicker of flame in years. The bare-bones living quarters included slumping cots, a dining table missing a leg and propped up using an old pick handle, some scattered trash. At the back corner, easily missed among the trash and other dusk-choked tools, were a couple of sad souls who hadn't made it out: skeletons clad in suits that matched the travelers', except theirs were torn from collar to crotch, everything edible to the Blatta gone.

They decided to take a break here, since they had heard a few scuttles and screeches in the passages ahead. It must've been nearing nightfall once again, and the insects were waking up to scout the tunnels for nourishment.

"Hopefully they've taken this dump off their list of places to check for food," Nevele said while barring the front doors. She collapsed into a chair by the front windows.

Between wooden slats nailed over the windows from the inside, precious little could be seen besides bleary reflections. Still, she remained, wordlessly volunteering for first watch.

Rohm hopped out of the breast pocket of Clyde's jumpsuit and navigated the corners of the way station, looking for anything that could be of use.

Clyde lifted the guardsmen helmet off his head and ruffled his hair, dragging his fingernails across his scalp. He liked the comfort in knowing his noggin was being protected by the helmet, but the itchiness he could do without.

Nevele knotted her hands and stretched her arms overhead. "We'll park it here for a while," she said through a yawn. "Take a load off for a minute." She knocked on the armrest of her ramshackle chair. "I was dreaming about a good sit-down like a dog dreams of buried bones."

Clyde, meanwhile, couldn't take his eyes off the two people in the corner, huddled together, reduced to nothing but bones. They looked like they were screaming, with their jaws hanging open like that. He hoped they were openmouthed because they had no muscle any longer to keep the bottom and top rows of teeth together, that their lives were taken painlessly, maybe even in their sleep: a dream that slipped into another, just of a more permanent variety.

He noted that Nevele and Rohm seemed not at all bothered by the fact that two skeletons occupied the way station with them. He tried again to paint a happy picture for them. He imagined them as friends, just two fellows seated side by side sharing a reflective moment of silent, humble company. They died laughing, not screaming. Maybe.

It didn't work. It was a disheartening sight either way. He turned his back to them, unable to help thinking of his own mortality. "What if we don't succeed?"

Nevele dropped her boots to the dusty hardwood with a clunk. "What sort of talk is that?"

He hadn't even realized he'd said it aloud. He cleared his throat and took a seat on the floor. "I mean, what if we don't make it to the surface? What if Gorett knows where we're coming from and has his men ready? I saw the Patrol shortly before we found you at the hospital. They had enormous guns and gray light lanterns mounted to their autos. They were covered head to toe in armor that looked impenetrable, even from cannon fire . . ." His voice cracked.

"Don't be a pessimist. I thought our talk earlier put the pluck back into your spirits; now here you are again thinking we're sure to fail."

"But we'll be outnumbered when we reach the surface."

"I know you've been *literally* living under a rock, Clyde. And I know you spent a lot of time in seclusion with all your comforts provided by Mr. Wilkshire, but out here in the thick of things, you have to carry on no matter the odds."

He let that sink in, but it couldn't melt the iceberg of defeatism. "And what keeps you going?"

"Hope," she said brightly, leaning back in her chair so it was on only two legs. "Hope is all you need. Think of yourself as a strong individual, rely on your own wits and strengths, and keep putting one foot in front of the other. If you lose hope and lose faith in yourself, then there's nothing anyone can do for you. Focus on the light on the horizon. If there isn't one, you've got to *put* one there." She patted his cheek, her hand warm.

And then he found himself with the power of the suns to take on that iceberg. Easy as that. He smiled.

A rumble shook the station, glass sconces shattering onto the floor.

Nevele threw out a hand to grab onto Clyde to keep her chair from overturning.

Beyond the walls of the way station, Blatta screeched. Clyde stood.

Nevele scrambled to get her boots on.

Rohm scampered into the room, climbed Clyde's entire body, and burrowed into a pocket. Clyde buttoned the pocket and noticed Nevele at the window.

Beyond her, a few shadows flitted by, darker than those around them. The scuttle of wings. The tramp of countless, bony feet. The Blatta didn't seem to be in their predatory mode, as they had been in the cavern when Nigel removed the digger's blade, bolting in straightforward trajectories; these were sporadic and mindless movements. Panic.

"They're unsettled," he said.

"Naturally. Their world is breaking down around them."

"They deserve to be scared, doing what they did to all the miners like this." He gestured at the two in the corner without actually looking at them. "They're monsters."

Still at the window, Nevele shook her head. "True, they're monsters. But they have hope—at least some version of it." She turned around. "They believe in something—survival of the fittest—and they're seeing to it that they remain at the top of the food chain here. You have to admire them in a way, doing what they do."

"Admire them? Are you serious?"

"Sure. I mean, I don't exactly want to run out there and make friends with them, but you have to give them at least a shred of credit. They're protecting something, taking a stand in the way that comes natural to them."

"I suppose. They do seem kind of like proud creatures. Even if they are just dim killing machines."

Nevele smirked. "They probably think the same thing about us."

A loud slam directly above their heads made both of them reflexively duck.

Nevele drew a pistol.

Clyde did the same, with some difficulty. Wrestling Commencement out of the too-small holster was difficult if he didn't pull at exactly the right angle.

They listened as six-legged footfalls went from one side of the roof to the other. One of the Blatta issued a trumpeting sound, and from deep within the caves came a response of blats and cries. This exchange continued, with each reply closer.

"It seems your honorable friends heard us gossiping about them."

"No one likes a smart arse."

Apparently the Blatta atop the way station was accompanied by a second, then a third. Then a slew all at once, slamming simultaneously. Each clanging arrival was accompanied by a scream from the others, as if in welcome. Once in a pack of what Clyde calculated to be at least ten or more, they scuttled around the exterior of the building, occasionally darting past the windows and giving every knick and knothole in the exterior a cursory prodding. They each took a turn with the front doors, feeling around under the door itself as well as poking an antenna through the keyhole before moving on. They each did this but never two at the same time.

Clyde nearly jumped when he felt something tickle his chest. He looked down to see Rohm attempting to work deeper into his breast pocket, even though he had already hit the bottom. Clyde gently patted the lump and whispered, "Stay calm. Everything's going to be fine." He tried his best to make it sound true.

Upon the last word leaving his lips, one of the Blatta dropped into the fireplace with a sooty whoosh.

Nevele spun and opened fire, putting bullet after bullet into the insect. She'd rendered it dead before it had taken a single step into the room.

"We can't stay here," she said, panting. "They'll call for more, and we have only so many bullets."

"What are you suggesting? Go out there and run . . . in the dark?"

She lowered her gun with obvious reluctance and faced him. "Better than here."

"No," Clyde said. "We'll stay here. We have the walls, and the door is locked. They won't be able to get in except through the chimney." He holstered Commencement. "Here. Help me move this table."

Together, they flipped it and pushed its top against the fireplace. It was barely in place before more thumping and screeching sounded outside, even more panicked.

"This is suicide," Nevele spat.

To their left, glass broke. In nary a second, a Blatta collapsed into the room with them, the opening behind it immediately becoming crowded with others trying to charge in.

It didn't hesitate. It spotted Clyde and Nevele and lunged in the same second, its mind clearly only on the kill. Luckily for Clyde, Commencement was feeling cooperative and slid from the holster on the first tug. He fired once, halting the Blatta's careening dive, and then again and again as it fought to regain its feet.

Nevele shouted, "I'm *telling* you, this is a bad place to stay."

He stared at the thing he'd just killed, his stomach turning. His voice came out soft. "I really don't think going outside will be any better than this."

Nevele growled.

Another Blatta dropped through the chimney and at once set to work chewing its way through the table blocking the fireplace. The ones at the window apparently decided who would go first and another plopped onto the floor. Nevele fired three times, then at the next preparing to push its way in.

The one in the fireplace speared a hole through the tabletop with its pincers.

Jamming a boot against the table's underside to keep it held flush with the hearth, Clyde opened fire through the table. An emptied chamber gifted him with a silent fireplace. Still, his stomach twisted a little.

"I suggest blocking off a single room and remaining there," said Rohm, muffled inside his hiding place. "It has proven to be fortuitous in the history books on military strategy that we've . . . I've . . . read."

Nevele and Clyde took the advice. Together, they grunted and dragged a heavy crate of mining picks in front of the door to secure it.

"This is stupid. So very, very stupid," she kept saying.

But he could scarcely hear her over the growing noise outside. "Get that end," he shouted.

She obliged, and they moved another crate in front of another window that, to their horror, just had its glass shattered and rained to the floor. Nevele used one of the picks this time to impolitely dissuade the next Blatta from entering. But it was nearly pointless given how many were crowded right outside, waiting to take the place of their fallen.

The harder Clyde and Nevele worked, the harder the

Blatta did as well. It wasn't long before their barbed arms were jamming through all the available holes in the walls and gaps in the blockades. Razor mandibles gnawed at the openings. Deafening shrieks from every angle poured in.

This is hopeless, Clyde thought, backing away from a wall bristling with twisting insect legs.

Nevele took one of the shovels from the box and ran its blade up and down against the crumbling door to scare the bugs out of losing a limb, but it was tiring work. Every time she paused to catch her breath, they'd start again.

She threw down the shovel and began rolling up her sleeves.

Clyde blurted, "What are you doing?"

"They're going to get in."

She unwound herself a little, allowing a few yards of thread out and then bringing life into them with a twitch of her wrist. With a sweep of her arms one way, then the other, the front door was soon webbed. With some exertion, Nevele bound the thing up tight, using her threads as a glue between the broken pieces of the door as well as the pick handles and other pieces they were using for a blockade.

Clyde could hear them chew right through her threads, severing them with a single flash of their serrated mandibles.

Nevele unraveled more and continued, patching when one part broke down. Even as her right ear began to slide down her neck.

The fireplace became the Blatta's next focus. Clyde left Nevele to tend to the front door. He drew Commencement but, with one pull of the trigger, realized no bullets remained.

The table blocking the fireplace scooted aside. Insect arms inched from the new gap.

He fumbled for ammunition, jamming it in backwards, frantically trying to remember his quick firearm lesson. He got the gun half reloaded, snapped it closed, and eyed the sights.

The fireplace was empty.

Outside, the noise began to dissipate. The scratchy flutter of Blatta wings was the only sound.

Daring a peek out the windows, Clyde saw all of them lifting off and collecting in a cloud at the far end of the cavern.

Once they had gathered into a solid pack, they set off, leaving their potential meal inside the way station.

Doused in abrupt silence, ears ringing, they listened.

"What happened?" Nevele said, approaching the window next to Clyde. "Did they decide we were too much of a fuss for such a small meal?"

Rohm peeked out from under the pocket flap. "They left?"

Nevele chuckled. "Maybe the mama Blatta rang the dinner bell?"

Although the imagery was funny, Clyde didn't have time to laugh, for the most likely reason the insects took off so fast hit him like a ton of bricks.

"Flam . . ."

CHAPTER 42

The Encounter

The pregnant Blatta encircled by the dancing Lulomba bellowed, a hellish noise that set Flam's teeth on edge. Covering his ears didn't block it out.

Greenspire took to his feet and hobbled across the camp toward the bridge to the wendal stone deposit. Flam joined him. Even on the far end of the deposit, the echoing noise was unbearable.

"How is it that an insect is going to give live birth?" Flam said, still grinding his teeth. "Do you mean to tell me these people have . . . ?"

"No, no." Greenspire chortled. "Nothing like that. Over time, I've dropped my Mouflon ignorance and have become much more open to ideas that differ from the teachings of Meech that are hammered into us. I've come to understand—and believe with all my heart—the stone's power has rubbed off on these people and their insect friends and has melded two coexisting societies into one."

"Rubbed off? Do you mean that . . ." He had to find the right words. "This sounds a lot like fabrick to me, Uncle." He looked at the rock beneath their feet. Besides being flecked with flashes of the more precious ore within, the dark blue was otherwise unremarkable. Flam never questioned why wendal stone was so highly coveted, but if what his uncle was saying was true . . .

Greenspire threw his arm over his nephew's shoulder as they walked on. Flam wasn't sure if he did it so he could lean on him to speak confidentially or if he genuinely needed the aid. Either way, for a flash, Flam marveled at how much smaller his uncle seemed now—how they were now roughly the same height. He used to think of Greenspire as a giant among Mouflons, and now Flam easily outweighed his uncle by fifty or more pounds.

"Fabrick," Greenspire chimed, tasting the word. "It's not the term they use for it, but I suppose that's the closest there is, really." Greenspire led them around the circle, giving the dancers and the Blatta at its center plenty of room, as if he and Flam were surveying some casual event, like a band of jugglers in Geyser's square, like he used to take Flam to see way back when.

"Anyway, the Blatta and the Lulomba are becoming a unified race," Greenspire continued. "The Lulomba can communicate with the insects. And, as it is with their fabrick, for lack of a better word, a gift is given to the Blatta for sharing their dialect: the live birth of the first of a new race." Greenspire took a second to breathe deep. "Simply a most wondrous time, Tiddle. It is truly great that you showed up when all this is happening. Kismet, it must be."

"Yeah, lucky me," Flam said, watching the dancing tribe members fan their arms out at the Blatta in the middle, skitter away, and then dance back in pulsing expanding and contracting circles. "Does this mean you, a Mouflon, can control fabrick now?"

Dismissively, Greenspire walked on. "Mouflon skulls are too thick for that, I'm afraid, but I can talk with the Blatta. I can have meals with them, speak, and comprehend their tales about the things they've discovered within the caves. Some of it can be interesting; some of it not. Tales of their existence are what you'd expect from any society that's lived in close quarters for so long." He paused, his opaque eyes looking side to side.

Flam wondered if he was doing the math on how long he himself had been down here.

With a grunt, he went on. "But as far as being able to fully communicate with them, that is where the Lulomba's gift is readily evident. *Bzzt.*"

"And this offspring, this live birth, what will it be?" Flam asked, partly nauseated at what his imagination conjured. A human baby body with buggy eyes, a million lenses, and snapping jaws? Or worse: the reverse. He tried to hide his shudder.

"The crusher of men," his uncle replied, the already rumbling timbre of his voice dropping an octave. "It will be a great warrior from the second it draws breath. I'm honored, for when we go into battle tonight, I will be the one the child will ride with. I have been chosen to present it to the topside world and bask it in the suns' glare and herald for all Gleese to behold what'll become their undoing."

Flam ducked out from under his uncle's arm. "Hold on. There really are some good men, Uncle. I hope you're hearing me when I tell you that. Not all of them need to be *crushed.*"

Greenspire grinned knowingly, as if to say, *Stop fooling yourself, Nephew.*

Flam was about to explain his point when the noise around them thickened. Twisting to look, he noticed the cavern above the wendal stone was becoming clouded with more Blatta. They were filing in from the gap he had fallen through, joining the others in their endless swirling near the ceiling.

It was hypnotic: the Blatta flew in a tight spiral a few yards above the heads of the Lulomba in matched tempo with their dancing. It was hard to tell who was setting the pace: the insects or the strange people. Flam put a paw to his face and rubbed his eyes, forcing himself to look away.

There was no way this could turn out well. He hoped Clyde and Nevele were safe. If Meech was up there looking out for them and liked what they were doing, possibly he'd already seen to it that they were outside.

His uncle thrust his spindly arms above his head. "It comes!"

Turning, Flam forced himself to look upon the Blatta, which let out a piercing screech. The ones flying above gave an equally shrill rejoinder. The Lulomba chanted, danced, and waved their arms about, the dance becoming disorganized, and the whole cavern was suddenly a riot of movement and noise.

The only things staying still were the pregnant Blatta and Flam. It was hard to tell, but she seemed to be watching him as he watched her through all the thrashing movement. Her expression seemed a mix of pain, worry, and discouragement, but it was hard to judge. Dismally, Flam came to a realization. The Blatta probably wasn't making a face at all. It was probably just Flam projecting what his own face was doing.

Clyde stared into the darkness in the direction the Blatta had gone. There'd been so many of them, and even though

Flam was the toughest person he knew, he wouldn't stand much of a chance. Nevele's hand on his arm snapped him out of his reverie.

"Do you want to go back?" she asked gently. "I know I was the one who said we should leave him, but . . . do you want to see if there's anything we can do?"

Clyde estimated the distant calls of the insects. They sounded like they were really tearing into something down there, more raucous than he'd ever heard them before. As much as it hurt, he decided to face the hard truth of the matter.

"If we go back and there's too many of them, and we die too . . . then there'll be no one to stop Gorett." He looked at her and made himself say, "We should keep going."

She nodded. "Okay."

He drew a deep breath and returned his gaze toward the distant noise spilling from the darkness. "I'm sorry."

When they turned to walk on, a glimmer of metal on the ground caught Clyde's eye. He stooped to pick it up and found it was one of the robotic sparrows. It must've smashed itself on the wall when the group was making its approach through the caves, having made a zig when it should've performed a zag.

"It looks like they came this way," Clyde said, showing Nevele the broken bird.

"Then we're closer to *him*," Nevele answered dully. "When we face him, I want you to stay behind me, all right?"

Nodding at the weapon on his hip, he said, "I know how to use this now. I'm not completely useless, you know."

Nevele closed her eyes for a moment, then said, "I know you're not, but I don't really think you know how awful a man Vidurkis truly is. He'll take any opening he can get. He'll try to get us apart. He was always quite the tactician, and I do *not* mean that as a compliment."

"I understand." Clyde stepped aside to let Nevele lead the way.

They went on for a few more chambers, then had to climb the sheer wall of a drop-off to continue. They reached an opening where some daylight filtered through the atmosphere bugs' mist. A few more twists led to the end of one tunnel where they saw not a sewer but an enormous floodway of the plugged geyser. Even though they were desperate to keep moving and wanted to make good time, both were struck dead in their tracks at the sight.

It went up forever, a corkscrew all the way up to the midmorning sky, just a glowing white dot high above. It hurt his eyes, but he couldn't help but look. He guessed this was the same splendor Flam felt each morning.

Nevele tugged at his sleeve and pointed down. He followed the direction of her finger. Stretching from one side of the geyser to the other were narrow bridges the Blatta had apparently made. Farther down, the bridges overlapped in escalating numbers until they became one solid mass, a floor blocking up the entire geyser floodway. It looked like the papery membrane of a hornets' nest, like the one his master pointed out to him in the gardens right before the husk split and a thunderhead of angry insects came out. The idea of the same thing happening here, except with Blatta, made the back of Clyde's head go numb.

"We're close," he said and carried on, not wanting to look down for a second longer.

They made it three steps up the corkscrew before they stopped, slapping out hands for something to grab onto.

The entire world around them quavered.

"It's just the backed-up pressure," Nevele said.

"That was worse than the other times," Clyde said, tentatively letting his hand off the wall.

A pebble somewhere struck a wall and landed on the organic plug below with a wet thump. A puff of steam came by, a shrill whine. More rock rained down, having been sent skyward from the temporary leak in the plug.

The mist that fell on them stung, not like hot water but an itchy, noisome burn.

He wiped the back of his neck where the smattering of mist had reached, then adjusted his guardsman helmet so the neckpiece was covering him better.

Nevele wiped at the backs of her hands, her patchwork skin blotchy with red marks that weren't there a moment before. "We should keep moving. When it finally gets too much for even that Blatta's biological . . . cement, or whatever you want to call it, this whole chamber will be flooded with boiling, acidic water." She ran her hands down the sides of her suit and daintily wiped off each eyelid.

"I thought the geyser gave off natural spring water, though."

Some of it must've gotten in her eye, because she blinked over and over, though she didn't seem to be in any serious pain. "It does, but there are traces of acidity in it. It's diluted when the pressure can be let go regularly. But when it's been held back this long, the stuff that'll come out of there now . . ."

"Yeah, let's keep going."

Bang.

The stone wall between their heads sparked, the bullet

singing as it ricocheted away. Nevele dragged Clyde behind a pillar of Blatta muck. Clyde fumbled with his gun, choking for breath. Nevele crouched beside him, pistol expertly drawn and cocked. She took a deep breath and risked a peek around the slimy, wet pillar.

A second shot.

Nevele pulled back, eyes wide.

"Is it him?"

She nodded.

"Is he alone?"

Nevele swallowed, her hand pulsing upon the grip of her gun. "It appears so."

A third shot struck the wall beside them.

Clyde flinched, gripping his gun as the shot ricocheted around them. He felt the heat from it as it skimmed past his left ear. It pinged and panged a few more times before coming to a stop a few yards away. Only then could Clyde breathe again.

"The pathway's a spiral," he sputtered. "There's no way to get around him."

Nevele's voice was dull when she answered. "I know. We'll have to fight him."

They could see their path ahead without risking their lives by ducking out from behind the pillar of stone. The corkscrew set into the floodway went up a few more turns until it reached a dark spot, where the path stopped.

Nevele pointed. "That must be how he got in here—the sewer. That'll take us right inside the palace. We're close."

Clyde stared. As much as he wanted to be optimistic, it was hard. Their goal, even their exit from this place, might as well have been on the other side of the planet.

"Put your visor down." Nevele hopped out and fired twice, her gun making the equivalent of an annoying pop in comparison to the boom of Vidurkis's rifle. She ducked back in.

Stealing a glance around the pillar, Clyde saw Vidurkis was now on the bridge made of the Blatta building material, keeping low, his rifle tucked tight to his shoulder. He was walking with his head cocked sideways, as if to hear them better. He really was going blind.

Clyde's boot scraped a rock.

The Executioner narrowed his sights toward the sound and fired.

Clyde felt a terrible strain in his neck as his head violently snapped back, the rifle shot deflecting off the helmet. He took cover and frantically undid the straps of his guardsman helmet. He felt all around on his forehead where he was positive the bullet had cleanly passed. He turned the helmet around and saw a smoldering square dent, the bullet a bent, alloy nub lodged firmly in place.

"My word," he breathed.

"Put it back on." Nevele squeezed off a few more rounds, blindly firing in her brother's general direction. She blinked with every shot.

Between the shots, for a couple of moments, there wasn't any shooting and each party listened to the other reload.

It was Vidurkis who spoke first, his voice echoing and dividing in the chasm of the plugged geyser.

"Where is the Mouflon, Sister? Didn't you bring him with you?" Clyde wasn't sure but thought Vidurkis sounded scared.

"What did you do to him?" Nevele shouted from cover. "He nearly killed us."

"Just something I've been tinkering with during my time in the stockade. Now where is he?"

For a moment, Nevele seemed to mull that over. A small grin materialized on her face before she called back, "Okay, so you learned a new trick. But does it still work the way it used to? What happens if you don't get him in time? We've been underground for a while, and I do believe you tagged him nearly three days ago."

There was no verbal response, just a shot from his rifle. Then he began shouting, nearly incoherently, "Give him to me. You and the pale man can go as you please. Just give me the Mouflon."

Nevele looked at Clyde. She handed him her pistol and began unzipping the cuffs of her miner suit, then the elbow vents as well as the clasps in the armpits.

Clyde's eyes went wide. He was barely able to keep his volume reined in. "What in the world are you doing?"

"Run when you get the chance. I'll hold him off. You get to the surface and find Gorett. Your safety is more important than mine."

"But I . . ." Clyde looked into her eyes. "We left Flam. I can't leave you too."

A shot rang out.

Vidurkis ranted chaotic curses, then fired again.

Clyde's focus remained on Nevele. "I can't. I care too much about—" He clamped his mouth shut. He took a deep breath.

Her eyes took on a heavy sheen, and she closed them. Her hand found his cheek. "I know. Me too." She pushed herself near, crushing a small, warm kiss on his lips. "Now run."

He had to force himself up and away from her. As he

jumped out of cover, Vidurkis got him in the sights. Clyde could feel the man's gaze on him as he charged ahead, leading him. When Clyde dared steal a glance, he saw Vidurkis's focus was being tugged away. He twitched his head birdlike, apparently operating almost entirely by sound now.

He lowered the rifle as something gripped his forearm. His gaze dropped out from behind his rifle sights. He was unable to ignore that his entire right arm and leg were being entangled in a netting of coarse, black thread.

Clyde continued, praying Nevele knew what she was doing, but his feet failed to find their next step. He couldn't go. He watched from above, scant yards away, heart in his throat.

Vidurkis tugged his knife free and swung at the threads climbing his arm. He cut himself more than the reaching tendrils, but didn't seem to care.

Nevele stepped out of hiding while her brother was preoccupied, continued to hold out the arm from which she was sending the threads, and pulled the trigger of the pistol.

Vidurkis ignored his cocooned arm and made himself into an impossible target by moving this way and that, ducking and dodging, all the while progressing toward her in long, erratic strides.

She tried to plant her feet and continued to fire.

One bullet caught Vidurkis in the abdomen. Slapping a hand over it, he roared. A sound not of pain but intolerable frustration. He threw the dagger down, and it stuck into the macrobiotic bridge walkway. He reached for the threads and began to spiral his arm, gathering and pulling more and more onto himself. He began sidestepping to the edge, sneering as he led her into an involuntary sidestep.

"Nevele, let him go," Clyde shouted.

The ends of the threads unraveled through Nevele's chest, pulling out of her neck, unreeling out of her arm. She cast her pistol aside and clutched the threads in both white-knuckled fists a mere foot or two before they slipped out entirely. An alabaster square fell from her forehead, then a panel from her neck. A small, plaintive moan escaped her. She let herself be pulled in another few feet as Vidurkis wrapped another revolution of her threads about himself, all the while pulling her nearer to the edge.

Boot heels straddling the edge, Nevele looked over the gap to her brother. "I'm not scared of you anymore."

"No? Funny. I am." And with that, one last angry grunt and tug.

Nevele tipped forward but kept hold on her threads.

Clyde's heart stopped as she fell.

Vidurkis braced for the sudden pull and locked his legs. Nevele stopped with a jerk at the length of her stitches, a fatal sixty feet above the Blatta-made cork.

No. Clyde's feet pounded as he ran back down the incline, stomping into a stop at the edge of the bridge. Everything around him sounded muffled, his pulse was racing so hard. He cried out to Nevele and ducked down, snatching the dagger from the muck. He held it against the strings like a cellist ready to summon a note with a simple pull of the bow.

Vidurkis flinched at the sound and angled his head toward Clyde. His face was dead, his lifeless eyes staring. "If I drop her, I don't know how much weight that Blatta 'comb can withstand. The Mouflon, you hapless shite. Where is he?"

"He fell. He's gone."

"If he were dead, I wouldn't have these spots in my eyes, liar!"

Clyde glanced down at Nevele, hanging by her handful of threads.

As she gazed up at him, her left cheek slid away. She couldn't let go to grab it. She had to let it fall.

Clyde gave her a resolute stare, trying to will her to chase away any thought of letting go to save him. When he shook his head, she looked away, down to where she'd fall. If it came to it, he knew she'd do it.

"Pull her up," Clyde said, the attempt at bravado abandoning him halfway through the shouted order.

"Give me the Mouflon!"

"I don't know where he is. He fell into this hole and . . . he's down there and . . ." For a moment Clyde considered suggesting taking Vidurkis to the spot where Flam had fallen in, but there was no way he would do that either. Flam was still a friend, and Clyde wouldn't betray him. There had to be some way out of this mess.

"Then she dies," Vidurkis said plainly, bending over the edge of the bridge with his sister hanging far below. He held out the dagger. He wiggled it between two fingers so she could see it all: the hilt, the handle, the blade itself. "You remember this one, don't you? You were good practice. Of course, since you never healed up, Mum and Dad always knew who it was who had cut up their little precious baby. The reason I got sent away." He turned the blade around and looked at its dented, blunted edge. "But not just you. Your blood—and the blood of a lot of others—was drunk by this blade. Most recently, fellow guardsmen who seemed bound and determined to hamper my progress. Before that, Gorett only let me out for special assignments, you see. There was the old man, though. He put up quite the fight—"

Something strange was happening. Clyde stood with his hands out, begging, begging, when he felt it. The same as when Flam had confessed, got on a good spiel, and just kept talking and talking . . . Clyde's pounding heart eased a little. There was hope; there was a chance. He just had to keep him talking.

"What was his name?" Clyde shouted, stepping onto the bridge.

"Clyde, no," Nevele shouted, trying to retain her grip. "Stay back."

"Yes, Clyde. Stay back," Vidurkis spat, aping Nevele's voice. "Can't you see I'm trying to have a word of farewell to my sister here? Have some manners, man."

"Was it Mr. Wilkshire?" Clyde barked. "Did you kill King Pyne as well?" He reached to his hip, drawing his friend's citizen dagger and Commencement at once. Attempting to distract the murderer, Clyde threw the citizen dagger.

Without even rising from his bent posture, Vidurkis lazily slapped it out of the air. It landed at his feet on the bridge. So this would require using a gun after all, Clyde surmised and raised the emerald revolver and trained it on Vidurkis's chest. For her, he'd kill. "Pull her up." He thumbed back the hammer. "Now."

With cloudy eyes, Vidurkis gazed at the gun as nonchalantly as one would study a pineapple. "I don't like guns pointed at me, boy." But then his fixed stare returned to the gun, and pearlescent eyes softened in sudden reverence. He began to blink rapidly, his face softening. "Where did you get that revolver?" His expression went slightly slack, and his eyes pinched tight. "The Sequestered Son. I thought it was only . . . a story. King Pyne, the milquetoast that he was, could never do a thing like that . . . send away his eldest son for safekeeping. You're supposed to be dead."

"Pull her up," Clyde said. He decided to try a phrase on for size. "By the order of the crown, I command you to pull my friend up." He stepped forward onto the bridge, narrowing the gap between them. "Do it."

"Fine," Vidurkis said dejectedly and began taking one handful of Nevele's strings at a time and pulling her up.

She struggled onto the bridge and darted away from her brother. She moved toward Clyde, where the bridge connected to the corkscrew path. As she limped, the threads dragging behind her became shorter and shorter, retracting as she got to safety. She stepped out of what could easily become the crossfire and went to retrieve her own gun from the ground. Clyde could see her in his peripheral vision, getting the gun trained on her brother once more. Her movements were languid; she was clearly exhausted from having been terrified to the core.

"Now drop that," Clyde said, jerking the barrel of Commencement at the knife in Vidurkis's clutch. "And anything else you have."

Vidurkis sheathed the blade, drawing back his cloak, revealing the rifle on his back, the pistol in his holster. He undid a few straps and let everything fall over the edge. The heap of equipment hit the enormous cork below with a soft flump. The smell of acid eating through leather and steel wafted up a second later.

Clyde kept the sights on the Executioner, unsure what

to do next. He stepped backwards until he wasn't on the bridge but on the solid pathway with Nevele.

She was steadily trying to get her torn sutures to go back into her flesh correctly, slapping loose scraps of skin into place, the retracting threads zipping everything into order, all while keeping one arm outstretched, pistol aimed.

"So what now?" Vidurkis asked. He shrugged. "Want me to jump?"

"I want you to confess it," Clyde said. "I want you to tell me what you did."

A smirk brushed Vidurkis's pale lips.

Clyde turned the barrel aside and fired once. Commencement was loud in here.

Vidurkis visibly recoiled.

"Say it! Tell me you killed Mr. Wilkshire and King Pyne."

"And what? You'll kill me in return? Not very kingly of you. Especially if you're the kin of Pyne. Never saw such a pushover in all my life. He couldn't give a demand or boss anyone around. Even when Gorett gave me the order to go and pay the git a visit—" Vidurkis cut himself off. "Are you doing this?"

"Go on."

Vidurkis puffed his chest out. "Well, I stuck him good. He was just dozing in his bed like a fat pig, and I ran in and jibbed him like he was a thief caught in my pantry."

He stopped and blinked. He brought a hand to his head as if he suddenly felt dizzy. After shaking it off, he continued, his voice sounding as if it were being drawn from him—like he was no longer speaking on his own accord but the words were on fishing lines being reeled up his throat one at a time. "And . . . he bled to death. I watched it till the job was done and he was just about gone. Then I called Pitka in, as I was told to do. And then, after he had done his business receiving the old codger's soul and whatever pomp and circumstance needed doing, words said and all that shite, I was put back in the cell. I was released after everyone was getting booted out because of the Blatta infestation. And . . . and . . . I was told to go to Albert Wilkshire's place a week later, on a Sunday bright and early. 'Gun him down, and make it look amateurish,' Gorett said." He tapped his brow. "Two bullets. And I did it. I went there. I killed him." By the end, he no longer had a hiss in his voice. He sounded tired. Fading. Almost . . . sorry, maybe.

Clyde slowly lowered Commencement's barrel. Next to him, Nevele stammered, "What are you doing? Shoot him."

"Just wait," Clyde whispered.

Vidurkis took the opportunity to make a move. With a winning smirk, he threw his hand down to cross draw a hidden pistol.

Clyde let it happen.

Nevele gasped.

As his hand went down, Vidurkis's weight shifted on the crooked organic bridge. Just a momentary lapse in his equilibrium. He threw a boot forward to get a better stance, his foot landing upon the flat of the citizen dagger's blade. It skidded forward, out from under him. His arms pinwheeled, his aim momentarily thrown off. He wobbled, nearly fell over the edge of the bridge, but regained his balance. He took his foot from the blade that had so nearly made him topple into the ravine.

He smiled again. Eyes set upon Clyde, ready, he aimed.

The citizen dagger teetered on the edge. It hung there, seesawing for a moment, before its handle went skyward like a capsizing vessel, cutting in deep swings as it sailed out of reach.

Vidurkis cocked the hammer.

Nevele grabbed her friend. *"Clyde . . ."*

Clyde remained, Commencement lowered at his side. He had been feeling weak since they had started into the mine, almost sick. Now he understood. Even though he didn't ever require food or drink to refresh himself, his sustenance came from elsewhere. The taste of Vidurkis Mallencroix's confession had enticed him. He knew what would happen when Vidurkis admitted it all. As much as he wanted to hoist Commencement, he did not. He hoped his fabrick would not fail him now, if it truly worked as he understood it. *Please do this for me now.*

"Good-bye, my dear sister and her fair-skinned prince. It's a crying shame it had to come to this." Vidurkis smirked, blinked, savoring the moment.

Below, the citizen dagger tip struck into the surface of the muck. Boiling water pushed up, squirting around the blade. A loud ping rang out in the empty geyser.

Vidurkis, his resolve softening for only a moment, looked over the edge to the source of the noise. The dagger rocketed up and lodged squarely in his forehead, burying itself to the hilt.

Nevele gasped—perhaps in shock or some lingering love for her brother, Clyde didn't know. She turned away.

Clyde forced himself to watch. This was what his fabrick could do. The jinx had been set.

The Executioner remained standing for another second, his pearlescent eyes crossing as he looked at the dagger lodged in his head. His fists tightened, and his gun discharged without being aimed, the shot smacking the space behind Clyde, having missed him by a fraction of an inch.

Vidurkis wheeled drunkenly, took one last lazy glimpse at Clyde and Nevele, and then went slack, shoulders slumping, hands falling open, back arching unnaturally. Gravity caught him and lulled him off his feet.

As Vidurkis's body began its tumble, Nevele wrenched Clyde by the arm, pulling him up the pathway. "We have to go."

Running up the corkscrew path, they heard the heavy thud of Vidurkis landing on the spongy membrane. It didn't splinter or burst but somehow managed to take his weight. They didn't stick around to question this lucky turn of fate but continued to run, ascending. It wasn't but a moment before distinct pops and hisses announced that the plug was crumbling.

The Executioner was a few pitiful seconds away from death, still seeing the world before his eyes. He felt the water come boiling up under him. His head hurt. Bad. He could feel the dagger in there, chiseled in place. His thoughts were loopy. His eyes caught white flashes where there shouldn't be any. He heard himself breathing, groaning. The pain came and went sporadically. Something was clearly broken inside his brain. He considered yanking the dagger out but knew this was the end. He smelled the water, like rotten eggs, like sulfur.

When his dying eyes cooperated and weren't cluttered with fuzzy swaths, he watched the two running up and around, his sister and the Sequestered Son, still alive. Amazing.

What a week. Not only had he unearthed an urban myth, but he was undone by it as well. Not a bad way to go, as far as these things went.

And then shadows scattered across, startling him. Dozens of naked people with painted bodies and two Mouflons as well, all saddled upon Blatta with their wings flapping furiously, soared over. The last thing Vidurkis Mallencroix thought about was that saddle he had discovered in the sewers upon that one Blatta.

Two urban myths unearthed.

"My Goddess, how curious—"

It was all he managed before the membrane ruptured and incalculable gallons of boiling acid-rich water rushed around him. The Goddess would accept him. He'd had a function in death, setting off the geyser.

Right?

That's all she wanted from him, from any of her followers. *Can you hear me? Will you accept me?*

He wasn't sure if he was thinking or speaking. And in a half-second-long fizzy burst, it didn't matter as Vidurkis Mallencroix was blasted into nonexistence.

Flam rode on the back of the Blatta, holding on for dear life as the whistling air pushed beneath the creature's wings and launched him up. His uncle was at the lead, hollering for the uprising of the Lulomba, the swaddled insect infant clutched to his chest. Flam rushed up in the pack along the wall and caught a fleeting glimpse.

Clyde and Nevele.

He steered his Blatta and saw they had spotted him as well. He gripped the beetle and reached out two hands for his friends to take.

They gripped on to the Mouflon and, together, rode up the remainder of the hollow shaft and out the top of the geyser, launching high above the city into the radiant sunlight.

"Hold on," Flam shouted, and Nevele and Clyde clutched his suit's straps.

The circular city below kept falling out from beneath them, the hot air pushing them into the sky.

The Blatta didn't have to beat their wings except to perform minor corrections to stay level. Together, they rode up through the cloud bank, Geyser washing out of sight.

Flam couldn't help but let out a whoop. They were genuinely flying, and what a thrill it was.

CHAPTER 43

The Reemergence

The light of the suns warmed their skin. They soared until it seemed if they dared go any higher, they might leave the planet. The three, upon the overburdened Blatta, held on for dear life but couldn't help but laugh. It was such a relief to be out of the mines, and what better way to make an exit to a new place of such high contrasting scenery?

Clyde saw the strange people Flam had apparently befriended, all lithe and with matted hair. They looked happy, though. Not a single sad face among them. And if they could tolerate Flam for any length of time, well, they couldn't be all bad. He spotted a hunched, gray-haired Mouflon riding a Blatta hands free of the reins, and Clyde's mind reeled. Could this be . . . Flam's uncle?

Before he could ask, he was interrupted when he felt a stirring in his guts. It was the same sensation he'd felt when they were saved by Nevele's net when the elevator gave out. But it wasn't as bad. He just felt weightless all of a sudden. Flam's satchel levitated. They were falling. He took two fistfuls of Flam's back hair and held on for dear life.

The Lulomba landed among the Patrol autos on the roof of the palace, the stairs, the balconies. There was no one there to fight. All the guardsmen's guns had been cast aside, their helmets scattered all over. A pyre roared, a heap of Patrol armor melting down to liquid metal.

Flam steered the Blatta to touch down softly in the courtyard. Clyde and Nevele climbed off and surveyed the empty palace grounds.

"Did we strike so much terror into the men that they vaporized?" Greenspire inquired proudly.

Clyde looked to Flam, who was still seated atop the Blatta, nearly crushing the poor thing. It was a remarkable sight.

Flam nodded at the strangeness of it all. He dismounted, letting the saddled insect scurry away. "Looks like there won't be much of a fight."

Clyde surveyed his surroundings. He couldn't remember the palace at all, even though apparently it had once been his home. At the arched front doors, he saw a group of men stripped down to their chain mail tunics and breeches, standing together in a loose knot. They all looked terrified, backing away as a group of saddled Lulomba approached, arrows ready.

Flam, Clyde, and Nevele—and Rohm, on Nevele's shoulder—pushed through the collected Lulomba and made their way up the stairs to meet the guardsmen.

In the weird clicking dialect of the cave people, Greenspire gave the word to stand down.

The guardsmen looked dejected and apologetic, noticing Clyde step up to the balcony with Commencement in his hand. They seemed to silently debate who would step forward to explain themselves.

"What's going on?" Clyde said. "Where's Gorett?"

One of the guardsmen, young with blond hair and shining blue eyes, stepped forward. "He's abandoned us. He decided to align with the Odium and flee. He feared this would happen—that the Blatta would invade." He looked them over. "But I'm sure he never expected all this."

A Blatta clicked its pincers, the guardsmen recoiling as one.

Glancing at the bug riders and then Clyde, the guardsman added, "We don't serve him anymore. No. Not after today. Honestly, a lot of us wanted to quit when he sent everyone away, but because of the wages and his threats . . . Forgive me, but it's been a long few months." He rubbed his temple, sweat dripping from the tip of his nose. He seemed nearly in tears.

"I understand," said Clyde. "So what next?" He looked at Flam, then at the older Mouflon, who bore a faint resemblance.

They returned stoic Mouflon stares, studying Clyde as he studied them.

Next, he surveyed the pale individuals with the ratty hair and painted bodies, still saddled on their insects. They seemed to have no opinion either but crowded around the older Mouflon as if waiting for a cue.

Lastly, he looked at Nevele and Rohm, but they gave no indication as to what Clyde should do either.

This was truly up to him, entirely in his hands.

For as long as he could remember, he was the one who jumped when asked and took confessions when barked at. Now he was the one responsible to issue a decision. It was a weighty feeling, as if he were holding Geyser together. He felt, for the first time, as if he had gravity. Not the same that kept everything from spiraling into the starry airless yonder but a different kind. A scarier kind.

He turned to the guardsman and took a moment to form his question. "Is he coming back?"

Another guardsmen stepped forward to answer, this one older. "I was a communications officer for Gorett. He sent a message to the Odium, said that if they helped him he'd give them a share of the wendal stone deposit. I'm sure, being who they are, they'll want to make good on that contract and return."

"And he didn't take any of you with him?"

"No," the officer said, jaw tight. "Gorett has revealed himself as a traitor. A wretch like him is unworthy of our service. He turned on his own people not once but *twice*." He noticed Clyde's gun and scowled. "That's Commencement, King Pyre's royal sidearm. Why do you have it?" But his anger was quickly ushered away. With eyes big, he moved his mouth but couldn't speak the words: *Sequestered Son*.

Clyde, not wanting a big rabble to come out of this, continued at once. "You men worked in allegiance to Gorett, not because you were honoring him, but because you were working for the palace. While you may have been doing wrong, you had to obey him or be killed. You can stay in Geyser, but not one of you will be allowed to wear the uniform of the Royal Patrol again."

All the guardsmen nodded.

The communications officer said, "That's quite a good amount of pity you're showing us, sir. We truly appreciate it, and we understand your decision. I don't think any of us would want to put the uniform back on, even if you asked us to."

Not one among them argued this statement.

"Please go," Clyde said and waved them on. "Remain in the city, though. If what you say about Gorett is true, then he'll be back soon. The quarantine is still in effect, and there won't be any way off the island for a while. As a matter of fact, you there," he said, taking the communications officer by the arm as he passed, "let's rectify that problem right now. The geyser is flowing again. Power will be restored. Contact the encampment where the citizens are being held, and call them back immediately."

The guardsman, in plain tunic and breeches, turned and headed up the blond stone steps in tired strides.

Clyde looked back at Flam and Nevele, and together they followed the guardsman inside.

The palace was cool and dark, its architecture strangely curvy. No hallway was a straight shot. No corridor had a single corner. Yet it didn't have the feeling of being obscure or mazelike at all. If anything, it felt naturally made. As power came back and electric candelabras and chandeliers sprang to life here and there, Clyde noticed the walls had the same glimmer to them that a majority of the structures around the city did, shimmering flakes set into the stonework.

They followed the communications officer as he loped along, a visible hitch in his step.

"My name is Alan," he said without turning around, his voice boomeranging behind him to Clyde and the others. "I served the Royal Guard since I was sixteen. I won't say how many years that's been." He chuckled and gave Clyde a glance.

Clyde offered a smirk and noticed Alan's smattering of gray hair. He didn't entirely trust this man yet. Not after what they'd been through.

"I suppose you'll probably want to see the main chambers," Alan said, stopping at a set of impressively large doors with wrought-iron hinges. He nodded at the emerald gun tucked in Clyde's holster. "If you are who I think you are."

"I'd rather not let that be known just yet," Clyde began.

Alan nodded vigorously with a big smile on his face. "I understand. No need to explain. Just let me say, though, if you are, you know, *him* . . . let me be the first to say it'll be an honor being in the same city with a man who bears the name Pyne." He seemed to want to touch Clyde, to pat him on the shoulder or even embrace him like an old friend but refrained. "I really liked him." Blinking, he collected his posture and took a step back. "I'll get on the horn with Adeshka and let them know it's safe for our citizens to start heading back. I'm sure they'll be happy to get the news."

"Thank you," Clyde said as the guardsman walked off.

He turned to the giant doors, reached for the handle, but didn't take the big metal ring in his hand just yet. Facing the door, he heard Flam shuffle forward. A big paw clapped him on the back, nearly knocking the wind out of him. Looking away from the handle, he saw Flam's big smile.

"Well, what are you waiting for, Pasty? Let's check out your home."

Clyde felt a burst of enthusiasm. "All right," he said, and pushed through.

Inside was bigger than any room he had ever been in before. The walls held a tableau stretching from one wall to the next as a continuous piece of fantastic creatures, darting starships, and winged maidens. Above, more murals. A man and a woman, she with cascading raven hair and he with a slicked-back silver coif. Together they clutched a longsword made of a deep emerald-colored metal. Together they beamed benevolently, their gazes earnest and loving.

Nevele stepped next to him. "There they are. Lord and Lady Pyne."

"I can see where you get your hairstyle from now," Flam teased.

Below the king and queen, seeming to float within this painting's beatific world, were four swaddled babies. None of their faces could be seen.

"Tym, Raziel, Moira, and you."

Clyde's focus returned to the sword, the centerpiece of the painting. His hand trailed to his side and brushed Commencement, lodged firmly in its holster.

"It was a sword," he said.

"Could be again," Nevele suggested. "Once the smithy gets back."

"Geez, Pasty. What'll you ever do with this place? What a dump." Flam guffawed at his own joke, walking to the throne and approximating it from a safe distance, hands on hips. He looked over his shoulder. "I'm kidding."

Clyde smiled. "I know."

They continued to tour the chamber, looking at all the leather-bound books on the shelves, the immaculate stonework, Nevele providing trivia on the things she knew. And finally at the front of the room, she pressed a button, and shutters rose from the floor-to-ceiling windows spanning the far wall. Clyde approached, suns blaring into the room. The view overlooked Geyser, all of it at once. Night was falling, and every streetlight glowed without flickering or dying out. Every bulb upon the geyser itself was illuminated.

The entire city was glowing in white light.

An hour later, the palace security walls at the edge of the front gardens were dropped. Anyone could come up as they pleased, which Clyde wanted. They had little in the palace pantries that hadn't spoiled, but he requested some coffee and tea be available at the very least. His heart swelled when the first elevator in the courtyard was lowered and even more so when the first load of people were brought up from the island docks. They looked both crestfallen at the broken state of their city and happy to be home.

Clyde and the others had gone off to help make the city as respectable as they could for the returning citizens, activating custodial bots and the like, but the place was too much of a mess to tackle all in one day.

It didn't take long for an infectious relief to spread among them, and more people were brought up one elevator trip at a time. Happiness began to take hold. Children chased each other, taking to familiar streets and recovering lost toys and belongings. Adults walked around, hugging loved ones. Tears were shed, Clyde noticed, but the smiles far outnumbered them. To his eyes, they seemed to look at Geyser not as one would look upon ruins beyond hope but as a project that—while big—just needed to be started and taken one thing at a time.

Clyde returned to the palace, to his father's chamber, and saw Nevele typing at a processor. She turned the monitor around, showing him the image of a microphone on the screen. Wide eyed, she urged him over.

He looked at it, then at her, confused.

"Say something," she whispered, waving toward the

monitor. "It's on."

"Like what?" Clyde said, and that was when he heard his own voice, a half beat later, booming over the city.

Out the windows, he saw some of the citizens standing around the functioning geyser, looking around in a concerned way as if they were about to hear another speech that began, "Please gather only what is necessary . . ."

Nevele raised her hands and backed away, a playful smile on her face. "Hey," she whispered, "you're the big cheese now. Not me."

Clyde looked at one couple in particular out in the square, spied from all the way across the front gardens. He focused on them as he spoke through the citywide PA system. "Welcome home," he said, sharing what he felt in his heart. "Welcome home, everyone."

An official reception was held the following day. Even though a majority of the city's people were bone tired, there was still a good turnout at the great hall.

One woman charged up the palace's front steps, and a few volunteer guards tried to bar her entrance.

Clyde had been sitting outside with Nevele when he heard the commotion. Even more startling was that he recognized the woman. Miss Selby.

"It's okay," he told the men trying to hold her back.

She squealed at the sight of Clyde, overjoyed. They let her go, and his dear friend leaped up the last few stairs. She nearly strangled him with her overzealous embrace. "I thought that was your voice. Thank goodness. I was sure you were—" She was smiling, but tears were in her eyes. "I went to the house, and . . . Do you know about Mr. Wilkshire?"

All he could do was nod.

She thumbed his chin so he'd look at her. "It's okay, Clyde. It's okay. He's in a better place now." She embraced him again. "I'm just glad you're here."

"I'm glad you're here too."

Voice muffled in the hug, Miss Selby said, "Dear, I have to say, I'm very confused about what's going on around here."

Clyde chuckled. "Me too."

"Will you explain it to me when it's all sorted out?"

"I will."

"Clyde?" Nevele said.

Miss Selby released him, and he looked at Nevele at the top of the stairs, her thumb pointed over her shoulder. Despite the bandages on her face and neck, she wasn't wearing her hood and her hair was swept out of her radiant eyes. "I'm really sorry to interrupt, but I think everyone's ready now."

"Go ahead, dear. I'll be in there too, cheering you on the entire time."

"Thank you, Miss Selby. I'm very happy to know that you're . . . that everything went okay . . . that you . . ."

"I understand, dearie." She kissed him on the cheek. "I love you too."

When Clyde arrived, Flam was on the dais, examining the throne. Noticing Clyde had arrived, he stepped out of the way to give him full view of it and the changes they'd made to it.

The seat was heavily padded in red leather, the massive chair set on top of a tablet of marble. When Clyde entered this room, the commotion stopped. Not even a murmur passed as all waited for the Sequestered Son to say something, do something, even so much as look at them.

Clyde had heard of stage fright, but this was ridiculous. There must've been a thousand people in this room. He trained his gaze on his feet. He was still in his ripped miner's suit. He had been looking for something more suitable but had simply run out of time. Getting a city back on its legs was no small chore.

Clyde approached the throne and put a hand upon its armrest, feeling the various temperatures of the natural materials: stone, metal, wood. He held his hand there and stared at the seat a moment. He didn't step up onto the tablet, didn't ease himself into the chair. For the first time, he acknowledged the crowd head-on.

The crowd began to talk among themselves. Many of them claimed he looked like his mother, while just as many claimed he looked like King Pyne. Altogether, though, no one seemed repulsed by his ashen face or dark eyes. "Sequestered Son" was what they said most. He must've heard it uttered three dozen times before he said a single thing.

"It wouldn't be right," Clyde said, standing alongside the battered old throne.

The murmuring became honest noise. Some displeasure, some blatant confusion.

One person deep within the throng shouted, "What do you mean?"

Nevele must've understood throne room etiquette. It made sense. She worked in the palace for years. She walked to the edge of the crowd, flashed her eyes wide at Clyde, and made a funny face by pulling the corners of her mouth down. *Well now, isn't this embarrassing?* she seemed to say to him. She pointed at herself, tapping the tip of her finger against her own forehead, then back at Clyde. She mouthed, "Just look at me, okay? Ready? Here we go."

She drew a deep breath and shouted through the competing noise, "Why not? Gorett's gone; you have Commencement. You *are* King Pyne's son, right?" It seemed she was attempting to mimic a man's voice by dropping her voice low, her chin held to her chest to eke out the necessary depth.

"I am," Clyde announced, fighting a smile. "But I won't take Gorett's place. Not until it's official."

Nevele looked perplexed at his answer, but Clyde gave her a stealthy wink.

Someone shouted, "Why should we trust him?"

"So you're going to continue to chase Gorett, the bugger?" Flam's voice boomed from somewhere way in the back.

Clyde was glad Flam was aiding him in this way but wasn't too pleased with the question. But it was a good move. Send out a question that involved action instead of suspicion, and that would surely prick up more ears. When Clyde answered, he focused on Nevele.

She looked back at him, nodding encouragingly as he spoke.

"No, I'm not going to chase him. And I'm not going to take the throne, either. Gorett can run all he wants. He can even return with the Odium in his allegiance if he desires. Given enough time, Geyser will be strong enough for any foe, with all of you back safe and sound now . . . I will never make any of you leave your homes."

Far back, beyond even Flam, Greenspire and his group of skittish underlings edged back out of the hall, went to the doors, and quietly excused themselves. They left the hall but didn't turn left toward the palace's exit. They were going deeper into the palace, but what for?

Clyde realized he was getting distracted. "There . . . there will be plenty of time for all that. I think this is just the beginning of a new age for Geyser. And unless you're a weaver who can see the future, no one knows what'll happen next. And to be honest with you, I like it better that way. We'll just take it as it comes. Whatever Gorett does, we'll be a reaction to it. We'll not seek him; nor will we invite him to fight us. We'll take it one day at a time."

For a moment or two, everything seemed good, the crowd at ease.

But then things took a strange turn.

A middle-aged woman toward the front stepped forward. "My son was killed by the Odium. Don't his killers need to be brought to justice?" She held a bloodstained knit cap with limp, dangling straps.

Clyde clutched the arm of the throne. "I'm sorry for your loss, ma'am, and I assure you we will find the individual or individuals responsible and do something about it. Geyser, as I understand it, had a court system, and at once we'll get that up and running again and—"

Another voice. "What about my husband? He died trying to keep those hateful men from burning down our house."

His face felt hot. "Again, if and when they return—"

A man cried out, "So you're not going to chase them? You're just going to let them show up and do what they did again? I thought this city was going to be safe. I thought you said—just a minute ago—that things were going to be *different!*"

More people cried out.

"We have to do something."

"I won't live here if I can't send my kids to school without wondering if they'll ever come home to me!"

"We can't let them continue to do this!"

"If you choose to do nothing, you're a fraud. Pyne never would've sat back and let them come to us!"

The room erupted into cheers.

Clyde simply stared at this sea of angry faces.

Nevele was covertly waving him on.

"One at a time," he said.

No one stopped shouting.

Clyde raised his palms, his hands twin white blossoms unfurling as he stretched his fingers out as far as they'd go. "One at a time."

When they noticed him, the noise tapered off and soon the hall was silent again.

"One at a time," Clyde began for a third try, "tell me exactly how you feel."

"What good will that do, huh? Will it mean you'll actually do something?" one sweaty man barked. "Because talk is cheap, and after what Gorett put us through, we've had more than enough of that shite."

A few bellowed their agreement.

Looking at that man, balding and hollow in the cheeks, Clyde drew a deep breath. "If you wouldn't mind," he said as pleasantly as he could, "I'd like it very much if you went first, sir."

The man scoffed. "And do what? Tell you how I feel? What I—?"

"Yes." It felt rude, but Clyde had to interrupt. Otherwise, they'd be there all night.

The man softened slightly, but he still looked wary. "And will that bring back my house, my job?"

"No, it won't. But to make progress, to get over any problem, one has to go about things with the right mindset. We can't hope to get back the things we lost"—for a flash he saw Mr. Wilkshire's face—"but all we can do is move forward. And that, I know, is hard to do. Quite possibly one of the hardest things to do that there ever was. But it cannot be done with a head full of bad thoughts, regrets, anger. And while I won't take the throne, I'd still like to be a person of service. I'd like to help all of you the best I can. And that is all I can promise—that I'll always be here to help."

Nevele moved forward, took one step onto the dais, and turned around to face the group. "Gorett couldn't take the city from us. We're Geyserians. We know what it means to be a tough lot. Spend a couple of summers up here, and you'll know that."

The people, ever so quietly, let out chuckles.

"And Clyde is a Pyne. He's technically next in line for the throne, but he doesn't want it. He wants to help all of you first because that's more important than any . . . stupid chair." She waved dismissively at the throne.

"Just give him a chance, okay? I know a lot of you folks know me, have seen me around, and even if you don't trust weavers, ask a certain Mouflon at the back of the room and you'll learn that anyone can have their mind changed. Give him a try, okay? Just . . . talk to him, and you'll see."

The man wiped sweat from his brow with the back of his wrist. "What'll happen to us when we get our concerns off our chests, though? Will we—?"

Clyde stepped forward. "You'll feel better. That's all that'll happen."

Nevele angled herself close to Clyde's side and whispered in his ear, "You're about to have a few thousand people telling you all sorts of things. I hope you know that. I mean, is it going to work, even? What about the people who are just mad and didn't do anything wrong? I thought you were a *conscience* sponge, not a . . . grump sponge."

The crowd shifted, talked among themselves.

Flam, all the way in the back, offered a wave.

Clyde peered at the man at the front, still sweating, but his face was somber and his eyes at half-mast, a mask of impatience. He wanted answers—and he deserved them.

"All I can do is try," Clyde said. "One at a time, please come forward and state your concerns."

The surging crowd began to form a line.

Clyde sat on the top step of the dais and listened to each concern, Nevele next to him. After a few minutes of elbowing, Flam sat at his other side. They heard them out one at a time. As they mentioned the names of those they'd lost, Flam pricked his tongue and jotted down the names on a piece of parchment from his satchel.

Each story was sadder than the last. Some people confessed to having looted their neighbors' houses. Some confessed having set up friends to take the fall for their own crimes. Some even breathlessly admitted to murder, unraveling horrid and sad stories of vengeance.

It was dawn by the time the last person finished speaking with Clyde and departed.

Flam had fallen asleep a few times, and Nevele had long ago run her hands ragged from all the seamstress work she'd performed—a small service she offered to those waiting in line.

Exhausted, Nevele fell onto Clyde and rested her head on his shoulder.

He put his chin on the crown of her head and threw an arm around her. Outside, beyond the open doors, he could see that hardly anyone had gone home. Everyone was still outside on the palace lawn. He heard laughter, story swapping. They were not at all the same crowd they had been.

He just hoped they would not suspect him of causing the epidemic of untied shoelaces and random tripping for the next week.

Even if they did, he'd take it in stride. He had his friends to help him now.

EPILOGUE

Landing Is the Hard Part

The citizens returned to their homes, power restored. Banners on every post called for strong men and women, fabrick weavers or not, to come to the palace to take up arms against the inevitable return of Gorett. Clyde had appointed himself the steward, the temporary holder of the throne, until it could be officially reclaimed. The title of Executioner was retired altogether, but Tiddle Flam felt quite comfortable being known as Sir Flam, Chief Security Officer of the Patrol.

Nevele reprised her role as the Royal Stitcher, mending and repairing clothes not only for the palace workers but offering her services as a seamstress to the townsfolk as well, even setting up a shop in the town square. Margaret's Mends, it was called.

It was there that Clyde found her the day he stopped by the blacksmith's to pick up Commencement, a sword once again. The smithy on duty had warned him when taking on the project that doing this would weaken the metal, but Clyde didn't care. He would lead by example, even if the Odium would continue to use guns. When he'd given the thirty spots to the smithy for the work, he'd said, "Only bad guys use guns."

Nevele came around from behind the counter. Every

wall of her shop was crowded with the various types of garments she could create. Enormous spools of thread in varying colors and types hung throughout, the strands running every which way about the shop in a system only Nevele understood.

She was still wearing bandages on her face and neck to cover the sections of herself that she hadn't been able to retrieve. They would grow back in time. Though she was, for now, incomplete, she was in the habit of sweeping back her hair. *Accept it,* she seemed to say each time. *I have.*

She'd been busy. So many citizens had lost their homes and, with them, their clothes. She clearly found peace in her part-time role outside of the palace as entrepreneur. She'd even found time to assemble a new wardrobe for herself. None of her new clothes had hoods, including the gown she now wore.

"How's it feel?" she said, tugging at the hem of Clyde's new embroidered jerkin, complete with ox hide shoulder pads and silk cuffs. Geyser fashion was always strange, but Clyde felt it necessary to appear as a man of the people.

"I adore it. But honestly, I miss the tails."

She laughed, cupping his cheek. "Seriously?"

"Yeah." He shrugged, slightly embarrassed. "I kind of do."

"Well, the next one, then, maybe." She noticed the sword at his back. "Is that it?"

"Yep." He drew Commencement from its sheath—careful to not slice any of Nevele's new garments hanging around him. He offered it to her to hold. "This is it."

"They kept the handle." The swirling souls were still there, the only part of Commencement Clyde insisted they not rework for fear of losing its original artistry. "It's heavy." She weighed the longsword resting in her open palms. "But I suppose that's appropriate, given its history and all."

He developed a faraway look in his eyes.

She smiled and touched his arm.

Clyde snapped to, nodded, smiled. "Yes."

"Hey, look at me. You'll do fine."

"I know. And so will you."

She smirked. "I am already doing fine."

She set the sword aside and sent her threads to the corners of the shops, pushing the drapes closed one by one. When they had sufficient privacy, she pulled her to him by his tunic and brought their lips to collide.

The bells rang outside the shop, marking the noon hour. Music played from street performers entertaining the lunch crowd seated at sidewalk cafés. Autos rumbled past Margaret's Mends as the steward and the Royal Stitcher shared a kiss.

After closing up shop, they would return home to the chateau and share a moment in the garden, standing side by side while looking at the grave among the rosebushes and sculpted hedges made to look like dragons, enormous rabbits, and the like.

They would share tea there, mint of course, making sure to add the sugar before the tea, a tradition.

They would watch Rohm assemble igloos on the table-top with sugar cubes and ask his permission before taking one for the next cup of tea.

And before the first sip of each fresh cup, Clyde and Nevele would raise their cups to their friend Albert Wilkshire.

Awake.

Awake and . . . wet? Aksel tried to sit up and found every square inch of his body was being stabbed simultaneously by what he could only imagine to be a million tiny spears. Looking around, he decided he hadn't landed in some thorny hell for his afterlife but had splatted squarely in a patch of cacti.

He hadn't had much choice where he landed, but he had to admit falling in this cactus patch was slightly better than slamming arse first into the Lakebed's rocky floor. He tried three times to sit up and finally made it.

After moving himself around so that he was on his hands and knees on the shattered heap of cacti, he ducked and weaved through the branches until he could see soil that didn't have something pokey growing out of it. Before long, he was cut to ribbons, but soon the thorns didn't bother him so much. The pain in his hand was much worse, after all.

Every few steps, he'd look at it: Dreck's mark in his palm. Bright red and already scabby, the one-by-one-inch square in his palm would scar. But until then, every little breeze and accidental bump made it come alive as if he were giving a high five to, well, cactus thorns.

He got lost in the patch more than once. The problem was that the farther he crawled, closer to the outermost edge, the larger the thorns became. Three times he had to stop and reevaluate his path. He looked around. *Forward. Just keep going.* Exactly as he'd told Ricky when they'd been chained to the stationary bikes. He took his own advice and barreled on, one agonized pull at a time.

Light up ahead. He chased it.

He felt like the cacti patch spit him out, as if it were birthing him.

Sunlight poured over him, and he lay in it, flat on his back. He laughed stupidly. Happy, in the face of all.

Here he was, ending up just as Moira said he would if he chose not to help her and Karl. Without weapons, in the desert, shoeless. He double-checked if he was in fact shoeless, because he'd certainly have a laugh if he were. Well, he had one boot on still. So that much was a step up. He laughed some more.

But his laughing subsided.

Ricky.

He didn't get expelled from the camp; he didn't volunteer for the nomad's life. He got killed. Aksel couldn't help but blame himself for that.

He got to his feet and turned to the cactus patch. Carefully—very carefully—and with the foot that still had the protection of a boot on it, he kicked one of the half-broken limbs until it snapped free. He upended the thing, ignoring the pricks it gave his palms, squeezed despite the pain, and drank the surprisingly tart cactus water.

A strange breeze tickled his face. Feeling for his eye patch, he confirmed that it too had been lost. "Come on."

Of course, patch or no, he was better off than he was before. Sure, he was penniless, cast out of the Odium after being in their service for less than three hours, but still, he was alive.

Neck Steve was dead, killed by Aksel's own hand. That was no good. Aksel would have the hardest time of all with that, he knew. He wasn't the first man he killed, but he'd try to make damn sure from this point on he was the last.

He would've preferred Dreck to occupy that position. Even falling to what he assumed was his death at the time, Aksel had scolded himself for barely winging the pirate.

He tossed the drained cactus aside, wiped his chin with the back of his wrist, and looked to the sky. There would be no way to summon a ride from down here. And by the look of his immediate surroundings, there was nothing to see whatsoever. He turned in a circle, just to verify. Yep. Nothing. No people, buildings, vehicles. His shoulders dropped, and he blew out a sigh.

"Quite the fall."

Aksel gasped and spun—his DeadEye telescoping out.

Moira stood before him, Karl at her side. Karl snapped some device shut—undoubtedly what they were using to follow him—and pocketed it.

But how? Oh, right. They hadn't removed the Dead-Eye to disarm him. They'd removed it to make an addition onto it.

Aksel groaned and turned away. Where could he dramatically stomp off to? They were in the middle of nowhere. He turned back to face them, sighed in frustration. His DeadEye ratcheted back into his head, and he closed the eyelid over it. He sized up Moira and Karl, letting it be known in his face he wasn't happy about how things had gone with his time as a pirate.

Moira wasn't wearing any sort of hood. Too windy out here to keep one up, anyway. Her face was like a freshly bleached tunic. Her eyes were like black marbles from corner to corner. She swiped raven hair behind her ear. She looked as if she wanted to say something, but her lips—just a touch pinker than the rest of her—remained closed.

He tried to play off the startle of seeing her unhooded but doubted it was effective.

"You did well," Karl said.

"You call that well? Were you not watching? They threw me out of the ship, man."

"Still," Karl said pleasantly, "you did well."

"How do you know? I haven't even told you anything yet."

Moira took a moment before saying, "You didn't have to."

Aksel's brow furrowed. "You knew what was happening? The whole time?"

She offered a small nod.

"Well, in that case, thanks for all the help." He snapped off another piece of cactus and squished it in his palm to use its water to wash his face. "Really. I mean . . ." No sarcastic line found him. Ricky was dead, and Aksel had barely escaped with his life. The reality of it hit him now. Hard.

He had to sit.

Karl stayed put, but Moira stepped closer. She moved her cloak to one side so she could kneel in front of him, revealing a black flight suit underneath. She was small. She said nothing, just stared at him.

"So. Did you bug me?"

"Yes."

"And you saw everything?"

She nodded, a dagger of black hair falling in front of her eyes. "Well, heard, but yes."

"And you heard it when Ricky *died*. Am I right in that assumption?"

Tiny nod. "You are."

"Way to show some sympathy. Why the blazes didn't you two do something, then?" He picked up a handful of sand and considered throwing it in her face.

"I wouldn't," she said, her bottomless gaze never moving from his.

Aksel let the yellow fistful flow between his fingers. "Forgot you can read minds."

"It's not exactly mind reading; it's more like . . . Listen, we couldn't risk the Odium knowing anything about us. Intervening would've blown our cover."

"Speaking of cover," Aksel snapped, "did you know they would check my record? If you wanted me in there with them, playing spy for you, you probably should've done something about that. They knew I was in the Fifty-Eighth."

Moira's lips pressed together a little harder. She blinked.

"Good comeback," Aksel scoffed. He threw up his hands. "So what now, huh? Any more fun and excitement in store for me? Should we go pay my mum a visit, put a bullet in her? I mean, we keep on like this, I should warn you, I *will* eventually run out of people I care about."

"Nothing of the sort," she said flatly, a vague smile playing on her lips. "Now we'd like you to come along and tell us what you learned."

"Why bother? You were apparently listening the whole time, weren't you? They didn't know a thing about the Sequestered Son, never even mentioned him." He ran a hand up the side of his head where the DeadEye was installed, feeling for little bumps where a tiny microphone may have been added.

"We want you to come along," she began with gritted teeth, "because you weren't just a mole for us, Aksel." She was still crouching there and so alabaster white she could've been a statue. The only way to tell her eyes were moving in their sockets was how the shine on them flicked about on their glossy jet surfaces. "When we said we hired you for your special set of skills, we meant that. We could've sent anyone in there to spy on the Odium. And we could only hear, not see, what you saw. We still need your firsthand report on any weaknesses in the Odium you observed."

"Then you'll let me go?"

"Well, no, we'd like you to stick around if you would. We'd like to ask for your help again." She reached behind her to retrieve something. She extended it toward him: a dangling satchel, plump and bumpy. Right now, he wanted nothing from her.

Apparently bored with holding the satchel out to him, she let it fall before him. When it landed, it made a familiar sound—one that made Aksel's ears prick up. That crunch all men crave hearing: that of a whole lot of spots falling into a heap. He ran his gaze over the satchel, guessing at how much was in there.

"A lot," Moira said. "For helping us with that, with them." She jutted her chin toward the sky. "The first phase."

"First phase?"

She stood, silent in her movements, each of which was steady and deliberate. "Yes, and that's followed by a second. Calling it a first phase would be stupid if there weren't a second planned." She reached out an arm, indicating something in the distance.

Aksel sat up, an arm shielding his face against the gritty wind.

When the sandy haze shifted again, he noticed a waiting starship, shiny as the day it rolled off the assembly line, angular and pointy. Its side hatch had been rolled aside, and